THE

UNDOING

OF VIOLET

CLAYBOURNE

Emily Critchley grew up in Essex and has lived in Brighton and London, where she worked as a bookseller in one of London's largest bookshops. She has an MA in Creative Writing from Birkbeck, University of London. Her young adult crossover debut *Notes on my Family* was nominated for the Carnegie Medal, longlisted for the Branford Boase and Book of the Week in the *Sunday Times*. *One Puzzling Afternoon*, her debut adult novel, was Indie Fiction Book of the Month and named a must-read book by *People* magazine. Her latest novel is *The Undoing of Violet Claybourne*.

First published in the UK in 2024 by
ZAFFRE
An imprint of Zaffre Publishing Group
A Bonnier Books UK company
4th Floor, Victoria House, Bloomsbury Square, London, WC1B 4DA
Owned by Bonnier Books
Sveavägen 56, Stockholm, Sweden

A CIP catalogue record for this book is
available from the British Library.

Hardback ISBN: 978-1-80418-510-0
Trade Paperback ISBN: 978-1-80418-749-4

Also available as an ebook and an audiobook

1 3 5 7 9 10 8 6 4 2

Typeset by IDSUK (Data Connection) Ltd
Printed and bound in Great Britain by Clays Ltd, Elcograf S.p.A.

Zaffre is an imprint of Zaffre Publishing Group
A Bonnier Books UK company
www.bonnierbooks.co.uk

Emily Critchley

THE UNDOING OF VIOLET CLAYBOURNE

ZAFFRE

THE

UNDOING

of VIOLET

CLAYBOURNE

ZAFFRE

Part One

Part One

Chapter One

1999

SIXTY YEARS AND I HAVEN'T returned. Not once. Not until today.

The National Trust café is not particularly busy for a Saturday in March. I sip my tea and pick at a piece of lemon and poppy-seed cake. From here I can see the park. A few of the ornamental trees have gone but the landscape is the same: the slope of the mount that leads down to the lake, the copse, and the beech woods beyond. I look away. Apparently they have Easter egg hunts in the woods now.

Last June my husband died and I am now finally in the process of having a clear-out. *It's a new phase, Mum,* one of my daughters said helpfully.

There was a box on top of the wardrobe in the spare bedroom. Nestled among a handful of loose photographs, postcards and an old instruction manual for a Hoover I haven't owned for over forty years, I came across a tiny, faded-green school diary with *Heathcomb, Autumn term, 1938,* printed on the front along with the school crest.

How had it survived? I'd wondered.

I noticed my initials, in pencil, on the top corner of the front inside page: *G. F. Larking*. I hadn't written much else in the diary. It was mostly full of the printed text that outlined the term's activities: *Tuesday, 13th September, Pianoforte recital; Thursday, 6th October, Upper School Debate; Monday, 14th October, Prep B excused for Choral Society*.

As I flicked through the diary, the only words of any interest were those I had written on Tuesday, 20th December, the first day of the Christmas holidays. *Thornleigh Hall*.

I'd quickly closed the diary and returned it to the box.

But then, this morning, I found myself driving to North Oxfordshire. Parking in the car park (once a field belonging to the tenant farmer) and entering through the large oak, iron-studded doors. I paid an entrance fee and was given a guidebook. I wandered the rooms, avoiding the smiling, enthusiastic volunteers.

Looking around Thornleigh Hall, I felt suspended in time. Here I was, an old woman in sensible shoes clutching a guidebook, and yet there in the dining room was Emmeline drinking her morning coffee, Lord Claybourne reading his paper, Lady Claybourne complaining about her eggs, Violet tucking in to toast and blackcurrant jam. And there was Laura in the library, her stockinged feet up on the sofa arm, leafing through a magazine. 'Oh, hello, Gilly,' she said, seeing me standing there. 'I wondered where you'd got to.'

I moved from room to room, pressing my nails into my guidebook. I watched the other visitors with their rucksacks and cameras. Babies strapped to the chests of men. Mothers gripping the hands of small children. *Look at that clock, darling, isn't it beautiful?*

As for me, I felt like a traveller returning to a faraway land, only to find it a pale shadow of what it once was. I was reminded of a time in my life that was both full of possibility and fraught with the anxieties of the very young. Thornleigh Hall – my visit in the winter of 1938 and the events that followed – had been the marker that forever divided my life. After Thornleigh, there was simply a before and an after.

In the café, I finish my cake then set my fork down. On the table in front of me is a cut daffodil in a single stem vase and I admire its bright resilience. I never got to see the park in spring. The daffodils. No doubt there will be bluebells in the woods soon too. Sitting alone at my table I can hear gentle chatter, the clinking of teacups, the whir of a coffee machine. Feeling better, a little less discombobulated, I refill my teacup. Perhaps I was only in need of sustenance.

The waitress walks past me, carrying tea and cake to another table. With her rare combination of blonde hair and brown eyes she reminds me of Laura. She looks so young, but then I suppose we were all young then.

Laura.

I can still picture her, the last time I saw her in 1943, walking up the steps to the house in Richmond, fumbling for her key with a shaky hand. She'd turned and given me a small wave.

Less than a month later she was dead.

Laura's death made all the papers. *Countess's sister involved in fatal accident. Society girl's tragic death.*

She had picked a spot along the coast from Brighton after driving all the way down from London. Petrol was still rationed then. She must have been saving it up. It was the end of the summer – the grassy clifftops were sprinkled with white sea campion, pink thrift, wild garlic and daisies. The blue water sparkled under the bright afternoon sun.

Lines like 'grief stricken' and 'recently widowed' appeared in the papers, although no publication went as far as to say Laura had taken her own life. Laura's brother-in-law, Viscount Cadwallander, was well connected, and things may have been hushed up. I read the statement Emmeline had given to the Sunday papers: Laura must have lost control of the car; she was driving too fast. The road should be better signposted.

Despite the statement though, there was much speculation around Laura's 'accident', especially after the testimony of the family who had been picnicking on the cliff top. I read their account of how Laura sped past them, her gloved hands gripping the wheel, her scarf flapping behind her in the breeze, her mouth set in a grim, determined line (or perhaps this is how I imagine it, anyway). She turned sharply off the road. The engine roared. The picnickers, their boiled eggs suspended halfway to their mouths, shielded their children's eyes as the car sailed over the edge.

Poor Laura.

Like the picnickers, I was in no doubt that Laura's death had been intentional. I knew something of her state of mind, especially after the day we'd left Wynscott. I should have kept a closer eye on her.

No invitation to the funeral arrived and I have to say I was glad. I could just see Emmeline, her dark hair – so different to Laura's blonde – sculpted tastefully into a low chignon at the nape of her neck. She'd be wearing a black two-piece, gloves, and a tasteful pillbox, greeting the mourners with a steady hand as the first autumn leaves blew across the churchyard.

I wanted to remember Laura in my own way. Dancing to her jazz records in the tower bedroom, striding across the park in her wellingtons, smoking a cigarette by the drawing-room window in the blue dusk of a winter afternoon.

How had it come to this? I'd wondered.

Now, in the café, I glance at my handbag and the pieces of paper folded inside.

Of course, it wasn't only the discovery of my school diary that had brought me back to Thornleigh Hall today. It was the letter I'd received from Henry.

I had glanced, a few days ago, at those opening lines: *Dear Mrs McCune* (my married name), *I am writing to you at the request of my aunt, Violet Claybourne. This is a somewhat tricky letter to write—* I had dropped the letter, as if scalding hot, onto my kitchen table, then picked it up, stuffing it back in the envelope and hiding it behind the fruit bowl where I'd left it festering beside the browning bananas for several days. But then today, on my way out of the door, I'd put it in my handbag, slipped it among the throat sweets, pocket tissues and my spare driving glasses. Perhaps, I thought, when I get to Thornleigh, I'll know what to do with it.

I take the envelope out of my handbag and stare at it for a moment or two.

'Can I take that?'

I look up, startled, to find the young Laura-like waitress, gesturing to my empty plate.

'Oh, yes,' I say. 'Thank you.'

The girl smiles, sweeps up my plate, and I reach for my tea, tepid now. I glance again out of the window, across the park, to the dark glitter of the lake and the woods beyond. I can see us there in our Christmas dresses, Laura clutching her flask, Violet in her woollen hat, Emmeline bending down to untie the boat from the landing stage.

The past, of course, is a different place, a place inhabited by people who would be completely at sea should they find themselves here today. We were different people back then, products of our time – and of our circumstances.

But that is no excuse.

I realise my memories of that winter, through never being summoned to the forefront of my mind, are hazy and out of focus, mere impressions, as when my daughters were small and liked to rub their crayons over paper, revealing the ghost of the leaf below. When I think of the Christmas of 1938, what comes to mind is the sound of the dinner gong, the shine of the silverware, the rustle of Emmeline's dress as she swept up the central staircase. Jazz music drifting through draughty shut-up rooms, scarlet-clad figures galloping across snowy fields, and Violet sprawled, star-shaped, across her bed. *How good it is to be home, Gilly.*

But these are nothing more than scrambled snapshots, a slideshow of disordered images on a fuzzy projector screen. If I am to remember, to *truly* remember, I must go back to the very beginning. I must remember not only the glamour, the decadence, and the sense of wanting so desperately to belong that I felt in the company of the Claybourne sisters, but also the darker side of our story, what really happened during that winter break, and the events that led me to flee my life as I knew it. Only then will I know what to do with the letter.

Chapter Two

VIOLET CLAYBOURNE WAS MY ROOMMATE and that's why we became friends.

I was a quiet, bookish sort of girl, of average height, mousy brown hair, hazel eyes. Prone to freckles. At school, I longed more than anything to fit in, but so often found myself on the margins. There were girls I would sit with on the long wooden lunch benches in the dining hall, those I would gravitate towards at break time where we stood in small gossipy groups sharing our news and opinions, trying not to let ourselves down. But until Violet came along, there was no one I could really call a true friend.

Violet arrived on a sunny September afternoon. The trees outside yellowing. That familiar nip of autumn already in the air. It was the first day of a new term, and the beginning of my sixth year at Heathcomb.

Violet dragged her suitcase into our tiny dorm room then stopped, clearly surprised to see me, as if she had been expecting the room to be unoccupied.

'We're roommates,' I explained.

Dropping the suitcase, she grinned and stuck out her hand, still gloved in red cashmere, a startling adornment to Heathcomb's dowdy uniform. An inch or so taller than me, she had green eyes and thick, wavy brown hair.

'Violet Claybourne.'

'Gillian Larking.'

'I like Tuesdays, purple, and *Atropa Belladonna*,' she said, whipping off her gloves.

I stared at her. '*At-rop—*'

'A tall bushy plant belonging to the nightshade family.' She flung her suitcase onto the bed. 'Highly poisonous.' She turned to me, her hands on her hips. 'So we're to share a room, are we?'

I nodded. 'We're in the same form. Form B.'

'How original,' said Violet dryly. She glanced around the small, bare space. 'Well,' she said, 'if we're stuck together we may as well stick together. Do you want cake?'

She opened her suitcase and produced half a yellow sponge cake, wrapped in brown paper and secured with a ribbon.

'Mrs Frith – that's our cook – insisted I take it with me,' Violet said, unwrapping a cake knife from a chequered handkerchief. 'Mother doesn't like us eating cake. She takes these slimming pills the doctor gives her. They affect her nerves. She's terrified we're all going to get fat and no one will want to marry us. Sounds like a reason to eat more, if you ask me.'

'We're not supposed to bring food in.' I stared at the cake with its rich cream filling.

Violet grinned at me. 'Well, we'll just have to hide the evidence then, won't we?' She sliced a great chunk then licked the cream from her fingers. 'Here. Have this bit. And don't worry, I've just washed my hands in the bathroom three times, so you won't get any germs.'

I furrowed my brow. 'Right.'

We sat on the floor, eating our impromptu picnic. I kept a fearful eye on the door, praying Matron wouldn't discover us. I wasn't worried about spoiling my appetite for dinner. The food at Heathcomb was dreadful.

'Where have you come from?' I asked between mouthfuls.

Violet swallowed. 'Come from?'

'Which school?'

'Oh, I've never been to school,' Violet replied dismissively. 'We had governesses, tutors, you know. Not that *they* lasted long. Emmeline knew it all already. She started working her way through Father's library when she was five.'

'Emmeline?'

'My sister,' Violet said, messily eating her cake. 'I've got two of them. Emmeline – she's the eldest. Almost twenty-three now. And then there's Laura. She's just turned eighteen.'

I tried not to show how impressed I was with Violet having older sisters. I was an only child. My mother had died during my birth and I had lived in Egypt until I was nine years old, before my father decided to send me to boarding school in England. He had since remarried and his wife had given birth to a little boy. I'd never met either of them. Although he wrote me short, termly letters, I got the impression my father didn't want much to do with me and was preoccupied with his new family. I felt I had been a disgrace to him from the moment I was born. I had, after all, killed my mother. Even so, I knew my father was a cold and distant man. He had lost the ability to feel too deeply. First the war, then the death of the woman he loved. Something inside him had cracked like an egg, leaving a vacancy that could never quite be filled.

Being, in my mind, an only child, I could think of nothing better than to have sisters. I often wondered what it would be like to be a part of a larger family, to have siblings with whom you shared your intimate thoughts and secrets, and who would defend you to the last should you ever need defending. I imagined sisters gave a person an extra layer of protection against the world and I longed for that protection. Life, for me, always felt a little too raw and sharp at the edges. Having sisters, I thought, would be like putting on another layer of much thicker skin.

'Laura's still at home,' Violet went on. 'But Emmeline's at Oxford studying Classics.'

Once again, I was impressed. I knew of very few girls who had gone to university and I hardly dared dream it might be something I could one day do myself. A teacher had suggested it could be a possibility for me, but I was unsure. I did well enough in school, but not exceptionally well, and I doubted my father would pay for me to stay on. I would have to ask him, which would require a carefully worded letter, and I hated asking my father for anything.

'Your sister must be very clever,' I murmured.

'Oh, she is,' replied Violet. 'Too clever for her own good, Mummy says. And there was an awful row about Oxford. Mummy didn't want her to go. She thought Emmeline would become too lofty and that no one would want to marry her. But Daddy said Emmeline could go if she wanted. He's a soft touch, you see.' Violet smiled. 'Anyway, Emmeline was always going to get her own way. She usually does.' She paused to pick a few stray cake crumbs from her dress. 'What a nuisance it is we have to wear these itchy frocks. Do we have to keep them on all the time?'

12

'I'm afraid so,' I said. 'Except for games, of course. Why? What do you go about in at home?'

Violet grinned. 'Slacks – if I can get away with it. They're much more practical. I've a lovely pair of brown ones. But Mummy is always trying to get me into a frock.' She laughed.

I smiled uncertainly.

'You've got a lot of books,' Violet said, eyeing my night table.

'Only a few favourites,' I said. Piled up there was *Jane Eyre*, *Great Expectations* and *The Woman in White*. I had been an avid reader since I was a child. Books had always been my companions, a way of escaping my dreary and very ordinary life – not any better in England than it had been in Egypt.

'Mummy says Emmeline's nose is permanently stuck in a book and it will do her no good.'

'And your other sister – Laura – does she read?'

Violet frowned. 'Laura reads *Tatler*. She loves the society pages.'

I had magazines too but I didn't admit this to Violet. The magazines were my guilty secret. I bought them (along with Fry's chocolate bars) from the village shop using the small allowance my father sent me, stuffing them up my pinafore and carrying them furtively back to my room. The magazines featured true romance stories with titles like 'A Night Too Long' and 'The Test of Love', along with fashion and beauty tips. Although I enjoyed the stories about breathless aching women caught in the arms of unsuitable men, what I really loved were the advertisements: glamorous models in red lipstick, telling me that the right face cream, pair of silk stockings, or a Camel cigarette could change my life. I believed in them. I would gaze at my favourite models over and over,

13

scrutinising their faces, the sharpness of their cheekbones, the thickness of their eyelashes, their coy smiles. I sat in front of the mirror holding my hair up to my chin, imagining what I might look like without my pigtails and freckles, with my lips painted and my cheeks rouged.

I swallowed another mouthful of cake. It really was delicious. 'What about you then?' I asked. 'Do you like books?'

Violet reached into her suitcase and produced an extremely tatty copy of *Peter Pan and Wendy*. 'It's my favourite,' she announced. 'We went to see the play at the theatre in London.' She waved the book at me. 'After I read it, I knew that no book could ever be as good, so I stick to this one. I must have read it a hundred times.'

Before I could comment, Violet had moved over to the window and was throwing it open, letting in a chilly blast. She stuck her head out, peered upwards, then turned to look at me.

'I wanted to ask you, Gilly,' (no one had ever called me Gilly) 'how do we get up on the roof? I was looking at it from the drive when Higgins was fetching my things from the car. You'd be able to see the whole grounds from up there. It must be a splendid view.'

'It *is* possible to get up there,' I said, pleased to be given the opportunity to tell Violet something I knew. 'There's a staircase at the end of the fifth-floor corridor. But of course we wouldn't be allowed.'

Violet looked surprised. 'Why ever not?'

'We just wouldn't be.'

'At least show me the staircase,' she said, grabbing hold of my arm. 'Show me now.'

'I really don't think we should,' I said. 'We're supposed to be in our rooms. Settling in.'

'I only want to see the staircase. And you're meant to be showing me around, aren't you?'

*　*　*

The hallways and stairwells were busy with girls arriving, hugging each other, expressing joy or dismay over their new rooms. Violet, I noticed, kept close to me. She seemed alarmed by the cacophony of excited girls.

'Gosh, it's loud,' she said, her eyes darting from left to right. 'In my house people creep about the place and keep to their own quarters. My mother would never stand for any of this screeching.'

'It's because they've just arrived,' I told her. 'Matron will soon quieten them down.'

We continued to weave our way through the throng and up to the much quieter fifth floor.

'Shh,' I said, placing a finger over my lips. 'Some of the teachers have their rooms up here. I doubt anyone is in now, but still ...'

Violet nodded, but as soon as we reached the little staircase she let out a squeak of enthusiasm. Before I could stop her, she was leaping up the stairs two at a time.

'Violet, no!' I said, panicking.

It was too late. She was at the top of the stairs, rattling the door handle. To my surprise, the door opened and she disappeared.

'Violet!' I called after her. 'You mustn't!'

15

I ran up the stairs and out onto the roof. Violet was standing next to a chimney stack, her face to the sun, the breeze lifting her hair. 'Isn't it marvellous, Gilly? I told you it would be.'

I stopped and looked around me, amazed at how much sky there was. I could see the chapel, the tennis courts and the playing field that stretched to the trees.

Violet walked to the edge and put her hands on the low lip of the wall.

'Be careful,' I said.

She turned and grinned at me. 'Are you always such a worrywart?'

'We must go back,' I said, ignoring her. 'We'll get into an awful lot of trouble if we're caught up here.'

Violet sighed. 'If we *really* must. But we should come up here again, Gilly. Just think, at night we could see the stars.'

I shook my head. Clearly Violet had no idea what punishments would be bestowed on us if we were caught out of our rooms at night, let alone on the *roof*.

'It's the perfect place for Elvore,' said Violet.

'Elvore?'

'A magical land. Full of enchanted forests and castles and dragons. I go there often with my sisters.'

Before I could reply, a stern voice called out from somewhere behind us. 'Hello? Hello? Is there someone out here?'

Startled, Violet and I immediately ducked down behind a chimney stack.

'A teacher?' Violet whispered.

I nodded, my heart in my mouth.

The door closed with a bang. Neither of us moved. We sat there, waiting until we were sure the coast was clear.

'Do you think they've gone?' Violet asked.

'Yes, I should think so.'

'That was close, wasn't it?'

Come on,' I said. 'We'd really better go back now.' I returned to the door but when I tried it, I couldn't get it open.

'Violet,' I called to her in dismay. 'The door is stuck. Come and help me.'

Violet bounded over and rattled the handle. 'Gosh, do you think it's possible that teacher – whoever they were – might have locked the door?'

I looked at Violet, the horrible realisation settling in my stomach.

'I think we're probably locked out, Gilly,' Violet said.

I could feel the panic rising in my throat. 'No,' I said. 'We can't be.' I pushed my body against the solid door but it didn't budge. I tried the handle again. Nothing.

'Yup, we're definitely locked out,' said Violet cheerfully. 'They'll have to send someone to rescue us.'

I could feel my eyelids pricking and, not wanting Violet to see, I turned away. 'No one will know we're even up here,' I managed to say. 'We might not even be missed until they do the head count at lights out.'

'Then we *will* get to see the stars,' said Violet.

'You don't understand ... We'll be punished. Maybe even expelled.'

'Well, that's all right,' said Violet, pouting. 'I never even wanted to come to this stupid school in the first place. I already miss Fee Fee.'

'Who's Fee Fee?'

'My pet rabbit.'

17

I put my face in my hands. It was too much. To be stuck up here. To get into this kind of trouble on the first day of the new school year. Even if we weren't expelled, we'd be laughed at by the other girls for weeks. The thought of being excluded sent a cold shiver of fear up my spine. If I was going to support myself after leaving Heathcomb, I needed to finish school, to complete my exams. It wasn't that the thought of staying on appealed to me; I despised school. But I knew I needed options. 'Marry well,' had always been Aunt Ada's advice. I wasn't sure this was something I could rely on.

Violet, sensing my distress, touched my shoulder. 'I'm sorry, Gilly,' she said softly. 'I didn't mean to . . .'

I wiped my eyes on my sleeve and took a few shaky breaths. Violet was still looking at me.

'I'll make it all right, Gilly. I promise. Please don't be upset.'

'You can't,' I said. 'It's done now.'

Violet walked briskly to the edge of the roof. 'We'll call for help,' she said, peering over the edge. 'When we see someone.'

My heart was heavy. I thought of us waving and shouting like victims of a sinking ship. I imagined the door opening, Miss Tankard's stony face. *I think you had both better come with me, girls.*

Violet was still leaning over the edge of the roof.

'Please,' I said, sniffing. 'Be careful.'

'Look,' said Violet. 'There's a window open just below us. See?'

I peered cautiously over. A few feet below us was a window. Below it, a thick concrete ledge.

'The fifth-floor lavatories,' I said glumly.

'I think we could get down,' said Violet.

I looked at her in disbelief. There was no way I was climbing over the edge of the roof and dropping onto a windowsill. If we slipped, we would certainly fall to our deaths.

'I'm sure we could do it,' said Violet. 'We just need to hang on to the drainpipe. Once we're on the ledge, we'll be fine.'

I looked at her, aghast.

'And we'll easily get through the window. We're hardly heifers, are we?'

Violet had a foot up on the low lip of the wall. She began to tuck her pinafore dress into her knickers.

'Violet, please. It's too dangerous.'

Before I had a chance to say anything else, she'd hopped over the edge.

I let out a cry of alarm then leaned over, half expecting to see her crushed body lying on the gravel below. But there she was, clinging to the drainpipe.

As I watched, she shimmied down until she reached the deep sill. I could hardly bear to look as she transferred her grip, one hand at a time, from the drainpipe to the top of the window.

She managed to get a leg through, then sort of slithered in, feet first. Her face appeared a moment later, beaming up at me. 'I told you it would be easy, Gilly. Come on.'

I shook my head.

Violet sighed. 'I'll have to fetch a teacher then. Tell them you're locked out.'

I shut my eyes. This couldn't be happening. I'd be known as a troublemaker for the rest of the school year. The other girls would avoid me, not wanting to be damned by association. I almost felt death would be preferable.

'It's perfectly all right. I promise,' Violet called up to me. 'I know you can do it, Gilly.'

I glanced back at the locked door, then took a deep breath. What choice did I have? But there was no way I was tucking my dress into my underwear. If I fell to my death, at least my dignity would remain intact.

I gripped the top of the roof as Violet had done, then swung my legs over, lowering myself down and feeling with my feet for the bracket that held the drainpipe to the wall.

'That's it, Gilly,' Violet called out. 'Now just wriggle down.'

The drainpipe felt rough and flaky under my hands. I had my arms and legs wrapped around it. It wobbled a little on a loose bracket. I looked down and gasped. The ground was a very long way below me. Suddenly, everything was spinning – a confusion of sky, brick and gravel. I closed my eyes.

'Come on, Gilly, you have to keep going.'

I opened my eyes. Violet, still craning her neck up at me, looked worried. I stared at her. I couldn't move. My limbs had frozen. The sensation was terrifying. I had visions of the whole school out on the lawn staring up at me as I clung, petrified, to the rusty drainpipe. I'd be there for hours. I imagined fire engines. Reporters. The locals in the village who had all come to get a good look at the girl stuck between the roof and the lavatory window. The crowd would part as I finally slipped and fell. They wouldn't even bother to put a bench up in my name. *She brought it on herself with her foolishness*, our teachers would say. *Let that be a warning to you, girls.* I'd exist only as one of those school legends, like the story of the girl who was flung from a deranged horse and killed in '23, and who was said to haunt the stables.

'Put your left foot on the window ledge,' Violet instructed. 'It's easy. Come on now.'

I shook my head. I could hear the ringing of the bell and thought, vaguely, of girls rushing towards the dining hall, unaware that I was out here, my hands growing sweaty as I clung desperately on to the drainpipe.

'Put your foot on the window ledge, Gilly,' Violet said again. 'Let go of the drainpipe and hold onto the window frame.'

I moved my foot a fraction towards the ledge.

'That's it,' said Violet encouragingly.

I really am going to die, I thought. I'm never going to see my sixteenth birthday. I'll never have known anything but Heathcomb; cold dorm rooms, rows of giggling porridge-scoffing girls with hockey-bruised legs, winter mornings spent lunging pathetically at lacrosse balls, the grey soap smell that permeated the dingy corridors. This will have been my entire life. And now it was over.

The thought was such a depressing one that I heaved myself onto the ledge, gripping the top of the window and squatting down. Violet cheered and guided my shaking legs through the window. I tumbled through, falling on top of her. After a stunned moment, I struggled to my feet.

Violet was brushing herself off. 'See. I told you I'd get us out of it. You just had to trust me. Now, what was that horrible ringing sound?'

'The dinner bell,' I choked, overcome with relief that I had done it, that I was still alive. My heart beat furiously in my chest. Heathcomb would not, I decided, be my life. There was more, there *had* to be. And now that I wasn't lying dead on the gravel outside the gymnasium windows, I vowed I would no longer be poor, quiet, shy, put-upon Gillian. I would rise to whatever heights I might be capable of rising to.

'Well, come on then,' said Violet, untucking her dress. 'Let's go to dinner, shall we? All that clambering about has worked up my appetite.'

I stared at her, unable to work out if I liked her, or if she was completely mad.

Chapter Three

WE WERE LATE TO DINNER, of course.

'Girls,' barked Miss Tankard, glaring down at us, 'you're *ten* minutes late.'

It had to be Miss Tankard. Head of games. Hairs growing out of her chin. A shelf of bosom before you reached her small, mean face. Some of the girls had nicknamed her 'The Tank'. She was known for sending pupils who had displeased her out onto the hockey field in their gym kits to cut the grass with nail scissors. I also knew she didn't tolerate lateness. I had once been late to chapel after misplacing my hymn book, and she had made me stand in the aisle, facing the wrong way, for the entire service.

Now Miss Tankard loomed over us, her arms folded, her mouth set in a thin, hard line. I tried to speak but Violet got there first.

'I'm new,' she said quickly. 'I lost my way and Gillian came to find me. It's my fault we're late. I'm terribly sorry.'

Miss Tankard moved her steely gaze from me to Violet. 'And who are you?' she asked Violet.

'Violet Claybourne. It's my first day.'

Miss Tankard considered us both. 'Very well then,' she said, her eyes still narrowed. 'Hurry up and join the queue or there'll be nothing left for you but gravy.'

As we reached the serving counter and grabbed our plates, I glanced at Violet. 'Thank you,' I whispered.

Violet smiled. 'I told you, we'll stick together.' Her expression changed as she looked in horror at what was being spooned onto her plate: chunks of unidentifiable stewed, gristly meat and lumpy mashed potato.

'Goodness, what is *this*?' she said loudly. 'Look at that potato. Do they not have any butter? And it's cold,' she said, prodding it with her finger.

'Shh,' I said.

'I'll starve,' said Violet in dismay.

'You get used to it. It's not so bad after a while. And if you get a piece of meat you can't chew, you can fling it under the table or put it in your pinafore pocket and flush it down the lavatory later.'

Violet made a face. 'I never thought I'd say this, but I miss Mrs Frith's cooking already.'

I took two forks and two knives from the pile and handed Violet her cutlery.

'Just think,' she said, studying the fork with a worried expression, 'this fork must have been used thousands of times by thousands of mouths. I hope they wash up well and use lots of soap.'

'I'm sure they do,' I said, looking around the dining hall for a suitable spot for us to sit.

'Let's go over there,' said Violet, pointing.

I followed her gaze. 'Oh no, we can't sit there. That's where Eliza West and Ursula Harryman and the others all sit.'

Violet frowned. 'But there's plenty of room.'

I didn't know how to explain. Clearly, Violet had a lot to learn about school hierarchy.

'Over here is better,' I told her firmly.

'If you say so,' said Violet with a sigh.

*   *   *

Violet, I soon discovered, was socially clueless. At first I put it down her not ever being at school before, but I then began to wonder if it was just a part of her personality.

She wasn't at all good at the general sort of chit-chat girls enjoyed. She asked direct questions that made the others glance at each other and giggle and, when in company, she often repeated the same old jokes and anecdotes.

It was difficult to say exactly what it was about Violet that was different. She was just always slightly out of step. I could see she tried to mimic the way the girls at school spoke, the gestures they made, the way they laughed. I knew all the copying she did was tiring for her and, knowing she wasn't at ease in groups, it was usually better if we kept to ourselves. Worried that, if left alone, Violet might be teased, I suppose I became protective of her. I didn't mind it being just the two of us. I wasn't particularly attached to any of the others, and now, more than ever, I had the sense that I was only biding my time at school, waiting for life, *real life* to begin.

We were passing the science classrooms one afternoon when we encountered Eliza, Ursula and Hilary giggling outside the equipment cupboard. They glanced at us then quickly moved on, their laughter echoing along the corridor.

'What's that sound?' asked Violet.

I could hear it too. A faint wailing coming from inside the cupboard. I knew immediately who it was: Angela Burke. The girls were always terrorising poor Angela.

'There's someone in there,' said Violet, pointing at the cupboard.

'It's Angela Burke,' I said calmly. 'They've locked her in, I expect.'

Violet was horrified. 'We'd better find the key and let her out, then.'

'Oh, no,' I said quickly. 'We can't do that.'

Violet stared at me.

'They'll know it was us then. Eliza, Ursula, Hilary and all the others.'

'Well, so what? Listen, she's *crying*. We have to get her out. We have to do the right thing, Gilly.'

Violet headed towards the cupboard but I caught her arm. 'No, Violet, really, we mustn't. You don't understand. If we let Angela out, it might be us locked in there next time.'

* * *

It wasn't just Violet's lack of understanding about the way social hierarchy worked at school and her awkwardness in company that made her a little odd: she had her rituals too. She had to do certain things at certain times, like twirl around on the spot before she flushed the lavatory or touch a door handle twice before she opened a door. I often caught her whispering certain words to herself three times or counting to fifty on her fingers. When I asked her why she had to do these things, she struggled to tell me. *For protection*, was all she would say, or *so that nothing bad will happen.*

The daily paper could usually be found in the dining room at breakfast. Violet would snatch it anxiously and leaf quickly through it, her eyes scanning the headlines. At first I thought perhaps she was interested in current affairs, but it soon became apparent to me that she possessed extremely scant knowledge of any recent events. She raced through the paper, reading very little of it.

'What are you looking for?' I asked her once.

'I'm just checking.'

'Checking what?'

She sighed. 'I know it sounds a bit funny, but I like to check through the papers to make sure I haven't done anything bad.'

Before we went to bed each night, Violet spent a good half hour performing her 'checks': looking under our beds and behind the curtains, rummaging through our chest of drawers, then glancing from left to right a number of times before she was finally able to get into bed. I had no idea what she was doing but it seemed important to her so I didn't intervene.

She also had these strange episodes where she would get overwhelmed by something relatively trivial and completely fall to pieces. The first time it happened, we were in the art room before dinner, finishing off our drawings. Miss Clarke had made a still-life scene comprising of a vase of dried flowers, a fruit bowl and a small mantel clock. Violet was furiously rubbing out her dried flowers, her brow deeply furrowed. She was rubbing so hard I thought she would go through the paper.

'I've got to get it *right*,' she said.

27

'It looked fine to me as it was,' I replied. 'Now you'll have to do all the flowers again.'

Violet glared at me, then flung her rubber across the room, scattering her pencils. 'I can't do *anything*,' she cried, taking off her glasses and throwing them down on the art desk – she hated wearing her glasses and forgot them half the time, anyway. 'Why must we do all this pointless work, Gilly? It's just all too much!' She put her head in her hands and sobbed, her shoulders shaking.

I didn't know what to do. Her outburst seemed so unwarranted.

I often found my life at school lonely and repetitive but I only ever allowed myself to cry under the safety of my bedclothes after lights out. Luckily, we were alone in the art room but it still took me a good twenty minutes of persuasion to calm Violet down.

I knew our teachers would not be sympathetic to this sort of unjustified emotional outburst. We were, after all, the daughters of the upper and middle classes and it wasn't appropriate for us to express our emotions so vehemently. Heathcomb cultivated resilience, respectability, team spirit, and was meant to turn us into the kind of capable young ladies who knew how to keep smiling when our cooks burned the pie crust and our husbands missed the last train home. Violet's changeable moods, strange outbursts and emotional collapses would be seen as a weakness in her character. I tried my best to pre-empt them and save her from embarrassment.

I occasionally felt conflicted about my new-found friendship with Violet and feared it could be detrimental to my own social standing. Like bloodhounds sniffing out rabbits, schoolgirls have a tendency to sniff out strangeness, but the other girls mostly left Violet alone. I had heard that Violet's family were wealthy and well connected which may have had something to do with her immunity to being teased. Even at our tender age, the girls at Heathcomb would never have made an enemy of a girl they knew they may later bump into in society and perhaps need a favour or an introduction from. Still, I once overheard some of the girls referring to Violet as 'an odd fish'. When I told Violet this, I worried she might be upset but instead she gave me a steady look and said, 'Well, I wouldn't want to be like them.'

*   *   *

'There are things you should know about me, Gilly,' Violet said to me at the end of our first week. 'If we're to be permanent roommates and the very best of friends, then you really should know them.'

We were lying in our beds, just before lights out. I shot her a questioning glance.

'I sometimes have nightmares,' Violet said. 'Terrible ones.'

'I can wake you,' I said. 'If I think you're having a bad dream.'

'And Gilly . . .'

'Yes?'

'My thoughts often run away with me and I can't stop them.'

'How do you mean?'

She hesitated. 'I think about doing something terrible, and then I worry I've really done it. Like I see an old lady waiting for a train and I think that I might push her onto the track. And then, later that day, I think of it again and I can't be sure that I *didn't* push her. Do you ever get that, Gilly?'

'No,' I said.

Violet sighed, clearly disappointed. 'And I sometimes worry I'm *going* to do something terrible. I have to do certain things – you know, my rituals – in order to undo what might happen. I call them my undoings.'

I frowned. 'In order to undo what *might* happen?'

'I know it's silly,' she said. 'I know what I believe can't *really* be true, but I have to do my undoings anyway. And there are special words I have to repeat before I go to sleep to make sure my loved ones won't get hurt.'

I rubbed my forehead; it sounded awfully complicated to me.

'I thought it might be best to tell you. And I wondered if you had it too ...'

'I'm sorry,' I said, aware I had somehow let her down.

Violet was quiet. I reached for my book, hoping to read a few pages before bed, but then she spoke again.

'Just imagine, Gilly. What if there was a plague or something and everyone died except us. We'd be all alone here. We wouldn't have to do any lessons, and we wouldn't need to sleep in our dorm room anymore. We could sleep wherever we liked.'

'I'd sleep in the library,' I said, thinking how nice it would be to go to bed surrounded by imagined worlds, secrets, magic, and other more interesting lives.

'We'd have to learn to grow food,' said Violet, becoming practical. 'In order to survive.'

'I'm sure we wouldn't be the *only* ones alive. Someone would come and rescue us.'

'No,' said Violet calmly. 'No one would rescue us. But at least it would just be us.' She paused, then whispered softly, '*Nos contra mundum.*'

I smiled to myself in the dark. Violet had clearly been paying attention during our Classics lesson. *'Nos contra mundam,'* I whispered back.

Us against the world.

*   *   *

Violet had a rich fantasy life and often wanted to engage me in games about Elvore. I quickly got to know the characters and the various plot strands. Violet would lapse into Elvore at surprising moments. She talked of it often, almost as if it were real, some other place we visited as often as we could, as though the real world were a mere inconvenience.

Violet was fiercely protective of Elvore and once grew cross with me when I referred to it as 'just a game'. After that, I always spoke of it as if it were a real place and the lives of its inhabitants were playing out alongside our own. The castle, the forest, Prince Caspian, King Luther and the purple knights all seemed more real to Violet than Heathcomb. Even though I knew we were probably too old for such fantasy games, I felt privileged to be let in on its secrets, and was always willing to play along.

I learned that the classroom didn't suit Violet; she preferred to be outdoors. We went on what our teachers called 'nature walks' across the school's surrounding countryside. Violet threw herself into these walks with relish, striding across the Sussex downs in her sturdy lace-up boots, splashing through puddles, hitching her skirt up and bounding over the stiles with the authority of a girl who had been brought up in the countryside. She seemed at home outdoors, unlike many of the other girls who complained bitterly during these walks of the cold wind and of mud-splatted stockings.

We were brushing our teeth one evening before bed when Violet, after putting her toothbrush back in the glass with a clatter, said, 'I'm sorry I bumped into you during games today.'

'What?' I said, my mouth full of toothpaste.

'You know, when we were running.'

I spat into the sink then washed my mouth out. Violet was still looking at me with a concerned frown. I had a vague memory of her shoulder bumping against mine during our warm-up exercises. 'It's fine,' I said.

'But, Gilly, I might have bruised you.'

'I don't think so,' I said.

'But you should check,' she insisted.

I slipped my nightgown over my shoulder and we both peered at my upper arm. 'See? Nothing there.'

Violet nodded. 'You should check again in the morning. Sometimes bruises come up later. I really am sorry, Gilly.'

I gave her a baffled look. 'There's no need to apologise.'

But she did.

Often.

And not just to me. Concerned she had offended or hurt someone, Violet often apologised for her actions, actions no one else but her had even noticed. Most of the girls just shrugged and told her there was no need to apologise. Others gave her strange looks and a wide berth. But even after she'd apologised, I knew these inconsequential incidents still bothered Violet. She appeared to analyse her daily interactions in minute detail. *Do you think Hilary was cross I pushed past her in the lunch queue? Do you think Margot would have preferred the seat next to the window in prep this evening? Do you think Louise will get sick because I sneezed next to her in chapel?*

Once again, I put this down to Violet not having been at school before. I could, after all, understand her desire to fit in, and had experienced similar anxieties about social faux pas myself, but then one night I woke and, once again, heard her muttering to herself in the dark. I checked my watch: it was nearly two hours after lights out.

'Violet,' I whispered. 'What are you doing? Are you still saying your undoings?'

'No,' she whispered back. 'I did that already. Now I'm going through my list.'

'What list?'

'The list of all the things I did wrong today. I have to go through each thing then say the special words three times.'

'But why?' I asked.

'I don't know,' she said quietly.

* * *

On Saturday mornings, any letters that had arrived for girls throughout the week were placed on the table in the hallway by the front staircase.

That first Saturday, Violet fought her way through the crowd and returned clasping a letter in both hands. 'I'm sorry, Gilly, I couldn't see anything for you.'

'I wasn't expecting anything,' I said, used to the familiar feeling of disappointment.

'Well, let's go up and read my letter together then,' Violet said, linking her arm through mine.

Once in our room, Violet tore open the letter and laid it on the bed. I could see the return address in the top right corner. *Thornleigh Hall*. Was that really where Violet lived? It sounded very grand.

'It's from Laura,' Violet exclaimed happily. 'Emmi won't write, of course. She's too busy with her studies.'

I peered over Violet's shoulder.

Dear Piff (apparently a pet name for Violet since childhood),

All very quiet here this week. Dreadful dinners as Mrs Frith has a cold and simply refuses to cook and so there's been absolutely nothing hot. Keeping everything crossed she's on the mend as can't abide the thought of another slice of pork pie with pickles. Of course we've had an invite to the Chester-Barnes' hunt ball at Branwood. I've ordered a new dress from Chatsworth and Hyde's. The Most Beautiful blue. (Emmeline will be wearing white, of course.) Should be a good crowd. Some chaps coming from Oxford, and several cousins of the Chester-Barnes'. Old Mr Linwood will be there again, no doubt breathing down the necks of all the young girls, holding us too tightly. Father had a party down last week. Over a hundred grouse shot which wasn't bad but of course nothing like the old days, he says. We've got a new horse. Emmeline wants to call him Sigmund (Siggy for short). Jennings is trying to break him in. I've never known such a stubborn horse. Daddy bought him cheap, I expect. I do hope it isn't too dreadful at school. You'll soon be home for Christmas.

Chin up.

Love Lolly.

I began to look forward to Violet's letters even more than Violet did. The lives of her sisters at Thornleigh Hall sounded so far removed from our daily existence at Heathcomb. I enjoyed imagining the horses, the hunts, the dresses and the balls – it was like something from a fairy story or a snowy Russian novel. I could imagine Emmeline and Laura in a cosy lamplit sitting room in the evenings. Emmeline, home from Oxford, relaxing on the sofa, reading; Laura on the floor, dipping her pen into an ink pot, writing to the younger sister they both missed. Lady Claybourne would be sewing, Lord Claybourne, after engaging his daughters in lively conversation about their days and interests, settling in for the evening with his pipe, slippers and a hefty book on the Crimean War. I saw Emmeline out on Sigmund, galloping across the fields heavy with early morning mist. Laura, choosing the fabric for her new dress, leaving the shop with a handful of parcels, running to catch her train. They were characters in my own little stage play. The kind of family I longed to be part of.

I had built the sisters up in my mind, created the scenery, added in the set dressings, even given them dialogue *(Oh, you can't possibly wear green to the ball, Emmeline!)* that it came as something of a shock to learn I might actually get the chance to meet them.

Chapter Four

I FIRST FOUND MYSELF HURTLING TOWARDS Thornleigh Hall on a damp December afternoon (I say hurtling because with Higgins at the wheel we went at quite a clip). I had received a letter from my father a few weeks before the Christmas break. He'd suggested I go to Aunt Ada's for the holidays as I usually did.

Aunt Ada was my father's older, spinster sister. Her house was both stuffy and stuffed. China ornaments and lace doilies adorned every surface. She didn't believe much in fresh air, especially in the winter months, and I knew I would spend my holidays sitting in her frilly front room next to the gas fire, carefully piecing jigsaws together, trying not to be untidy. As each day wore on, I would have the feeling I was slowly suffocating under the weight of her heavy furniture, pinned by the eyes of her china dolls. I would almost have preferred to stay at school.

Violet had found me slumped at my desk, my father's letter in my hand.

'What's the matter?' she asked.

'I'm supposed to stay with Aunt Ada for Christmas.' I briefly described the doilies, the dolls, the jigsaws.

Violet shrugged. 'Well, why don't you come to Thornleigh?'

Although secretly thrilled by this proposition, I protested I didn't want to be a nuisance.

'Don't be silly,' Violet insisted. 'Mummy won't mind at all. I'll write to her tomorrow and you write to your father and tell him arrangements have already been made.'

My father wrote straight back and I got the impression he wasn't really concerned where I planned to spend the holidays, only relieved he no longer had to organise somewhere for me to go.

* * *

I gazed out of the car window at the anaemic landscape whizzing by; flat winter fields, slate-grey sky, trees as bare as sleeping maypoles.

I thought back to when I had first set foot on English soil six years ago at Tilbury docks. I had been bitterly disappointed. This was it? Where were the green hills, the trickling streams, the wild moors, the thatched cottages I had read about in the books my nanny, Clara, had given me? I found England damp and smoggy, full of pale, stout people who dashed about in long coats and turned-up collars under black umbrellas. Thick smoke curled upwards from red-brick chimneys. Cars, buses, horses and bicycles filled the roads and everyone looked like they had somewhere important to be. It was as if life had sped up before my eyes, whilst at the same time becoming a shade greyer like an old pair of socks washed too many times. Gone were the peasants working in the fields, the village children, the skinny pye-dogs, the donkeys and the gharry cabs pulled by the horned cows. Even the sun had paled.

'You look just like your mother,' Aunt Ada had said stiffly, as if she couldn't decide if this was a good thing or not. My father never spoke of my mother and I had not really considered that I might look like her. I had one photograph of her, which I had brought with me to England. In the photograph she sits, most likely in a photographer's studio, next to a leafy potted plant, her long, plaited hair resting across one shoulder. A flower had been pinned to her dress. I looked at the photograph often, taking it everywhere with me, wondering what my life might have been like if my mother had lived.

In Egypt, an acquaintance of my father's who worked for Shell had given me a set of Angela Brazil novels, left behind by an older daughter. The books all had titles like *A Fortunate Term*, and *The Nicest Girl in the School*. When my father announced I would be going to school in England, I imagined tree-climbing, horse-riding, midnight feasts, kindly teachers who let us into their rooms in the evening to sit by the fire as we developed our sewing skills and drank hot cocoa. I would make many friends and be celebrated for my unique and loveable character traits.

My father had chosen Heathcomb out of the Truman and Knightly school directory. Heathcomb advertised invigorating air and healthy outdoor pursuits, all of which to my father, mopping his brow under a glaring Egyptian sun, must have sounded like a good idea. But I hated the cold, hated hockey and lacrosse and the half-mile run up the drive we were supposed to undertake each morning before breakfast (unless we had the curse). In the winter months we slept with our school coats over the top of our bedclothes. One night my hot water bottle fell out of my bed and I found it the next morning on the floor, a solid lump of ice.

I felt a sense of disbelief, even mild outrage, that this was it: England, school, my life. I kept thinking there must have been a mistake, that another girl was living the life I should be living. I longed to escape the dreary existence I had mistakenly been assigned. My dull, lonely childhood in Egypt followed by the disappointment of boarding school in England had given me reason to believe my life was tainted in some way. Without really realising it, I had sunk into a permanent, numbing melancholy whilst I waited for something better to arrive. Perhaps Violet, my visit to Thornleigh Hall, would be that something better.

'I think I'm going to be sick,' said Violet.

Higgins pulled the car sharply to the side of the road. Violet rushed out and threw up dramatically onto a pile of brambles.

'I'm all right now,' she said, climbing shakily back into the car, her expression grim.

Higgins turned around. 'Are you sure, Miss Claybourne? We can stop for longer, if we must?'

'No,' said Violet firmly. 'Let's carry on. Mummy will be cross if we're late for dinner.'

I must have fallen asleep for when I woke it was late afternoon, the light was fading and the landscape had changed. The roads, fields and hedgerows had gone and we were driving through woodland, the branches of the bare winter trees silhouetted against the approaching dusk. Perhaps the bumpiness of the uneven track had woken me, although it might have been the intuitive sense that we were in the final stage of our journey. I wound down my window and breathed in the freezing air, the scent of woods and moss, then looked over at Violet who was still dozing, the tartan rug over her knees.

Suddenly the car swerved, jolting me sharply to the right. Higgins slammed on the brakes and Violet woke, letting out a cry of alarm. Higgins rolled down the window. 'For goodness' sake,' he called out angrily. 'Watch where you're going, man. You walked right out in front of me. Bloody fool.'

I could see a shadowy form in a large coat standing at the edge of the track. He turned and I saw his sad, startled eyes. They peered in at us from the gloom. Before I could get a better look, Higgins, with a shake of his head, had wound the window up and we were pulling away.

'Who was that?' I whispered to Violet.

'Oh, only Frank Marks,' she said, dismissively. 'He lives at the edge of the estate, in the old gate-lodge cottage. He walks through the park as it's a short cut to the village. It's trespassing, really.'

I nodded as if I knew about such things. The image of the man stayed in my mind, the way he had emerged, animal-like, from the trees. What had he been doing there anyway?

Further along the track, the thick woods gave way to an avenue lined with elms which curved to the left. We passed through a stone gateway embellished with wrought ironwork.

When Thornleigh Hall finally came into view, my breath caught in my throat. It was far grander than I had imagined. Built in a sandy grey stone, the house was bristling with turrets and spires and appeared to be made up of various different sections all stuck together. There was even a length of castle-like crenellations. I noticed a blackened section at the top of the house, giving one side of the place a diseased appearance. The overall look was far more foreboding, severe, and much larger than I had expected, certainly not the gentle chocolate box country house I had envisioned when reading those letterheads of Violet's.

The sky was beginning to blush at the line of the horizon. A low mist had crept in through the trees and I felt as though I had stepped into a dream, some other realm. Parts of the house were covered in a dense red leaf. I could see a number of chimneys, inside which I imagined sooty children had once crawled, brushes in hand. The vast lawn, studded with ornamental trees, conjured up images of a different season in a different time – Edwardian ladies under parasols taking tea, the sound of horses' hooves on the gravel.

As the car pulled to stop on the drive in front of the house, I saw a girl, a few years older than Violet and I, wearing a belted tweed jacket and riding breeches, standing next to a grey pony. A dead deer was slung over the saddle. I stared at the deer's vacant, lifeless eyes, the flop of its head, its lolling tongue, its neat little hooves. The deer had been shot. A wound was visible on its flank, a small burst of red and purple. A chill swept through me. I was not used to dead animals; had not grown up, as Violet had, in the English countryside, where hunting was a common pastime. The deer had no antlers and so I guessed it must be a female.

The girl was holding a gun, her blonde hair cut in a sharp, fashionable bob. Her cheeks were pink with exertion and,

I imagined, the thrill of a successful hunt. She turned and waved at the car as we pulled to a stop.

'That's Laura,' said Violet.

* * *

We climbed out of the car and stood on the drive outside the front of the house as Higgins fetched our luggage.

Laura rushed over, shook my hand vigorously, then airily embraced Violet, kissing her on both cheeks.

'It's great to have you home, Piff. Nothing's changed here as you'll soon see.' She gave a little laugh. 'A rather successful afternoon, don't you think?' She nodded at the dead deer then turned to me, her eyes bright. 'Lovely to meet you, Gillian. We just adore having guests at Thornleigh. And I'm so glad Violet's making friends. It must be awful to be away at school without a friend.'

'We're roommates too,' said Violet.

Laura smiled. 'How lovely. And do you have a last name, Gillian?'

'Larking,' I said.

'Hm. I don't think I know any Larkings. Lovely name, though. We hear skylarks in the summer over the meadow.'

I smiled politely, feeling tongue-tied. I was finally here: Thornleigh, with Violet's sisters. The half-baked figments of my imagination were slowly being replaced by what I saw in front of me.

'That's an interesting scarf, Gillian,' Laura said. I felt my cheeks redden. Knitted rather crookedly, the scarf was one of Aunt Ada's creations. I had never been sure about it. The colours were a little odd – I expect she was using up leftover wool. But it was warm, and I hadn't wanted to be ungrateful. Now I wished I hadn't worn it.

At that moment the large oak, iron-studded door at the top of the front steps swung open with a creak. A tall young woman appeared. She was wearing a white dress that reached her black ankle boots. The dress looked like something from another time: a high collar, long sleeves and lace panelling. She would not have looked out of place on the front cover of a Wilkie Collins novel. Her hands were encased in a pair of black velvet gloves and she wore a matching hat with a wide brim. Her hair, thick, dark and wavy, cascaded over her shoulders. She looked very bohemian. *Emmeline*, I said to myself.

She was carrying a camera and tripod. My father had given me a box Brownie years before but I hadn't been able to take it to England as I hadn't the room in my suitcase. This camera looked much more professional, like something a real photographer would use. I watched her move with ease towards Laura and the pony. She set the tripod down on the gravel. 'Well done, Lolly. Didn't I tell you? You just needed to have patience, that's all.'

Laura blushed. 'It was mostly Jennings.'

'Nonsense. You must take credit for your achievements. Now, let's get a picture, shall we? Before the light goes.'

Laura obligingly began to rearrange herself next to the dead deer, smiling proudly. It was then that Emmeline glanced at Violet and me, as if noticing us for the first time. 'So you're back, are you?' she said to Violet.

'And she's brought a little friend,' said Laura, waving her hand in my direction. 'Gillian Larking.'

Emmeline's eyes briefly swept over me, taking in my sensible coat, my scuffed shoes and horrid scarf. She gave me a small, curt nod then resumed setting up her shot.

I felt disappointed by Emmeline's cool greeting, and by being described by Laura as a 'little friend'.

Lingering on the drive, I watched Emmeline expertly fiddling with the camera lens, adjusting the height of the tripod, giving instructions to her sister: 'That's it, Lolly. Move your hand to the left.'

How wonderful, I thought, to be beautiful, clever, artistic, and to live in such a magnificent place as Thornleigh Hall.

Laura assumed a new pose, tilting her head, smiling broadly as Emmeline swept her hair over her shoulder then clicked the shutter.

A man in ancient tweeds was coming through the gate, several stag hounds panting at his feet. 'Take the pony back once we're done, will you, Jennings?' Laura called out to him 'It's getting late.'

'Come on,' said Violet, catching my arm. 'Let's go in, shall we?'

*   *   *

I stood in the entrance hall with its tiled black-and-white floor and magnificent central staircase with a spiral of wrought-iron bannisters. A little paper ship in a stormy sea scene, secured behind glass, was suspended above the face of the grandfather clock. The ship swung from side to side, cresting a wave with each tick. I stared at it, having never seen anything like it before. A telephone sat on a hall table like a large back daffodil. Behind

45

it was the largest Christmas tree I had ever seen. The tree was decorated with blue baubles, red paper hearts, gold fairy lights and, strangely, pink flamingos and large playing cards.

'We went for an *Alice in Wonderland* theme this year,' Violet explained. 'Laura made the flamingos, and Mummy had the rest shipped in from Harrods.'

'Where are our suitcases?' I asked.

'Higgins has already taken them up, I expect,' Violet said, climbing the stairs. A grey rabbit appeared from behind the bannisters and Violet let out a cry of joy. 'Fee Fee!' She scooped up the rabbit and buried her face in its fur. 'Hello, Fee Fee. Did you miss me?'

'Does it wander around the house?' I asked, surprised.

'Oh, yes,' said Violet. 'The gun dogs live in the stable yard so he's quite safe. And Mrs Frith gives him titbits from the kitchen.'

As I was looking at the rabbit in Violet's arms, something huge, black and winged came flying towards me, squawking loudly. I let out a little yelp and ducked, my hands covering my face.

Violet laughed, setting Fee Fee down.

'Whatever was *that*?' I asked.

'Emmeline's jackdaw.'

I looked fearfully in the direction the huge, menacing bird had gone but could see no sign of it.

'Emmeline found him when he was a chick and fed him worms. He's quite tame, really.'

I shuddered at the thought of dropping live, wriggling worms down the throat of that ominous creature.

Violet led me along the first-floor landing, pausing several times to point out ancient family portraits or paintings by notable Dutch artists. I nodded politely, trying not to appear ignorant.

'You need to be careful around the house,' she told me. 'There are several shut-up, fire-damaged rooms. We have a problem with bats. They're always getting in. And the floor-boards of one of the west wing bedrooms are quite rotten; last year Ethel – one of the maids – nearly fell straight through to the drawing room. I should let you know – Mummy thinks central heating is awfully common but she gave in a few years ago: although it's temperamental and only a handful of rooms have radiators. You need to tell the maids a day in advance if you want a bath. And we don't have fires in the bedrooms as Mummy says it's bad for our health to get too hot at night.'

I nodded, following Violet along the landing, taking all this in.

At the bottom of another staircase there was a collection of photographs. One, in particular, caught my eye and I stopped to look at it. A large group of people stood outside Thornleigh on the driveway, some of them sitting in chairs.

'Why are there so many people?' I asked.

Violet shrugged. 'Staff. There were a lot more in those days. It's just the way it was. Those are my grandparents,' she said, pointing. 'And that's my father. You'll meet him at dinner. The boys next to him are his brothers. Both killed in the war. Father fought too, of course. He got shot in the leg. He's got a terrible limp. Did your father go?'

I nodded. 'Does yours ever talk about it?' My own father never did. Along with the subject of my mother, the war remained The Great Unmentionable.

'Yes,' said Violet. 'Although when he does, it's as if he's talking more to himself than to us. Anyway, it was yonks ago. All ancient history now. There'll never be another war. Not like that one.'

* * *

Violet threw herself down on one of the twin beds, her arms and legs spread out like a starfish.

'Oh, how good it is to be home, Gilly. Away from that beastly school at last.'

I smiled. It certainly was good to be away from Heathcomb.

And I was pleased we were sharing. I would have felt uneasy had I been given my own room in that huge house. A wallpaper of wide green stripes and falling roses made the bedroom feel cosy, although I noticed the paper was peeling at the edges. Towels had been laid out on the beds for us and a sprig of winter foliage was arranged in a vase on the mantelpiece. Violet had a writing desk. Old and ink-stained, it was littered with bits and pieces she must have collected: pheasant feathers, a cracked blue bird's egg, twigs tied with ribbons. Her labelled nature drawings – mushrooms, plants, and insects – were pinned to the wall behind the desk. I noticed a detailed drawing of her beloved deadly nightshade. There were several field guides, and two volumes of Andrew Lang's *Fairy Books*.

Candles and matches had been left on our dressing table and Violet warned me that the landings and hallways were rarely lit so I'd have to take a lamp or a torch with me if I needed to use the bathroom in the night.

'Laura hates the dark,' Violet said, 'but Mummy and Emmi think electric light is vulgar. Mummy says the electric wiring ruined our Venetian chandeliers.'

I took in the view from our high domed window. The light was fading fast but I could see that what Violet referred to as 'the park' stretched all the way to the trees. It was quite a distance, as far as several hockey pitches. In front of the woods was a great oval-shaped mass of water, half hidden by reeds and a black tangle of brambles, with a landing stage at one end. As I stared out, I thought I saw a figure move amongst the trees: a flash of white. I blinked. Was it Emmeline perhaps? I looked again, but there was nothing there.

'If you look out the window early in the morning, you'll probably see deer,' Violet said, coming up behind me. 'Let's change for dinner, shall we?'

I turned gratefully. I was feeling rather travel weary, and quite ravenous. I hoped there would be plenty to eat.

I put on my brown buttoned dress and was taking out the contents of my suitcase, when Violet turned to me said, 'Don't worry about putting your clothes away. The servants will do it.'

I immediately stopped what I was doing. 'Oh right,' I replied quickly. 'Of course.'

I was beginning to realise that although Violet and I were on fairly equal terms at school – if anything I was ahead of her in maturity, being almost a year older, ahead in my studies, and more socially adept, I liked to think – she lived in a world of which I knew very little. Of course in Egypt, I'd had Clara and there was a woman who'd come in each day to help with the cooking and housework, along with the gardener who serviced all three of the expatriate houses in our cul-de-sac, but we lived modestly. Here at Thornleigh Hall, in this great house with its art and sweeping staircases – which Violet seemed to take as a matter of course – she was above me. Her background and breeding were, I knew, far superior to mine. It wasn't just that Violet's father was titled, my family did not have land, host hunting parties, own art. I also remembered, with horror, that a sister of my mother's had been in service for a while before she married. Here I was, a guest of the Claybournes and yet I perhaps had more in common with their staff. The thought made me feel cold inside, and I decided I would put as much distance as I could between my relatively humble upbringing and the new Gillian I wanted to be here at Thornleigh Hall.

I pictured Emmeline and Laura as I had seen them on the drive. How Emmeline had barely looked at me, and how Laura had scrutinised my home-made scarf. I wanted desperately for Violet's sisters to notice me, for them to see me as more than a mere schoolgirl. I remembered the vow I had made after surviving my climb across the roof – my vow to do something with my life, to *be* somebody. I decided they would notice me. They had to. This was my opportunity, the one I had been waiting for, the chance to be someone different, someone better. This was real life beginning at last.

I took my hairbrush from my washbag and stood in front of the looking glass, trying to tidy my hair before dinner. My face, ordinary and familiar, stared back at me. I was too plain, too girlish. I did not possess Emmeline's grace or Laura's charm. But perhaps by spending time here at Thornleigh, I could develop myself into something that more closely resembled them.

I dropped my shoulders, lifted my chin, gave myself an encouraging smile. From somewhere downstairs there came the sound of the gong.

'Are you ready then?' Violet asked.

Chapter Five

WHEN WE ARRIVED DOWNSTAIRS FOR dinner, the Claybournes were evidently in the middle of a discussion.

'. . . simply have to invite the Naylor-Bests, they're such good fun,' Laura was saying.

'No,' said Emmeline firmly. 'We can't have their situation making other people uncomfortable. Besides, we're quite full as it is.'

'Such a ghastly business, divorce,' Lady Claybourne murmured with a shudder. 'Emmeline's right. We won't invite them this year.'

The dining room was filled with a long mahogany table and a breakfast cabinet along one wall. The table was draped with red damask. There were candles, heavy silverware, and a fire crackling in the huge fireplace. The faces of the Claybournes in the firelight were pale and luminous.

As we slipped into our seats, Emmeline's eyes fell briefly on me before her attention returned to her mother.

With her height, vivid green eyes and razor-sharp cheekbones, Emmeline was really quite striking. She wore another white lacy Edwardian-looking dress with long sleeves and a high ruffled collar, and she'd put her hair up for dinner. I wished I was out of pigtails and able to wear my hair in such a grown-up style like Emmeline.

Laura was in a sleeveless blue flapper dress with gold beading that made her look like she should be stumbling out of a Soho nightclub. She wore a blue feather in her hair and a fur stole draped across her shoulders. A white fox. The fox unnerved me: those tiny dead teeth baring down at her dinner plate.

Perhaps, I thought, if I can get close enough to them, a little of their beauty and elegance might rub off on me, like when you walk through a spider's web and the silky strands cling to your clothes.

'You'll have to excuse us – Gillian, isn't it?' Lady Claybourne said. 'I'm afraid invitations and preparations for the New Year's Eve ball are all you'll hear over the coming weeks. You must think us very rude.'

I shook my head, sneaking a look at her. Her hair was piled on top of her head. A shawl of lilac and gold was draped over her shoulders, a necklace with a dark red gem at her throat, all making her look, I thought, rather like a queen residing over her court.

'It's wonderful to have you at Thornleigh for the holidays,' she said. 'We were all so pleased when Violet told us she was bringing a friend home.' Lady Claybourne glanced at Violet and gave her a thin smile before returning her to gaze to me. 'But won't your mother miss you very much at Christmas?'

I looked down at the tablecloth. 'Oh, no. My mother died at my birth.' I tried to keep my tone neutral, the words brief, but I braced myself for the uncomfortable offerings of sympathy that usually followed this admission. I always felt embarrassed, not for myself, but for those who struggled to know what to say to a child who has lost a parent. 'I'm afraid I don't remember her,' I added, which usually softened things.

'Oh, dear, I *am* sorry.' Lady Claybourne peered at me over the table. 'Your father?' she asked, tentatively.

'He's in Egypt.'

'Fascinating country,' Lord Claybourne murmured, spreading a napkin over his knees. He was a tall, thin man with hollow cheeks, balding on top, and with little greying tufts of hair that stood on end. His moustache gave him a military air. I noticed the cuffs of his dinner jacket were fraying. His cane leaned against his dinner chair, its top a brass fox head.

Looking at Lord Claybourne, I found it difficult to believe he owned Thornleigh, that he was an aristocrat, had been an officer in the war, that he rubbed shoulders with earls and viscounts. I thought he looked more like the sort of man you might find huddled in the corner of the reading room at the British Library, trying to discreetly unwrap a sandwich. When in London, Aunt Ada occasionally took me on what she called 'cultural outings'. We wandered through the British Library, stood across the road from the newly built Carreras Cigarette Factory and admired the regal Egyptian cats, then ate our lunch – meat paste sandwiches – by the Thames, gazing at the Houses of Parliament. 'What a nice day we've had, Gillian. And we've only spent our bus fare,' Aunt Ada would say with satisfaction.

'I played cricket once against Sir Lee Stack,' Lord Claybourne said. 'Of course this was when we were boys,' he went on hastily. 'Such a pity. Poor old Stack … Still, we need the Suez, of course. Got to maintain our interests. I know several government men who have been posted in Cairo.'

I realised Lord Claybourne assumed my father had some kind of senior government position, that he worked for the embassy or the consulate. I didn't correct him and, never being quite sure exactly what it was my father did (something to do with irrigation and canals?), I decided not to attempt to explain.

Luckily, I was saved by our driver, Higgins, now in his liveries, who had assumed the role of butler (or was it footman?) and was bringing in several bowls of soup balanced on a silver tray.

I glanced down at the vast array of cutlery around my place setting and found myself staring at a little silver fork. I'd never seen such a beautiful fork. A pearly, engraved handle, elegantly shaped prongs, so well polished I could see my reflection in it.

'Gillian actually *lived* in Egypt,' Violet said.

I glanced at my friend, feeling grateful. Here was something about me other people appeared to find exotic.

'Did you?' Emmeline asked with mild interest.

'I've heard all these places are quite similar to England, really,' said Laura. 'Only the weather is hotter and you get a bigger staff.'

Laura was, I saw, picturing me living in some magnificent colonial house, the Egyptian equivalent of a larger and less crumbling Thornleigh, and with twenty staff, like the photograph Violet had shown me upstairs.

I gave the usual spiel about my childhood; weekend picnics in the desert (we went once – Clara found it too sandy), archaeological expeditions to newly discovered tombs stuffed with ancient treasures, cocktail parties full of diplomats and film stars onboard luxury, privately owned boats; the stunning sunsets over the Nile.

This colourful, fabricated childhood was far more interesting than the reality. What I really remembered of Egypt was long, hot, dreadfully dull days spent gazing at the mimosa leaves floating in the pond in our garden, wishing I had a companion to play with.

'How fascinating,' said Lady Claybourne, when I had finished my little speech. 'I can't see *us* there, of course. We would miss England, and Thornleigh.'

'We could never leave Thornleigh,' said Emmeline.

'I'm afraid you'll think this very rude of us, Gillian,' Lord Claybourne said, 'but Olivia—' (apparently Lady Claybourne's first name) '—and I are going away tomorrow. Just for a few days—'

'London,' Lady Claybourne interrupted, setting down her fork. 'We've had an invitation we can't get out of. You know how it is at this time of year.'

Violet pouted. 'We've only just got here.'

Lady Claybourne ignored her. 'It will give you girls a chance to catch up.'

I thought I saw Emmeline roll her eyes.

'We'll be back by Christmas Eve,' Lord Claybourne added. 'We wouldn't miss the Boxing Day hunt.'

'Have you ever seen a hunt before, Gillian?' Laura asked me. I said I hadn't.

Our soups bowls were cleared and a girl wearing an apron and an old-fashioned mob cap entered the dining room carrying huge plates of food. Higgins was close behind her with more. I stared at the sliced beef, pigeon breasts, smoked salmon, roast potatoes and buttery winter greens that were being piled onto the table. There seemed enough food for twice as many of us. I knew Aunt Ada would think it ridiculous.

'Thank you, Mary,' said Lady Claybourne.

After Mary and Higgins had served us, Violet tucked into her meal, already spearing additional roast potatoes off the platter with her fork.

'Goodness, Violet, anyone would think you hadn't eaten for a week,' said Lady Claybourne disapprovingly.

'I haven't really,' said Violet, with a mouthful of potato. 'The food at Heathcomb is horrible.'

'I'm sure it isn't,' said Lady Claybourne.

Violet was right but I kept quiet. I sensed some friction between Violet and her mother and didn't want to add to it.

'We had a manservant, down in the trenches,' Lord Claybourne said, his fork poised in mid-air. 'That fellow was a fine cook. I've never known anyone be able to do so much with tinned ham. He was killed one night when he insisted on going back to the reserve trench to fetch the pepper. "You've got to have pepper, sir," he said, and off he went. A German sniper got him. We had to make do without the pepper.'

There was an uncomfortable silence.

'Well . . .' said Lady Claybourne.

'Gillian can cook,' said Violet.

The Claybournes all looked at me in surprise.

'Really?' said Laura.

Lady Claybourne frowned. 'They're not teaching you that at school, are they?'

'Oh, no,' I said quickly.

Miss Eldridge, our headteacher, thought Domestic Science beneath us, and deemed it unnecessary for the sort of lives we were being groomed for. Lives with servants, presumably. Aunt Ada, a practical woman of the lower middle-classes, had thought this dreadful. 'Don't they teach you anything?' she'd asked me when she discovered, on one of my visits, that I couldn't boil an egg.

'I can only cook a little. Eggs and bacon . . . My aunt taught me.'

'Well, I suppose it could come in useful,' said Lady Claybourne, looking doubtful.

Lord Claybourne glanced up from his beef as if remembering we were all there. 'Mrs Frith is a good plain cook,' he said. 'Fancy food never did anyone any good.'

Emmeline and Laura exchanged a glance, and I saw Emmeline lift her napkin to hide her smile.

Laura cleared her throat. 'So have we decided about the ball? I really think it should be fancy dress. It's all the rage at the moment. *Everyone* is doing fancy dress.'

Emmeline made a face. 'All those cowboys and Cleopatras. If we have to have fancy dress, can't it be Regency?'

Lady Claybourne considered this. 'No,' she said finally. 'I think Laura's right. Every ball I've been to this year has been Regency, and our guests will enjoy the freedom to get creative with their costumes. Besides, I can't stand the Regency dances. All that sidestepping.' She shuddered.

'I know what I want to go as,' said Violet.

Emmeline raised an eyebrow.

'Peter Pan.'

Laura laughed. 'That's perfect for you, Piff. You do like to be original.'

'I'm going to make an outfit of red leaves and cobwebs,' said Violet. 'Just like when we saw the play.'

'Don't be silly, Violet,' said Lady Claybourne. 'That's an outfit for a boy. I'll get Ethel to help me make a costume for you. Something suitable.'

Violet's face fell. 'But when we went to the theatre, Peter Pan was played by a woman. Don't you remember?'

'Theatre people are a law unto themselves,' said Lady Claybourne stiffly.

'And what about you, Gillian?' asked Emmeline. 'We'll have to think of something for you.'

'I know,' said Laura, excited. 'How about Cinderella? I think Gillian would make an excellent Cinderella.'

I blushed furiously. Was this Laura's way of saying she knew I didn't belong here? That I was not like them? Only a younger, poorer, relation.

'We'll get you a ballgown,' Laura went on. 'You must be Cinderella at the ball. Cinderella *after* the fairy godmother has worked her magic. Every girl must get a chance to be a princess.'

I smiled, feeling relieved.

There was some kind of commotion in the hallway outside the dining room, a scuffling and a strange cry. To my astonishment a duck flew in and dived under the table. I caught a flash of brown and white, the flapping of wings. We all leaped up, dropping our napkins.

'Really!' exclaimed Lady Claybourne. 'Rabbits. Jackdaws. And now ducks. This place is a zoo!'

From beneath the table the duck quacked loudly. I lifted the tablecloth. It was a female mallard and seemed rather surprised to have found itself under our feet.

Mary, the maid, appeared at the doorway, her face flushed. 'I'm dreadfully sorry, your Ladyship. The duck – he went up the stairs before we could stop him.'

'It's a her,' said Emmeline dryly.

'We'd better catch it,' murmured Lord Claybourne.

'Oh, no, sir,' said Mary, panicked. 'It'll only flap and try and get away. Robin will have to do it. It's his duck, you see.' She turned back into the hallway and called out. 'Robin! Come here, please.'

A small dark-haired boy, around six years old, came skidding into the room. 'Bertha!' he cried. 'Naughty Bertha!' He stopped and blinked when he saw us all looking at him.

'And what, exactly, is the boy doing with a duck?' Lady Claybourne asked, her eyes narrowed.

Mary swallowed nervously. 'He found it, your Ladyship. Down at the lake. It had lost its mother. But it's growing up quite well now.'

'So I see,' said Lady Claybourne.

Mary turned to the boy. 'It's all right, darlin'. Fetch him quickly now.'

The boy gave us all a wary look, then crawled under the table. He emerged with the duck. 'There, there, Bertha,' he said. 'Nothing to be scared of.'

'I think,' said Lady Claybourne, tersely 'that it is *our* nerves that need to be soothed. Really, Mary, a duck under the dining table. It's not civilised.'

Whilst Mary was apologising and with the Claybournes distracted, I glanced down again at the little fork that had caught my eye. Making sure no one was watching me, I managed to slip the fork up my sleeve. Immediately after I'd concealed it, I felt my cheeks burn. Why had I done such a thing? I had wanted a little piece of Thornleigh to be mine, a memento of this lavish dinner that although I knew to be nothing out of ordinary for the Claybournes, was everything to me.

*　*　*

'Gilly, wake up.'

I rolled over and opened my eyes to find Violet holding a torch and peering at me.

'What is it?' I asked, blinking and trying to shield my eyes from the light. 'Did you have a bad dream? Are you still doing your undoings?'

Violet moved the beam of the torch away from my face and shook her head. 'No, nothing like that. I just want to show you something.'

'Now?' I asked, sitting up and glancing at the clock on my night table. It was a little after midnight. We'd gone to bed at ten.

'Yes,' said Violet. 'Come on.'

I got out of bed, wearing my winter pyjamas and thick bedsocks. I put on my slippers and reached for a cardigan. Violet was already at the bedroom door.

We crept along the third-floor landing, Violet holding the torch, passing paintings of storms at sea. Boats with taut sails being tossed among huge leaping waves. Then there were the brown Dutch landscapes – tiny seventeenth-century peasants walking along muddy riverbanks – and, finally, more gloomy portraits of the Claybournes' long-dead relatives.

60

We ascended a staircase to the upper floor. I noticed a thick line of black soot on the dado rail and realised we must be entering the damaged, blackened wing of the house I'd seen from the drive.

'Where are we going?' I whispered softly, catching up with Violet.

She put her finger to her lips. She opened a tiny door at the end of the landing and I found myself in a narrow, winding stairwell, the steps polished smooth with age.

I could hear something now. Music. It seemed to be coming from all around us. We reached a door at the top of the torchlit stairwell.

The room was lit with candles, some of them shoved into old wine bottles, wax dripping down the necks. An ancient oil lamp sat on a low table that was littered with overflowing ashtrays and empty glasses. The room smelled of cigarette smoke and another, deeper scent – something smoky and burned, long ingrained, a smell that had got into the very fabric of the walls. Much of the furniture was covered with sheets. A black mark, shaped like a winged creature, was spread across the wall like a huge inkblot.

Laura was standing by a gramophone, playing something slow and jazzy at a low volume. Holding a drink in one hand and a cigarette in an ebony and ivory cigarette holder in the other, she swayed in time to the music, the hem of her long silky nightdress sweeping across the bare floorboards.

Emmeline was sitting on a threadbare chaise longue reading a large hardback with *Oresteia* embossed in gold on the spine. She looked luminescent and ethereal; all the candlelight in the room appeared to be drawn to her.

'I knew you'd be here,' said Violet triumphantly.

Emmeline lifted her eyes slowly from her book. 'Isn't it past your bedtime?'

Violet frowned. 'I wanted to show Gilly.' She turned to me. 'This is the tower bedroom, Gilly. Emmi and Lolly come here sometimes after Mummy and Daddy have gone to bed. It's their secret hideout.'

Emmeline reached for a large crystal glass and took a sip of something – a dark, golden liquid that looked like the whisky my father used to drink. 'It's where we come for a little peace,' she said.

'And to play music,' said Laura happily. 'Mummy despises jazz. Divorce, jazz, fast cars, girls in slacks. She thinks the world's going to hell in a handcart. She won't even listen to Noël Coward. I just adore Noël, although he is rather louche.' She let out a little giggle.

Violet had sunk into an old button-back sofa, curling her feet up underneath her. I sat too.

'Would you like a drink, Gillian?' asked Laura, gesturing to the table of half-empty spirit bottles.

'Oh, no, thank you,' I murmured.

Emmeline shook her head a fraction. 'Lolly, they're only fourteen.'

'Fifteen,' Violet said grouchily.

'Nearly sixteen,' I said.

Emmeline smiled. 'Still. Far too young.'

Laura changed the record on the gramophone. 'Aren't the Boswell Sisters fabulous,' she said, wriggling her hips as a silky female voice sang about an evening in Caroline.

'I like your music,' I told Laura.

My voice sounded small and girlish. I wished I was more sophisticated, more worldly. I didn't know much about popular music.

'I bought this record in Paris,' said Laura dreamily.

'You were in Paris?'

Laura exhaled a plume of smoke. 'Last summer. I returned from finishing school in Switzerland – Emmi and I both had to go – and then I came out, you see. I went to Paris, then Venice, and Capri. Oh, Capri was wonderful. Full of writers and queers, but simply divine. The eldest du Maurier sister was there. You know, the less interesting one. Then I went to Berlin. Germany was magnificent. Everything runs so smoothly and the people are so *optimistic*. I attended a rally in Nuremberg with the friends I was staying with. People were going crazy for the Führer. It was difficult not to get swept up in it all. All that cheering and saluting. And all those lovely men in their shiny boots. But this was before Munich, of course.'

'The man's completely mad,' interjected Emmeline. 'I don't know why people can't see it.'

'At least he's enthusiastic about something,' said Laura, pouting.

Emmeline took another sip of her drink. 'Evicting people. Stealing their property? Because that's what he's doing over there, you know.'

'Well, *anyway*,' Laura continued. 'I loved Germany, but of course Paris stole my heart.'

'Yes, we heard all about *that*,' said Emmeline.

I gave Violet a questioning glance but the comment seemed to have gone over her head.

'Have you shown your friend the park yet?' asked Emmeline.

'Of course not,' Violet replied. 'There's been no time. I'll show Gilly around tomorrow.'

'I hope you'll find enough to do,' said Laura. 'It can be awfully boring at Thornleigh in the winter months. I suppose you can ride, if you like?'

'Gilly doesn't ride,' said Violet.

I knew Violet was only stating a fact but I wished she hadn't made me sound so silly. The truth was, I hadn't been brought up around horses, and had always been rather frightened of them and their size.

Laura took another long drag on her cigarette. 'Well, there's always skating if the lake freezes. You can borrow my skates. I've got a lovely pair. But you won't get Violet on the ice, I'm afraid to say.'

Violet's jaw tensed. 'You always have to bring that up.'

'Violet had an accident,' Laura told me. 'She was on the ice – this was several years ago now – practising some kind of twirling manoeuvre. The ice broke and she fell straight through.'

'Goodness,' I said.

Laura turned the music down then came to sit with us, her cigarette smoke trailing behind her as she crossed the room. 'Luckily Emmi was there.'

Emmeline smiled. 'Oh, it was really nothing.'

'I might have been fine,' said Violet.

Emmeline raised an eyebrow. 'You didn't say that when you were gasping and shivering on the bank. And you didn't look fine – thrashing about like that – you looked like you were drowning.'

'What did you do?' I asked Emmeline.

Laura stubbed her cigarette out in a stuffed ashtray. 'Emmi grabbed a branch and managed to pull Piff from the water.'

'I got extremely wet,' said Emmeline. 'And of course I had to give Violet my coat.'

'She saved Piff's life,' said Laura, matter-of-factly.

I looked at Violet who was pressing her lips together. I felt irritated with her for not appearing more grateful, for not appreciating what she had. I knew I'd be proud as anything if my sister had saved my life.

Violet doesn't know what she's got, I thought.

Chapter Six

THE FOLLOWING MORNING, LORD AND Lady Claybourne departed for London and Violet insisted on giving me a full tour of the house and grounds. I followed her along dim passageways and dark landings as she threw open door after door, ready for me to peer appreciatively inside. *Just another guest bedroom. This is a room we don't use much. This arch leads to the servants' quarters. We've no need to go down there and, anyway, it's only Higgins, Mrs Frith, Mary and Ethel nowadays. Mary and Ethel are our maids. They don't get on. Ethel thinks Mary is lazy, and Mary thinks Ethel has ideas above her station.*

She'd shown me the orangery (*Emmeline grows orchids and dahlias*), the blue drawing room, and the billiard room with its red velvet curtains and musty cigar smell.

In the gunroom, paintings depicting hunting scenes, along with a map of the estate, hung on the walls. The guns were displayed in cabinets.

Violet pointed out a smallish grey gun with a black handle and a seahorse snout. 'This one is Father's service revolver. It's a Webley.'

Looking at the gun, I experienced an ominous feeling. Although the weapon was now retired, I tried not to think about when and for what purpose it would have inevitably been used.

She went to the desk drawer and produced a key which she used to unlock a tall wooden cupboard. Inside were three long shotguns. 'Daddy's Purdeys. Do you want to hold one?'

I shook my head. 'I don't think so.'

Violet laughed. 'They're not loaded, silly. Although I know how to do it. Here.' She thrust the gun into my hands and I took a step back, startled by the weight of it.

'We sometimes use them to shoot rabbits. Jennings, that's the keeper, taught us how to shoot. The woods get overrun with rabbits. They eat the crops, so the farmers are pleased if we keep the numbers down. Of course the farmers want to shoot them themselves, but they're not allowed. It's our land, see. They only rent it. And we have terrible problems with poachers. Frank Marks poaches – you know, the man we saw on the track last night – but Father turns a blind eye. It's dreadful, really.' Violet shuddered, perhaps thinking of Fee Fee.

'Is Frank Marks a farmer?'

'I don't know what you'd call him. He doesn't work for us, exactly, but we always use him as a beater during the October shoot, and he helps the farmers in the summer. His mother worked for my grandparents for years. She was Daddy's nanny and Daddy was awfully attached to her. That's why, when Frank's mother died, Daddy rented the cottage to Frank for a pittance.' Violet shut the shotguns away, replacing the key in the drawer, and we left the room.

'This is the lounge hall,' Violet said, leading me into a vast room just off the main hallway.

I peered around the door. Clumps of furniture sprang up in various places like shrubs in a desert. Two huge, dusty chandeliers hung from the ceiling spotted yellow and brown from years of fires, cigarette and pipe smoke. Mounted above the mantelpiece was a cream skull with antlers that looked too large to be a deer.

'A moose,' said Violet, following my gaze. 'Daddy brought it back from a hunting trip to Canada. We've got relatives over there.'

On the oak-panelled walls, along with several threadbare tapestries, hung old grey armour and a number of ancient and terrifying looking weapons: swords, muskets and something that looked like a giant, rusty spade.

'That was used by my grandfather during the Boer War,' said Violet, following my gaze. 'He murdered several Boer guerrillas with it. If you look closely enough you can still see the bloodstains.'

There were stuffed stags' heads, a tiger-skin rug, and, over by the grand piano, a snarling brown bear clinging to a branch. 'Mummy calls this room the heart of the home,' Violet said.

It seemed a rather chilly heart to me.

As Violet turned back to the hallway, something caught my eye. A movement in the corner of the room. It was Fee Fee, I saw, nibbling the curtains.

Up on the first-floor landing, Violet paused outside a door, touched the doorknob three times, spun around on the spot, then opened the door a crack. 'This is the butterfly room.'

I peered inside. The walls were full of frames of pinned butterflies. 'Who collected all these?'

'My grandfather,' Violet said, then quickly pulled the door tightly shut.

'Can't we have a look?' I asked. This room, for me, was far more interesting than the gunroom and the dusty bedrooms and reception rooms Violet had insisted on showing me.

She shook her head. 'I hate the butterfly room. I never go in there. It gives me the creeps.'

So we headed up to the second floor as Violet wanted me to see the nursery, a large, cold room with a bare fireplace and elaborate cornicing. The room smelled of damp and mildew. A table and chairs sat in one corner next to an old rocking horse with a missing ear and a matted grey mane. There was evidence of teaching: a blackboard, abandoned chalk sticks, a Victorian-looking abacus, a wooden painting chest and a French dictionary.

'Did you used to have lessons in here?' I asked, gesturing to the blackboard.

'Well, not me so much. Emmeline and Laura had lessons in the schoolroom across the hall but that's empty now too.'

Violet wandered over to the window. She put a finger in the fur of dust on the sill, grimaced, then wiped it quickly on her dress.

I noticed that someone had made a procession of small toy soldiers. They snaked their way across the floorboards.

'Emmeline and Laura have never been to school?' I asked.

Violet shook her head. 'Mummy doesn't go in much for education for girls, despite how clever Emmi is. Mummy believes all the games at school give girls thick ankles and rugged complexions and makes them unattractive for marriage.'

I wondered why Lady Claybourne hadn't been worried about Violet getting thick ankles.

'Emmi and Laura had an English and Languages master in for a while. I suppose he would have taught me too if he'd stayed but Mummy sent him away.' Violet paused and wrinkled her nose. 'Let's get out of here, Gilly. It smells.'

*　*　*

We were out in our coats, boots and scarves, stomping around the vast grounds. Although it was now mid-morning, a pearly mist still hung over the park and the woods. The landscape was sepia toned, as though the rain had washed all the colour away, the woods and the grass covered in a slimy, dank film.

We had come a long way from the house. Violet had shown me the stables, the greenhouses, and the outhouses. The clock over the stables clearly hadn't been serviced for years and was stuck permanently at five to twelve.

Then she showed me Emmeline's aviary.

'What are they?' I asked, peering through the wire at the small birds hopping about or sitting on branches.

'That's a laughing thrush, I think.' Violet pointed to a brown and white bird with a tufty head. 'And that's a fairy-bluebird. But I don't know the others.'

We walked through a small copse. On the other side was a wooden hut where Violet said the keeper, Jennings, lived. Outside, animal corpses in various stages of decomposition hung from a makeshift gibbet; rabbits, stoats, a weasel, and something that looked like it might once have been a mole. Three crows were strung up by their feet, two with tail feathers missing. A voice coming from behind the hut made me start. Violet put her fingers to her lips, and we crept around the side wall.

There, by the water pump, was the boy from yesterday evening. Wearing a brown jacket and matching short trousers, he was playing by himself with a stick, thrusting the stick out in front of him, leaping around, slashing at the air. He hadn't seen us.

'Who *is* that boy?' I whispered.

'Oh, that's just Robin,' said Violet.

I gave her a questioning glance.

'He's Mary's child. One of our maids.'

I remembered the girl who had served us our main course last night, the one who had called Robin to come and collect his duck.

'Mary was engaged to Ned Barrow who worked for us,' Violet said as we walked. 'Ned died in the fire. He was trying to help us put it out and rescue the furniture and he got trapped. Mary was awfully upset about it, then she told Mummy and Daddy she was pregnant with Ned's child. Of course under any other circumstances Mummy would have told Mary to pack her bags, but Daddy said how could they? With Ned dying like that in a fire in *our* house, and everyone in the village being so fond of Ned. So they had to let Mary stay, even though it is a great inconvenience to us,' Violet said primly, giving me the impression she was repeating her mother's words. 'And Ned and Mary weren't even *married*. Robin is an illegitimate. Mary says they were engaged to be married but who knows if that's true.'

I thought this harsh and felt sorry for the boy. 'But who looks after him when Mary is working?'

Violet shrugged. 'No one, really. He spends a lot of time in the kitchen with Mary and Mrs Frith. But he's always running about the woods and grounds and getting under everyone's feet. And he plays in the nursery.'

So that explained the toy soldiers.

'I think it's kind of your father to let them stay.'

'Well, don't say that to Emmeline. She's on Mummy's side. She says we should let Mary go and get another groundsman to help Jennings. Poor Higgins is the only manservant we've got left in the house, and Jennings has to do everything on the estate. Father says there isn't the money for any more staff but I'm sure that can't be true.' Violet sighed. 'You know, Father was the youngest brother and he never thought he'd inherit Thornleigh. Lucky for us, I suppose. I can't imagine living anywhere else.'

I looked across the lawn to the hall, at its turreted and jagged silhouette against the ice-blue sky.

'Emmeline says Thornleigh is getting difficult for Mother and Father to manage,' Violet said. 'You know, all the costs.'

'Might you have to sell it?' I asked anxiously. I had heard about similar large properties being turned into schools or residential homes, or worse, demolished. I couldn't imagine Thornleigh being sold or razed to the ground. Through Violet's letters, Thornleigh Hall had ignited my imagination, become a source of wonder and mystery. The house had been in my consciousness, along with Violet's family, long before I'd actually arrived. Now I was here, it had seeped into my blood. I couldn't bear the thought of bedrooms being turned into dorms, or trucks and wrecking balls reducing it to rubble. Surely the Claybournes wouldn't let that happen?

'No,' Violet said fiercely. 'We won't sell it. Even though Father keeps talking about it. Emmeline says she will *never* let that happen.'

*   *   *

The lake sat in front of the beech woods, circled by a worn, muddy path. Violet and I proceeded to follow it, heading towards the trees on the far side. I looked into the inky-black water at the still reflection of the winter trees, their branches reaching towards us like long bony fingers.

At the top of the lake, there was an old oak arbour. 'Emmeline likes to read there in the summer,' Violet said, pointing it out. I imagined Emmeline, lounging on a pile of cushions, wearing one of her flowing white dresses, book in hand, the lilies in full and lovely bloom.

I noticed Violet doing the strange darting thing she did with her eyes and realised she was making the most of the quiet moment to do her rituals. I knew she stored them up, made lists of all the things she'd done that she felt she needed to be forgiven for, undone by completing her strange compulsions.

'I wondered if you weren't doing your rituals so much, recently,' I said. 'I thought perhaps it was different for you, now you're home.'

'No, I still need to do them, Gilly,' she said quietly. 'If I am doing them less, it's not because I'm home.' She turned to me. 'It's because of you, Gilly. I know it might not seem like it, but I do them less when I'm around you. I don't feel the need so much. I feel better,' she said, 'knowing I have a friend.'

'Me too,' I said softly.

She squeezed my hand.

We reached the landing stage, almost hidden by tall fawn-coloured bullrushes. Violet stepped onto it and I followed her. There was a rowing boat floating on the water, tied to the post with a piece of rope.

'Do you use the boat?'

'Oh, yes. We take it out quite often. We don't tell Mummy, though. She doesn't like it.'

'Why not?'

'Well ...' Violet glanced behind us as if someone might be listening. 'Mummy is frightened of water. She was pulled under by a wave at the beach once when she was a child and has never been in the water since. And then there was my accident on the lake.'

I thought of Violet falling through the ice and shivered. 'It was so fortunate, wasn't it,' I said, 'Emmeline thinking quickly. Saving you like that.'

Violet was gazing across the lake with a faraway look in her eyes. 'It was,' she said, but her voice was strained.

'It was very heroic,' I went on.

'Yes,' said Violet. 'It's just ...'

'Just what?'

We stopped walking. 'You mustn't *ever* repeat this, Gilly.'

'Go on.'

Violet drew in a breath. 'I really thought I was going to drown. And then Emmi was there. I saw her on the bank with the branch, only ... Only I'm sure she hesitated.'

'Hesitated?'

'Before she pushed the end of the branch towards me. I've just ... I've always thought there was a moment when she considered *not* passing me the branch, when she considered doing nothing at all.'

I stared at her for a moment. 'Oh, be reasonable,' I said. 'You were struggling in the water. How could you have seen anything clearly?'

Violet sighed. 'I'm sure you're right. And I know I was very lucky.' She paused and looked across the water. 'Bad things are always happening to country children, you know. There was a boy, only a few years ago. One of the farmers' sons. He was in the barn sliding down the haystacks. He fell onto a pitchfork. It went straight through him. They found him like that. Speared.'

I grimaced.

'Let's go into the woods, Gilly.'

Violet turned away from the lake and headed towards the beech woods. I went to follow her, then noticed the solitary figure. He walked slowly, along the other side of the lake, scouring the ground, perhaps for animal tracks. I recognised him as Frank Marks. He wore the same large brown coat and flat cap as when we'd almost run him over the night before. He was some distance away, but I was sure he gave us a nod.

I caught up with Violet. She was heading into the trees. The mist deadened the sound of our footsteps as we walked among the black maze of bracken and copper-coloured ferns.

'Do you want half a rock bun?' said Violet, producing the bun, wrapped in a handkerchief, from her pocket.

I continued to follow Violet, nibbling at my half-bun. It was rather stale.

I could hear a lone bird chirping, the steady drip-drip of water falling from the last clinging leaves. We ducked under bare branches sprinkled with furry, open-mouthed beechnuts, Violet striding on ahead of me. In the damp and the mist, the woods felt more solidly ancient, the thin line between the past and the present blurring. I inhaled the musky decaying smell of leaves returned to the earth. We headed deeper into the woods. There was something of a path, perhaps made by Frank, or Jennings, or by badgers, but after a while it seemed to disappear and I worried we wouldn't find our way back. I didn't entirely trust Violet's navigational skills and I didn't like the thought of being lost in the never-ending woods.

'Maybe we should turn around,' I suggested tentatively.

'Don't be silly. I know where we are.' Violet glanced at me over her shoulder. 'We played in here all the time when we were little. Emmeline, Laura and me. We made a den. I think it's still here somewhere. I expect Robin uses it now. He's always in the woods.'

I carefully stepped over a tree root speckled with yellow fungi. 'It must be lonely for him, having to play on his own.'

Violet shrugged. 'I suppose he'll go to the village school in a year or two.'

'Did you ever go there?'

Violet pushed aside a low branch and shook her head. 'Of course not. Mummy wouldn't have thought it right, us mixing with the riff-raff. You know, the famers' children and—'

She let out a sharp, piercing scream and pitched forward into the ferns.

I rushed up to her. 'Violet?'

She was lying amongst the leaves and the bracken, making strange gasping noises. 'My foot,' she said. 'My *foot*.'

I knelt down. The first thing I saw was the blood. It was startlingly red against the white of Violet's woollen tights. Her face was screwed up in pain. The blood was pouring out of a deep gash above her ankle, yet there was something bedded in there. Then I saw the wire. 'Oh, God,' I said.

Violet was twisting her body, trying to see. 'What is it, Gilly?' she choked. 'Oh it hurts. *It hurts.*'

The blood was seeping down into her boot. 'Wire,' I told her. 'It's wire.' I looked around desperately, and yet I knew no one would hear us if I called out. Frank would be long gone by now. The keeper's hut, even if he was there, was beyond the lake and the copse, and Thornleigh felt as if it was miles away.

Violet was writhing around and making little moaning noises. Her face had gone white. 'It's a trap,' she managed to say.

I looked at the wire embedded in her leg. Although I'd never seen such a thing before, I knew it must have been meant for animals. There had to be a way of releasing it. I felt along the wire, my hands getting wet and slippery with Violet's blood. 'Stay still,' I ordered her. 'I need to free your foot.' I tried to keep my hands steady.

Violet whimpered. 'Please, Gilly.'

I found a piece of metal attached to the wire and when I pressed it, felt the wire release. As carefully as I could, I tried to ease it out of Violet's flesh. She cried out, and I fell back, the bloody wire in my hand.

'It's out,' I said, breathless.

Violet was gasping from the pain. She kept squeezing her eyes shut. Her stockings were dark and sticky with blood and I didn't know if she'd severed an artery. Drops of blood kept running down her boot and falling into the mud. Remembering a first aid lesson we'd had at school, I quickly took off my knitted scarf and wrapped it several times around her ankle, tying it as tightly as I could.

'What are you doing?' Violet asked feebly.

'It's a tourniquet,' I said. 'Here.' I held out my hand. 'You have to try to stand.'

Violet's face was wet with tears. She shook her head. 'I can't,' she said. 'It hurts too much. Go get someone, Gilly. Please. Run as fast as you can.'

I looked into the trees, in the direction we'd come from, my stomach churning. What if I got lost? I couldn't bear the thought of leaving Violet alone. How long would I be? I had visions of myself running around Thornleigh, from room to room trying to find someone.

'I'm not leaving you,' I said firmly. 'Take my hand.'

She did, and I managed to get her to her feet. She leaned heavily on me, her arm draped over my shoulders. We tried to take a few steps, but she kept crying out in pain. '*I can't*, Gilly, I really can't.'

I crouched down, bending over. 'Get on my back then.'

She managed to flop herself over me and I steeled myself. 'I'm going to straighten up. Hold on.' She clamped an arm tightly around my neck and I stood, bearing her weight.

We made our way through the woods like that, Violet heavy on my back. I was terrified I was going to trip over a branch or tree root, or stumble head first into the bracken. I wanted to tell her to relax her grip; it felt as if she was choking me, but I carried on, putting one foot in front of the other, trying to balance myself, Violet whimpering in my ear, occasionally offering directions. 'This way. Just go straight.'

Finally, we reached the edge of the woods and were back by the lake. Once we'd passed the lake there was only the south section of the park to cross to the house. Still it seemed so far, and the mount was steep.

'Shall we stop, Gilly?' Violet said, her voice shaky. 'You can leave me here if you like.'

'No,' I said through gritted teeth. 'I'm not leaving you.' As we passed the stables we saw a figure dressed in white coming out of the stable door.

'Emmeline,' Violet whispered, close to my ear.

I called to her and at the same time she turned and saw us. We must have looked a strange sight, emerging in the mist from the woods, me stooped over, my knees buckling, Violet clinging to my back like a limpet.

Emmeline rushed to us, stopping when she saw Violet's ankle, the blood on her tights, my scarf wrapped around her foot, its end trailing through the muddy grass. 'Violet! Goodness, what have you done?'

'I stepped in a trap. It hurts, Emmi, it really hurts.'

'Here.' Emmeline was removing Violet from my back. 'Put an arm around each of us. That's it. We've got you.'

I couldn't have walked another step. It felt as though Emmeline had rescued me as much as Violet.

With Emmeline and I on either side of a trembling, wincing Violet, we half carried, half dragged her into the house.

Chapter Seven

'**B**LOODY POACHERS,' SAID LAURA UNDER her breath. We were sitting in the library, a healthy fire burning in the grate.

'Do you think that's who it was, then?' I asked.

'Of course,' Laura replied. 'Must have been. Jennings knows we like to walk through the woods. He wouldn't leave traps lying around. Poachers are always sneaking onto our land. We have a terrible problem with them.'

'Jennings doesn't need to set traps. He knows how to use a shotgun,' Emmeline said, her eyes not leaving the book she was reading. She had one leg curled beneath the other, the fabric of her muslin dress ruffled up around her.

Laura threw Emmeline a harsh glance. 'I don't how you can read at a time like this.'

'She'll be fine,' Emmeline said, turning a page. 'You heard what the doctor said.'

'Yes ... but still.'

Laura, on seeing us enter the house, had called immediately for the doctor. We'd placed Violet on the Chesterfield in the library, her foot elevated on a stack of towels. Emmeline had summoned Ethel to light a fire, and we'd tried to keep Violet warm with blankets as we waited, with some anxiety, for the local doctor to arrive.

The doctor untied my scarf and poked and prodded at Violet's ankle as she yelped and squirmed, then pronounced Violet's injury to be a flesh wound and perhaps 'a bit of a sprain', but nothing worse; no broken bones.

'You were lucky,' he told Violet.

'It was Gillian who pulled the wire free,' Laura said. 'She used her scarf. And she carried Piff all the way from the woods to the stables.'

The doctor had looked up at me. 'Well, Gillian, you certainly thought on your feet.'

'Oh, it was nothing.' I blushed.

Although I wouldn't have wished Violet's accident to happen, I had to admit it was nice to finally be noticed by Emmeline and Laura. They both seemed suitably impressed by my heroic actions. Even Emmeline, glancing at my scarf around Violet's ankle had said, 'Good thinking, Gillian.'

The doctor, before he left, had instructed Ethel on how to change the gauze bandage and had given Emmeline something for Violet, 'for the shock' he said, recommending she rest as much as possible over the coming days.

Now, after taking the prescribed pills from the doctor, Violet lay asleep on the Chesterfield, a cushion beneath her head, her ankle elevated. Emmeline's jackdaw was perched on the bust of Milton on the mantelpiece. A huge portrait of Lord Claybourne's father – a stern-looking Victorian – loomed over us.

'I bet it was Frank Marks,' Laura whispered. 'Putting traps down.'

'He'll deny it,' said Emmeline flatly. 'And I think he uses ferrets for rabbiting, anyway.'

Laura sighed. 'Still, maybe Father will have a word this time. I wish he'd tell Frank not to use the park as a cut-through, not to use it *at all*. He swans about as if he *owns* the place.'

'I don't like it any more than you do,' Emmeline said. 'But Frank's always been here and that's the way it is.' She turned to me. 'His mother worked for us, you see. And I suppose Father must have known Frank about the place when they were both boys.' She glanced at the fire. 'Really, though, given everything, you'd think Father would hate Frank Marks. But no, he gave Frank the cottage to live in as soon as Frank got out of prison.'

'Father's soft,' said Laura. 'That's always been his problem.'

'Did Frank Marks really go to prison?' I asked, surprised.

'During the war,' said Emmeline. 'Frank was a conscientious objector. He was lucky he wasn't shot. A lot of the villagers don't speak to him.'

'But the war was years ago,' I said.

Emmeline smiled. 'Emotions still run deep around here, Gillian. Many women lost husbands and sons.'

The jackdaw flew over to the sofa and Emmeline reached out and stroked him gently with one finger.

Laura had been frowning at the fire but then she shifted her gaze to me. 'Your poor scarf, Gillian.'

The scarf, bloody and tattered, still lay on the pile of blood-soaked towels.

'It wasn't a very special one,' I said.

Laura shook her head. 'We can ask Mary to wash it of course, but I'm afraid it won't be quite the same.'

'It *was* very quick thinking of you, Gillian.' Emmeline had placed her bookmark in her book.

'Anyone would have done it,' I said modestly.

'But I'm afraid Laura's right,' Emmeline continued. 'You've probably lost that scarf. I don't think soaking it will do much good, either.'

'We'll have to get you another one,' Laura said, turning to me, her face animated in the firelight.

Violet stirred.

'Keep your voice down, Lolly. You'll wake her.'

'Sorry,' Laura whispered. 'But we should. Why don't we go tomorrow? We'll take the train to Oxford and choose a new one. It'll be fun.'

I felt I should protest but, at the same time, the idea of going out with Emmeline and Laura appealed hugely to me. To spend time with them, even time without Violet; I felt I would like that very much. I shot Violet a guilty glance.

'You'll have to count me out, I'm afraid,' Emmeline said.

Laura rolled her eyes. 'I'm sure your incestuous Greek plays and Austrian mind doctors will still be there after *one day*. Emmeline has gone mad for psychoanalysis,' she explained to me. 'It's all the rage at the moment. She's reading everything by that Austrian chap. Before too long, she'll be *analysing* us all.'

Emmeline smiled wryly. 'Actually, I've got an essay to write on Plato's presentation of Socrates.'

Laura sighed, then turned to me and smiled. 'So it will just be you and me then, Gilly,' she said.

I felt my heart warm; only Violet called me Gilly.

* * *

Going shopping with Laura was something of a revelation. *Well, the sleeves are a little long now but it ought to last two winters*, was the sort of thing Aunt Ada would say to me when we went shopping for the essential items that would 'see me through'. Shops were not to be lingered in. Clothes were purely practical.

Laura, by contrast, was not in any hurry. She chatted to the sales assistants about current trends in fashion and what had been featured in what magazine. She held scarf after scarf up to my face before finally deciding on the one which best suited my complexion and brought out the colour of my eyes. 'Clothes have to *do* something for you, Gilly.'

The scarf was a foamy turquoise blue cashmere, softer than anything I had ever owned. Laura draped it elegantly over my neck and declared it was 'absolutely perfect', causing the sales assistant to rush over to the desk and begin cutting ribbon and paper to wrap it in. I walked out of the shop, my head high, carrying a branded paper bag.

The day was dismal and cold but we didn't let it spoil our jovial mood. By early afternoon we had visited a great many shops. 'The overpriced shops', Aunt Ada would have called them. But Laura went into them all, and it seemed we still weren't done.

In a small, fashionable boutique, she reached for a dress and held it against me. 'Well, this would suit you very much, Gilly.'

The dress was dark green with a tiny print of white leaves and red berries. Pretty and seasonal, it had a contrasting, velvet yoke, and a matching trim. I reached out to touch the soft fabric at the neck.

'Why don't you try it on?' Laura asked.

'Oh, no, I couldn't.'

Laura lowered her voice. 'The brown frock you wear to dinner, Gilly, it's the only one you brought with you, isn't it?'

I nodded, embarrassed. 'I didn't get time to pack,' I murmured.

This was not true. The brown buttoned dress was my best, the only dress I owned aside from my school pinafore. Neither my father nor Aunt Ada would have thought it necessary for me to own anything more than what I had: an outfit for Sundays which doubled as travelling wear, two blouses and two cardigans, my games kit, practical flannel undergarments, two nightdresses and sturdy shoes. A dress to be worn for dinner at a large country house would not have featured on Aunt Ada's twice yearly shopping list (she sent the bill to my father).

Laura nodded as if she suspected as much. I could see she understood that I did not have a wardrobe of expensive dresses waiting for me somewhere, that I had not simply been careless and forgotten to pack them all. She turned to the sales assistant who was hovering discreetly somewhere behind us and told her I would be trying the frock on.

I glanced at the price tag and balked.

Laura took the dress from me, tucking the tag back into the collar. 'No one ever looks good in cheap clothes, darling. One must have nice things. Go on.' She gestured to the fitting room.

Of course Laura bought me the dress. 'Consider it a Christmas present,' she said.

Before I could stop myself, I threw my arms around her, inhaling her floral perfume. 'Thank you.'

Laura looked surprised. I drew back and she patted my shoulder. 'It's nothing, Gilly,' she said, clearly amused by my show of affection. 'Just a little gift, that's all.'

On our way out of the shop, Laura stopped to admire a plum-coloured hat sitting on top of a display chest next to a pair of matching gloves, gently stroking its brim then picking it up. 'Ooh, this is a lovely hat.'

'You're welcome to try it on if you like, miss,' the assistant said eagerly.

Laura removed her own hat then put the plum on, standing before the shop's mirror just as I had done in my dress. 'It *is* sweet, but I'm not sure it's really my colour.'

'I might have it in blue,' the assistant said. 'If you'll wait a moment.'

The assistant scuttled off out the back and Laura replaced the hat. She glanced in the direction of the open doorway the assistant had gone through, then slipped the matching gloves into her pocket.

I blinked in surprise, then quickly lowered my eyes as the assistant returned with a blue hat identical to the plum, unwrapping it and handing it triumphantly to Laura.

'Oh, no, I don't think it's *quite* right,' Laura said, turning her neck and checking her reflection in the mirror. She took the hat off and smiled genially. 'But thank you anyway.'

As we walked along the street, my heart was racing. I kept expecting someone to come after us. Laura had a fixed, euphoric expression on her face.

Once we were around the corner, she burst out laughing.

'Oh, isn't it a *thrill*, Gilly.'

I laughed too. I could see what she meant. It did feel exciting to be reckless, even though I felt sick to my stomach.

Laura took the plum gloves from her pocket and admired them before dropping them into one of our shopping bags.

'Goodness, it's after two,' she said, glancing at her wristwatch. 'Let's get tea, Gilly. We'll go to The Randolph, shall we? It's really the only place to go in Oxford.'

I had never had afternoon tea in a hotel before and felt like royalty. The way the waiter swept the napkins over our laps and poured the tea, the elegant cake stand full of tiny pastries and cucumber sandwiches, the pretty china plates, it was all wonderful. There was a bar with expensive-looking liquors, huge leafy plants in alcoves, high ceilings, decadent lights and the prettiest wallpaper: tropical birds and flowers. A man with a waxed and twirled moustache was playing the piano in the corner and the music was gentle and soporific.

The waiter seemed to know Laura. 'Can I get you anything else, Miss Claybourne?' or 'I hope everything is to your satis-faction, Miss Claybourne?' he asked, sidling up to our table, his back as straight as a board, a napkin folded over one arm. Imagine, I thought, walking into a place like this and the staff knowing your name. I wished I had Laura's confidence, the confidence to know that if you walked into a hotel bar or a fancy shop you were going to get immediately served, to dress in such beautiful clothes, and to walk around as if you had a perfect right to everything life had to offer. Even taking things that didn't belong to you and you didn't need.

'I suppose you eat out with your father when he comes to England,' Laura said, adding another drop of milk to her tea.

'Oh, yes,' I lied, casting my eyes down. My father never came to England and Aunt Ada never ventured further than the Lyons Corner House.

Laura was looking around for the waiter. 'I think I'll get a G & T. Of course you can have one if you like.'

'Oh, no thank you,' I said quickly, not having much experience or taste for alcohol. On the rare occasions Aunt Ada had allowed me a drop of sherry before dinner, I'd felt woozy, and I wasn't sure that was the sensation I wanted right now.

The waiter nodded as Laura put her order in. The hotel lounge had acquired several more customers. I could hear the clinking of glasses, low chatter, the soft music coming from the piano.

Laura leaned forward, resting her elbows on the table, a thin silver bracelet sliding down her wrist and clinking against her teacup. 'So tell me, Gilly, what is Violet like at school? I simply can't imagine it. I think we all expected her home after a week or two. I can't believe she's managed a *term*.' She chuckled.

I swallowed a mouthful of tea, pleased to be asked something I could comment on. 'I don't think Violet enjoys school.'

'I should think she's quite unsuited to it. All those girls. All that chatting.'

I hesitated, wondering how much I could say to Laura about Violet's lack of social skills, her nervousness and strange compulsions. 'I think she finds school overwhelming at times,' I said finally. 'She doesn't have any other friends.'

Laura nodded as if she had been expecting as much and I felt a tiny stab of betrayal. I reminded myself that Laura was Violet's sister and naturally concerned about how Violet was fairing at school, probably more so as she had never been to one herself.

'Well, it was always going to difficult for her,' said Laura. 'Violet is confident enough in her own little world, and I know she puts on the bravado at times, but she's really quite sensitive. She doesn't mix well. We had a rather insulated childhood at

Thornleigh, you see. We only had each other and our games for company.'

'Elvore,' I said.

Laura smiled. 'Emmeline created Elvore. After reading about the Brontes' Gondal. Do you know, I think Emmeline actually managed to convince Violet that Elvore was real?'

'I think she might still believe it's real.'

Laura laughed. 'That's Piff all over. When Emmi told her Father Christmas didn't actually exist, she cried for a week. I don't think she's ever got over it. She went straight to Mummy and Mummy said, "I'm afraid it's true, darling." Poor Piff felt awfully betrayed.' Laura's gin arrived and she took a large sip. 'It's still hard to believe Violet is the one who gets to be properly schooled. Emmeline used to beg Mummy to let her go. Poor Emmi. She was awfully frustrated by our hopeless governesses and longed for a proper education. She couldn't believe it when Mummy announced Violet was going to school, although we all knew why it was.'

'Why?' I asked.

Laura smiled sadly. 'I think Mummy wanted Piff out of her hair for a while. It's an important time for Emmi and me. Coming out. All the social events and the entertaining. Violet, well ... she can be unpredictable in company. She does odd things, and she gets upset easily, as I'm sure you've seen.'

I thought of Violet in the art room, collapsing into tears over her drawing.

'It drives Mummy mad,' Laura went on. 'All Violet's fidgeting. She's always on edge, isn't she? Always frightened of things. The only fear one should ever really have is a fear of being dull, don't you think, Gilly?'

I nodded solemnly.

'Of course, Emmeline has always been Mummy's favourite. Even as a small child, Emmi was so clever and refined. She could talk easily to adults, and she was so *perceptive*. Nowadays, it's Mummy who looks to Emmeline for advice.' Laura paused. 'You see, Gilly, between us, Mummy's father was only a shop-keeper. He owned a department store in the north of England. Oh, he had a bit of money, but absolutely no breeding. I know Mummy's upbringing makes her feel dreadfully inferior at times. She overcompensates. She's obsessed with appearances. Apart from their disagreements over Oxford, Emmeline is really the perfect daughter for Mummy, full of ease and grace, sharp as a pin, but Violet is problematic.'

'I don't think Violet means to be difficult,' I said, trying, half-heartedly, to defend her.

'Oh, I know,' said Laura, rattling the ice around in her glass, 'but it's been hard for Mummy. When Piff was little, Mummy said it was unnatural for a girl to run around dressed like a boy, to not be able to sit still for five minutes, to be so anxious. Piff embarrasses Mummy.' Laura lowered her voice. 'You must admit, Gilly, Violet can be peculiar. All her little habits ... Counting on her fingers and muttering to herself and checking everything a thousand times.'

'Her rituals.'

Laura sighed. 'At one time Mummy wanted to call the doctor in to have Violet examined but Daddy wouldn't hear of it. That's always been our way, I suppose. Keep it all in the family.' She leaned forward. 'Great-aunt Verity once told me that when Father came home from the war he was completely shattered.' She lowered her voice. 'You know, *mentally*.'

Of course I had heard of shell shock, and it was common knowledge that a great many men were not the same as they had been before the war, my own father most certainly being among them.

'Well, Aunt Verity wanted to get Daddy help,' Laura said. 'Send him off to one of those convalescence homes for soldiers or something like that, but my grandmother wouldn't have it. She hired a nurse to tend to him. Prescribed long, brisk walks, plenty of fishing and a double whisky before bed.' Laura shrugged. 'Perhaps she was right. Father did get better in the end.'

'He seems well,' I said, trying to sound reassuring. I had a vision of Thornleigh falling down around Lord Claybourne in great chucks of brick and plaster, and him standing in the middle of it all steadily cleaning his glasses with a handkerchief, shaking his head and saying, *Oh, dear, what a mess this is.*

Laura sighed. 'Daddy is *mostly* fine, but he buries his head in the sand if there's even the tiniest hint of a problem.'

'What about you?' I asked.

Laura smiled. 'Oh, I just go along with things. Here, do you want this last little sandwich?'

Before I could say anything she dropped a cress and mustard sandwich onto my plate.

'Violet told me things are tricky at Thornleigh,' I said in what I thought was a diplomatic and sympathetic way.

Laura leaned back and touched the pearls at her throat. 'Things certainly aren't what they were back when my parents were young. A few years ago Daddy said we ought perhaps to rent Thornleigh to Americans. Lots of people are doing it. Emmi says they'll rent any old English house if you tell them

Cromwell once watered his horse at the lake, or Queen Victoria stopped over for tea or something. But Mummy can't abide the thought of some overenthusiastic American ripping out the panelling, throwing away the tapestries, only using the house at alternate weekends for parties and installing a cocktail bar in the lounge hall. Although *that* doesn't sound so bad … But you see, Gilly, the park, the land, the house: they're a part of us, of our family. They have been for hundreds of years. And where would we go? Can you imagine us all? Squashed into some little apartment on the Continent, eating spiced sausage or goodness knows what.'

She looked so horrified, I almost laughed. But I could see how much of a wrench it would be for the Claybournes to give up Thornleigh.

'Thank goodness we put Daddy off the idea. But there are so many costs to running a place like Thornleigh. We rack up debts and then the tradesmen are reluctant to come out. A great disappointment to Mummy, of course. She does so enjoy flirting with the tradespeople.' Laura smiled wickedly.

I had never known anyone talk about their mother in such a frank way and felt embarrassed at the thought of Lady Claybourne giggling with a handyman.

'And poor Daddy,' said Laura. 'He keeps selling fields to pay the servants' wages.'

'Couldn't you perhaps make do without them?' I suggested.

'What, the servants?' Laura looked aghast. 'Goodness, no, darling. We couldn't do without Mrs Frith and the maids. Daddy would never let Jennings go. Jennings is really the only person who listens to Daddy's suggestions and pays him any attention. And Higgins has been at Thornleigh for as long as anyone can remember. He's a part of the furniture. He slithers around Thornleigh like an old reptile, getting into all the cracks. But, anyway, we needn't worry too much about money,' she said cheerfully. 'Not anymore.'

I must have given her a puzzled look as she smiled again. 'Not now Cadwallander is on the scene of course.'

'Cadwallander?'

'Oh, I thought Violet might have told you. Mummy hopes he'll propose when he comes back in the spring. He's out in Africa for the winter. Shooting rhino or whatever it is men like him do out there. Marriage has been on the cards for a few months now. He came down to stay with us in the autumn—' Laura's second drink arrived on a silver tray and she thanked the waiter. 'He was dreadful at tennis,' she continued. 'Emmeline thrashed him and Mummy was cross but Cadwallander was very jolly about it.'

I furrowed my eyebrows, the word 'propose' gathering momentum in my mind. 'Do you mean, you and him...?'

Laura laughed. 'Oh, goodness, no, darling. Not me. He's far too old for me. He's far too old for Emmi, really, but you know ...' She gave a small shrug of her shoulders.

I couldn't hide my surprise. So this *Cadwallander* (I wasn't sure if this was a first name or a surname) was planning to propose to *Emmeline*? It was difficult to imagine Emmeline married. She seemed so focused on her studies, so fiercely independent.

'But do you think Emmeline will say yes. If Cadwallander does propose, I mean?'

Laura took a large sip of her gin. 'Of course she'll say yes.' She leaned forward and lowered her voice. 'It's the only way, you see. Cadwallander, well he's ... very rich. He's recently inherited Chaseley House. Do you know it?'

I shook my head.

'Well, it's *huge*. Tons of land. They've other houses too. A place in Scotland, I think. *And* he's a viscount, which Mummy is thrilled about. She thinks it's a perfect match.'

'Oh.' I paused to consider this. So this was what Violet had meant when she'd said Emmeline wouldn't let Thornleigh be lost.

'Is Cadwallander his first name?'

Laura laughed. 'It's Hugh. But we all call him Cadwallander. Viscount Cadwallander is such a mouthful, although I suppose we'll have to start calling him Hugh. At least Emmi will.' She reached forward and took a small fruit scone from the cake stand, sliced it in half with her knife. 'Oh, have some of this, will you, Gilly.' She nudged the bigger half onto my plate and reached for the butter. 'Emmeline is desperate to hang on to Thornleigh. We've got a second cousin in London, Sebastian – an utterly urban creature – who will eventually inherit the title. Luckily for us, he's already said he has absolutely no interest in the house. He visited once a few years ago and got rather a shock when he found a bat in his wardrobe. Daddy tried to get him to take an interest in the estate and took him to visit the tenant farmer, but poor Sebastian couldn't understand a word the man said. He told me the farmer's damp children pawed at his boating blazer. Yes, the entire visit thoroughly traumatised him. He was appalled at the thought of inheriting Thornleigh and all its problems and told Daddy if he was in his position he would most certainly get rid of it. Sebastian has plenty of money and property already and so Thornleigh will most likely be given over to Emmeline and Cadwallander.'

'But would Emmeline really marry just to keep Thornleigh?'

Laura daintily buttered her scone. 'Of course she would. She loves Thornleigh more than any of us. She hardly leaves it. She loves the woods and the house. She couldn't bear it if it were lost. I mean, it's old England, isn't it?'

I nodded, agreeing that it would be ghastly if Thornleigh had to be sold. I added a blob of cream and jam to my half a scone and took a small bite. Laura had finished her second drink now and was waving our over-attentive waiter down for a third.

'But is he nice?' I asked.

'Who?' She turned back to me.

'Mr, um, Viscount Cadwallander.'

Laura smiled. 'He's all right, I suppose. A bit wet, if you ask me.'

'Is he very much older than Emmeline?'

Laura dug her knife into the jam. 'About forty or so, I think.'

I put my scone down. In my eyes, Emmeline was much more an adult than a child but still, to me, forty was very old, almost double Emmeline's age.

'Does Emmeline love him?' I asked.

Laura considered the question. 'I don't know about love, Gilly, but I expect they'll get along well enough. Last time he was at Thornleigh he was falling over himself to please her. It was quite funny, really, especially as Emmi mostly ignored him.' Laura pushed her plate away, evidently done with the scone. She hadn't eaten much at all, just nibbled at things. I wondered if she worried about her figure the way her mother did.

Something behind me must have caught Laura's eye as she smiled, then began frantically waving.

I turned, following her gaze. A young, light-haired man, wearing a Fair Isle jumper and a mustard-coloured tie, was striding quickly towards us, an umbrella hooked into the crook of his elbow.

'Hullo, Laura. I thought it was you!'

Chapter Eight

LAURA LEAPED UP. 'CHARLIE! How lovely to see you.'

'Fancy bumping into you here,' the young man said, enthusiastically. 'I was passing and I saw you through the window.' They exchanged elaborate air-kisses.

'This is Gillian Larking,' Laura said, gesturing to me. 'She's a friend of Violet's, staying with us over the holidays.'

Charlie stuck out his hand and I clambered to my feet to shake it, stumbling over my chair.

The young man grinned at me. 'How do you do, Gillian Larking. Gosh, it looks as though you ladies are having a rather nice day out.' He surveyed our little scene: the cake stand half full of fruit scones that we hadn't managed to eat, the pot of tea, now gone cold, Laura's gin glasses, our shopping bags under the table.

'This is Charlie Chester-Barnes, Gilly,' Laura said, placing a hand on his arm. 'From Branford Manor.'

'Middle son,' Charlie said cheerfully. 'That's how my mother always introduces me.' He turned to Laura. 'Of course Laura knows all about being in the middle. We've got to stick together, haven't we? Us middlers. Do you have brothers or sisters, Gillian?'

I shook my head. It felt too awkward to go into the details of my family and the baby half-brother I had never met.

'Gilly's an only child. Imagine that, Charlie.'

'Sounds like pure bliss,' he said.

Laura gestured to our table. 'Oh, do sit down, won't you, Charlie. Let's not stand about like this.'

'Are you sure . . .' He hesitated, glancing at me. 'I don't want to intrude.'

'Nonsense,' Laura said firmly. 'If you've got the time, that is?'

'Oh, I've got the time,' said Charlie, picking up a chair from a neighbouring table and placing it firmly down in our corner. 'My brother is always late.' He set his newspaper down then hooked the umbrella over the back of his chair. 'Thought I'd pop in for a drink, take a look at the paper – I wasn't expecting to run into company. This is splendid, just splendid. Let's get some drinks in, shall we?'

* * *

At first, Laura and Charlie tried to include me in their conversation, explaining who this or that was, but after a while I think they forgot about me. What I do remember is that the drinks kept coming. Lemonades I didn't want piled up around me and I struggled to drink them, the sugar coating my tongue, making me feel queasy. Laura and Charlie seemed to grow closer together at the table even though their chairs hadn't moved, and their laughter became louder.

I began to watch the clock above the bar, longing for one of them to notice how much time had passed, but they were so wrapped up in each other, they didn't notice a thing.

At one point, I began to feel rather hot and uncomfortable. I excused myself and went to the Ladies' where I splashed a little water on my face and gazed at my reflection in the glass. I straightened my shoulders and told myself not to be a bore. Laura was having a good time. It wasn't their fault I was struggling to follow the conversation. I was a guest at Thornleigh. Laura had taken me shopping and bought me beautiful things, the least I could do was be good company for her and her friend. Wasn't this, after all, what I'd come to Thornleigh for? Here I was sitting in a salubrious hotel with glamorous people, wearing a beautiful scarf, a scarf that cost more than Aunt Ada would spend on me in a year. So why did I suddenly feel so uncomfortable, so alone? In that moment, I longed to be back at Thornleigh, sitting in the library by the fire as Emmeline underlined pages in a book. The jackdaw on his perch, ruffling his feathers. Violet petting Fee Fee.

It wasn't long after I returned to the table that Charlie announced he had better be going. His brother had clearly stood him up. Saying goodbye took a long time. There were more kisses. Charlie grasped my hand, pumping it up and down, telling me how jolly good it had been to meet me, before giving Laura a final peck on the cheek and tucking his umbrella under his arm.

'I suppose we ought to be getting back too, Gilly,' Laura said once Charlie had gone. She stood, unsteady on her feet, almost knocking the glasses off the table. I had to catch her arm.

She struggled into her fur coat, her brow creased in concentration, then laughed loudly. 'Hasn't this been *fun*, Gilly. It's so nice to *get out*. We hardly ever do, you know.'

The waiter was watching us and I could feel my ears growing hot. He approached tentatively and asked if we wished to settle up. 'Oh, send us the bill,' Laura said dismissively. 'We've got an account, haven't we?'

The waiter nodded. 'It's just that a payment is due, Miss Claybourne. There are several, in fact—'

'Oh, send it on,' said Laura, feeling around the chair legs for her handbag.

The waiter must have realised his task was fruitless. He slunk back to the bar, but I could still feel his eyes on us.

As we were walking out of the hotel, Laura stopped in the foyer, picked up a small potted plant and, to my astonishment, walked straight out the door with it.

She held the plant firmly against her chest as we made our way unsteadily down the street. I hoped the cooler air would help bring her back to her senses, but she clung onto my arm, giggling. 'I do wish it would all stay *still*, Gilly.'

I tried to remember the way to the station. Perhaps it might be best to call a cab, but I didn't have any money and I worried that Laura didn't either. In each shop we'd been into she'd told the salesperson to 'put it on the account'. I imagined a bureau drawer, somewhere in the library, or in Lord Claybourne's study, full of unpaid bills. I now felt slightly sick that I had contributed to Thornleigh's financial problems, but it was hard to believe, when you considered the size of the estate, that whoever lived there could possibly have any money trouble.

'Let's not go back just yet, Gilly, I can't stand it. Look—' Laura stopped and pointed to a dingy-looking pub across the road. 'Let's just have one last drink. Before we go.'

'I really don't think—'

But Laura was already stepping into the road. An angry motorist honked his horn and I ran after her, waving an apology.

The pub was full of men in tweed caps and rolled shirtsleeves, scarves knotted around their necks. The air was thick with smoke. Laura rested her elbow on the bar and ordered a brandy from the bartender, a beefy man, wearing braces. His eyes fell on Laura's pearls and fur coat.

'Aren't you having anything, Gilly?'

I shook my head. 'Laura, I really think we ought to—'

'You best go in the snug,' the bartender told us, his expression hostile. 'Out back. There's a fire. Out front here is strictly men only.'

'Oh, lovely,' said Laura. 'A fire and a snug. That'll suit us very well, won't it, Gilly?'

I nodded stupidly.

'We don't do supper,' the barman said, his eyes still narrowed.

'Luckily we don't require any,' said Laura, laughing.

'Only pork scratchings,' said the man.

'Oh, pork scratchings!' said Laura loudly. 'Wonderful. We'll have some of those then.'

We sat next to the fire in the little room behind the bar. Laura set the potted plant down on the table between us then leaned back in the worn leather armchair.

The fire crackled, warming my feet, and I couldn't help admitting to myself that, despite my anxieties about us getting back, and Laura's intoxicated state, it was fun to be out with her. And I felt much more at ease in this room with its worn furniture and faded rugs than I had in the posh hotel bar.

'Isn't Charlie a darling?' Laura said, sipping her drink.

'He seems very nice.' I hesitated. 'I think he likes you.'

Laura blushed. 'Emmi says the greatest power is knowing you can attract people. She positively *thrives* on it. But then she has that effect on everyone.'

I leaned forward, wanting to know more.

'Men are always so dreadfully nervous around Emmi. They're in awe of her. But I don't know, Gilly. It's about ... well ... *connection*, isn't it? That's what we're all looking for.'

'I suppose it is,' I said. All the same, I wished I could have an effect on people, like Emmeline did.

'You're such a good friend, Gilly,' Laura said, smiling at me. 'It was so brave of you, saving Piff like that in the woods yesterday. And isn't this nice? The two of us sitting here chatting away like old chums. I didn't want to go home. I wasn't quite ready to face Emmi yet. No doubt she'll be *very* cross.'

I must have looked alarmed because Laura laughed. 'Oh, not with you, darling. With *me*. Goodness, what are these?' she said dipping her hand in the paper bag the barman had given her. 'They're awfully crunchy. You must try one.'

I took a piece of the salty crackling and chewed slowly, thinking of Emmeline. I wished she were here too, that she might laugh with me the way Laura was. 'Emmeline does look rather stern sometimes,' I said thoughtfully.

Laura set her drink down. Her cheeks were pink. 'Oh, Emmi wasn't always this way. Of course she was still *Emmeline*. Still interested in all her books and her piano, and her horse, and all of that. But there was something lighter about her. She wasn't as – spiky.' Laura flopped back into the chair. 'Emmi got her heart broken. That's what did it, Gilly. She was in love and it all ended in rather a mess. After that she was different.'

I sat up, alert. Emmeline in love?

'What happened?'

'You must promise not to breathe a word of this, Gilly. You must never mention this at Thornleigh, and you mustn't speak with Violet about it. Promise me.'

I nodded, worried Laura would change her mind about telling me this secret about Emmeline, but already feeling guilty that I was promising to keep something from Violet. I felt bad enough that I was here without her.

'I promise,' I said.

Laura took another sip of her drink, gathering her thoughts. 'Mr Lempstead was our English and Languages master. He knew all the poets, and Shakespeare and Latin, and he could speak four languages. He was a good drawing master too. Oh, and he played the piano.'

'When was this?' I asked.

'A long time ago,' said Laura dismissively. 'Before Emmi came out. I know Mummy wanted a lady tutor for us, really. But Mr Lempstead had such good credentials. Emmeline was already quite far ahead and protested she didn't need anyone to teach her, but it turned out there was really quite a lot Mr Lempstead knew about. He came to live with us. It was meant to be a six-month position.' She stopped and put her hand to her head as if she had a headache, then glanced in the direction of the bar. 'I think I need another drink. Wait here a minute, Gilly, will you?'

She returned a few minutes later with a glass in each hand. I briefly wondered if she meant one of the drinks to be for me, but it soon became clear they were both hers.

'We had our lessons with Mr Lempstead in the schoolroom,' she went on, reaching into the bag for another pork scratching.

'Two lessons in the morning before lunch and one in the afternoon.' She chewed, took a swig of brandy, then cast her eyes down into her drink. 'They fell in love. Mr Lempstead and Emmeline. Looking back on it now, it seems obvious.' She glanced up at me and gave me a small smile. 'I knew they had become great friends, of course. That much was evident. They would spend their evenings sitting in the library reading together and talking. Sometimes I was there too. Then Mummy would come in and tell us to let Mr Lempstead get his rest, and that he wasn't employed to teach us in the evenings, but I could tell he didn't mind, that he liked being around Emmeline. I suppose I didn't think much of it at the time. But when I think about it now, Gilly ...' She shook her head. 'Well, I can see their faces, the way they looked at each other. It was all there. You know, little things. A look, a gesture.'

'What happened?' I asked, hardly daring to breathe. I could picture the whole thing: the squeezing of hands under the schoolroom table, stolen kisses in the dark passages of Thornleigh, clandestine moonlit meetings in the oak arbour down by the lake. I decided that this Mr Lempstead must have been really something special for Emmeline to fall in love with him.

'It was Violet,' Laura said.

'Violet?'

'She must have got out of bed for something. I suppose she heard them. Anyway, there they were, in the butterfly room. I mean, I don't know *exactly* what Violet saw, but of course we can imagine.'

I could feel my pulse racing.

'You know about the birds and the bees, don't you, Gilly?'

I nodded. I had read, last Christmas (with wide eyes and a racing heart) a rather tatty copy of *Lady Chatterley's Lover* I found inside Aunt Ada's hardback *Illustrated Birds of the British Isles*. I was aware of the startling and rather random nature of love and physical passion, or so I thought.

I did not imagine Violet to know about such things. Not now, and certainly not then. She just wasn't the type. She wasn't yet curious in that way, and was the sort of girl to make a face if kissing, boys, marriage, or anything remotely along those lines was mentioned.

Laura fumbled in her handbag, producing her cigarettes. She lit one, tossed the match on the table then inhaled deeply.

'When Violet saw Emmi and Mr Lempstead, she screamed,' she said slowly. 'She dropped the oil lamp she was carrying and it smashed. She ran off along the landing and Mr Lempstead went after her. As Emmeline was gathering herself together, the landing rug caught alight, then the curtains. That's how the fire started. Emmi was trapped in the butterfly room.'

'But she got out,' I said, my throat tight.

Laura took another drag on her cigarette. 'Yes, but she was badly burned. Haven't you ever wondered why she always wears long sleeves? Her right arm and shoulder are scarred. She was lucky it wasn't worse. The fire spread quickly through the west wing. Ned Barrow in the servants' quarters smelled the smoke. He woke me by banging on my door. He woke my parents too, then he tried to rescue some of the pictures and things ...' Laura gazed at a fixed point beyond me, then shook her head, tapping ash onto the carpet and rubbing it in with the toe of her shoe.

'That's when Violet started up with her odd compulsions.'

I took a shaky breath, imagining it all: Violet opening the door, Emmeline's hitched-up nightdress, Mr Lempstead's firm grasp.

'It's so awful,' I said. 'To be discovered like that.'

'Of course it all came out a few days later – about Mr Lempstead. By then he had disappeared. Violet said she'd seen him in the butterfly room, hurting Emmeline. It was terrible for Mummy. She couldn't bear it, you see. Emmeline, her eldest daughter. Spoiled.'

'Spoiled?' I wanted Laura to spell it out for me.

'For marriage. Emmi was always supposed to marry well.'

I leaned back in my chair, trying to take it all in.

'Apparently Emmeline had been planning to run away with Mr Lempstead,' Laura told me. 'That was the rumour, anyway.'

I considered this. 'Don't you think Emmeline would have been happier if she'd gone with Mr Lempstead? If she loved him, I mean?' I was picturing Emmeline, what her life might have been like had she gone away from Thornleigh. I could see her living in some cosy cottage by the sea, perhaps teaching in the local village school. Maybe she would have had a child by now.

Laura considered this. 'I don't think so, Gillian. Emmeline's place is here at Thornleigh. She would have come to realise that. Even if she'd gone, I believe she would have come back.'

'But we don't know that for sure.'

Laura looked at me through a haze of cigarette smoke. 'No,' she said.

I sat there, mulling it all over.

Laura threw her cigarette end into the fire. 'Emmeline is twenty-three now, which is why Mummy is so keen for her to marry. In our world, Gilly, once you're over twenty-five, well it's all a bit late, really.' She gave me a small smile.

In our world. Her words were a sharp reminder that I wasn't one of them.

'And it was around that time that Emmeline started wearing mostly pale colours. It was like a light going out. She became a paler version of herself.' Laura sighed. 'Anyway, that's all in the past. Mummy is incredibly anxious about Cadwallander proposing. She wants it to all go smoothly.' She drank the last of her brandy. 'Emmeline likes beautiful things too, you know, Gilly. She isn't all in her mind, although that's the impression she likes to give. She's used to a certain amount of comfort. We all are. She wouldn't have lasted with a penniless tutor.'

I nodded. But I was still thinking of Emmeline and Mr Lempstead, of Violet's discovery, of her words, *I never go in the butterfly room.* Violet, along with Lady Claybourne, had exposed Emmeline, ruined her plans, caused her to lose the man she loved. If Violet had only kept quiet. If only she hadn't reacted the way she did, then Emmeline wouldn't have lost Mr Lempstead and wouldn't have been hurt in the fire. Ned Barrow wouldn't have been killed. Mary wouldn't be without a husband, Robin without a father. No wonder Violet had to do her undoings, why she constantly worried about being responsible for something bad, why she needed to make amends with herself for the tiniest inconsequential mistakes.

'Mr Lempstead was a fad, Gilly,' said Laura. 'A crush. We all have them. I was completely in love with Terrance Stokes, one of the farmhands, last year. The sight of his muscly back, that piece of corn he used to chew, made me go quite weak.'

She shrugged. 'But these obsessions pass. Emmeline will make a sensible marriage to Cadwallander. Probably in the spring.'

'Poor Mr Lempstead,' I murmured, imagining Lady Claybourne telling him to pack his bags, then perhaps, later, intercepting his desperate lovelorn letters to Emmeline.

'The strange thing was,' said Laura, 'that Violet dreamed it. She told me she had a dream that Mr Lempstead was standing on the landing outside her room and that behind him everything was burning. When Violet looked into Mr Lempstead's eyes, they were as black as two pieces of coal. Well, that's when Violet woke up. She knew she had to get out of bed. That's what she said, anyway.'

'Violet often has strange dreams,' I said.

'She dreams things before they happen, although her dreams are never completely accurate. It's as if she dreams the sense of the thing, but not the thing itself.'

'Do Emmeline and Violet get on?' I asked. 'You know, after what happened. The butterfly room ... The fire...'

'Of course they get on,' Laura said brusquely, as if the question was absurd. 'They're sisters.'

Chapter Nine

SOMEHOW, I GOT LAURA TO the station. She sat there in the carriage, slumped against the red plush seats, still holding the potted plant, looking unwell. We returned the same way we had come: first class.

When we finally arrived at our stop, I managed to get both Laura and our shopping bags off the train, the guard frowning at us, impatient to blow his whistle and get moving again. Once the train had departed in a cloud of white, oily smoke, Laura sat on a bench, setting the plant down next to her. She put her head in her hands. 'Gosh, you know, I feel rather ill, Gilly.' She stood up, stumbled a few paces towards the bushes and was sick.

I realised I had no idea how to get us home from the station. What had the plan been? Was Higgins supposed to be here waiting for us? Had she given him a specific time? I expected that time had long passed. Whatever the arrangement had been, there was no sign of Higgins now, just a cold dark platform and a chill wind. I shivered, pulling at my coat.

'Wait there,' I told Laura, who had found her way back to the bench and was sitting with her eyes closed, surrounded by our shopping bags.

I walked a little way along the platform and entered the guard's office. The guard, a thin man with a few dark hairs swept over his bald head, was sitting at a desk reading a cowboy novel. My eyes fell on the telephone.

'Excuse me. I need to borrow the telephone.'

The guard looked up at me. 'I'm afraid it isn't for public use.'

'It's an emergency.' I glanced out of the small window, towards Laura sitting on the bench next to the potted plant, her head between her knees. The guard followed my gaze.

'It's my sister. She isn't well.' The lie was out of my mouth before I could help it.

The guard placed his book down on the desk then eyed me suspiciously. 'You'll have to reverse the charges.'

'Of course,' I said as if it was the sort of thing I did all the time.

The guard stood outside the ticket office, lighting his pipe, stamping his feet to keep warm, waiting for me to finish the call.

After I had given Thornleigh's address to the operator, the best I could remember it, I was put straight through. Mary answered.

'It's Gillian Larking,' I said. 'I'm at the station. I'm afraid Laura isn't very well and I'm not sure ... Well, I'm not sure how to get us back.' I let my words linger, feeling rather foolish.

Mary did not seem at all perturbed, but then wasn't that the requirement of a good servant? Discretion. Or perhaps, I strongly suspected, it was just that she had other, more important things to be getting on with. She briskly told me Higgins would come and collect us. Before I had a chance to thank her, she'd hung up the phone.

Laura straightened up as I approached and gave me a somewhat lopsided smile.

'Higgins is coming,' I said.

'Oh, wonderful,' she murmured. 'It was good to see Charlie again earlier. Sorry about all that.' She waved a hand in the direction of the bushes. 'Damn hotel. Cream must have been off. Or maybe it was those scratchy things we had.'

I didn't say anything.

After twenty minutes or so, during which time we sat shivering on the bench, our breath visible in front of us, we finally saw the headlights of the Bentley, two needlepoints of light in the dark. We left the station, opening the gate and taking the path down to the street. I could see Higgins at the wheel. There was someone in the passenger seat: Emmeline.

She got out and, without a word, helped Laura into the car. I climbed in, slotting our shopping bags in around our legs, the plant tucked under my arm. I was dreadfully embarrassed and didn't know what to say. I felt ashamed, as if I was responsible for the state Laura was in, as if it was all my fault. I couldn't help thinking I should have said something about the gins and the brandy. But what could I have said? *Haven't you had enough now?* I wasn't her mother or sister, or even a friend.

'Did you have a nice time, Gillian?' Emmeline asked. I thought there was an icy quality to her voice but I may have been mistaken.

I said, quietly, that I had.

'Sorry, Emmi,' Laura was saying, each word a great effort. 'Missed the earlier train. Feel rather wretched.'

Emmeline said nothing. The drive was painfully silent. I could hear only the murmur of the engine, an owl hooting somewhere in the darkness, the occasional cough from Higgins.

When we arrived at Thornleigh, Emmeline helped Laura from the car, into the house, and up the staircase. She had her arm around her waist. Laura's head was slumped against Emmeline's shoulder. When they reached the top, Emmeline saw me standing there in the dark hallway, still holding our shopping bags and the plant.

'You'll get yourself to bed, Gillian?'

'Yes, of course.'

Laura muttered something indecipherable.

Emmeline hesitated then turned back to me. 'Best not to mention to this to Mother and Father when they return.'

I nodded. I wanted Emmeline to know she could trust me, that I could keep a secret.

She gave me a thin smile then shifted Laura's weight to accommodate her better as they began to slowly ascend the next flight of stairs.

* * *

'I had the most awful dream last night,' Violet said, tucking into her eggs.

I was about to make my way down to breakfast. Violet was still in bed, propped up by pillows, eating from a tray Mrs Frith had brought. I felt she was laying on the whole invalid routine a bit thick; limping about (but often forgetting her limp) asking for constant cups of weak milky tea and biscuits to be brought to her. Breakfast in bed.

I had shown Violet the scarf Laura bought for me but not, for some reason, the dress which I had carefully hung in the section of wardrobe Violet had allotted me, amongst my other things, as if it had been there all along. I don't know why I didn't show it to Violet. I think I had the idea that when I appeared in it, Laura would say nothing except perhaps 'What a lovely dress, Gillian.' A knowing twinkle in her eye, as if I had owned it all along.

'I didn't hear you cry out,' I said, referring to Violet's dream.

She swallowed her mouthful then looked up at me from her nest of pillows, her mad hair sticking up from sleep. 'We were all there. Me, you, Emmeline and Laura. We were running down the park towards the woods and there were dead birds everywhere.'

I went to the window and peered out. The park was silver with frost, broken by green criss-crossing rabbit tracks. I looked for deer, as I had done every morning since I'd arrived, but there was nothing. 'Dead birds?' I asked.

'Pheasants, I think. The park looked just like it does after the October shoot, after the final drive. Dead birds *everywhere*. A massacre.'

I grimaced.

'But then we were in the woods and I don't know what had happened but Emmeline was covered in blood. Her dress and her hands . . .'

I thought of what Laura had told me about Violet's dreams and a chill swept through me. I turned away from her, pulling at my cardigan. 'Maybe it's something to do with your ankle,' I said. 'With what happened the other day. You had a shock. Then we saw Emmeline. You know how dreams can distort things.'

Violet frowned. 'Maybe.'

'Or perhaps you dreamed of the dead birds because the fox hunt is coming up.'

Violet shrugged and went back to her eggs, digging her spoon around to scoop out whatever was left. 'Are you going down to breakfast then?'

*　*　*

I came across Robin at the top of the stairs. He was sitting fully clothed in a little empty tin bath that I felt sure must be intended for a much younger child, holding what looked like fire pokers and swinging them about. I noticed someone had draped a white sheet over the top of the bannisters.

'Are you all right there?' I enquired.

Robin looked up at me. 'It's a boat,' he explained, gesturing to the little bath. 'We've left the main ship in search of seals.'

'Who's we?' I asked.

'Me, Captain Scott, and what's left of the crew.'

'I see.'

He held a drinking tumbler up to his eye. 'Land ahoy!'

Peering inside his little boat, I could see a jar of plum jam, a compass and several pieces of orange peel. 'What's that?' I asked, pointing to the plum jam. 'Provisions?'

'Rum,' he said proudly.

'And your orange peel?"

'Protects the men from scurvy.'

I nodded. 'A terrible affliction, I should think.'

'Their teeth fall out,' said Robin solemnly.

'And is that to do with your expedition too?' I asked, pointing at the white sheet.

'That's a polar bear,' said Robin. 'Only we haven't encountered him yet.'

116

'I can tell someone has been reading adventure stories to you,' I said with a smile.

Robin stood up in his vessel, puffing his chest out. 'I can read myself. Mother and Mrs Frith taught me. I started with all the jars in the kitchen then I went on to real books. Lord Claybourne let me choose some from the library. I've got *Scott's Last Expedition*, *Ivanhoe* and *Tom Brown's Schooldays*.'

'That should keep you going,' I said.

'I can read more words than Mother now.'

Using his hand as a visor, Robin pointed at something invisible along the landing. 'Iceberg ahead!'

'And who's this chap?' I asked, noticing one of Robin's tiny toy soldiers in the bottom of the bath.

'This is the Major General,' said Robin. 'My highest-ranking officer. He goes everywhere with me.'

'Well, good luck,' I said, manoeuvring myself around the bath. 'I hope you catch your seal. And watch out for that bear.'

As I approached the dining room, I could hear voices: Emmeline's and Laura's. I paused. Their discussion sounded heated.

'I can't believe she slipped it in like that,' Laura was saying.

'Because she knows we'll be upset. She didn't want to tell us face to face. Easier to drop it casually into a letter.'

'And bringing Daddy into it. *Your father and I have decided . . .*' Laura said, mimicking her mother's voice. 'We *always* ride. Really, Emmi, it's too much.'

'I know,' said Emmeline. 'But she's clearly made up her mind.'

'For goodness' sake, *why?*'

'She doesn't think it appropriate. Young ladies, eligible for marriage, galloping about over the fields with wild hair and muddy faces.'

'She's never stopped us joining in with the hunt before.'

'You know what she's like when she gets an idea into her head,' Emmeline said. 'Anyway, what was all that about yesterday? It was completely irresponsible of you. You never know when to stop.'

I heard Laura sigh loudly. 'Oh, don't go on, Emmi. You know how it is for me. I had to go. It was my only chance to see him.'

'But taking Gillian with you on the pretence of a new scarf—'

'Well, we *did* get her a new scarf. Gilly had a lovely time. I don't know why you're being so tiresome about it.'

'I suppose you said you just happened to bump into Charles by chance, did you?'

Laura was silent.

'You took advantage of Gillian simply to protect your reputation.'

'I don't care about *that*,' said Laura.

'Well, you should. Especially after Paris.'

'Oh, *Paris*,' said Laura with a little laugh. 'I've already forgotten about it.'

'Well, Mummy hasn't. And you know what she thinks of the Chester-Barneses. It's all new money. They believe having a house full of staff and drinking Maderia wine is enough to make them aristocrats. You could do better than Charlie.'

'You're just upset about not being able to ride,' said Laura.

At this point, feeling self-conscious about loitering in the hallway, and concerned one of the servants might pass me, I entered the room.

'Oh, hello, Gilly,' said Laura.

'Good morning,' I said cheerfully, as if I had just arrived.

The dining room was bright and cold. The wintery sun coming in at a slant fell across the table illuminating Emmeline, creating a watery halo around her head and shoulders, as if she were a girl in a painting: *Young Woman at Breakfast*.

On the breakfast cabinet were various dishes; bacon, eggs, porridge, kedgeree, all in silver platters with spirit lamps underneath. The table was laid with tea and coffee, jams and marmalades. It was the same every day, whoever was in the house. The floors may have been falling down but there was plenty of food.

Emmeline was eating half a grapefruit with back coffee, whilst Laura was adding fresh cream to hers. I wanted to be like Emmeline, so I poured myself a cup, took a sip, and winced, finding the taste bitter and nutty.

Emmeline laughed then set her cup into its saucer. 'Here, have it with cream and sugar, Gillian.'

I did as she said, dropping two lumps into my coffee cup and stirring in the cream.

I realised Emmeline had been implying that Laura had used the purchasing of my scarf, as an excuse to see Charlie. Could this be true? Hadn't Charlie said he'd been waiting for his brother? It was funny how the brother never materialised. Was it so terrible that if Laura had used me that I really didn't mind very much?

'You must get something hot, Gilly,' said Laura, gesturing to the platters on the breakfast cabinet. 'I don't feel so good myself, but you must be starving. We didn't get much dinner, did we?'

'And whose fault was that,' murmured Emmeline.

Laura shot her sister a look.

It seemed a shame not to sample the hot food. It was so much better than the lumpy, watery porridge at Heathcomb. I filled my plate, then returned to the table.

Emmeline glanced over. 'I'm glad to see you're eating well.'

I blushed.

'We've had dreadful news, Gilly,' said Laura. 'You simply won't believe it.'

I looked up from my breakfast.

'Mummy isn't going to let us ride this year. The hunt,' she explained, on seeing my blank expression.

'Oh,' I said, feigning ignorance.

'It's very disappointing,' said Emmeline. She had finished with the grapefruit and was now tapping the top of a boiled egg. 'We always look forward to the hunt.'

'It's simply awful of Mummy,' said Laura.

Both the sisters were clearly upset about this news but I didn't really understand it myself. I couldn't see what was so exciting about chasing a fox to its death.

'I don't know what we'll do,' Laura moaned. 'It'll be dreadfully dull, having to sit around and not take part.'

'I'm sure we'll find some way of amusing ourselves,' said Emmeline, swiftly decapitating her egg.

*　*　*

We were in the bedroom. Violet at her desk working on a map of Elvore. Two squares of bright winter sunlight lay on the rug where I was drawing the forest. We were planning to stick all the squares of paper together when we were done. It had been

Violet's idea and I had gone along with it as usual, but now I was beginning to feel restless. I wanted to be wherever Emmeline and Laura were. Particularly Emmeline who was still such an enigma to me. I thought of her on the stairs last night, helping Laura to bed. *Best not to mention to this to Mother and Father when they return.* I longed for another opportunity to prove to her my worth.

Violet was working on the castle – the most interesting part of the map. This was typical of Violet. Whenever we played Elvore she always took the best parts: Prince Caspian, King Longhorn, or Mogwart the sorcerer, whereas I was left with the role of an errant knight, disobedient servant, or ailing princess.

After spending the day with Laura, I felt changed. She had taken me into her confidence. We'd been equals. Two friends having a delightful day out. The train guard had even believed we were sisters.

Whereas before, at school, I had thought Violet amusing and unusual, I was beginning to realise that, with all her games and childish interests, she was actually rather immature. Certainly her sisters saw her that way.

I could also see now that Violet and I were really quite different. I couldn't wait to leave behind the confines of child-hood, whereas Violet was frightened of growing up and all that meant. I suspected she wished to stay a child forever, like her beloved Peter Pan.

I knew it would be impossible to distance myself from Violet when I was here at Thornleigh as her guest, but I longed for Emmeline and Laura to see me as one of them, or at least recognise my potential; that I could be nurtured and moulded into something that resembled them.

I put down my pencil, got to my feet, then looked longingly towards the windows. 'Why don't we go out?' I suggested. The winter days were short and I knew the sun wouldn't be out for long.

'I'm in the middle of doing the castle,' said Violet. 'Anyway, I don't think my ankle is up to it. I'm supposed to be resting.'

I sighed.

'I know why you want to go out anyway,' she said. 'You want to see if you can find Emmi and Lolly. You'd rather be with my sisters than with me.'

'That's not true,' I lied. 'I just want some fresh air.'

Violet stared at me for a moment, then turned back to her map.

'Go on then. If you really want to. Why don't you go for a walk? Just don't get lost. And be back in time for lunch.'

I decided I would go. Violet's generosity might be short-lived. And perhaps, whilst out, I might accidentally bump into the older Claybourne sisters.

* * *

There was something liberating about striding out down the mount and across the park by myself. I could almost pretend the whole place belonged to me, that it was my own private kingdom. I was wrapped up in my coat, new scarf and mittens. I'd borrowed the same pair of gum boots I'd used the last time we'd gone out. I followed the same path too, around the copse and down to the lake. The frost sparkled in the winter sunlight.

As I approached the water I saw him: a small figure running alongside the bank on the far side. Robin. He was wearing the little brown jacket and matching short trousers with his thick wool socks. He held something in his arms, only I couldn't make out what it was. I saw the branch on the ground before he did and winced as he tripped and let out a cry of surprise. He was lying flat out, face down, in that sprawled way young children land when they fall.

I rushed around to the other side of the lake. By the time I got there he was picking himself up. He stood blinking at me as I approached.

'Are you hurt?' I asked.

He shook his head, then looked down at his damp, grassy knees.

'It's all right,' I said. 'It'll brush off. Worse things happen at sea,' I added, remembering his game from earlier.

Robin glanced about as if he'd lost something then let out a squeal of distress. 'My boat!'

I saw he had been carrying a wooden sailing boat. It had clearly been crushed in his fall. The sails were slack and the part that held them up had snapped off.

'It's broken,' he said picking it up and staring at it, wide-eyed. His bottom lip trembled. 'I was going to sail it across the lake to the new world.'

'It's only the mast,' said a voice behind us.

I turned to find Frank Marks, wearing his peaked cap. He must have come out of the woods. I hadn't even heard his footsteps. Looking at him more closely, and in the light of day, I could see there were deep wrinkles in the corners of his eyes but that his face was kind. It was the face of a man who had seen a great deal of life, I thought.

'It's broken, Frank,' said Robin miserably.

'Let's have a look then.'

Robin handed Frank the boat and the broken mast pieces.

'This is a fine boat,' said Frank. 'Where did you get it?'

'It was my father's,' said Robin quietly.

'I expect *his* father made it for him,' said Frank, examining it. He looked down at Robin and smiled.

I thought of Robin's father, Ned Barrow, how he had died in the fire at Thornleigh, and felt a rush of tenderness for this small boy with his broken boat. Like me, he had never known one of his parents and although it was clear Mary did her best, she must have little time for him working so hard at Thornleigh.

I wondered if Robin ever fantasised that his father was still alive, that there had somehow been a mix-up. I had thought this often when I was small, that my mother was living, not dead, somewhere far away, having a wonderful time, her only sadness being that she was separated from me. Or perhaps my mother had been told it was me who had died – *We're sorry, Mrs Larking, the baby didn't make it* – and was living her life, elsewhere, unaware of my existence.

I no longer entertained such fantasies – had even come across my mother's death certificate in my father's study – but the daydreams had existed in my childhood as an opportunity to break away from the chilly brokenness of my father into something wholly peaceful and complete.

Perhaps Robin had his own fantasies. Perhaps he sailed to distant lands in search of his father, staging heartfelt reunions among great mountains and rivers as wide as England, or perhaps his father was the Major General, always tucked safely into his pocket.

'Well, come on then,' said Frank to Robin. 'Let's get her fixed up.'

Frank began to walk away, whistling to himself. Robin glanced uncertainly at me then trotted after him. I stood there for a second or two watching them, until Frank turned around. 'You can come too, miss, if you like.'

Frank's cottage smelled of wood shavings, beeswax and apples. He had a stove, a table, and an armchair with a woollen antimacassar. A hammer and saw lay on his workbench and there were jam jars full of nails and screws and other items I couldn't identify. A shotgun hung on the wall, and I noticed a small shelf of books. I peered at the titles; mostly they were Thomas Hardy novels.

Standing in Frank's cottage, I felt awkward, an intruder in his small, private world, and yet there was something about the cosy cottage that made me feel immediately at home.

Frank was rifling through a box by the stove. He turned and looked at me. 'Staying up at the Hall, are you?'

'Yes. For the holidays. I'm a friend of Violet's. From school, that is.'

Frank smiled. 'Can't say I spent a lot of time at school.'

I glanced again at the books.

'Taught myself,' he said.

'I might go to school,' said Robin. 'Mother and Mrs Frith say I might.'

'Well, I hope you like it all right,' said Frank.

'I've borrowed three books from the library.' Robin had taken the Major General from his pocket and was walking him across the table.

'Is that so,' said Frank.

'And I might get a book on Sunday. For Christmas. Mother says I might. Are you excited about Christmas, Frank? We've only two days to go you know, if you count today.'

Frank smiled.

'I'd like a car too. One that you wind up.' Robin blushed. 'But a book would be the best. I like adventure stories.'

Aware of me loitering by the stove, Frank said, 'You can sit if you like, miss.'

I perched on the edge of a stool.

'Here, this ought to do it.' Frank was holding a large twig. 'Ash,' he said. 'Nice and strong.' He turned to me. 'Look in that drawer over there, miss, and see if you can't find me a bit of twine.'

I got up, opened a kitchen drawer and searched through the contents: a letter opener, two screwdrivers, a tube of glue, and small paper box that had 'Eley, Grandprix, shotgun cartridges' written on the front. I opened the box and ran my finger across the smooth paper casing of one of the cartridges, then quickly replaced it. I found a ball of twine and handed it to Frank. As I shut the drawer, I saw something on the flagstones, peeping out from under Frank's chair. A slim light-coloured glove. It seemed out of place in the small rustic cottage. Not wanting Frank to realise I had noticed it, I quickly looked away.

Frank sat at the table, took a knife from his pocket and began to shape the twig. Robin watched, hovering between us.

'You must know the woods well,' I said to Frank.

'Aye,' he said, smiling. 'They're a part of me, these woods, and all that live in them.'

Looking at the pots and pans hanging above the stove, the tools on the workbench, the threadbare armchair where

I imagined Frank sat in in the evenings, I felt transported back in time. I doubted the cottage had changed much in fifty years or more. It made me think of life before the Great War, a time of long golden summers and harvest dances, a time when my mother would have been a young woman and would have felt her life stretch out before her, a time when all things seemed possible.

I thought of how I had ripped through my mother's body, killing her from the inside out, snuffing out her existence with mine. The truth of the matter always made my stomach churn. I tried to push the thoughts away but they were always there.

Watching Frank at work steadied me. The warm cottage was so very different to the cold, formal atmosphere up at the Hall where everything was fixed and rehearsed: gongs sounding for mealtimes; chilly, empty rooms; social customs I was expected to get right; the impenetrable barrier that existed between the Claybournes and their servants. Here, with the embers of a fire glowing in the grate, the smell of old wood, Frank's agile fingers carefully working the knife, none of that mattered. It struck me that Frank appeared happy with his lot, certainly happier than any of the Claybournes who kept to their own quarters, and their own silent lives.

Frank was now digging out the remains of the original mast and attaching the new one. 'That's it. There's your new mast, Robin. We'll wedge it in nice and tight. Come and help me thread these sails, would you?'

Robin went obediently back to the table.

Next to Frank's books was a long white feather. I picked it up and brushed my fingers along its edge. 'Did you find this?' I asked Frank.

Frank glanced up from his work. 'I was given it,' he said slowly. 'A long time ago. It was meant to shame me, to humiliate me, but I kept it anyway.'

Robin looked at the feather too. 'What's hu-mil-iate?'

'To make me feel unhappy in myself,' said Frank.

Robin frowned. 'Why did you keep it then, Frank? If it was meant to make you feel bad?'

Frank smiled. 'Because I thought it was beautiful. And because it reminds me of who I am, what I stood for, and what others did too.'

I wanted to ask Frank about the war, about why he hadn't fought, but I felt it wasn't my place to ask these things. Then he was standing, presenting the boat to Robin. 'She's all fixed up now, lad. You'll be able to sail her again tomorrow.'

* * *

As I walked slowly back up the mount for lunch, I decided I wouldn't tell Violet where I had been. She would no doubt say it wasn't right for me to be associating with someone like Frank Marks, and she was probably right. But I also wanted to keep something for myself: my encounter with Frank, with Robin, the smell of apples and wood shavings, the white feather on Frank's bookshelves, they didn't mean much but, as with the fork I had taken at dinner and hidden in the lining of my suitcase and the romance and beauty magazines I kept under my bed at school, they were mine. Just mine. And for those brief moments in Frank's cottage, for the first time since I'd arrived at Thornleigh, I hadn't needed to try and fit in.

But the feeling was already fading. I looked up at the Hall ahead of me. Laura and Emmeline were beginning to notice me, to accept and trust me. I must remember that I was a different Gillian now, one who did not need to associate or empathise with the servants and the lower classes. I mustn't let the Claybournes or, perhaps more importantly, myself, down.

Chapter Ten

ON CHRISTMAS EVE, LORD AND Lady Claybourne returned from London, then it had snowed. We'd been in the library, roasting chestnuts: Laura pricking the tops, Emmeline holding them over the fire, Violet burning her fingers with impatience. It was Violet who wandered to the window and called out to us.

'Look, it's snowing!'

We'd rushed over. Fat white flakes falling from the sky, settling on the park, the drive and the bare trees.

'A white Christmas tomorrow then,' Laura had mused.

Then, early this morning, we'd woken to find the park covered in a thick white blanket.

The Claybournes had exchanged Christmas gifts after breakfast, mostly cashmere and crystallised fruits. There was a box of fruit for me too.

Although the food had been plentiful, the atmosphere at lunch had been strained. Emmeline and Laura were still clearly put out about not being allowed to take part in the Boxing Day fox hunt.

Now we were in the drawing room, our stomachs full of Christmas lunch and pudding. Lord Claybourne had retired to his study and Lady Claybourne had gone for one of her lie-downs. I wore the dress Laura had bought me in Oxford.

Laura, in blue velvet and a silk scarf worn as a headband, was draped over the chaise longue, smoking a cigarette. 'It always makes one feel rather flat, doesn't it? Christmas. Nearly over already. And I was *so* looking forward to riding tomorrow.'

Emmeline got up and stood by the window, looking out over the snow-covered park. 'I was too,' she said.

Violet, over by the hearth, had removed the fire screen and was poking around in the embers with a stick. 'Well, I think it's cruel. The poor fox.'

Laura tapped her cigarette holder against the ashtray. 'Nonsense, Piff. The foxes quite enjoy it, you know. You can see it on their faces. And it's tradition. Anyone who doesn't like it has clearly never tried it.'

'Country sports are a part of country life,' said Emmeline. 'Besides, we have to control the wildlife.'

I said nothing, although I secretly worried that one day all the foxes would be hunted out of the English woods, like the whales were being hunted out of the sea, and the pharaohs had hunted all the lions out of Egypt. But I kept my opinions to myself.

'You're still too immature to understand,' Emmeline said to Violet.

Violet scowled at her sister.

'And what are you doing over there? Poking around with that stick.'

'Saving a woodlouse,' said Violet.

Laura sighed. 'At least we've got the ball to look forward to. Although tomorrow will be ghastly. I'm not sure I even want to watch if we're not allowed to ride.' She blew out a few deliberate and careful smoke rings.

'Got it,' said Violet triumphantly, presumably talking about the woodlouse.

I glanced at Emmeline who was still at the window. The kitchen garden was white and fluffy-looking where the snow had settled over the hedges, shrubs and urns. There wasn't much growing at this time of year, only a few hardy herbs and Brussels sprouts.

As I watched, Emmeline picked up one of the tiny soldiers that stood in a row on the deep sill. I'd seen the soldiers: lined up on the stairs, on the side table in the parlour, crossing the first-floor landing. Robin seemed to be always staging some battle or other. A few days ago, Mrs Frith had almost stood on one when carrying a tea tray up the stairs to the drawing room. I'd heard her mutter something unsavoury under her breath.

Emmeline held the tiny soldier in her hand, looked at him for a moment, then set him down again. She turned from the window and for some reason I averted my gaze, not wanting her to know I had been watching her. 'Let's take the boat out on the lake,' she announced.

Laura was absent-mindedly threading her beaded necklace through her fingers. 'Really, Emmi, it will be freezing.'

'The fresh air will do us good. I'm going to fall asleep if I stay inside much longer.'

'But we've got a good fire in here now,' said Violet. She nudged a log with the poker and a few cinders fell onto the tiled hearth.

Emmeline crossed the room. 'We can ask for a fire in the library when we get back.' She glanced towards the windows again. 'It'll be dark in a couple of hours and then we'll be sorry we didn't go out.'

'What do you think, Gillian?'

'I'd like to,' I said, hoping to please Emmeline.

'Well, that's settled then. You can't visit Thornleigh and not go out on the lake. We'll take blankets with us.'

'If Gilly really wants to . . .' said Violet.

Emmeline glanced at Laura. 'Of course you can stay here, Lolly, if you think—'

'No, I'll come,' said Laura, putting out her cigarette. 'But for goodness' sake let's take something to drink. To keep us warm.'

'All right then,' Emmeline said. 'Go and see what you can find. And be discreet about it. I'll get the blankets.'

We went off in our separate directions, to fetch additional layers and provisions, then assembled downstairs in the boot room where we pulled on our boots, coats, hats and scarves and set off for the lake, Emmeline carrying two blankets under her arm, Laura a plaid-patterned flask.

The snow was soft and powdery and made a satisfying squeaky crunch beneath our feet. The air was clean and brittle. When we reached the small copse, I turned around and drew a breath. Against the white ground and pale grey sky, Thornleigh looked magnificent. With its turrets and jagged edges it appeared like a thorny weed sprung miraculously from the frozen ground. Yet, there was also something foreboding about the way it sat, up there on the mount, watching over us.

The others were now skirting the copse: Emmeline striding ahead in her black velvet coat with an embroidered collar, holding a corner of her long pale dress to stop it dragging in the snow. Laura in her Russian hat and furry muffler. Violet skipping along behind, her coat flapping open.

Laura hung back, waiting for me, and we walked by the rest of the copse together. Two crows were pecking around beneath a tree. They squawked and flew off as we approached. 'Silly birds,' said Laura. 'Although actually,' she added thoughtfully, 'they're not. Crows are very intelligent according to Emmi. More intelligent than they need to be to survive, in fact.' She linked her arm through mine and giggled. 'That's just like Emmeline, isn't it?'

At the sound of our laughter, Violet turned and called to us to hurry up.

The lake was covered in patches of thin ice. Frosted bullrushes and reeds bent in the middle like old men gave the place a still, graveyard-like air.

'Do you really think we can row through that?' Laura asked.

Emmeline walked onto the landing stage. 'The ice is very thin, look.' She poked a patch of ice with an oar and it broke and fell easily apart.

'I'm not sure about this,' Violet said uneasily.

'Don't be silly, Piff.' Emmeline hopped down into the boat and Laura handed her the tartan blankets and the plaid flask.

Violet sat, huddled in the boat, giving both the ice and Emmeline reproachful glances.

I was last to get in. Emmeline held out her gloved hand to help me as I stepped off the landing stage.

I sat next to Violet in the middle. Emmeline and Laura were at either end. We swept our coats underneath us and covered our knees with the blankets.

Emmeline began to row. We moved smoothly across the lake, the oars cutting through the still black water, breaking up the occasional patches of thin ice. I thought Emmeline in her pale dress and waist-length hair looked like the Lady of Shallot. Aunt Ada had taken me to view it at the National Gallery. It was most beautiful painting I had ever seen.

As Emmeline rowed, Laura produced her cigarette case from her pocket and lit one of her gold-tipped cigarettes. She took a few puffs then handed it past my shoulder to Emmeline who rested the oars on the oarlocks.

'Isn't it beautiful,' Laura said. 'And isn't it funny how calm the snow makes you feel. You might think there isn't a trouble anywhere in the world. That it's all like this: perfectly white and clean and pure.'

Emmeline raised her eyebrows, handing the cigarette back to Laura. 'Didn't you see Father's paper this week?'

Laura sighed. 'Of course. I was just saying, you know. It's all so peaceful.'

'What was in the paper?' I asked, realising I hadn't read one since I'd been at Thornleigh, or heard the radiogram. It was sometimes difficult to conceive that there was a world beyond Thornleigh.

'Chamberlain has ordered the construction of air-raid shelters,' Emmeline said.

Laura puffed on her cigarette. 'I thought we were done with all that.'

'Maybe he's just being cautious,' I said.

'Who's Chamberlain?' Violet asked.

Laura snorted.

'Our prime minister, Piff,' said Emmeline dryly.

'Well, how was *I* supposed to know.' Violet pouted, her arms folded across her chest.

'Perhaps you ought to try actually reading the papers as opposed to just rushing through them in that odd way you do,' Emmeline said.

Laura tapped ash into the lake. 'Aren't you supposed to know these things, Piff? Now you're at school?'

Violet shook her head. 'We only learn sums, and which bits on the map still belong to us.' She looked to me for confirmation. 'Don't we, Gilly?'

'We don't learn much about current affairs at school,' I said, feeling it wise to defend her, although Violet's general knowledge was pretty poor.

'You've *heard* of Hitler, I suppose,' Emmeline said.

Violet glared at her sister. 'Of course. And we were given gas masks, weren't we, Gilly? Horrible things. Then we were told we wouldn't need them anymore.'

Laura leaned back and flicked the stub of her cigarette into the lake. 'Really, he's such a silly little man. All that stomping and shouting and waving his arms in the air.'

'I thought you said it was exciting,' Emmeline said.

'Well, it was *then*. All those hysterical women trying to catch a glimpse of him. It rather drew one in.'

'You sound like a Mosleyite.'

'I certainly *am not*,' said Laura huffily.

'What's a Mosleyite?' asked Violet.

They both ignored her.

Laura rubbed her hands together. 'We had a party here, Gilly, after Munich. It coincided rather nicely with the first shoot of the season.'

Emmeline looked at Laura, then said darkly, 'Bits of paper won't stop a man like that.'

'Yes, no doubt you have something dreary to say about it all, Emmi.' Laura sighed.

Emmeline picked up the oars again, gazing off into the middle distance. 'War's coming all right.'

Laura stamped her feet in the bottom of the boat, trying to keep warm. 'Don't be so pessimistic. Have a little faith in old Chamberlain, will you? I'm sure he knows how to handle a silly little German.'

'Let's hope so,' I echoed feebly. A small part of me thought a war might be quite exciting. I quickly berated myself for the thought, reminding myself of my father's war.

'See, Gilly knows,' Laura said. 'Now, let's not talk of it anymore, not on Christmas Day. Who wants a drink?'

When the flask reached me, I peered inside at the blood-coloured liquid. The port burned my throat but warmed my insides, a pleasurable feeling when my hands and feet were growing numb with cold. Even Violet seemed to enjoy the drink although she grimaced on her first sip.

'Let me have a go with the oars then, Emmi,' she asked, handing the flask back to Laura.

Violet and Emmeline changed places and Violet took up the oars. 'This is hard,' she declared after only a few minutes. 'You can have them back.'

Before any of us could stop her, she'd lifted the oars from the oarlock and was trying to get past Emmeline.

'No!' shouted Emmeline.

It was too late. One of the oars slipped from Violet's gloved hands and into the water. Her hand flew to her open mouth.

'Violet, you *idiot*,' said Emmeline.

Laura peered over the side of the boat. 'Oh, Piff, you really are a nitwit.'

'I'm sorry, Emmi ... I didn't mean to ... It just fell.' Violet sat down, her face pale. She secured the other oar in the oarlock. 'We can row back with one, can't we?'

'Don't be stupid,' hissed Emmeline. Her nostrils flared. 'We'll just go around in a circle.'

We were all silent for a moment. We were out in the middle of the lake. It was nearly four o'clock and the light was already beginning to fade.

Emmeline turned to Violet. 'I think you should swim to the bank and get help, seeing as *you* dropped the oar.'

Violet's chin trembled. 'Emmi, you know I can't swim. None of us can.'

'I've heard it's quite easy,' said Emmeline. 'Once you start splashing about.'

Laura rubbed her forehead. 'Oh, don't tease her, Emmi. Besides, she'd freeze solid before she reached the bank.'

Violet swallowed nervously.

'Nonsense,' said Emmeline coolly. 'Some of the *Titanic* victims survived for thirty minutes in the North Atlantic. It'll only take Violet few minutes to swim across the lake.'

'No one is *swimming*,' said Laura. 'And we're not sinking. We're just a little stuck.'

'Up the creek without a paddle,' said Violet, stifling a giggle.

'Oh, do shut up, Piff!' snapped Emmeline.

After that, we sat, silent again, hunched into our coats, looking across to the rushes, the oak arbour, and the beech woods beyond. I glimpsed a dark figure emerging from the woods.

'Look,' I whispered.

The others followed my gaze.

'It's Frank Marks,' said Laura.

We watched him making his way slowly alongside the trees. It was clear he had seen us; he glanced inquisitively in our direction several times.

'Quick,' said Laura. 'We'll have to catch his attention.'

'I don't know there's much *he* can do,' said Emmeline.

'Don't be silly, Emmi,' said Laura. 'He'll be able to get help. We can't just sit here.'

Laura began to wave. 'Yoo-hoo!' she shouted. 'Over here!'

Frank stopped and looked across at us as Laura continued to wave. She cupped her hands around her mouth. 'We've lost an oar! Got ourselves into a bit of a pickle!'

Emmeline groaned.

Frank took several steps towards the bank, still looking over at us. Then he knelt, disappearing into the rushes.

We all strained to see.

'What's he doing?' asked Violet.

Emmeline blinked. 'He's unlacing his boots.'

Frank was up again now, shrugging his coat off.

Laura bit her lip. 'Goodness, he's not getting in the water, is he?'

'It certainly looks that way,' I said.

'Emmi, we must stop him,' said Laura, alarmed. 'It'll be freezing.'

Emmeline shifted her weight in the boat. 'I don't know, Lolly. He's pretty hardy. He's out here in all weather.'

Laura blinked at Emmeline. 'Emmi, come on now. You make him sound like a sheep. We can't let him get in the water.'

Frank had his jumper and shirt off and was unclipping his braces. His figure was lean and muscular. As he stepped out of his trousers, we all averted our eyes.

'I think he's really going in,' whispered Violet.

In only a vest and long johns, Frank walked to the end of the landing stage then, like a fish, dived straight into the water.

Laura gasped and we all held our breath.

Frank's head quickly emerged and he swam stealthily towards us in long, elegant strokes, barely rippling the surface.

'Quick. There's a rope.' Emmeline was rummaging around beneath her seat. She attached the rope to the bow then threw the other end into the water. When Frank reached us, he took the rope and trod water for a second or two whilst he tied the rope around his waist. He began to swim again. This time we went slowly with him. When we reached the bank, Frank clambered out, dripping wet and shivering. He secured the boat to the landing stage, then dried himself off with his coat. We sat nervously, unsure of whether to leave the boat while he was still undressed. Wrapped in his coat, Frank held out a hand and motioned to us to step up. We alighted the boat, one at a time. I noticed both Emmeline and Laura avoided Frank's eye. I was last off. When it was my turn, Frank nodded at me. 'Thank you,' I whispered.

At the sound of my voice Emmeline turned. She opened her mouth and I thought she was going to say something but then she didn't.

'You saved us,' said Violet breathlessly, staring wide-eyed at the shivering Frank.

Frank shook his head, an indication, I thought, that he didn't want our gratitude. I noticed his teeth were chattering and his lips were turning blue. Without a word, he collected his boots and trousers then set off, almost at a run, in the direction of his cottage.

'Do you think he'll be all right?' asked Violet, watching him go.

'Of course,' said Emmeline, although she looked uncertain.

Laura stared after Frank. 'Poor man,' she whispered. 'Imagine, getting in the water in this weather. He'll be lucky if he doesn't catch pneumonia.'

Emmeline inhaled deeply then straightened her shoulders. 'Well, we didn't ask him to, did we?' She paused. 'Look, I think it's best if we forget this. The whole thing was dreadfully embarrassing.'

I blinked in surprise but Laura was nodding, still clutching her flask. 'Oh, do let's get back to the house, Emmi. I couldn't feel my feet half an hour ago and I certainly can't feel them now.'

As the four of us walked soberly back to Thornleigh, all I could think of was Frank. How he had leaped straight in without a second thought. How he had left without a word. The sisters had barely thanked him.

Chapter Eleven

I STOOD BY THE WINDOW IN the tower bedroom looking out over the park, still blanketed in white. The hunters and their horses were gathered outside: straight-backed men calling to each other and downing small glasses of sherry to sustain them as they prepared for the chase. Lord Claybourne was there amongst the riders, wearing a Norfolk jacket and tweed knickerbockers, waving his cane around animatedly. Apparently he didn't hunt himself, not since the war, Laura told me.

Higgins had the car ready in order to drive Lady Claybourne and two other ladies down to the village so they could watch the hunt from the bridge. The atmosphere was lively and I could see why Emmeline and Laura were so put out not to be allowed to join in. I did see a few female riders amongst the men but thought it wise not to point them out.

The hounds were as eager to get started as the men, their white-tipped tails high and wagging, their noses to the ground. I watched Jennings striding down the mount in his cap and tweeds, two small white terriers running along beside him, almost camouflaged by the snow. 'To burrow the fox out,' Violet replied when I asked.

I saw a man I recognised. 'Laura, look, it's Charlie.'

'I know,' said Laura glumly. 'I was planning to ride with him. I do hope he stays for lunch. Not that I expect to get much of a chance to speak to him with Mummy hovering about.' She sighed heavily.

Violet had told me Mrs Frith had been down in the kitchen with Mary and Ethel since five o'clock. On the lower floors of the house, the scent of roasted duck and pheasant drifted through the long passageways. 'Keep that bird out of the way,' I'd overheard Mrs Frith say to Robin when he was playing in the hallway with his duck, 'or it will go in the oven with all the others.'

A blast from the horn and the riders set off towards the woods. Scarlet figures bright against the white of the snow. I was still secretly sorry for the poor fox and hoped, rather sentimentally, that he'd be able to escape, although watching the riders with their horses and hounds tearing across the park, out for blood, this seemed unlikely. I kept my feelings to myself. I knew, somehow, that it was important to Emmeline and Laura, important to Thornleigh, that the hunt was a success.

'At least it will be easy to see the fox against the snow,' said Laura, her chin resting in her hand.

We watched the riders from the window as they skirted the copse, some of them turning towards the village lanes, others heading out across the field, jumping the fence that separated the park from the farm, the hounds tumbling over the hedges like salmon over a waterfall. Eventually, they disappeared from view.

'How long will it all take?' I asked.

'Ages,' said Violet with a yawn.

Emmeline set her book down on the table amongst the empty bottles and the cigarette packets. 'Well, I'm not going to sit around here until they return.'

Laura wandered over to the table in search of a cigarette. 'I don't think we have much choice, Emmi.'

'I think we should go out,' said Emmeline.

'I don't mind,' I said, trying to be amenable.

'I thought you didn't want to watch the hunt?' Laura said to Emmeline.

'I don't. I just want to get out.' She looked towards the windows. 'Why don't we take a gun out?'

Laura tilted her head. 'What, look for rabbits?'

'Yes, why not?'

Violet was twirling a loose thread around her finger, turning the tip white. 'Count me out. I don't like it. I don't like to see them dead.'

Emmeline laughed. 'How do you think food ends up on your dinner plate?'

'Won't they all be in their burrows, keeping warm?' Laura said.

Emmeline folded her arms across her chest. 'No, the sun will bring them out.'

'They'll hear you a mile off in the snow,' Violet said.

'Yes, really, Emmi,' said Laura. 'I'm not sure it's a *very* good idea.'

'The snow won't be as thick in the woods,' said Emmeline. 'What do you think, Gillian?'

'Oh, I don't know ...' I wasn't sure I wanted to go hunting rabbits. But Emmeline's comment from yesterday about Violet being too immature to understand echoed in my mind. I wanted

145

Emmeline to see that I wasn't afraid of their way of life. This seemed like a good opportunity to please her.

'We could go out,' I said.

'Gillian and I will go then.'

Laura sighed. 'Well, if you're *both* going. Perhaps I will after all.'

Violet shot me a hurt look. I knew she felt betrayed, but Emmeline seemed pleased. 'Well, that settles it. If Mother won't let us join in, we'll have our own hunt. Our guest would like to.'

'Oh, Gilly, are you really going out?' Violet said. 'I thought we could stay in and play a game.'

Emmeline stood. 'Of course she's coming. She just said so.'

I followed Emmeline and Laura to the stairwell, avoiding Violet's gaze.

'I don't know why you're bothering,' she called after us. 'You won't kill a thing, you know.'

* * *

Down in the gunroom, Emmeline took the key from the desk then opened the long cabinet, lifting out a shotgun and handing it to Laura.

'Damn,' she said, rummaging around in the desk drawer.

'What is it?' asked Laura.

'The key to the cartridge box isn't here. Father must have it on him.'

'Well, that rather scuppers our plans,' said Laura, passing the gun back to Emmeline.

I thought of the box of cartridges I'd seen in the kitchen drawer at Frank's cottage.

'I think I've seen some cartridges somewhere,' I said slowly.

Laura brightened. 'Oh, have you, Gilly? That's typical of Father. He's so scatty these days. He leaves all sorts lying about.'

'Do you want to get them then, Gillian?' Emmeline was peering down the barrel of the gun. She took a handkerchief from her pocket and begin to clean it.

I went quickly along the hallway, heading for the boot room. The sisters had assumed I'd seen cartridges in the house. It would take longer than they would be anticipating for me to get all the way down to the cottage and back. I must be very quick.

Without even bothering to fasten my coat, I ran outside and hurried down the mount. The morning was hard and bright, the snow sparkling so brilliantly I could almost taste it, a sharpness at the back of my throat. The park was still beautiful in the snow, despite much of it being churned up by the hunters. The freezing air was harsh in my lungs, and by the time I reached the cottage I was out of breath.

I stopped. What was I going to say, exactly? Would Frank give me the cartridges if I explained we were going out to shoot rabbits? I had no idea. What if he said no? I'd have return empty handed. I'd let Emmeline down.

I crept up to the window and chanced a look inside. I could see Frank's chair, the workbench, the fireplace and the stove. No smoke coming from the chimney. No sign of Frank.

I knocked and waited. Nothing. I gently tried the door handle and, to my surprise, the door opened. Before I could think about what I was doing, I dashed across the room to the drawer. I took two cartridges from the box then quickly shut the drawer and let myself out again.

When I reached the house, Emmeline and Laura were in the boot room putting their coats on. Emmeline had the gun.

'There you are,' she said. 'We wondered where you'd got to.'

'Yes, where have you been, Gilly?' asked Laura.

'Will these do?' I showed them the cartridges.

Emmeline took them from me. 'That's funny. These are paper cased. Father usually uses brass. He's so traditional. Perhaps they belong to Jennings.' She shrugged then put them in her coat pocket.

We set off wrapped in our coats and scarves, crunching our way down the mount. Emmeline carried the gun over her arm. Broken in two, it looked like a limp, dead thing. The hunt must have moved beyond the fields as we could see or hear nothing of it, the only evidence being the horse and dog prints and piles of kicked up snow.

As we headed away from the house, and from where the riders had been, the snow become undisturbed, broken only by rabbit tracks, tiny bird prints and, now, our own footprints.

We went by the stables, the clock still stuck at five to twelve.

'You can't shoot, I suppose, Gillian?' Emmeline asked me.

I shook my head.

'We can show you if you like.'

'Oh, no,' I said quickly. 'I'm happy just to watch.'

'Only Emmi's a good shot,' said Laura. 'I'm quite useless.'

'That's because you don't practise enough,' Emmeline said. 'But you got that deer the other day.'

'Yes,' admitted Laura. 'But that was mostly Jennings. He has such a scent for them. Better than the dogs.'

A figure appeared from a clump of trees: Frank Marks, looking perfectly fine and thankfully not at all worse for wear after our escapade at the lake yesterday. He tipped his hat at us as he passed but I avoided his eye, thinking of how I had let myself into the cottage and stolen from him.

Emmeline's face flushed. 'We can't go anywhere without seeing that man,' she said once he'd gone. 'Walking around our park. Bold as brass. Anyone would think he was taking a stroll across his own land. And tipping his hat like that. *Really*.'

'He did rescue us yesterday, Emmi,' said Laura quietly.

Emmeline humphed but said no more. I got the impression she hadn't enjoyed being rescued.

Today, the lake was fully frozen. There would be no chance of us taking the boat out. A mallard sat amongst the bullrushes, his head huddled into his body. From somewhere in the trees, I could hear a wren singing.

We entered the beech woods, eerily silent given that the hunting party and the village spectators were only several miles to the west of us, according to Emmeline. A crow cawed, making me jump.

As we plunged deeper into the woods, they became darker and denser. Tangles of bracken between the trees made it more difficult to find a path and we fell into single file, treading as carefully and silently as we could. The woods were as still as a painting. Shafts of sunlight streamed down through the gaps in the trees, illuminating reddish ferns, frozen leaves. Snow-laden branches fixed against the paper-white sky. We wove through the ancient beeches, silver birches, and the standing deadwoods with their peeling bark and trailing branches like limp fingers.

Emmeline stopped, turned around, and whispered to us. 'We're coming up to a good spot. Remember, rabbits are tricky, they can bolt from any angle and at any time. They've got good eyesight too. If we miss, they'll all go back to their burrows and we'll have to wait forever until they emerge again.' She loaded the gun, taking the two cartridges I'd given her from her pocket and dropping them into each of the barrels. 'Lolly, why don't you take it?'

Laura shook her head. 'I'm not a good a shot as you. Not for rabbits. They're so small. Anyway, I don't really feel on form today.'

Emmeline shook her head. 'That's rubbish. Go on.' She handed the gun to Laura who took it reluctantly.

'We need to keep back a bit, Gillian,' Emmeline told me. 'Laura won't want anyone right behind her when she's ready to fire.'

I nodded. I could feel the adrenaline coursing through me. I suddenly understood why the Claybournes enjoyed these kinds of sports so much.

'Remember, Lolly, there's a different trigger for each barrel.'

'I know,' said Laura impatiently.

We crept on, keeping our eyes peeled, the gaps between us lengthening. We seemed to have walked for some time and I wondered when we would give up, but no one said anything and I didn't want to be the first to break the silence. I kept my eyes on Emmeline ahead of me, making sure I didn't lose her, being careful of where I put my feet, trying not to make a sound, trying not to trip over the tree roots or put a foot through an icy puddle. I ducked under a low branch as Emmeline had done moments before me, but a twig caught me in the face, scratching at my cheek. I pushed it away, making no sound, not wanting to let the others down.

Suddenly, Emmeline stopped and stood, stock-still. Craning my neck, I could see Laura ahead. She'd stopped too, poised, gun in hand. I held my breath.

After that it all happened in a matter of seconds.

I saw something moving amongst the trees: a flash of brown. Emmeline saw it too. The tops of the ferns fluttered slightly leading me to believe that maybe it wasn't a rabbit at all – something taller. A deer? A fox? But I couldn't see clearly. Whatever the animal was, it didn't fully emerge. Perhaps it had sensed us and had already bolted. Laura raised the gun and was pointing in the direction of the movement. I assumed she could see something Emmeline and I couldn't.

There was a moment's pause, a suspension in time. The woods too appeared to be holding their breath. *What is it? What do you see?* one of us should have whispered to Laura. She might have turned crossly (*Well, it's certainly gone now*), lowered the gun.

But we made no sound.

There was a click as Laura pulled back the hammer. She fired the gun. The sound was much louder than I'd anticipated, a boom that seemed to shake the trees and the ground beneath us. I felt a throb in my chest and in my ears. A handful of crows flew up into the air, squawking and flapping.

There was a long pause.

'Did you get it?' Emmeline asked, peering ahead.

Laura lowered the gun. 'I don't know.'

'Well, let's go and look then.'

Laura began to crunch through the undergrowth. In that moment, I hoped she really had killed a rabbit. At least our walk out wouldn't have been wasted, and I knew she'd be pleased if she'd shot something, especially after not being able to ride.

Ahead of us, Laura pushed aside a clump of ferns. She stopped, rather abruptly, her posture rigid. She didn't move, just stood, staring. She let out a shrill cry.

Then I was there with Emmeline and we saw him too: Robin. He was lying on his back, his eyes open and unblinking, a dark red stain blooming across his chest. He was wearing his little brown outfit. The jacket and short trousers. Wool socks and scuffed boots. His right hand was lying limply on the snow, the fingers loose. Inside his palm lay a tiny toy soldier: the Major General.

I heard a strange noise, a sort of low moan, and realised it had come from Emmeline. When I looked at her, she had her hand over her mouth.

All the colour had gone from Laura's face and yet she hadn't moved an inch. Her eyes were wide and unblinking.

There was, what seemed to me, a terrible long pause. Then I heard Emmeline whisper, 'Lolly, you've killed him.'

Part Two

Chapter Twelve

HOW LONG DID WE STAND there staring at him? It must have only been a few seconds, but it felt like an eternity.

Laura had begun to shake. 'Emmi, I didn't know he was there. I . . .'

Emmeline was staring, wide-eyed, at Robin. 'What have you done?' she whispered.

Rooted to the spot, I felt barely aware of Emmeline and Laura, of anything else but Robin amongst the ferns. The blood. His limp hand. He was right there in front of me and yet I couldn't believe what I was seeing. It simply couldn't be true. My muscles felt weak. A tight pain in my chest. *No, no, no, no, no . . .*

Laura stumbled a few paces. She leaned against a tree. She was shivering violently.

Emmeline had knelt down next to Robin and was peering closely at him. Numbly, I watched her as she removed her glove, reached out, touched his hand, then picked up the Major General and put him in her pocket. As she pulled her glove back on, I could see her hands were trembling. She rose, rather stiffly, and turned to us.

'I-Is he . . .' I stammered although, somehow, I already knew.

'Yes,' Emmeline said. 'The shot went straight through his heart.'

Laura let out a wail. 'I'm sorry, Emmi. I'm so, so sorry. Oh my God. Oh *my God*.'

Emmeline looked at Laura. 'Please,' she said. 'Please stop that.'

'We need to get help,' I managed to say. 'Someone – someone from the hall . . .'

Emmeline looked vaguely in the direction of Thornleigh, then back at Robin.

Laura was still trembling all over.

I had a strong desire to run. I needed to run as fast as I could back to the house, shouting for help as I went. Someone would hear. Someone would help us. And yet I didn't move.

'What do we do?' whispered Laura. 'Oh God, Emmi, what do we do? Is he really . . . Are you sure? He *can't* be. Try to help him, please, Emmi. Do something. We must do something.'

Emmeline didn't move. She swallowed, blinking rapidly. She stared at Robin for a moment or two longer, then averted her eyes.

'What do we do, Emmi?' asked Laura again. Her voice caught in her throat and she let out a choked sob.

Emmeline slowly shook her head.

I couldn't seem to speak. I was still unable to comprehend what was happening, that this might actually be real.

We stood around, as if waiting for some sort of sign. Robin didn't move. The sun blinked through the trees.

I could see Emmeline thinking, weighing something up in her mind. 'I believe it would be best,' she said finally, her words coming out slow and forced, 'if we went back.'

'We'll have to carry him,' Laura whispered. She wiped her eyes with the sleeve of her coat. 'Oh, this is awful, Emmi. It really is. This is truly terrible.'

Emmeline put her hand to her temple. 'No,' she said loudly. She cleared her throat, then looked at Robin again. 'I mean, it would be best if we left him here.'

I thought perhaps I'd misheard her.

'What on earth do you mean, *leave him*. We can't *leave him*.' Laura's voice was shrill. She stumbled forward a few paces and gripped Emmeline's arm.

Emmeline shook her off. 'I'm trying to think, Lolly. For goodness' sake.'

A lump of snow fell from a tree branch, a dull thud in the silence. Robin was lying in a shaft of sunlight. The blood was everywhere now, pooled around him. There was a strange metallic taste in the air, the smell of copper pennies.

'We can't take him back,' Emmeline said, turning to Laura. 'Just think about it, Lolly. Can you imagine? We can't take him back to the hall and casually tell everyone you *killed* him, can we?'

'It was an accident,' I said desperately, sure that this one simple fact would mean that everything would somehow be all right again.

Emmeline shook her head. 'No one will see it like that. This—' she gestured in the direction of Robin. 'We can't say this was *us*.'

The silent woods, our strained, cracked voices: it all had an unreal quality. One minute I had been walking through the woods, enjoying the sun streaming through the branches, the challenge of walking silently in the snow – then, somehow, I had stumbled unknowingly into a horrific and violent dream from which I would surely soon wake, sweaty and relieved, sheets twisted, throat dry. This couldn't possibly be happening. In just a moment, Robin would leap up laughing, telling us it had all been a joke, or we would be back to where we were half an hour ago, sitting in the tower bedroom discussing our plans for the morning. I think we were all waiting for the mechanic click, the flicking of the switch that would propel us away from this awfulness and back into reality, but of course that never came.

From somewhere in the distance, the hunting horn sounded. A sparrow landed on a branch, tilted its head, then flew off. Somehow, life was still going on. I looked again. Robin was still there, lying motionless in the snow, that awful red bloom on his chest.

'I thought he was a muntjac,' said Laura lamely. 'I'm so sorry, Emmi, really I am.'

Emmeline turned her back on Robin and Laura, and looked towards the trees. 'We must leave him here,' she said firmly. 'I need time to think. We must return to the house *and think.*'

Out of the corner of my eye I saw Laura flinch. 'If you're really sure, Emmi ...' Her voice was shaky, uncertain.

And so, somehow, we left him there.

* * *

I see the three of us from above – a bird's eye view – walking away from the woods, across the park and up the mount, our heads bowed, our faces a mask of shock, but also set in a grim kind of determination. We would not panic. We would not fall apart. We would simply, as Emmeline had said, *return to the house*.

We entered quietly, not wanting to alert anyone to our return, creeping into the library and sitting in stunned silence. Emmeline went down to the kitchen (for a brief moment I thought she had gone to tell someone) then returned with four cups of warm cocoa on a tray which she placed on the footstool. Laura and I stared at them as the jackdaw eyed us all with a look of contempt.

'I asked Ethel for cocoa,' Emmeline said simply. 'I said I would take it up. They're very busy down there.'

The room was cold, the servants too busy today to be lighting fires. The longer I sat, with each second that passed, I felt a rising panic in my chest. Robin was still out there in the woods, and we were here, doing nothing, drinking *cocoa*.

Laura, clutching her drink, said, 'We should fetch Daddy. He'll know what to do.'

'We need to tell someone,' I echoed weakly. All the muscles in my body felt numb. I'd never been in shock before. Was this it? The complete inability to function? Why wasn't I screaming and crying? Why weren't we *all* screaming and crying? I gazed into my cup, at the brown milky liquid. Had we really *left* him there?

Emmeline ignored us both, taking her own cocoa and sitting on the green sofa. *Eau de Nil*, I'd heard Violet call the colour when she had showed me around the house that first afternoon. *In the Chippendale style, Gilly.*

'No one saw us go out,' Emmeline said. 'No one knew we took a gun. What with the hunt, and soon lunch . . . It's likely he won't be missed for some time. I've put the gun back, disposed of the cartridges. Father rarely uses that shotgun. He likes his Purdeys for the birds, and the season is over now anyway ...'

We were both staring at Emmeline. What was she saying?

'No one saw us leave the house,' she said firmly.

I had no idea whether anyone had seen us or not, but I wanted Emmeline to be right. I wanted her to know what we should do. I wanted it all to go away.

Laura was staring at her hands. 'Mrs Frith, Mary, Ethel, even Higgins – they were all down in the kitchen ...'

'And everyone else had gone to watch the hunt,' Emmeline went on, her voice gaining conviction. 'Jennings is master of hounds today. He's been asking Father for years ...'

The jackdaw squawked.

'But, Emmi, what are you *saying*?' pleaded Laura desperately.

Emmeline turned and looked at us. 'It was an accident,' she said flatly. 'No one is to blame, and although it's a terrible, terrible thing, we don't deserve to be punished for it.' She glanced towards the closed library doors and lowered her voice. 'Don't you see?' she told us. 'This can't possibly have been anything to do with us.'

I stared at her, trying to comprehend what she was saying, but I felt cold and numb, and her words made no sense.

'But it *was* us,' Laura whispered, her eyes brimming. 'It was *me*.' She let out a sob.

I wanted to put my arms around Laura, to comfort her, but the gesture felt too dramatic, too familiar, and besides, I didn't know if I had the strength. Also, to do such a thing, to comfort one another, would be an acknowledgment of what we had experienced. It would be a betrayal to Emmeline who, I sensed, did not, or *could not*, allow us an admission of guilt.

'No one needs to know that,' said Emmeline.

Laura wiped her eyes on her sleeve. I saw her take a breath, as if steeling herself. 'Are you sure he was dead?' she whispered.

'Yes,' replied Emmeline. 'Quite sure.'

This prompted a further sniffle from Laura, quickly stifled by her handkerchief.

No one spoke for several minutes. The jackdaw ruffled his feathers. Laura tried to light a cigarette – the flame from the match creating a brief orange glow in front of her face – but her hands were shaking and the match kept going out. Eventually Emmeline got up and lit one for her, cupping her hand over the flame as Laura leaned forward.

Emmeline took the spent matches, tossed them into the fire, then put the heavy glass ashtray on the arm of Laura's chair. Laura didn't seem to notice. She stared blankly at a spot on the rug as she put the cigarette to her lips with shaking fingers, taking several tiny puffs to keep it alight.

'We won't receive an ounce of sympathy,' Emmeline said.

I looked to Laura but she wouldn't meet my eye.

'Not outside the family,' Emmeline said. 'I can tell you that. Imagine how it will look? Three upper-class girls out with guns accidentally shoot a servant's child on their father's estate. The papers will love it. Remember what a fuss they made when that beater was injured over at Lord Fairclough's shoot last autumn?' She turned to her sister. 'Really, Lolly, just think about it. The villagers will probably come for us with pitchforks. The public hate the landed classes enough as it is right now without *this*. They hate our way of life, our traditions, our sports. And now this happens, on a hunting day, of all days.'

'I don't see what that's got to do with it,' said Laura, her voice trembling.

'We'll have to go to trial,' Emmeline said, her voice rising. She glanced at her sister.

'I could go to prison,' whispered Laura. 'Couldn't I? What would it be? Manslaughter?'

I felt a chill snaking its way through my core. Trial? Prison?

'Involuntary manslaughter, I should think,' Emmeline said. 'You could still be liable. I expect they'd want to make an example of us.'

I set the cocoa cup in its saucer with a loud clatter, the handle slipping from my fingers.

Laura was ghostly white. 'Even if they understand it was an accident, even if I get off, everyone will despise me,' she whispered.

'Yes,' Emmeline replied. 'Do you think we'll ever be free of this? Do you think anyone will want to associate with us, *marry* us?' She took a long, deep breath. 'No one saw us go out, and if we say nothing there is a chance, a *good* chance in fact, that no one will ever know it was us, whereas if we fetch someone now, if we explain ...' She shook her head again.

'But it was an accident.' My voice wobbled. I couldn't help thinking of the girls at school, how they would stare at me when they knew what had happened on my winter break at the Claybournes', and of my father, of the letter that would arrive in Egypt, how he would open it in his study using his silver letter opener with the carved wooden handle. I pictured his shocked face, the way his hands would tremble as he set the letter down, the shame it would cause him, his disappointment that I could have been involved in something like this ...

'It will ruin our lives,' Emmeline said simply. 'And for what? For ...' She made a slight gesture with her hands.

Laura was staring at the hearth. A lump of ash fell from her cigarette onto the Persian rug. She glanced up as Emmeline spoke and I could almost hear her finishing Emmeline's sentence in her mind: *for an illegitimate servant's child? A child no one wanted in the first place?*

I sat with my hands knotted tightly together. I thought of Robin sailing across the landing in his imaginary boat, of his provisions, the polar bear. I fought back my tears. The clock on the mantelpiece ticked on, jarring and arrhythmic. I wanted to smother it. This wasn't just about Laura, I realised. It was about all of us. Emmeline certainly wouldn't want Hugh Cadwallander to know what had happened. What if he no longer wanted to marry her? Thornleigh might be sold, or destroyed.

'It was *because* it was an accident that we don't deserve to be punished,' Emmeline said firmly.

Neither Laura nor I made any response. I had no idea what I wanted to do with my life, but I didn't relish the idea of it being tainted by this one awful event. I didn't even know how to fire a gun. What was I even *doing* here? I should never have come. I didn't belong. I looked down at my lap to find I was digging my nails into my hand, that I had created a row of deep half-moons in the fleshy part between my thumb and forefinger. I didn't want my life to be ruined before it had even started. And Emmeline was an adult. Emmeline knew what we should do.

'What about Violet?' asked Laura faintly.

Where was Violet? I wondered. Had she not heard us come in?

'Of course we must not tell Violet,' said Emmeline.

I looked up, startled.

Emmeline noticed my expression. 'I think it's vitally important,' she said slowly, 'that Violet, like everyone else, does not know we went to the woods, that we ...' She swallowed, unable to finish her sentence.

I tried to understand Emmeline: Violet was emotional, anxious and overly transparent. She saw things in black and white. She wouldn't be able to tell a lie to save her life. She would never be able to keep this a secret. She would be upset enough as it was about Robin, without knowing our involvement. Still, I couldn't imagine keeping such a thing from her.

'Perhaps I could talk to Violet,' I said.

'No,' said Emmeline. 'We'll tell her we decided not to take a gun. We just went for a walk. But it was too cold so we turned back quickly.' She stood and reached for a packet of cigarettes behind a vase on the mantelpiece. Laura passed her the matches with a shaking hand.

'We'll act just like everyone else,' Emmeline said. 'As if we know nothing. As if we were never there.' She lit her cigarette, paused, then took a long slow drag. 'If Violet makes the suggestion it was something to do with us, well, we'll cross that bridge when we come to it.'

'What if she makes the suggestion it was us to *someone else*,' said Laura softly. 'What if she says, Emmi and Laura and Gilly were out with a gun this morning ...' She stopped talking and swallowed hard.

Emmeline was frowning. 'I think she would speak to us first. She would surely know that if she went and said something like that, she would be seriously implicating us.'

Laura took in a deep breath and I knew she was thinking this was a risk.

'I still think I could speak to her,' I said in small voice.

Emmeline shook her head. 'I'm sorry, Gillian, I don't want her to know. We'll always have the worry that she'll lose control of her nerves and tell someone. It will be easier if she doesn't know anything.'

Laura put her head in her hands and let out a loud sob. Emmeline turned sharply. 'Really, Lolly. I know it's hard, but you mustn't get upset. We need to behave as if we know nothing at all. It's the only thing we can do. Of course it's been a terrible shock for all of us, and it will be for the house, for everyone, but we can't be getting hysterical.'

Laura nodded and blew her nose. Folding the handkerchief, she dabbed under her eyes. 'Sorry, Emmi.'

There was silence for a moment, then, 'Poor Mary,' I said.

Emmeline and Laura said nothing. What was there to say? At some point the news would be broken to Mary. I felt sick thinking of it. She was currently down in the kitchen, preparing the final touches to the meal, stirring sauces, making gravy, turning the potatoes, and all the time not knowing ... I squeezed my eyes tightly shut.

'And Mrs Frith,' said Laura. 'She's awfully fond of him.'

'It will be hard on everyone,' said Emmeline.

At that moment the library door flew open and Violet was there, holding Fee Fee in her arms, looking pleased with herself to have discovered us but also annoyed. She set Fee Fee down then folded her hands across her chest. 'Well, you could have told me you were back.'

Laura smiled thinly and I attempted to take a normal nonplussed sip of cocoa, but Violet must have become aware of the tension in the room, of our pale, shocked faces.

'Goodness, look at you all. Who died?'

I choked on my cocoa and Violet came over and thumped me playfully on the back. 'Go down the wrong way, Gilly? Oh, you've got cocoa,' she said, put out.

'There's some for you,' Emmeline said, gesturing over to the tray.

'Well, thanks.' Violet glanced suspiciously at Emmeline then went to get her drink. 'You could have told me you were back,' she said again, huffily.

'We haven't been in long,' Emmeline replied.

Violet was looking at Laura. 'What's the matter?' she asked, narrowing her eyes. 'Something *is* the matter.'

'Oh, no,' said Laura, letting out a nervous high-pitched laugh. 'It was coming in from the cold. It's made me sniffy.'

Fee Fee darted under the sofa.

'Didn't shoot anything then?' Violet asked.

I watched Laura briefly close her eyes. The blood drained from her face.

But Emmeline barely flinched. 'No,' she said.

'I told you that you wouldn't, didn't I? But you insisted on going out all the same. You could have stayed here with me and played—'

'In fact, we decided not to take a gun,' said Emmeline, interrupting Violet. 'We thought it would be pointless in the snow. The sound of our footsteps—'

'Well, that's what *I* said.' Violet sunk crossly into a chair. 'If I'd known you were just going for a walk I might have come with you.'

I gave her a small, apologetic smile but I don't think she noticed. There was some commotion outside the French doors on the gravel. Violet bounded over to the window, almost spilling her cocoa. I could hear men talking, dogs barking, the stomp of horses.

'Oh good, they're back,' said Violet. 'That means lunch will be ready soon. I'm famished.'

Chapter Thirteen

I T WAS WHILST THE HUNTERS were entering the hall, hanging up their coats, taking their drinks from the silver trays carried by Higgins and Ethel, that I managed to slip quietly away.

With all the commotion in the hall, no one noticed.

I had to get out. I felt if I stayed inside a moment longer, I would be sick. I left via the boot room, through the kitchen garden, unable to even look in the direction of the beech woods.

I ran as fast as I could, praying that no one could see me from the house. It was difficult to move quickly in the snow and once I fell, my hands reaching out to break my fall. I got up quickly and ran on, flying over the white ground.

I could hardly think what I was doing. My thoughts were scrambled. I pictured Frank's kind face, the cottage with its rustic furniture and comforting smell of wood shavings, the way he had mended Robin's boat with such skilled and steady competence. I knew I had agreed with Emmeline that we should tell no one. I had decided she knew best. But neither was I sure I could do nothing. Frank Marks felt somehow removed from the hall and from the family. I felt sure a man like Frank Marks would know what to do, how to make it all right, how to fix what we had done.

A curl of smoke could be seen from the cottage chimney and I felt relieved he was in. I banged on the door and he opened it, peering down at me. He was wearing a flannel shirt and braces. I could smell something cooking on the stove.

He looked surprised to see me.

'It's ... We...' Before I could help myself, I burst into tears.

Frank ushered me inside. I sat down at his little table and continued to cry, burying my face in my arms. He didn't try to comfort me or press me as to what was the matter, only went off to find a clean handkerchief which only made me cry even harder.

'You have to help,' I managed at last. 'We've ... Something terrible has happened.'

Frank sat opposite me.

'Take your time, miss. Go steady now.'

I tried again, blinking through my tears. I caught sight of his armchair. For some reason the woollen antimacassar on the already worn chair made my heart ache.

'In the woods. We ...'

I looked up into his kind, crinkled eyes.

'It was Laura. She ...'

'Laura?' Frank asked, a brief flash of alarm crossing his face.

There was something about his expression that made me stop talking. 'No, she's fine, but ...' I couldn't go on. It was too dreadful. I thought of Emmeline's words in the library. *Do you think we'll ever be free of this? It will ruin our lives.*

What right did I have to appease my guilt, to appeal to kind, gentle Frank, when Laura and Emmeline's futures were at stake?

How could I have been so selfish? How could I have considered, even for a second, betraying them?

I stood up and looked wildly about. What was I doing here? I wasn't thinking clearly.

'Steady there,' said Frank, watching me. 'You're not yourself, miss. I think you'd better stay for a minute or two. I can walk you back to the hall when you're feeling fit.'

I shook my head violently. I had to go.

Without saying anything more, I flung open the cottage door and ran.

*   *   *

A huge fire roared. Crystal glasses clinking. Laughter. A babble of upper-class voices. The table dressed with white linen, garlands of berries and holly. The best silver. I felt I was in a dream, that nothing around me was real, that if I tried to touch it, it would all melt away. Hams, sides of beef, duck and pheasant, crispy potatoes, roasted vegetables with butter, little frilly pastries filled with mince, and a creamy yellow soup that might have been parsnip.

When I looked along the table at Laura, she was staring at her dinner plate, her shoulders curled forward. It was as though she was in pain. Like a shard of glass was sticking into her and she was having to bear it. Several times she dropped her fork. Someone tried to engage her in conversation and I could see that her responses were forced and minimal. Charlie and his father had been seated at the other end of the table, as far away from Laura as possible. I knew this was most likely orchestrated by Lady Claybourne: I had overhead Emmeline talk about how Laura could do better than Charlie. No doubt, Lady Claybourne shared this view. Although I'd liked Charlie, I thought it was for the best that, today, he wasn't seated next to Laura. He would surely have noticed how distressed she was, how little she ate.

Emmeline was too far along the table, sitting next to a red-haired gentleman, for me to see her clearly. I only managed to catch a glimpse of her when the man leaned forward to reach for a dish. She was nodding at something a lady in a grey silk blouse was telling her, a faintly amused expression on her face, as if she had nothing at all to worry about in the world. But when her eyes briefly met mine, I could see what lay beneath her placid exterior: *Don't mess this up, Gillian*, she seemed to be saying. I went back to my soup, taking another nauseous mouthful. The shock and unspeakable horror of what had happened only an hour before swam up inside me and caught in my throat. I could barely make the movements required of me for consuming food.

I have no idea how I got through that lunch. Without Emmeline and Laura there I am sure I could never have done it without breaking down, without screaming out at the top of my lungs, or sobbing uncontrollably into my dinner plate.

I imagined taking Lady Claybourne aside. *I'm terribly sorry to interrupt your lovely lunch, Lady Claybourne. It's Robin. Yes, you know, the servant's child. I'm afraid he's lying out there in the woods, dead. Your daughter shot him, you see. But don't worry, it was only an accident – she thought he was a muntjac. Oh, no, we decided it was best to leave him there.*

How could *I*, a guest in this great house, an insignificant person, say something like that?

Sitting next to me, Violet talked and ate enough for the both of us: 'Are you going to have those potatoes or not, Gilly?' – and when I confirmed she was welcome to them, discreetly spearing them with her fork and slipping them onto her plate under the cover of her elbow so as not, presumably, to alert her mother.

I caught Emmeline's warning look when Higgins appeared behind Laura with the wine bottle, a white napkin over his arm. Noticing Emmeline's glance, Laura shook her head and continued to methodically chew.

After lunch, the men retired to the billiard room in order to smoke and drink brandy, the women to the drawing room. Emmeline and Laura were permitted to go with them, but Violet and I, still being too young for drawing-room talk, were not. My heart lurched. How was I going to manage on my own?

We went up to our bedroom. Violet wanted to play Elvore but I couldn't. To lose myself in another fantasy when reality already felt so distorted was inconceivable.

'Oh, all right,' said Violet huffily when I told her that I wasn't in the mood.

We sat on the rug playing whist. I tried to concentrate on the game, only the game. My stomach was queasy, knotted with anxiety, and I had pains like a bad stitch.

'Are you ill?' Violet asked me suspiciously. 'You're awfully pale. And you're not concentrating at all.'

'Oh, no, I just ate a lot at lunch, that's all.'

'You hardly ate a thing.'

'Well, I ate a lot for me,' I said weakly. 'The food was very rich.'

'It certainly trumps Heathcomb, doesn't it?' said Violet, taking this as a compliment. 'I don't think I'll be able to face that awful porridge again.' Her face clouded. 'I can't believe I have to go back to school. I've *tried* to tell Mummy how horrible it is. It's so unfair that I have to go when Laura and Emmi didn't.'

'I know,' I said quietly.

'At least I have you,' Violet said warmly. 'We have each other.'

I tried to smile.

'It's snowing again.' Violet went to the window where soft fat flakes, as large as petals, were falling steadily. I joined her and we stared out. I could see the edge of the woods, the trees spindly grey etchings against the white sky. I swallowed hard, trying to loosen the tightness in my throat. Why had nothing been said yet? Had Robin not been missed? An image of the flakes falling and resting on Robin's still body sprang into my mind and I recoiled from the window, bile rising in my throat.

'Oh, look,' said Violet, 'people are leaving already. They're probably worried about getting snowed in. Just think, Gilly, *we* might get snowed in!'

Yesterday, I might have thought this fun. Now, the idea filled me with dread. I didn't want to be stuck here. I wished I could leave, write to Aunt Ada, have her come and meet me at Paddington. And yet I knew I couldn't. Emmeline and Laura were relying on me. Hadn't that been what I'd wanted? Wasn't that what I'd wished for? An opportunity to show them my loyalty?

Down below us, the guests, gloved and hatted, were getting noisily into their motor cars. The riders were being brought their horses by groggy grooms who had not long finished their own lunch down in the kitchen with the servants. Had Mary not noticed Robin wasn't there? Were they so busy they hadn't even thought of him? I pictured Mrs Frith as I so often saw her: red-faced, puffing and wheezing up and down the stairs, that slightly lopsided gait she had, the way Robin followed her around. And Mary. His mother. All the things she would never do for him again. Mary, who had already lost Ned. Now she had lost her son too.

I wanted to find a hole to crawl into and stay there for a very long time.

Violet stepped away from the window. I could feel her eyes on me. 'What's wrong with *you*?' she asked sharply. 'You're acting all funny.'

'No, I'm not,' I said, with little conviction.

Violet continued to study me. I turned from her gaze, lowering my eyes to the floor.

'I know you, Gilly. Something's wrong.'

I shook my head. 'It's just ... It's just been a lot to take in. All those people at lunch ...'

Violet frowned. 'Let's go and find the others. I expect they're in the library again now everyone has gone.'

* * *

In the library, the fire was roaring. Laura was on the footstool, sitting as close to it as she could. She had her knees pressed together, her arms wrapped tightly around herself. Emmeline was on the chaise longue, her pale dress trailing the floor. The snow beyond the window was falling heavily in the soft, late-afternoon light. 'Close the doors,' Emmeline told us. 'To keep the heat in.'

I pulled the doors shut.

'Have they all gone then?' asked Violet, sitting down on the wingback chair. She flung one leg easily over the chair arm. Mindful of her bad ankle, she manoeuvred her other leg more carefully then sat with both legs dangling.

'Yes, I believe so,' said Emmeline. 'It was a successful hunt by all accounts. But I expect you heard that at lunch.'

I hadn't. I'd barely registered any of the talk around me.

I took the other chair next to the fire. Laura leaned forward from her footstool, taking the fire poker and nudging a few burning embers back into the grate.

'And what's wrong with *you*?' said Violet to Laura. 'Your eyes are puffy, and you were acting strange at lunch, just like Gilly.'

'What?' said Laura, swallowing hard. 'I don't know what you're talking about, Piff.'

The library doors opened and Lady Claybourne entered. 'I don't suppose you've seen Robin, have you?'

'No,' said Emmeline, not blinking.

The rest of us shook our heads. There was an unpleasant squeezing sensation in my chest.

'Only Mary has got herself into a flap,' said Lady Claybourne. 'She says she hasn't seen him since this morning, and that his boots aren't there.'

'His boots?' said Laura in a small voice.

'Apparently he went out to play this morning and hasn't been seen since.'

'Surely he must have returned by now,' said Emmeline calmly.

Lady Claybourne glanced towards the French doors. 'Well, that's what *I* said. He wouldn't be out *now*, would he?'

Violet was swinging her legs whilst picking at a loose thread on the chair cover. 'He's probably just playing somewhere. Remember that time he played hide and seek with Ethel and Mrs Frith and they lost him. All that time, he was standing behind the curtains in the drawing room.'

Lady Claybourne looked vaguely to the bookshelves. 'It's really such a nuisance of the child to cause us trouble at the end of such an important day.'

'I'm sure he'll turn up, Mother,' said Emmeline.

I stared at her. My palms were sweating.

Lady Claybourne's gaze snapped back to us. 'Well, of course he will. But as I said, Mary is in a flap. So is Mrs Frith. The servants have searched the house. Mary insists he isn't here, that someone ought to go out and look for him.'

'Well, if that's what she thinks, then I suppose someone should,' said Emmeline.

No, I wanted to shout.

A similar flash of alarm crossed Laura's face and she quickly turned to the fire.

Lady Claybourne sighed. 'Yes, I suppose *someone* must go out and look for him.'

'There should be a search party,' Violet piped. She frowned, thinking of something. 'You don't think Robin went to slide down the haystacks, do you?' she asked nervously.

There was a long uncomfortable silence. I thought of the farmer's boy she'd told me about, the accident with the pitchfork.

Lady Claybourne frowned. 'Are you sure you haven't seen him, girls? Not even before lunch?'

'No,' said Emmeline quickly.

177

Violet furrowed her brow. 'But you all went out,' she said, looking pointedly at us. 'Didn't you see Robin then?'

'Oh, that was early this morning,' said Emmeline dismissively. 'We were cold and returned to the house after twenty minutes or so. No, we didn't see him.'

Violet knitted her eyebrows together but said nothing.

Lady Claybourne turned to Emmeline. 'Go and let your father know about this, will you? He's in the gunroom.'

'Are you sure Father will want to be disturbed?' asked Emmeline.

'No, but I think you ought to tell him anyway.' Lady Claybourne turned crossly to Violet. 'Violet, please stop picking at that chair. And for goodness' sake arrange yourself in a more ladylike fashion. I can see your undergarments.'

*　　*　　*

'Father thinks a search party should be organised,' Emmeline said when she returned to the library. 'It's too much for Jennings and Higgins to search the park and the woods on their own, he says. And you know how Higgins doesn't like to go outdoors.'

I shivered at the thought of a search party. *Maybe Robin won't be found*, I thought. *Maybe they'll search and search and find nothing.*

'I told you,' said Violet. 'I'm going to go down and let Ethel know. The men might want brandy. Are you coming, Gilly?'

'No,' I said, my hands clenched into fists. 'I'll stay here for a bit.'

Violet gave me a cold look then left the room. As soon as she did so, Emmeline got up and pulled the doors shut. 'Try not to get on the wrong side of Violet,' she told me. 'She mustn't suspect we're keeping anything from her.'

I blushed furiously.

'Emmi, what did Daddy say?' Laura was pacing in front of the windows.

'Jennings has taken the Daimler down to the village. He's going to round up a search party.' She paused. 'Mary and Mrs Frith insist Robin has been missing for hours.'

'Do you think the police will want to speak with us, Emmi? When they find ...'

'It's likely,' said Emmeline.

Laura put her head in her hands.

'If anyone asks, we'll just say what we agreed,' said Emmeline. 'We went out for a short walk, but when we got to the bottom of the mount we decided to turn back. This was around ten o'clock. We didn't get as far as the woods.' She lowered her voice. 'We never took a gun.'

No one spoke. The sky outside was lilac-coloured, the daylight fading fast. In an hour, it would be fully dark.

'It's a terrible thing we're doing,' said Laura quietly, 'leaving him out there to be found like this.'

'But we've discussed why it has to be this way,' Emmeline replied. She glanced towards the windows. 'The fresh snow will have covered our tracks at least.'

Laura turned to me. 'I'm so sorry you're mixed up in all this, Gilly.'

I didn't know what to say. I was sorry too.

'You're a true friend, Gillian,' Emmeline said calmly. 'I'm glad we can rely on you.'

I tried to smile but it froze on my face. *It's all my fault*, I wanted to say. *I took the cartridges. I wanted to belong here.*

'We've just got to stick together, that's all,' said Emmeline. 'No one will suspect we had anything to do with this, not for a moment, not unless we give them reason to. Understood?'

We both nodded.

Emmeline got up and opened the library doors. 'It will look odd,' she said quietly, 'if we keep shutting ourselves into rooms. From now on we need be extremely careful about when we talk. In fact, we really shouldn't.'

*   *   *

Wrapped in our coats, the four of us went out and stood around in the snow as Jennings shouted instructions as to who would search where, handing out torches and lamps to those who didn't have them. I imagined some of the searchers had been plucked from the village pub or from warm homes, from cosy evenings in with their families. It was bitterly cold out. The sky was opaque with clouds.

Lord Claybourne stood with us at the top of the mount, holding tightly onto his cane. 'We had a man once,' he said, staring vaguely off into the woods. 'Went out across no-man's-land in the dead of night to patch up a hole in the wire. He was one of my best men and, when he didn't come back, I sent out a search party for him. Four good men. Boche got them all.'

'It's all right, Daddy,' said Violet, touching her father's arm. She glanced at the three of us and I felt sure she was thinking of how she'd found us in the library when we'd returned from the woods, our pale, shocked faces. Perhaps she didn't believe Emmeline's firm assurances that we had turned quickly back to the house. After all, we must have been gone for some time before Violet entered the library. I avoided her gaze, yet I could feel her looking at me, her nervous, questioning glances.

We watched as the men set off at a sharp pace, keeping their eyes to the ground, spread out like soldiers in formation, those who had been dragged out of the pub now sober and solemn, focused on the task ahead. The moon, barely visible, was waning and it was a dark night, despite the snow which still lay thickly on the ground. I felt such an awful sense of dread I could hardly speak. Emmeline and Laura were also deathly quiet. Emmeline had brought an old Tilley lamp and I could see my breath coming out in front of me, a white mist against the freezing air.

'You girls should really go inside,' said Lord Claybourne. 'It's cold tonight. You'll catch a chill.'

'We're fine,' said Laura clutching at her coat. She didn't look at all fine.

We stood about, waiting, Lord Claybourne bumbling on about how Robin had most likely found himself a playmate in the village and stayed for dinner. His theories were unbearable to listen to. Finally, he fell silent and, after that, no one spoke. It seemed like we had been standing there forever.

'Perhaps we should go inside,' said Laura quietly.

But then, from halfway down the mount, came the sharp shrill of a whistle. Jennings was shouting something indecipherable. I could feel my heart, a wild thrumming in my chest, like a bird trapped in the corner of a windowpane.

'He's calling the searchers back,' Laura whispered.

'Already? Has Robin been found then?' Violet asked. 'What's happening?'

'I don't know,' said Emmeline, her gloved hands shoved deeply into the pockets of her coat.

'I should go and see,' said Lord Claybourne, breaking away from us.

We squinted into the darkness. I heard Laura's sharp intake of breath.

I saw it then too, the lone dark figure emerging from the trees, the shape of what he was carrying.

Emmeline strained to see. I watched her eyes widen. It was a chilling sight: the tall man carrying the small boy in his arms.

'It's Frank Marks,' Violet said. 'He's got him. Look, he's got him!' She paused. 'Why is he carrying him like that. Is he hurt?'

Lady Claybourne had appeared in a huge white fur coat. She stood at the top of the mount, and I noticed that as Frank lifted his head, his eyes met Lady Claybourne's. When she realised what he was carrying, her hand flew to her mouth.

'We should go inside,' Emmeline said firmly. 'It's freezing. We'll find out soon enough.'

'Yes,' said Laura faintly, although her eyes remained fixed on the dark shadowy figure of Frank Marks with Robin in his arms.

We watched Lord Claybourne approach Frank. Jennings was there too and I saw him remove his cap. Several of the villagers had come back from the woods. A few words were exchanged between the men who were now all gathered around Frank.

We watched as the small solemn party moved further up the mount. They crossed the kitchen garden, then disappeared into the house.

Lord Claybourne had peeled off from the group. He approached us. Lit by Emmeline's lamp, the lines on his face appeared exaggerated, as though someone had drawn him roughly with charcoal.

'What's happened, Daddy?' Violet asked. 'Is Robin hurt?'

Lord Claybourne hesitated, his face pained. He looked into the silent faces of his daughters. 'Robin ... He's ... He's dead. Frank found him in the woods. I'm so sorry, girls. I'm awfully sorry...' I noticed his hand, still holding tightly onto his cane, was shaking.

I was acutely aware of Emmeline next to me, of her body stiffening. Laura bowed her head. Only Violet was blinking at her father in disbelief.

'But *how*,' Violet whispered.

Lord Claybourne cleared his throat. 'It looks as though he was wounded,' he said simply. 'A gunshot wound. Dr Roach is on his way. I am sure he'll be able to tell us more.' Lord Claybourne looked, then, not in the direction of the house, but fearfully back, towards the woods, as if there might be some further horror concealed there. Shifting his gaze, he turned to us. 'It's a dreadful thing. A terrible shock...' He made a choking sound that caught in his throat.

'But how did it happen?' Violet's voice cracked. She was still staring at her father.

Lord Claybourne shook his head, unable to answer. He took a handkerchief from his pocket and dabbed at the corners of his damp eyes.

I had never seen a man cry before, had not known it was possible.

He put his hand over his face. 'Such a dreadful thing,' he managed to say through his tears.

* * *

That night we climbed under our blankets, trying to keep warm. Violet kept the lamp on. Her eyes were red from crying. She wiped her nose on the sleeve of her pyjamas.

'I just can't believe it,' she said, her chin trembling. 'I can't believe he's *dead*.'

I winced. I didn't want to talk. I only wanted Violet to fall asleep so I could bury my head beneath the covers and weep.

'Shot,' she said. 'Who would do that?' She let out a sob. 'And if it was an accident, why didn't they *tell* somebody?'

'I don't know,' I whispered, my throat tight.

She sat up, hugging her knees to her chest under the covers, then glanced over at me. 'This morning,' she said slowly, 'when you went out with the gun ...'

'We didn't take the gun,' I muttered. 'We didn't even make it to the woods. It was too cold out, and so we turned back.' My words sounded hollow.

I knew Violet was still looking at me, but I couldn't meet her eye. I wished she'd turn the light out.

She took a shaky breath. 'I was sure I heard a gunshot,' she said. 'About half an hour after you left. I was sitting over there at my desk—' she pointed to the corner of the room '—working on my map of Elvore. It could have been the one that killed

Robin.' She paused and I could feel her eyes boring into me. 'You were all out then,' she added.

I swallowed hard. 'We were only out briefly. And we didn't hear a gunshot. Only the hunting horn. That must have been what you heard.'

She sniffed, then frowned. 'I know what I heard.'

'Then why didn't *we* hear it?' I said. Our eyes met in the dim light and I tried to keep my features neutral, my gaze steady. 'You must have been mistaken.'

Violet slumped down into her bed then drew the blankets up under her chin. I thought she was going to turn the lamp out but then I heard her voice. 'If it was an accident,' she said slowly, 'if someone was in the woods, and they accidentally shot Robin, why didn't they get help? Why let him die there?'

He was already dead! I wanted to cry. *We wouldn't have left him there, not if there was a chance.*

'Everyone else was at the hunt. You, Emmi and Laura were the only ones in the beech woods this morning. The hunt never goes into the beech woods, only the big woods.'

I could barely make a reply now. My hands felt clammy despite the cold.

Violet rolled onto her back and blinked at the ceiling. 'Gilly, you would tell me, wouldn't you?' she said in a small voice. 'If something happened out there in the woods. If you, or Emmi, or Laura ...'

'What do you mean?' I asked sharply.

Violet hesitated. 'At lunch. You were all acting oddly. And before, when I came in and saw you all there in the library. Your faces. I remember your faces.'

185

'We were cold, so we came in to have cocoa.' My voice was strained.

There was a pause. 'I hope you know I'm your friend, Gilly, that *I* brought you here. Emmi and Laura, they don't have friends. All they do is take from people. Take, take, take. You'd see that if you stayed here long enough.'

'I'm very tired,' I said. 'It's all been dreadful.' I stifled a sob. 'I think I'll try and go to sleep now.'

I turned away from Violet and, after several long minutes, she turned the light off.

She doesn't believe me, I thought. *And neither will anyone else.*

* * *

I had to wait a long time to be sure Violet was asleep. I could hear her tossing and turning in her bed, snuffling and sniffing. Finally, her breathing evened. I lay flat on my back under the blankets, wide awake, listening to the sounds of the house: doors and floorboards creaking, pipes clanging, draughts blowing in from ill-fitting doors and window frames. I imagined the men from the search party had long been sent home, back to their warm beds and wives. *Tragic*, they'd say, removing their boots by the fire, pulling their shirts over their heads. *That boy never even had a chance at life.* I shuddered. And what about Frank? How could I have been so irresponsible? Surely he would tell someone I went to the cottage, that I was distressed and incoherent. He wasn't a stupid man. He'd work it out. Wouldn't he?

I also knew that somewhere in the house Mary was surely being consumed by the most horrific, unimaginable, gut-wrenching grief. I hid my face in my pillow, the nausea swelling in my stomach.

I pictured the grave, disappointed faces, the way every adult would look at me once they knew. *How could you have done such a thing? We thought you were such a nice girl.* And then, to each other, *Do you know those girls actually left him there?*

I had to be sure the rest of the house was sleeping or at least, by now, tossing and turning in their own chilly beds. Opening the bedside drawer as silently as I could, I took hold of the heavy torch, then crept across the room. My fingers made contact with the smooth cold metal of the brass doorknob and it turned without a sound. I slipped quietly onto the landing.

Only then did I turn on the torch, the single beam not providing as much illumination as I'd hoped. The house was in complete darkness and I kept the light low for fear of alerting someone to my presence. Feeling my way along the landing, I had the sensation of moving further and further into the deep, dark belly of the house. I took the staircase to the deserted west wing. The accusing eyes of the Claybournes' dead relatives stared down at me from the portraits hung along the walls. Eighteenth-century red-lipped gentlemen in buttoned jackets and frilly white neckties. Dark-haired, slender-necked women holding useless sprigs of flowers or resting their chins casually in their palms.

I reached the narrow staircase that led to the tower bedroom, treading carefully on the smooth wood, praying that my hunch was right.

At the top of the stairs, I could see a pool of faint yellow light creeping under the closed door. I turned the door handle.

Laura, wrapped in her mink coat, was sitting on the windowsill with her back to me, smoking a cigarette. She tapped ash out of the window, which she'd managed to open a crack, letting in a chilly blast. Emmeline, wearing a heavy knitted cardigan over her long white nightdress, was lying on one of the dusty sofas. There were two large oil lamps, one on the side table next to Emmeline and one on the floor, and a number of lit candles on the table amongst the overflowing ashtrays, empty glasses and half-drunk bottles of liquor. The lid of the gramophone was closed.

'Jesus,' said Laura, turning from the window, one hand on her heart, the smoke from her cigarette spiralling upwards.

Emmeline quickly recovered and gave me a small smile. The large black mark on the fire-damaged wall loomed behind her. 'You gave us a fright there, Gillian. We didn't even hear footsteps.'

'I thought you might be here,' I said.

'Did Violet see you leave the room?' Emmeline asked.

'No. She's asleep.'

Satisfied, Emmeline nodded. 'Here.' She tossed me a thick tartan blanket in a mustard check. 'Wrap this around yourself. You'll freeze.' Turning to Laura, she said, 'Shut the window for goodness' sake, Lolly. Use an ashtray.'

Laura pushed the window down then crossed the room and sat in an ancient armchair with leaking stuffing, curling her legs beneath her. Her teeth were chattering. I could hear the wind outside, and a faint murmur coming from the heavy brass oil lamp on the table.

Gratefully, I took the blanket from Emmeline and draped it over my shoulders. It smelled musty and stale, and vaguely of rodents.

No one spoke for a moment or two. Laura, still shivering, tapped ash into an empty sherry glass. Underneath her mink coat, she was wearing pyjamas in an emerald-green silk and what looked like Japanese slippers edged with fur. She held her ebony and ivory cigarette holder loosely between her fingers.

'Did Violet say anything?' Emmeline asked me.

'She heard a gunshot. When we were out.'

'Oh God,' muttered Laura.

'What did *you* say?' Emmeline frowned a little.

I felt a flutter in my stomach. 'I told her she must have been mistaken, that we didn't hear any gunshot.'

'And how did she take that?'

'I don't know. I mean, I think she was confused.'

'Good,' said Emmeline with a nod. 'It won't do any harm to unsettle her a bit.'

'But I'm sure she believes we know something,' I said.

Laura groaned. 'She's bound to tell Mummy. That's it, Emmi. We're done for.'

'There's no need to panic,' Emmeline said calmly. 'We just stick to our story, as we said.'

Laura stubbed her cigarette out onto the side of an empty wine bottle then dropped the butt into the dirty glass. 'Can I get anyone else a drink?' she asked in a shaky voice.

'Yes, please,' said Emmeline grimly.

'Brandy?'

'Scotch, if we have any.'

We watched as Laura rooted around in the cocktail cabinet and located three reasonably clean glasses. She set them on the table in front of us, then went about pouring brandy into two glasses and a Scotch for Emmeline. When Laura handed me the brandy, I felt too tired to protest but she must have noticed my uncertainty as she said, 'It will help you sleep, Gilly.'

I took the glass, and then a first tentative sip, the alcohol warming my numb insides.

'Violet looks up to you both,' I said. 'You're her sisters. And I'm her only friend at school. I'm sure, even if she does believe we had something to do with what happened today, she wouldn't say anything. But we'd have to tell her the truth.'

'Gilly might be right,' said Laura.

Emmeline shook her head. 'I'm not going to rely on Violet's loyalty. Besides,' she said darkly, 'Violet tells tales. We all know that.'

I wondered if Emmeline was referring to what Violet saw in the butterfly room all those years ago. Emmeline with Mr Lempstead.

Laura took a gulp of her drink. 'How can we make sure Violet doesn't say anything to anybody? If she does suspect we know something?'

'I don't know yet,' said Emmeline. 'I need to think, and we need to watch her carefully.' She lit a cigarette. 'And I also think that if the police *do* want to speak to us tomorrow, we ought to say a little something to distract them.'

We both looked at her.

'We saw Frank, didn't we?' she said. 'As we were heading towards the woods.'

I'd been thinking the same. If Frank told the police he'd seen us out with a gun that morning—and why wouldn't he?—well, that would be it, really.

'We need to get in first,' said Emmeline. 'We'll tell the police that when we were walking *back* to the hall, we saw Frank heading down *towards* the woods, and that he was carrying a gun.'

'Oh, no,' I said quickly.

'Emmi,' Laura murmured, 'do you really think ...'

Emmeline waved her hand, a cigarette between her fingers. 'Don't worry. Nothing will come of it. Frank was most likely heading to the pub where half the village will have seen him. It's just to keep the police busy for a while, so they don't have any reason to think about us. If Frank says he saw us, well, we'll have already said *we saw him*.' She took a sip of Scotch.

Laura frowned. 'What about if he tells them we were carrying a gun?'

Emmeline considered this. 'We stick to our story. As I said, a short walk. No gun. If Frank says he saw us with a gun, well, it will make him sound like he's trying to deflect the attention away from himself. We'll deny we had a gun with us and I'm sure we'll be believed over Frank Marks.'

The thought of doing this, of telling the police this awful lie about Frank, was making me feel ill. My skin prickled all over.

Laura also looked distressed. 'Poor old Frank. He's all right, really, you know.'

Emmeline sighed impatiently. 'It's just to distract the police.' She turned to me. 'And as I said, it won't do any harm to unsettle Violet, give her something else to think about.' She took another sip of her drink and I could see she was mulling it all over. 'Gillian, can you do something for me tomorrow?'

I looked up.

'Violet's book,' Emmeline said. 'I want you to take it and hide it somewhere.'

'Her book?' I stammered. 'You mean, *Peter Pan*?'

'You are not to tell her where it is. Just say you haven't seen it.'

I nodded, frowning. My head was swimming. Emmeline knows what to do, I told myself. Emmeline has a plan. If I followed Emmeline's instructions, put my trust in her, there was a chance it would be as she said: no one would ever come to know what had really happened in the woods today.

'Are you all right, Gilly?' Laura asked, peering at me in the dim light. 'You look a bit peaky.'

'I'm fine,' I'm whispered.

'And don't worry about Violet,' said Emmeline, exhaling a plume of smoke. 'She won't be a problem.'

Chapter Fourteen

THAT NIGHT, WE FELL ASLEEP in the tower bedroom. Emmeline woke us at around five thirty. For a moment, I wondered where I was, then I remembered. It all came flooding back; the three of us standing around Robin's body, the search party, Frank with that terrible shape in his arms. I had slept fitfully. The chair had not been comfortable, and now I felt thick-headed and disorientated. The brandy had made my tongue furry and my stomach unsettled.

We left the tower bedroom, creeping down the staircase, Emmeline holding the lamp, turning and placing her finger over her lips for silence as we parted and went our separate ways on the landing.

When I finally returned to my room and crawled under the covers, I was sure I wouldn't be able to sleep a wink and would only wait for it to grow light and for Violet to stir, but I promptly fell asleep.

When I woke, I remembered all over again. All I wanted to do was bury myself back into sleep in order to forget, but it was worse, somehow, lying there with my eyes closed, those terrible images flashing through my mind. I realised with a start that it must be quite late. The sun, creeping through the gap in the curtains, was cool and bitter. Violet was not in her bed. I groped for my wristwatch and was horrified to see it was almost nine o'clock. Why had no one come to wake me? I stumbled to the washbasin, splashed cold water onto my face and stared at myself in the glass. I looked pale, my hair was mussed and I had a line across my cheek, an indent from the lace edge of the pillow. Otherwise, I looked the same. The same light brown hair. The same hazel-coloured eyes staring back at me. The mirror lied. I was not the same.

I had the sudden thought that Robin was still in the house. Had they taken him to his room and laid him out on his bed? The thought of him lying not so far away from me made me nauseous. I had to get out of the room. I had to find other people to be with.

I hastily dressed, before running a comb through my hair and pulling on my stockings, and was at the door when I happened to glance back and notice Violet's tattered copy of *Peter Pan* on her night table. I was glad I had noticed it. I would have hated to tell Emmeline I'd forgotten her instructions, that I had failed at the one small task she had set me.

Violet's book in my hand, I looked desperately around the room. Where would I hide it? Under my bed? In the back of the wardrobe? No, Violet might find it if it was somewhere in the room.

I darted along the hallway towards the bathroom, terrified I would bump into one of the servants or, worse, Lady Claybourne. The bath stood on lion's claws and had been painted a dull dusty rose. I reached down behind it and found a ledge where the copper water pipes had been boxed in. I shoved the book onto the ledge, down behind the pipes, then quickly left.

Wandering through the dim corridors of Thornleigh, the air around me felt light and empty and I wouldn't have been surprised to have found no one else in the house, to discover I had woken in a different reality, one in which I was the sole inhabitant, like in some terrifying, silent horror picture. Or perhaps like Violet's idea that one day we might wake to find a plague had killed everyone but us. But as I descended the staircase, my hand on the rail, I could hear voices.

The dining room was occupied by Emmeline, Laura, Violet and Lady Claybourne. Pots of jam and honey, bread, tea and coffee, and various bits of cheese and cold meat had been laid out on the table, but I noted, for the first time during my stay, the absence of anything cooked. Emmeline was as immaculate as always. You wouldn't think she had spent the night sleeping in the draughty tower bedroom, huddled under dusty blankets. Laura looked tired and dazed, but had also made the usual efforts with her appearance.

'Gillian,' said Lady Claybourne with a small, tight smile.

'You were fast asleep,' said Violet.

I mumbled an apology, feeling extremely embarrassed.

'It's quite all right,' said Lady Claybourne kindly. 'I think we're all a little out of sorts today. It's hard to believe ...' She looked towards the French windows and lightly touched her neck.

Emmeline cleared her throat. 'Yes, I think we're all exhausted, after yesterday.'

This remark hung in the air for a moment before Lady Claybourne spoke. 'You'll have to help yourself, Gillian. It's rather primitive, I'm afraid. We've given Mrs Frith the morning off, and Mary will naturally need a few days.'

'Tea? I know you prefer it to coffee, Gillian.' Emmeline was leaning over, pouring tea into a teacup for me. 'There's a little milk left, but we can ring for Ethel to fetch more from the kitchen if you need it. One lump, or two?' She hovered over my teacup with the sugar tongs.

'One,' I croaked.

There was another awkward pause. Laura took a small, forced bite of a tiny piece of bread and chewed as if it were painful to do so.

Emmeline was now calmly spreading blackcurrant jam onto a muffin. Violet was looking at her sisters with a slight frown. 'They'll catch whoever did it, I'm sure,' she said pointedly.

I felt a horrible dropping sensation in my stomach and stared into my tepid, over-brewed tea.

Lady Claybourne gave Violet a fierce look. 'Really, Violet. It's quite obvious what happened. A poacher. It must have been. An awful shock to the man, I expect. But to just *leave him there*.' Lady Claybourne shook her head. 'I don't know what has become of the world, why people can't just do the decent thing anymore.'

Laura swallowed and looked down at her plate.

'I was always telling Mary the child needed more supervision. Letting him run all over the place like that.' She brought her teacup to her lips and took a sip. 'It'll be in all the papers, of course – they love this sort of thing.'

At the mention of the papers, Emmeline looked up. 'Do you think so?'

'You know what they're like,' said Lady Claybourne. 'Journalists. There was one here this morning. A young man in a striped suit with a camera, asking if he could "interview us about the tragedy". Ethel sent him away, of course.' She turned to Emmeline and gave her a reassuring smile. 'We shall just have to weather it out, I'm afraid. But it *will* blow over. And it won't spoil any of our plans for the spring.'

I knew she was talking about Emmeline's engagement.

'In fact,' she said firmly, 'by then, it will be the right time to perk everyone up, give them something else to talk about.' She paused, took another sip of tea. 'But I'm afraid it will all be rather ghastly for a while. And I do hope they catch the man quickly. It would be a terrible strain if the thing dragged on.'

I blinked and stared at the tablecloth.

'Where is Daddy?' Laura asked nervously.

'He went to the coroner's. And he's going to speak to the vicar. I expect we'll have to cover the funeral costs. There is no one else who will do it.'

I felt a tiny, awful wave of relief that Robin was no longer in the house.

There was a silence before Lady Claybourne turned to me.

'I'm sorry this happened while you are here, Gillian. What a horrid Christmas you'll have had.'

I opened my mouth in an attempt to say something to contradict this, although of course it was true, and she didn't know the full extent of it, but at that moment Ethel appeared at the door. She was neatly turned out, her clean white apron covering her dark maid's dress, but her eyes were red-rimmed.

'It's Detective Gamble, your Ladyship. And another policeman with him. Sparrow, I think he said. I've shown them into the morning room.'

Laura and Emmeline exchanged a glance.

'Oh goodness, already?' Lady Claybourne sighed. 'What a nuisance your father isn't here. Did you tell Detective Gamble that Lord Claybourne is with the coroner, Ethel?'

'Yes, your Ladyship,' said Ethel. 'But they wanted to come in anyway.'

Rising with a sigh, Lady Claybourne reluctantly left the dining room.

Laura put the piece of bread down on her plate and stared at it whilst Emmeline had become very focused on carefully stirring her coffee.

'Aren't you going to eat anything, Gilly?' Violet asked.

I could feel Emmeline's gaze on me. 'Oh, yes,' I said airily, reaching for a muffin.

'Try the blackcurrant jam,' Emmeline said, gesturing to the pot. 'Mrs Frith makes it every year. It's the last of the crop.'

I reached for the pot and slowly spread a little of the dark jam across the fluffy, snow-white muffin. The sight of the clots of blackcurrants and the purplish, seeping stain made me feel queasy. I took a small bite, forcing it down.

Why was the constable here so early? Would he want to speak to us? This last thought was petrifying. And if he did speak to us, what if Violet said something about us planning to take a gun out, or hearing a shot? I felt a roiling in my stomach.

Lady Claybourne swept back into the room.

'What is it?' Laura asked quickly. 'Has there been any news?'

'Oh, they wouldn't tell me much,' Lady Claybourne replied dismissively. She turned to Emmeline. 'They'd like to speak to you. I've put them in the library.'

Emmeline nodded. 'Certainly.'

'Why do they want to speak to Emmi, did they say?' Laura was pulling at her dress as if it was chafing.

'I should think it's just a formality,' said Emmeline calmly, although I could tell she was rattled.

'Such a nuisance,' said Lady Claybourne. 'I do despise policemen and such like. Digging around in everyone else's affairs ... I expect they want to speak with you girls as you were here in the house at the time.'

'Some of us were,' muttered Violet under her breath. She tapped her fingers methodically against the table. She's doing her rituals, I thought. She's cross, but also anxious. She knows we're keeping something from her and it bothers her that she doesn't know what.

Emmeline glanced at Violet, letting her gaze settle on her sister for a moment, before leaving the room.

Why did they want to speak to Emmeline in particular? Were they intending to call us in one at a time? What if I said the wrong thing? What if they saw the guilt written all over my face and it gave us away? It would be all my fault then. Our lives would be ruined because of me.

I looked over to Violet who had resumed messily eating her muffin. Surely, if she knew something, she would keep quiet.

As I watched her, I decided, like Emmeline, that I just couldn't be sure.

* * *

'What the hell is taking so long?'

We were in the lounge hall, waiting for Violet who was in the library with the two police officers. Emmeline was pacing up at down on the tiger-skin rug by the fireplace, Laura was on the window seat worrying at a loose button. I was perched on the piano stool. The sight of Emmeline agitated made me feel even more anxious. She was usually so calm.

'She's only been in there five minutes,' said Laura. Her face was drawn and her words lacked the intended reassurance. She reached for her cigarettes, took one out, then began to tap it against the side of the packet.

'Will you stop that,' snapped Emmeline. 'It's irritating.'

'Sorry,' said Laura, staring at the unlit cigarette for a moment before putting it back.

'How long were we in there for?' Emmeline asked.

'Not long,' I said. 'Ten or fifteen minutes at the most.'

Laura turned to Emmeline. 'Were they beastly to you, Emmi?'

'No, of course not,' said Emmeline tensely. 'In fact, I had quite a nice little chat with old Gamble about the hunt. He wanted to know all about it. Who was there, who had fared well, if anyone had come off. Of course he's absolutely delighted to be here, handling this. I bet he can't wait to tell everyone he knows he's been up at Thornleigh Hall rubbing shoulders with the landed gentry. He's probably hoping he'll get an invitation to the ball.'

I imagined Emmeline in with the two officers. She would have been polite, friendly and amenable, playing the part of the gracious and bright eldest daughter well.

Laura lowered her voice. 'Did you mention Frank? As you said—'

'Yes, didn't you?' Emmeline asked.

Laura nodded.

'Anyway, what do you mean beastly? What did they ask you?'

Laura looked uncomfortable. 'Well, it was all right in the end.'

Emmeline blinked. 'What do you mean, Lolly?'

Laura wouldn't meet her sister's eye. 'Oh, just that when I walked in, the younger chap, what's his name, *Sparrow*, said, "Oh, it's you—"'

Emmeline was now standing perfectly still. 'Sorry?'

Laura tugged at the cuff of her blouse. 'Well, you see, there might have been a little misunderstanding, a few weeks ago when I was in town ...'

'What misunderstanding,' asked Emmeline darkly.

'Oh, nothing much.' Laura fiddled with her watch. 'I was in that shop in Oxford. You know the one that sells undergarments and stockings and those dear little bags of lavender.'

Emmeline's eyes narrowed.

'Well, I had a little look, but didn't *quite* need to purchase anything on that occasion, only when I had got a little way along the street I heard someone calling at me to stop and when I turned around that officer – *Sparrow* – was steaming up behind me, red in the face. He said the shop assistant – I remember her, a vile, mousy girl – said I'd *stolen* something. He made me turn out my handbag, and do you know, there *was* pair of silk stockings in there.' She gave us a quick, false smile. 'Of course I told him it must have slipped my mind to pay for them. At first he was quite awful, suggesting I come to the station and what not, but after we chatted a little, and I gave him my address, and mentioned Daddy and various other things, he let the matter drop. Although he did escort me back to the shop and waited as I paid the dreary girl. And when the officer explained the misunderstanding on my behalf, she dared to accuse me of *lying*.'

'For goodness' sake, Lolly. Why do you take these damn things? As if we need the police to believe we are capable of lying right now.'

Laura looked hurt.

'Did they say anything else?' I asked Laura. I was breathing rapidly. The police had called each of the sisters in to speak to them in turn. Would I be next?

Laura shook head and looked down into her lap. 'No, I just told them about us watching the hunters arrive, our short walk, seeing Frank, and how dreadful it all was when we knew Robin was missing and everyone searching, and then ... well, I had to get my handkerchief.'

I could just picture it: Laura, smiling nervously, her fingers entwined in her lap, her damp eyelashes. She'd give the officers that wide-eyed look, the look I'd seen her give virtually every man she came into contact with, a look of pure innocence and loveliness, coupled with a fragility that had men falling over themselves to please her. It wasn't only Emmeline who had *an effect* on people. Whereas I imagined men longed for Emmeline to notice them, to respect them, they wanted to protect Laura.

Footsteps in the passage. We glanced at each other, falling silent. The door opened and Violet came in. She gave us a cool look. 'Your turn,' she said to me.

I stood, my legs jittery. It had been too much to hope for that the officers would have no interest in talking to me as I wasn't a resident of the house. I was going to have to go through with this. Laura attempted to give me a reassuring smile before I left the room, but my stomach was as tight as a drum.

I walked along the hallway towards the library, my tweed skirt hot and itchy against the tops of my legs. I could hear the steady tick-tock of the grandfather clock and glanced at the little paper ship swinging backwards and forwards across the top of the clock face. I knew I need only say one stupid thing and the truth might be guessed at. It was different for Emmeline and Laura. They knew how to talk to adults. From a young age they had been primed to flourish in any social situation, to handle the household servants, to deal with shop-keepers, waiters, railway ticket inspectors, and the world around them, when required. I had spent my life cooped up with girls the same age as me, and with terrifying teachers who had the capacity to take away my meagre privileges or dish out painful and humiliating punishments. Figures of authority made me nervous.

I paused outside the library doors, took a deep breath, and went in.

The older man, Detective Gamble, I assumed, was standing by the fire, his hands clasped behind his back. He wore a green three-piece tweed suit and a gold watch strung on a chain. I couldn't help thinking of Toad of Toad Hall. The younger man, Sparrow, in his navy uniform, was sitting in the smallest leather chair, his tall, lanky frame overspilling it. He was sipping coffee from one of the Claybournes' gold-rimmed teacups. On the side table was a silver tray on which sat a pot of coffee and a little bowl of cubed sugar. Ethel must have brought it.

Detective Gamble, I noticed, had put his cup on the mantel-piece and seemed quite at home, one foot resting casually on the fender as he studied the fireplace. He was a beefy, red-nosed man with deep fleshy jowls and small, sunken eyes. What was left of his hair was greying around his ears. He turned towards me as I entered and reached for a notebook from the inside pocket of his jacket. 'Ah, Gillian,' he said, glancing down at the notebook. 'Please, take a seat.' He gestured towards the tartan wingback. As I crossed the room I imagined I was Emmeline. She would not feel at all intimidated. She would sit down quietly, say nothing, wait to be spoken to. Smile pleasantly when required.

'You're a guest here?' he asked me.

'Yes,' I said.

'And how do you know the Claybournes?'

'I go to school with Violet.'

'Here for the Christmas break?'

'Yes.'

He paused and peered down at me from where he stood over by the fire.

'A terrible thing to happen,' he said.

'Yes.' I swallowed hard, trying to dispel the lump in my throat. Poor Robin. Poor, poor Robin. I could see him, chasing his duck into the dining room; his limp arm stretched out on the snow. No, I mustn't think of it.

'Can you tell us where you were on Boxing Day morning?'

This came from the younger officer.

'I was in the house.'

'And did you leave at any point?' Detective Gamble asked me. He'd put the notebook away and had his hands clasped behind his back which accentuated his protruding stomach.

'We went for a walk,' I said, in what I hoped was a casual way. 'We set off down the mount, but it was really very cold, so we turned back.'

'This walk,' said Detective Gamble, moving away from the fireplace and coming closer towards me. 'Did you see anyone?'

I exhaled a shaky breath. 'Yes. A man. Frank Marks. He lives in the old gate lodge cottage.'

Constable Sparrow wrote something in his notebook.

'Can you tell us, Gillian,' Detective Gamble said, leaning towards me. 'In which direction Mr Marks was walking?'

'He was walking towards the beech woods,' I said. 'At least, I mean, he looked like he was. But I didn't see where he went,' I added quickly.

Detective Gamble cleared his throat. 'And did you notice Mr Marks carrying anything on his person?'

I could feel my heart racing and I was sure it was beating loudly enough to give me away. I didn't want to say it. I really didn't. But I also knew I couldn't let Emmeline down. 'Yes,' I said. 'He was carrying a gun.'

Constable Sparrow scribbled something in his notebook.

'I believe he shoots rabbits,' I said feebly.

'Now, Gillian,' said Gamble, giving nothing away, 'can you tell us about the hunt?'

'Well,' I faltered a little. What was he asking me exactly? 'Well, we didn't actually see the hunt. We stayed inside.'

'But you saw the hunters arrive.'

I pressed my knees together. 'We were up in the tower bedroom.'

Gamble cut in. 'Did you know any of those ladies and gentlemen, Gillian?'

I shook my head. 'No.'

'And when you were up there – in the tower bedroom, watching the hunters arrive – did you notice anyone who looked ... how can I put it, as if they perhaps didn't belong?'

'No,' I said.

Gamble was fumbling in his jacket pocket. He brought out a crumpled packet of tobacco and began to stuff his pipe. I wished he'd sit down.

'How well do you know the Claybournes?' he asked, his eyes not leaving his pipe.

I shifted in the chair. 'I just know Violet from school.'

'Your father isn't a friend of Lord Claybourne's?'

'No. My father is in Egypt.'

Detective Gamble nodded as Constable Sparrow took a sip of coffee then wiped his mouth on his sleeve.

What did this all have to do with anything? I wondered.

Gamble puffed away thoughtfully on his pipe. His eyes landed on a photograph of Emmeline, Laura and Violet on the mantelpiece. It must have been taken six or seven years ago. Violet looked about eight or nine, Laura around thirteen. And Emmeline, I guessed she was sixteen. They were in fancy dress and had floral garlands in their hair. Behind them a curtain had been erected, upon which some kind of woodland scene had been painted. They had obviously put on a play. Two chairs had been pushed together and I could see the rocking horse from the nursery in the background wearing reins. I wondered what the performance had been and who had been there to witness it.

Detective Gamble turned from the photograph and gave me a kind smile. 'Do you have brothers or sisters, Gillian?'

I shook my head.

'Me neither,' he said. He paused and glanced at the photograph again. 'It must be interesting,' he said. 'To have siblings you are close to. To grow up with – all this.' He lifted an eyebrow and made a sweeping gesture with his hand. I supposed by 'all this' he was referring to Thornleigh Hall, and to the sisters' sheltered and secluded lives. 'I expect the girls have some tales to tell,' he said with a smile.

I swallowed hard. A lump had formed in my throat.

He took a step away from the fire. 'I think that's all we need for now, Gillian. You'll be returning to school in the new year?'

I said that I would and he gave a satisfied nod.

Assuming I was dismissed, I rose slowly. Pausing at the library doors, I glanced back. Constable Sparrow was downing the dregs of his coffee. Detective Gamble was once again peering at the photograph of the three sisters.

Chapter Fifteen

VIOLET INSISTED WE GO OUT. We went, just the two of us, down the mount towards the copse. The snow lay thick on the ground.

I was grateful Violet didn't want to go into the beech woods. I don't think I could have gone back there. Violet had barely spoken to me since the two police officers had left. She walked slowly, with hunched shoulders.

When we reached the copse, we stopped at the fallen tree in the clearing. Finally, Violet turned to me. 'I told Detective Gamble you were all gone for twenty minutes. That's what you've decided, isn't it?'

I didn't know what to say.

'I lied for you,' she said quietly. 'I lied for you all, and you won't even tell me what's going on.'

I cleared my throat. 'We *were* gone for about twenty minutes. We—'

'You were out for more than an hour. I know, because I was waiting. I lied for you all and you won't even tell me the truth, Gilly.'

'There's nothing to tell,' I said. I was tired and weary and I wished she would let it drop. I could barely deal with my own guilt, with the horror of it all. It was enough without Violet's incessant inquisitions.

'I saw your faces when you came in. Something happened in the woods, didn't it? You all know what happened to Robin, but you won't tell me.'

I prodded a pile of snow-covered leaves with the toe of my boot, not looking at her.

'And now you're all against me,' she went on. 'You're talking about me behind my back. I know you are.'

'Of course we're not,' I said, feigning indignation. 'We don't know any more than you do.' I swallowed. 'Perhaps your thoughts are playing tricks on you. It happens sometimes, remember? You told me about it.'

Violet stiffened. Her eyes met mine and we stared at one another. 'You're supposed to be my friend, Gilly,' she said quietly.

'I am,' I said, 'which is why I'm reminding you that you sometimes believe things that aren't true. I'm trying to help.'

She turned away, her face pained.

I stuffed my hands into my pockets. *It has to be this way,* I reminded myself. Emmeline was right. *It's better that she doesn't know.*

* * *

'Where's my book?'

Upstairs, we were peeling off our outdoor layers when Violet, glancing over at her night table, noticed the absence of her cherished book.

'I don't know,' I said.

'I left it right here,' she said, pointing.

'Perhaps you left it somewhere else?'

I wasn't sure what Emmeline hoped to achieve by me moving Violet's book, other than what she had said about unsettling her. Lying to Violet made me feel dreadful, but I had to have faith that Emmeline knew what she was doing.

'No, I told you.' Violet stared at the empty night table for a moment then picked up the corner of the bedcovers and peered underneath. She got down on her knees and checked under the bed, sweeping her arm across the floor. 'It isn't anywhere,' she declared, getting up. 'I do wish the servants wouldn't move my things. Can you go downstairs, please? Tell Ethel we'd like some tea – not too strong, you know I don't like strong tea – and ask her if she's moved my book.'

I didn't particularly like being ordered about in this way by Violet and wondered why she couldn't just ring the bell as she usually did. I gave her a frosty look, then set off down to the kitchen, taking the backstairs.

Ethel was in the laundry room, a sheet spread out over the ironing table, the iron heating on the range. Bedclothes hung on hooks from the ceiling.

'Hello, Ethel,' I said, ducking under a sheet.

'Oh,' she said, startled. 'Can I get you anything, miss?'

'Violet and I have just returned from a walk and would like some tea if it's not too much trouble.'

I was still uncomfortable when talking to the servants. And I disliked it when Ethel – barely much older than me – called me miss. I knew Violet would never feel awkward asking for a simple cup of tea, but I always had the sense, with the servants, that I was disturbing them, dragging them away from more important work. Especially Mrs Frith who I was rather frightened of.

'Of course, miss. I'll bring it straight to you. Will you be in the library?'

'Yes, I think so.'

I hesitated. Ethel watched me, waiting.

'Is there anything else, miss?'

'Well, yes. I was just wondering how Mary is?'

Ethel nodded as if the question was expected. 'She's still in her room, miss. Not come out.'

'It must be awful . . .' I murmured.

'Yes,' said Ethel. She paused. 'Well, to be perfectly honest, miss, I think she likes the rest. I don't think she's in any hurry to get back to work.'

I blinked. This seemed rather harsh, but then I remembered Violet telling me the two maids didn't get on, that Ethel thought Mary lazy.

'I'm sure she'll return to work when she can, when she's . . . ready.' I stumbled over my words, feeling foolish. How would Mary ever be ready to return to work? How could a person ever learn to live with a loss like that?

'Yes, miss,' said Ethel flatly. 'I'm sure she will.'

I thought again of Robin, lying out there in the woods in the snow and all the time Mary not knowing a thing about it. I shuddered.

'Are you all right, miss?'

Ethel was staring at me.

'Yes, fine,' I said, clearing my throat. 'Oh, Ethel, just one more thing . . .'

She waited.

'I don't suppose you've seen Violet's book, have you? *Peter Pan*? She can't find it.'

Ethel frowned, shook her head. 'No. I don't think so. I don't remember seeing any book when I did the bedrooms this morning.'

'That's fine,' I said quickly, turning to go. 'I'm sure she's just misplaced it.'

* * *

I decided to seek out Emmeline.

It was late afternoon; before long we'd be getting ready for dinner. I guessed, if Emmeline wasn't in the library, or out on Sigmund, she must be in her room. Violet had shown me, on my grand tour of the house that first day, where it was.

A glow coming from under the closed door told me she was there. I knocked softy.

'Yes?'

'It's Gillian.'

'Come in then.'

Outside the temperature was dropping steadily and Emmeline had lit the gas fire and several candles on her large mahogany desk where she sat, writing. The desk was covered in papers and books, including the blue Sigmund Freud volumes I'd seen her reading in the library. An old-fashioned quill pen lay resting on an open notebook, and a teacup and saucer were perched on top of a copy of *The Iliad* that had various scraps of paper sticking out of it, marking pages. Her desk may have been untidy, but the rest of the room was immaculate and unfussy, decorated in rich reds and golds. She was wearing a pale fawn-coloured dress. I noticed an ink stain on her thumb. 'Are you all right, Gillian?'

I lifted my shoulders. 'Yes, thank you.'

'Good.' She smiled. 'You're holding up remarkably well. As I said, I knew we could rely on you.'

For some reason, her words made me want to cry.

'I'm glad you've stopped by,' she said. 'I wanted to talk with you about the police. What did they ask?'

I cleared my throat. 'Just about how long we were out, and if I'd seen anything.'

'Did you tell them about Frank Marks?'

I nodded.

'Good. You've done well, Gillian.'

I blushed. 'I really came to speak to you about Violet,' I said. 'She thinks we know something more than we're letting on. I reminded her that she often believes events have happened, or might have happened, when they haven't at all. Her mind exaggerates the truth and runs away from her.'

'Oh, yes,' said Emmeline. 'She often believes she's done something bad, doesn't she? Or else she has to prevent something bad from happening. It's strange.'

'It's why she does all her rituals, her undoings.'

Emmeline looked thoughtful.

'I moved her book this morning, as you said.'

Emmeline blinked. 'Oh, right, yes. Well, great. Where did you put it?'

'Behind the bath in the first-floor bathroom.'

'Perhaps leave it there for a little while,' she said, turning back to her desk. 'Then put it back.'

I had hoped Emmeline might have been more pleased with me, for managing to take the book, for completing the task she had given me, for trying to convince Violet that she was being paranoid. But she was distracted. As if remembering I was still there, she turned to me again.

'Are you looking forward to the ball?' she asked.

'Oh, yes,' I said, because it seemed like the right thing to say. In truth, I was surprised to hear the New Year's Eve ball might still go ahead.

'We'll be able to introduce you to some fabulous people. Just think, your first night in society. A big moment for you, Gillian. And there'll be plenty of eligible bachelors there, of course.'

I tried to return her smile but struggled. At any other time, I might have felt a tingle of excitement at the thought of eligible bachelors – I remembered Aunt Ada's advice: *Marry well, Gillian* – but it was hard to think about meeting anyone now at such a terrible time.

Emmeline had gone back to her desk. I glanced over. It looked as though she was writing a letter. I could see an address written at the top corner.

'Is that to Hugh Cadwallander?' I asked boldly.

Emmeline smiled. 'Yes, as a matter of fact, it is.'

I looked at the letter, imagining it to be terribly romantic and wondering if I would ever write such a letter to a man.

'It's mostly arrangements,' Emmeline said. 'He'll come to stay at Thornleigh when he returns from Africa next month.'

'Do you think he'll propose then?'

'Yes,' Emmeline said, a smile playing at the corners of her lips. 'I believe he will. He's already written to Father.'

'But what about your studies?' I asked.

Emmeline's smile vanished. She pressed her lips together then smoothed a non-existent crease in her dress. 'Well ... we can't have everything in life, Gillian. Sometimes we have to make choices or sacrifices. We have to accept the role assigned to us.'

I nodded, biting my lip. This seemed so at odds with Emmeline's fierce determination and passion for learning. She seemed to me, despite her enthusiasm for her marriage, to be willingly sacrificing the most essential parts of herself.

'Do you think you'll enjoy being married?' I asked.

'Of course,' she said. 'Married women have more freedom. They hold a more respected place in society. Besides, I'm bored to death of being a debutante, of parties and egg rissole, of the endless mindless chatter of stupid girls, and of all those needy chaperoning mothers. Thank goodness it's almost over. I'll be married by the spring,' she said firmly. 'And nothing will get in the way of it.'

*   *   *

At dinner that evening, Violet was sullen. We sat around the huge table, a few candles flickering, a crackling fire, the scraping of cutlery, the occasional chink of a glass. Outside, a strong wind blew, causing the flames in the hearth to leap madly about. Laura was opposite me and the string of pearls she wore dazzled a brilliant creamy white against her pale throat. Lady Claybourne was wearing a large fruit salad brooch that sparkled in the firelight. The Claybournes often wore their jewels for dinner. 'All the best pieces are in the bank,' Laura had told me. 'Although our collection is greatly diminished now as Daddy keeps selling pieces off.'

'You probably left your book somewhere in the library,' Lady Claybourne was saying impatiently to Violet.

We were on to dessert: fruit crumble with cream and a quivering green jelly with tangerine segments floating about in it like stuck goldfish. I could see the orange glow of the fire in the smooth curved surface of my spoon.

'I didn't leave it in the library,' Violet said. 'I left it by my bed where I always do and now it's gone.'

'Easy to misplace things,' said Lord Claybourne vaguely.

I could see Lord Claybourne was terribly upset by Robin's death. He seemed even more vacant than usual, wrapped up in himself.

'And someone has moved my bed,' Violet said.

Lady Claybourne paused, her spoon halfway to her mouth. 'Violet, what on earth do you mean, someone's moved your *bed*.'

'It's closer to the window than it was this morning.'

'Perhaps Ethel knocked it while she was cleaning.'

I thought this unlikely. The beds were solid brass, laden with thick horsehair mattresses and piles of blankets. The only way to move one would be with two people, one at each end. What was Violet talking about?

I looked up just in time to see Emmeline and Laura exchange a glance. *They've moved it*, I thought. *Why have they done that?*

Lady Claybourne put her spoon down. 'Girls, we had a call from the coroner this morning. They're releasing Robin's body. We're to have the funeral on Thursday. Your father and I are dealing with the arrangements.'

'The least we can do,' murmured Lord Claybourne.

I looked from Emmeline to Laura but their faces gave nothing away. Surely this must be good news? We wouldn't be able to have a funeral if there was still an ongoing investigation, would we?'

'It's dreadful,' said Violet, throwing her napkin on the table. 'To think he'll soon be buried and forgotten about when we don't even know what really happened.'

Emmeline's shoulders stiffened. 'It's upset us all, Piff.'

'Really?' said Violet. 'Because you're all behaving as if you just want it to go away.'

'Of course we're not,' said Lady Claybourne sharply. 'But we must go on, Violet.'

'Age shall not weary them,' murmured Lord Claybourne irrelevantly into his crumble.

Violet glared at us all. She stood up, excused herself loudly from the table, then left the room, slamming the door behind her as she went.

I hesitated, unsure as to whether I should follow.

'I am sorry, Gillian,' Lady Claybourne said, perhaps noticing my unease. 'I'm afraid Violet is edging towards one of her moods again.'

Emmeline set her wine glass down. 'She gets worked up, Mother.'

'We hoped, of course, that school might be the best place for her,' Lady Claybourne said. 'The routine, the structure and discipline ... But Violet, well, she has these *compulsions*. Her nerves get the better of her. It's difficult to know what to do. I've always thought school quite unnecessary for girls ...' She glanced at me, realising her mistake. 'Of course it's different for *you*, Gillian,' she added quickly. 'I understand your father would want you to grow up in England. Somewhere civilised. But for my girls, well, school simply wasn't required.'

I saw Emmeline flinch and remembered what Laura had said about her begging to go to school. I felt another pang of sympathy for Emmeline when I thought of her impending marriage, and how she would have to give up her studies. I had never known a person make such efforts to go against the grain of their nature. She was clever and yet all that cleverness, the business of her mind, had never had any real outlet or encouragement. No wonder she fell for Mr Lempstead.

'Dr Roach thought school might do Violet some good, you see. And we think very highly of Dr Roach's opinion,' Lady Claybourne was saying. 'But I am now beginning to wonder if it is the right place for her. Her nerve trouble does not seem to have improved. And now these strange accusations . . .'

I thought of all the times Violet and I had eaten stolen biscuits in our dorm room, bounced on our beds, and laughed about our teachers, speculating about their lives. *Miss Dodds went out to dinner with the handyman last week. I saw them walking out together. Miss Beeton is livid. She wanted him for herself.* I suppose, if I'd thought about it, I'd expected my stay at Thornleigh to strengthen my friendship with Violet, bring us closer together, when in fact, the opposite had occurred.

'She has a difficult nature,' Lady Claybourne said firmly. 'We try to do what we can.' She stared at her wine glass. 'But it takes its toll on one.'

The door creaked open and Violet reappeared holding *Peter Pan*.

'You found it,' Lady Claybourne said. 'Didn't we say you would, Violet?'

219

'In the library, was it?' asked Lord Claybourne, squinting at Violet through his spectacles.

Violet stared at us through narrowed eyes, her jaw set. 'It was by my bed. Right where I left it. Someone must have put it back.'

I studied my dinner plate. I had fetched the book from the bathroom and replaced it before dinner, just as Emmeline had instructed.

Lady Claybourne pursed her lips. 'Oh, Violet, *really* ...'

'And it's *damp*. It smells musty. It's been moved and then put back. I know it has.'

I felt hot. I was sure my flushed face would give me away.

'Perhaps you left it on a windowsill,' said Laura helpfully.

Violet ignored Laura. 'I'm telling you, someone took it. And they moved my bed. Someone is playing tricks on me and I'm going to find out who.'

'You must have thought you left it somewhere else,' Lady Claybourne said, calmly taking a sip of wine. 'You're always in such a rush, Violet. You obviously didn't look properly.'

'Of course I looked properly. And Gillian was there. She saw it wasn't on my night table.'

I swallowed with some difficulty. 'I couldn't say for sure.'

The colour rose in Violet's cheeks. 'You're all against me,' she said. 'You're all lying to me.'

Lady Claybourne flashed Violet a warning look. 'That's quite enough,' she said curtly.

At that moment, Higgins appeared, carefully sidestepping around Violet. He surveyed the scene as if he had just stumbled upon it, but I suspected he had been listening from the hallway.

'Shall I clear the table, sir?' he asked Lord Claybourne.

'Oh, yes, very good, Higgins,' murmured Lord Claybourne who had taken to stoically cleaning his glasses with a handkerchief.

Before Higgins could begin clearing our plates, Lady Claybourne tossed her napkin down then rose from her chair. 'Yes, I think we are all done here.' She turned stiffly to her daughter. 'Violet, I won't stand for any more of this nonsense. It's been a trying time for all of us. You are to spend the evening in your room.'

*   *   *

After Violet had gone up to our room, and Lord and Lady Claybourne had retired to their various parts of the house, I found Emmeline and Laura in the library. They were sitting close together on the Chesterfield, talking in low voices, a newspaper spread out between them.

'Oh, it's only Gilly,' said Laura, looking up, with a short nervous laugh.

'What is it?' I asked.

She handed me the paper.

On Monday evening at around 9 p.m., the body of a six-year-old boy was found in the woods at Thornleigh Hall, the country estate belonging to Lord Claybourne. The boy, the child of a member of the Claybournes' staff, was found to have been killed by a shotgun. It is believed the boy had died sometime during the day, the time happening to coincide with Lord Claybourne's annual Boxing Day hunt meet, although the two events are seemingly unconnected. The boy was, by all accounts, friendly and well liked – 'always a cheery little soul' according to his mother who works as a housemaid at Thornleigh Hall and who sadly has no other children. Although believed to most likely have been an accident, the death is still being treated as suspicious, and local police are appealing to both residents of the area and those from further afield who attended the hunt at Thornleigh Hall on the 26th of December, to come forward should they have any information regarding the boy's untimely death.

I handed the paper back to Laura, not knowing what to say. I thought of Frank, sitting in his chair by the stove reading the paper, recalling my visit. *We've done something terrible.*

'You've gone pale, Gilly,' said Laura, looking at me with concern. 'Sit down, will you?'

I thought of my father. I knew he received the British papers in Egypt, albeit a week or so late. Would he see the article? Would the name 'Thornleigh' ring any bells for him? Would he remember it was where I told him I was staying for Christmas?

Our teachers and the girls at school were also bound to hear about what had happened during my stay here. There was a girl a few years ago called Kathleen Gibson whose brother and father had died in a sailing boat accident one summer. When she returned in the autumn, an air of tragedy hung over her, dark and impenetrable, and although she did her best to carry on with her life at school as normal, the other girls avoided her, as if her misfortune might rub off on them, or simply to avoid the embarrassment of not knowing what to say. What would it be like for Violet and me? I felt I couldn't bear it if I were ostracised. I'd always tried my best to blend in, to not stand apart.

'It was to be expected,' Emmeline was saying calmly. 'Nothing to worry about.'

I hoped she was right. At least it was on page eleven and barely took up half a page. Clearly no one thought the death of a servant's child on a country estate in Oxfordshire was huge news, even if the circumstances were being 'treated as suspicious'.

Still, I couldn't help thinking of Frank. A permanent knot of anxiety had formed in my stomach. What would Emmeline think of me if she knew I had almost let them all down?

'What I want to know,' said Emmeline, 'is when, exactly, Mary has spoken to journalists? I thought we'd made it clear she wasn't to.'

I looked over at Emmeline, surprised.

'They obviously got to her somehow,' said Laura, reaching for her cigarettes. 'There was a man here yesterday afternoon. Said he'd come to inspect the pipes or something. He was down in the kitchen. It could have been him.'

Emmeline let out a frustrated sigh. 'We really must be very careful about who we let into the house.'

There was a short silence, then Laura spoke again. 'Violet's very upset, you know. She hates being kept in the dark. The whole thing has shaken her up dreadfully, even though she wasn't even . . .' As she brought the cigarette holder to her lips, I noticed her hand was trembling.

'Yes,' said Emmeline simply. 'But we can't tell her, I'm afraid. Here.' She carefully tore the article out of the newspaper. 'You should have this, Gillian.'

'Me?'

'Yes. And when the time is right, you can show it to Violet.'

'But what should I say?' I asked, baffled.

'I'm sure you'll think of something,' Emmeline replied, folding the article in half and pressing it into my hand.

* * *

Later, upstairs in our bedroom, I could see that Violet's bed *had* been moved. Not by much, only a few inches, but the space between the bed and window was definitely smaller. I knew because I had often stood in that space in the mornings, looking out, scanning the park for deer. Violet must have seen me notice for she said, 'Look, Gilly, the bed's definitely closer to the window, isn't it?'

I hesitated. Some intuitive sense was telling me I should disagree with her, that it was what Emmeline would want. Could Emmeline and Laura really have crept into our room before dinner? Might they have moved the bed together? I couldn't see any of the servants doing it. It was the only explanation.

'I don't think it's been moved,' I said, looking away.

'Oh, come on,' challenged Violet, her hands on her hips. 'It *has* been moved. You can see that clear as anything.'

I forced myself to glance at the bed. 'It looks the same to me,' I said.

Violet's shoulders tensed, but she said nothing more. She got into bed with *Peter Pan and Wendy* and turned over so she was facing away. I longed to ease the tension between us. I wanted to say something kind but I didn't know what.

I was about to switch off my night light when we heard a light rapping at the door. Violet turned back to me and we looked at each other. The door opened and Emmeline stepped in holding a candle. In her pale dress, her thick hair around her shoulders, the candle illuminating her face, she looked like a spectre in a Victorian ghost story.

We stared at her.

'I came to say goodnight,' said Emmeline frankly.

Even in the dim light I could see Violet's features soften.

'Goodnight,' I said, because Violet hadn't spoken and was only staring at her sister.

Emmeline cleared her throat. 'How about we go out tomorrow morning, Piff? All of us. We could play Elvore in the woods?'

I bit my lip, surprised.

Violet nodded, her brow furrowed. 'Really, Emmi?'

'Of course.'

'And dress up?' she asked in a small, hopeful voice. 'Like we used to?'

'If you like,' said Emmeline. There was a pause. 'Well, goodnight then.'

'Goodnight,' echoed Violet.

Lying in the dark, I let out a deep breath. Emmeline was being kind to Violet, keeping her on side. She had it all under control. Emmeline knew best.

Chapter Sixteen

AFTER BREAKFAST, VIOLET BOUNDED UPSTAIRS and began to dress in her outdoor clothes. She seemed in a better mood than she had been the last few days. 'Well, where *is* she?' she said.

'Who?'

She gave me an impatient look. 'Emmeline, of course. Laura too. We should go and find them.'

I followed Violet up the staircase to the third floor. Outside Emmeline's bedroom door, she knocked loudly.

'Yes?' came an irritated voice from within.

Emmeline was sitting at her desk, pen in hand, scribbling away in one of her notebooks. The gas fire was on. A pot of coffee sat on the desk.

'Are you ready?' Violet asked.

'Ready for what?'

Violet frowned. 'To play Elvore, of course.'

'What?'

They stared at each other as I shifted my feet on Emmeline's tasselled rug.

'You said we could go out to the woods this morning. To play Elvore.'

Emmeline stared at Violet. 'I'm sorry, when was this?'

'Last night when you came to our room.' Violet shot me a baffled look then returned her gaze to her sister. 'You promised.'

Emmeline raised her eyebrows. 'I can assure you, I promised no such thing. I've told you before, we both have: Laura and I are really too old for such childish games now. Besides, it's completely inappropriate, what with the funeral tomorrow.' She shook her head. 'Anyway, as you can see, I'm busy.' She turned back to her desk.

Violet blinked rapidly. 'But you came to our room. Last night . . .' Her voice quivered.

'Violet, I really don't have time for this. Run along now, would you.'

Violet turned to me. 'Gillian was there. Gillian heard.' She looked back to Emmeline. 'You *promised*.'

I winced at the sound of my name but tried to keep my face as neutral as possible.

Emmeline gave me a quick glance then went back to her work. Somehow, I understood what was required of me.

'I don't remember,' I said uneasily.

Violet stared at me, open-mouthed. 'What? Come on, Gilly. You were there. Last night, just before we went to sleep. Emmi came in and said we'd all go out and play Elvore today.'

I avoided looking at Violet. 'I'm afraid I don't remember Emmeline asking us anything last night. Perhaps I was asleep?'

I could see Emmeline give me a tiny but very definite nod.

'You weren't *asleep*,' hissed Violet.

'Gillian wasn't asleep because I never came into your room, and I certainly never mentioned Elvore. Now please, I've got to get on.'

Violet stormed out of Emmeline's room and I reluctantly trailed after her along the dim landing.

I had been expecting a violent outburst, accusations of lies, but when Violet got back to our room, she sat on her bed and burst into tears.

I stood there, not knowing what to do as she sobbed into her pillow, her shoulders heaving. If I comforted her now, would it be an admission that I'd lied? I moved awkwardly towards her and she lifted her head.

'Tell me, Gilly. *Really*. Did Emmeline come into our room last night?'

I felt awful, my skin prickling, an ache in the back of my throat.

'No,' I said. 'No, she didn't.'

Violet gave me a long, hard look then turned away. She stared out of the window.

'You do have very vivid dreams,' I said. 'Perhaps you dreamed it?'

She said nothing.

I tugged at the collar of my blouse. 'We can still go outside?'

There was a pause and I wondered if she'd even heard me. She was still staring fixedly out of the window and across the park, and I felt she had gone somewhere else in her head. 'I don't think I want to,' she said, finally. 'I think I'll stay here. I'm not feeling particularly well.' She turned briefly towards me, her eyes misted. 'You can go now,' she added vaguely, as if she were speaking to one of the maids.

I did as she said, leaving her alone in our room, closing the door behind me. I stood on the cold landing wondering what had just happened.

The house felt oppressive. Despite everything, I longed to go down to the cottage. The smell of wood, the warmth from the stove, the steady scrape of Frank's knife as he worked at his table. I was sure it would calm me, that there I would be able to breathe a little easier. But how could I visit Frank? After what we had done? After we'd said we had seen him walking towards the woods with his gun. I was sure he knew what had happened that day in the woods. I had as good as told him. And he'd seen us. Why hadn't he said anything? Why hadn't the telephone call, the knock at the door, arrived?

I took the front stairs down to the entrance hall, moving as quietly as I could, my hand on the smooth wood of the bannister, my footsteps soft and light on the carpet. I was heading for the boot room.

A voice behind me. 'Ah, Gillian. Going out, are you?'

Lady Claybourne. I stopped and turned.

'And where is Violet?'

'Violet isn't feeling well,' I said. My voice sounded squeaky in the vast hallway.

Lady Claybourne frowned. 'Whatever is the matter with her *now*, Gillian?'

'I don't really know,' I said, lowering my gaze. 'She was crying. She got herself in rather a state. She said she wanted to be alone.'

Lady Claybourne pinched her lips. 'First last night. Those odd accusations about stolen books and moved furniture. Now this. *Crying.*' She spoke the word with distaste. 'I am sorry, Gillian. It's terribly impolite of Violet to leave you to fend for yourself when you are her guest.'

I murmured that it was fine, pulling at the sleeve of my cardigan.

'I think I had better call Dr Roach,' Lady Claybourne said. 'Perhaps he can take a look at her.'

*   *   *

It rained in the night and was still raining on the morning of Robin's funeral. The snow was finally melting. I could hear the sound of gushing water in the drains, the rain lashing against the window. The landscape was exposed now, beaten and raw looking. The park was sodden under a limp grey sky.

Evidently, the dining room roof leaked in wet weather. Several pots and pans and a tin bucket had been placed at intervals around the room. The Claybournes ate their breakfast, ignoring the constant dripping, splashing, and the puddles that were beginning to gather on the parquet. Higgins came in to serve the coffee wearing his black tailcoat and his wellingtons.

'I do wish he wouldn't make a point about things,' said Lady Claybourne, once he'd gone.

After breakfast, we gathered in the hallway by the open doors waiting for Violet, and for Jennings to bring the Bentley around to the front of the house. Lord and Lady Claybourne had already left in the Daimler. Higgins was driving them to the church.

Emmeline and Laura were barely speaking after an earlier argument. Laura had said she couldn't face the funeral and was planning on telling her mother she was ill. Emmeline had testily replied that Laura had better pull herself together and get dressed *right this minute*. Was she stupid? How would it look if she wasn't there?

We were all dressed in suitable, muted shades. Even Emmeline who I only had ever seen in pale colours wore a black dress.

Laura was in charcoal tweeds. They both had little black hats with veils perched on their heads. I was in my travelling clothes and my school beret.

Laura clutched hold of the bannister and moaned. 'I really do feel dreadful, Emmi. I don't think I can do it.'

It was true, Laura didn't look at all well. She was pale and jittery, her eyes unfocused.

Emmeline turned to look at her. 'For goodness' sake, Lolly, what did you drink last night?'

'Hardly anything. Really, Emmi. Just a little wine with dinner.'

Emmeline studied her sister carefully. 'You've taken something else then.'

'Nothing much,' Laura mumbled.

'You've raided Mother's medicine cabinet. I can see it in your eyes, Lolly.'

'I had to take *something*,' Laura wailed. 'How else I am supposed to get through this beastly day? Knowing all the time that we—'

'What did you take?' asked Emmeline sharply.

'Oh, I don't know.' Laura rubbed her forehead. 'Those little pink pills of Mummy's. You know, the slimming ones Dr Roach gives her. They're awfully good at perking one up.'

'Those are amphetamines,' said Emmeline, glaring at her sister. 'You shouldn't take them unless you know how they work.'

'*You* take them.'

'That's different,' she snapped. 'How many did you take?'

'Oh, I don't know. Three, maybe?'

Emmeline stared at Laura. 'For God's sake,' she muttered.

There was a noise behind us and we turned to find Violet standing on the stairs. A flash of panic crossed Emmeline's

232

face. I could tell she was wondering how long Violet had been there. What was it, Laura had said? *Knowing all the time that we . . .*

Laura swallowed. 'There you are, Piff.'

'I don't know how you can all do it,' said Violet, her voice cold. 'I really don't.'

Before Emmeline could answer, the door swung open and Jennings was there with a huge black umbrella, the Bentley parked outside.

'I'll drive,' Emmeline said to Jennings when we were by the car.

'I can take you if you want, miss,' Jennings replied.

'No, that's fine.'

Jennings shrugged, put his hands in his pockets, and began to walk back to the stables as the rain lashed down around him.

Laura sat up front next to Emmeline. I was in the back with Violet. The car smelled of old cigarette smoke and Laura's perfume. The rain beat down on the roof.

'I had a terrible dream last night,' said Violet quietly. 'I was in a room with green walls and I was mopping the floor. I was in my nightgown and my feet were cold but I kept on mopping. I knew the people outside the door were going to do something terrible to me and I thought that if I mopped the floor well enough they might do it to someone else.'

'We all have bad dreams,' said Emmeline stiffly. 'It's our minds needing to process our experiences and emotions, that's all. You should read Freud.'

'Mine aren't like that,' said Violet quietly. 'Mine are always about what's *going* to happen.' Her fingers were twitching and I knew she was trying to do her rituals. I'd noticed, the last few days, that they had been getting worse. I felt awful and wanted, more than anything, to be able to help her or at least comfort her. I knew she was feeling anxious and alienated and that I was partly to blame. It was terrible to see her in such a state and to do nothing. I imagined the voice in her head telling her all she was doing wrong and longed to silence that voice for good. It was impossible now, of course. There was a distance between us.

Laura was checking her watch. 'We'll be late. The hearse will be there before us.'

'No, it won't,' said Emmeline, putting her foot down purposefully, her black driving gloves firmly on the wheel.

We sped down the long driveway, splashing through puddles. As Emmeline swung out of the gates and along the road, Laura bowed her head as if she was going to be sick. I stared numbly out of the window.

Laura was reaching for her lighter and the smell of her expensive Turkish cigarettes filled the car. She took quick, tiny puffs, then stubbed the cigarette out, only half smoked, in the silver ashtray fixed to the dashboard.

We arrived at the churchyard and Emmeline parked the car at the side of the road next to the Daimler, pulling up the handbrake sharply.

We got out, holding onto our hats in the strong wind, Emmeline's dress whipping around her calves. We waited, huddled in the church doorway, with the servants who were wearing their Sunday bests. Mrs Frith had on a grey hat shaped like a mushroom. We all watched as the long, black, motorised hearse pulled up in front of the church.

Laura really did look as if she might be sick. Her face had taken on a yellowish tone.

I glanced at Mary, who was staring numbly at the hearse, and I felt a sharp ache in my chest. I could see the small coffin through the glass windows. The awful tragedy of it struck me as if for the first time and I felt as though I'd been punched in the stomach. *Oh, poor Robin. Poor, poor Robin.*

Higgins, along with several men from the village who I assumed had known Robin's father, acted as pallbearers, each taking one end of the coffin and carrying it into the church.

We joined Lord and Lady Claybourne at the door and made our way in. Violet was running her hand along the pews, making sure she touched each one as we passed, whilst whispering to herself. Lady Claybourne reached out and grabbed her arm. 'Violet, that's enough,' she hissed.

Violet yelped and struggled to get her arm free, but Lady Claybourne still had hold of her. She frogmarched Violet up to the gallery and into the family pew. I followed with Emmeline and Laura, and we took a seat behind a sniffing Violet and a stiff-backed Lord and Lady Claybourne.

Below us, a few villagers shuffled in. Wet umbrellas leaked onto the cold stone floor.

The coffin now stood alone, humble and bare, on a wooden trestle by the altar. I felt this was probably the only time in his short existence Robin had ever been the centre of attention.

Mary stood in the front pew, holding her hands neatly in front of her. I stared at her rounded shoulders, the frumpy cut of her dark dress, the thick, damp plait that fell down her back. A lump rose in my throat and I fought it down.

Laura's hand was shaking as she fumbled with her hymn book. She looked at me, her eyes wide and panicky. 'I can't *do it*, Gilly,' she whispered.

I placed my hand on her arm to steady her. 'It will all be over soon,' I said. My voice didn't sound convincing. Laura nodded but her whole body was trembling and I was sure someone would notice. I glanced at Emmeline but she was staring straight ahead, watching the vicar who was moving towards the pulpit in his robes, wiping the top of his head with a black handkerchief. A woman somewhere was coughing, a horrible hacking sound that made me wince.

'*Robin Barrow was brought into this world by God on 3rd March 1932. He returns to God—*'

'I think I'm having a heart attack,' whispered Laura.

Her face was pale now and her breathing had become heavy and laboured. She had one hand on her chest, the other on the back of the pew in front of her.

'You're not,' said Emmeline sharply.

Laura closed her eyes and I could see her chest rising and falling with the effort of regulating her breathing.

'*May help cometh from the Lord who made heaven and earth—*'

'I have to get air.' Laura's shoulders were shaking. 'Something is happening to me. I might *die*, Emmi.'

'You shouldn't have taken the pills. That's all.' Emmeline shook her head in exasperation. 'If you'd *asked me*, I could have got you something more suitable.'

Laura was gripping her clutch bag so tightly her knuckles were white. 'I really think something awful is happening to me, Emmi.'

Lady Claybourne turned around and gave us all a stern look.

'*I am the resurrection and the life saith the Lord.*'

I took Laura's hand. 'It's all right,' I whispered, my voice barely audible. It was rotten of Emmeline to make Laura come here, I thought. But then I reminded myself that Emmeline was her sister and that she knew what was best. She was trying to protect Laura, after all.

I held Laura's hand until the vicar had finished. The organ started up and then we were rising for 'Guide Me, O Thou Great Redeemer'.

Laura clutched her hymn book tightly but didn't make an attempt to sing. Two red spots had risen on her cheeks. She stood staring straight ahead as if trying very hard to concentrate on the design of the stained-glass window, her whole body rigid. Violet, in front of us, was also quiet. Her head was moving, just a fraction, from left to right, and I knew she was doing the eye thing she had to do, another one of her strange compulsions.

I did my best to sing for the both of them, and for Robin too.

* * *

We trudged out of the church in small groups, following the coffin to its final resting place. All except Violet who had been told to sit in the Daimler. The rain had eased but everything was sodden, the gravestones wet and shiny.

'My *shoes*,' said Laura in horror as we made our way towards the grave. 'They'll be ruined.' She seemed to have made something of a recovery now we were outside. Lady Claybourne, I noticed, was also looking fearfully at the ground.

'Come on, Mother,' said Emmeline, taking Lady Claybourne's arm and guiding her across the grass. We stepped gingerly around the overgrown, moss-covered graves until we came to the newer end of the churchyard, tidier, the inscriptions on the headstones still readable.

The wind blew and the church bell clanged disjointedly. I helped Laura along; her heels were sinking into the mud.

The sight of that awful hole in the ground made me feel nauseous. Laura gripped my arm.

We stood around the small, pitiful, freshly-dug grave as the men steadily lowered the coffin.

Behind me, I could hear some of the villagers whispering.

Thank goodness for the rain. The ground was frozen solid yesterday. Poor little mite.

His mother was never married, you know.

Mary was sobbing now and Mrs Frith, dabbing at her own eyes, had her arm firmly around her. I noticed Emmeline turn her head slightly, a flutter of disgust crossing her face. Just like her mother, she hated any show of emotion.

I turned away too, unable to look at Mary, then pulled my coat more tightly around me. The vicar's robes billowed. Lady Claybourne held grimly onto her hat.

When it was all finally done, the Lord's Prayer recited, the first handfuls of earth thrown over the coffin, we made our way gratefully back to the cars. Lord and Lady Claybourne were walking ahead of us. Lord Claybourne, slightly stooped, appeared to me to have aged significantly in the short time I had been at Thornleigh. Lady Claybourne, I knew, would now disappear for the rest of the day to have one of her lie-downs. Tomorrow, it would be as if the funeral had never happened. She would no doubt expect the house to be running as normal.

Chapter Seventeen

A T THORNLEIGH, FOR THE FIRST time in my life, I had become a light sleeper. I tossed and turned, my mind racing. Robin was buried and it was all over, but it didn't feel that way. My skin crawled and I was sick and hot. It was awful, awful. But surely it had to be this way. Telling someone now would be pointless – how could it possibly change anything?

I could hear something. Music. At first I thought of Emmeline and Laura playing records on the gramophone in the tower bedroom, but the tower bedroom was far above us. It was unlikely I was hearing music all the way from there. No, the sound was coming from below.

The music was so faint, I thought at first perhaps I had imagined it. Could it be Emmeline playing the piano in the lounge hall? Why would she be playing the piano in the middle of the night?

I fumbled for the torch on the bedside table, flicked the switch, but kept the beam face down on the bed. I didn't want to wake Violet.

Closing the bedroom door softly behind me, wearing a jumper over my pyjamas and my house slippers, I crept along the corridor then down the stairs to the first-floor landing. The floorboards creaked beneath my feet and I tried to tread lightly.

A pale shaft of light was coming from underneath the door of the billiard room. Although it was being played at a low volume, I could hear the music more clearly now too, something slow and jazzy, and with a slight crackle from the gramophone. I hadn't imagined it. I knew who liked jazz music, but I still wondered if perhaps it was Lord Claybourne sitting up with a cigar and a whisky, lulling himself to sleep after such an awful day. I hesitated outside the door, then slowly turned the handle.

The heavy red curtains had been drawn. The billiard table stood in the middle of the room on a burgundy and gold rug. There was a wooden cabinet for the balls and a forest of tall cues in a stand by two leather armchairs. A stuffed eagle surveyed the room from the mantelpiece, but otherwise the room appeared to be empty.

I went over and turned the gramophone off, carefully lifting the needle. A half-drunk bottle of brandy and various other liquors sat on a mirrored tray table, next to an empty glass and a full ashtray. The room smelled sweet and musty, of stale cigarettes, liquor and ancient cigar smoke.

At the sound of a low moan, I jumped and turned quickly around.

'Who's there?'

No one answered but the noise came again. I looked down and saw a pair of feet clad in Japanese slippers poking out from under the billiard table. Kneeling down, I found her.

'Laura, what are you *doing*?'

She was curled up on the rug, her hands tucked under her face in prayer position, like it was the most natural place in the world to sleep. I noticed she was still wearing the beaded peach-coloured evening dress she'd changed into for dinner. Her hair was dishevelled and the makeup around her eyes had smudged.

At the sound of my voice, she opened her eyes.

'Gilly,' she murmured, her voice thick. She tried to sit up, banging her head on the table. 'Ouch.' She rubbed at her crown. 'That *really* hurt.'

'I'm sorry.'

Laura looked steadily at me, trying to focus. 'I thought you were an angel,' she said, giving me a watery smile.

I held out my hand and she took it, crawling out clumsily, her long string of pearls dragging along the floor, her dress getting caught around her knees. We sat on the rug. She rubbed at her head again.

'What are you doing here?' I asked. 'It's very late.'

'Oh, *I* don't know,' she huffed. 'We were in the tower bedroom. Emmi was being boring as usual. I had a drink and a little dance and then I felt very glum. I came here in search of liquor and then, at some point, I think I decided it might be best if I slept here.'

Her words were slightly slurred and her breath smelled of alcohol. She looked at me and giggled, but then, without warning, she let out a terrible wail.

'I killed him, Gilly. *I killed him.*'

Alarmed, I reached out and touched her hand. 'Shhh.' I floundered, not knowing what to say.

'It was *me*,' she cried. 'He's dead because of *me*.' She leaned forward and began to sob onto my shoulder.

'Laura.' I tried to gently remove her. 'It was an accident. It's all over now.'

She pulled back. 'An accident,' she whispered to herself.

'A terrible accident,' I said. 'It was no one's fault.'

'But Violet knows. *She knows.* She's going to tell someone, I just *know* she is. I know Piff better than anyone. She can't cope with it. She'll either tell Daddy, or the police, or she'll confront Emmeline ...'

I hesitated. 'Emmeline will know what to do. She won't let anything bad happen to you.'

Laura shook her head. 'Gilly, you don't understand. How could you? Emmeline only wants to protect herself. Her perfect little future with Cadwallander and all his money. She doesn't care about *us*.' She made a wild dismissive gesture with her hand then tried to stand. I caught her arm and helped her to her feet. 'It's all gone wrong,' she said quietly. 'It's all gone terribly wrong.'

'Shh. Let's go to bed,' I said. I imagined creeping upstairs, entering the bedroom to find Violet awake and waiting for me. Perhaps, I thought, if she *was* awake, I would tell her everything. I thought of the relief I would feel, how much calmer Violet would be once she knew the truth and that nothing was being kept from her. I could hear her insisting it should all be out in the open, that Mary, at least, deserved to know what had really happened to her son. I thought of Laura and Emmeline and how I would have betrayed them after all I had promised.

'I don't want to go to bed,' said Laura swaying a little. Her face brightened. 'Let's have a drink.'

'I don't think so,' I said uncertainly. 'I think it would be best if we went to bed. It's very late.'

Laura made a scoffing sound, then poured us both a brandy.

I took mine with a sigh, but after the first sour sip, the drink began to make my head feel wonderfully fuzzy. The horrors of the day blurred, softened, and no longer seemed quite real.

We sat on the rug, the bottle between us, Laura leaning against the leg of the billiard table.

'I'm so glad you're here, Gilly,' she said, reaching out and patting my hand.

'So am I,' I said. Was that true? I no longer knew. I took another large gulp.

Laura leaned forward and topped up our glasses. 'Cheers,' she said. 'To us.'

'To us,' I echoed and took another sip of the brandy.

Laura clambered to her feet and put the needle down on the gramophone. The music started again and she began to skip, hop and twirl. She held out her hand to me. I took it and found myself upright. The room spun.

'I knew we would be sisters,' said Laura. 'We like all the same things. Or cousins, at least,' she said. 'Cousin Gilly.' She giggled loudly.

I smiled, my chest loosening.

'Doesn't it feel good to dance, Gilly? That's all we've got to do, you know. Dance, dance, dance.'

We danced around the billiard table, spinning and twirling to Laura's American jazz, voices that sounded like cigarettes and whisky and other people in other lives, a whole ocean away, forgetting their problems, just as we were.

A flash of blue dress. Laura's flushed cheeks. Her glimmering pearls. The eagle's beady, watchful eye. We danced and danced and nothing mattered but the colours in the room and the emptiness in our heads.

Maybe it really was all over. I had proved my loyalty, gained Emmeline and Laura's trust. I was a part of the family now, bound forever to the sisters by the secret we shared.

I was cousin Gilly.

I was somebody.

*   *   *

The following day, I felt dreadful. I tried to hide it, but Violet wasn't fooled.

'I know you went somewhere last night,' she said as we were getting ready for breakfast. 'I woke and you weren't in your bed. And you look terrible today. You were with my sisters, weren't you?'

My head was pounding. The last thing I needed was Violet's inquisitions. I ignored her, running the brush through my hair.

'It's rude, Gilly, that's what it is. *I'm* your friend. *I* brought you here. All you've done since ... since *that* day, when you all went off to the woods ... is ignore me and not tell me a single thing.'

'I was here asleep last night. We were both tired, weren't we?'

Violet bit her lip. 'I saw your bed. It was empty.'

'I might have got up to use the bathroom.'

'It's wrong,' said Violet, turning away from me. 'How you lie.'

Her words were like a stab in the chest. She was right. I hated lying to her.

'Well, I won't let it go on. People deserve to know the truth.'

I gave her a sharp look. 'What do you mean?'

'I'm sick of your lies, and my sisters'. It's time everyone knew what *really* happened to Robin.'

She held my gaze for a moment, then turned and walked out of the room.

I felt dizzy. Spots danced in front of my eyes. I took a deep, controlled breath. I could feel the hair lifting on the nape of my neck. What was Violet planning to do? Did she really know the truth? Or only think she knew?

I left the room, ascending the next flight of stairs, walking quickly along the landing, trying to keep my hands from shaking.

Emmeline was coming out of her room. I'd caught her just in time.

Her eyes met mine. 'What is it?' she asked.

'It's Violet,' I said, my voice trembling. 'She said she knows we're lying, and that people deserve to know the truth.'

Emmeline smiled calmly. 'She's testing us, that's all. We mustn't rise to it. And you don't need to worry. Laura and I have everything in hand. We're simply waiting for the right moment.'

The right moment for what? I wondered.

She rested a hand on my shoulder. 'Do you think you could do something for me, Gillian?'

'Of course.'

'I'm going to ride Sigmund after breakfast. Just around the park. He needs it as much as I do.' She checked her watch. 'I'll set off about ten. Do you think you could persuade Violet to go out with you?'

'I should think so,' I said uncertainly.

'Well, let's say at ten thirty you make sure you're down the mount, somewhere beyond the copse. I'll be there with Sigmund. Then Laura will arrive and say I've had a telephone call. I'll ask Violet to return Sigmund to the stables for me.' She paused then lowered her voice. 'After Violet's put Siggy away, I want you to go back and open the stable door. Do you think you can do that?'

'Yes, but what about Si—'

'Don't you worry about that. This is important, Gilly. We must keep Violet unsettled. We absolutely cannot have her voicing her suspicions, and if she does, well, we need to make sure she won't be believed.'

*   *   *

The rain had gone and it had turned cold again. We crunched over the damp, frosted grass. Violet had her hat pulled low over her forehead.

'Are you sure you wouldn't rather go find my sisters?' she'd asked peevishly, when I suggested we go out.

'No, of course not.' I'd stuffed my hands into my pockets then dug my nails into my wrist. But Violet had voiced what we both knew: my allegiance was to Emmeline and Laura. I felt nauseous at the thought of what I was about to do. 'I really think *we* should go out,' I said quickly. 'Just us.' I lowered my gaze unable to meet her eyes. 'You're right, you know. I've been selfish. Let's get out of the house. We can talk then.'

Violet's forehead creased. 'Fine. You know you can trust me, Gilly. I'm supposed to be your friend, remember?'

I nodded humbly.

Now, as we walked, I glanced at her. We were almost at the lake and she hadn't yet said a word. Perhaps she thought her earlier threat had been enough to remind me where my loyalties should lie. Or perhaps she was just biding her time. Her hands fluttered; she was doing her rituals. I knew she saved up her lists so she could go through them, perform her undoings, whenever she had an opportunity. I felt a flood of sympathy; it must be difficult being Violet. I knew I was not helping her and the guilt gnawed at my insides. I felt trapped, caught in a web of lies that seemed never-ending.

As we walked, Emmeline came trotting along on Sigmund. The horse was a beautiful dappled grey, almost lost against the frosted landscape, the dirty white sky, and the winter trees scratched onto the horizon. Emmeline pulled gently at the reins then waved to us. We watched her confidently dismount. I could see the horse's breath steaming at its nostrils.

'Hello, you two,' she said cheerfully. 'Isn't it beautiful? I love these bright winter mornings.'

Violet gazed across the still, smooth surface of the lake. 'I keep expecting to see Robin,' she said sadly.

For just a moment, Emmeline looked as though she'd been struck. She swallowed and I could see her tightening her grip on Sigmund's reins.

'Yes,' she said. 'It is very strange – without him about the place.'

'I keep thinking of his duck,' said Violet. 'The one he was looking after. I wonder what happened to it.'

Emmeline faltered. 'I expect it's around somewhere. The servants might know. Oh, look, there's Laura.'

Laura was rushing down the mount, waving at us. She cupped her gloved hands and called out, 'Emmi, telephone for you. It's Cadwallander. I told him to hold on.'

'Goodness,' said Emmeline. 'How nice of Hugh to call when he's away. Will you girls take Siggy back to the stable for me?'

I looked to Violet who nodded numbly.

Emmeline passed the reins to Violet, then went at a brisk pace up the mount towards the hall.

When we reached the stables, Violet undid the various buckles and straps and unbridled Sigmund. She led him in, turned him around, then bolted the stable door.

'Wait,' I said, as we were walking away, fumbling in my pocket. 'I think I must have dropped my handkerchief by the lake.'

Violet sighed impatiently. 'Well, come on then. Let's go back and look.'

'No,' I said, moving quickly away from her. 'You carry on. I won't be a minute.'

I began to run before she had a chance to follow me. When I knew I was out of sight, I turned left by the greenhouses, circling back to the stables. I unbolted the stable door as Emmeline had instructed.

'Did you find it?' Violet asked when I caught up with her again, slightly breathless.

'Oh, yes,' I said. 'It was just lying on the ground.'

*　*　*

Several hours later, I was with Violet in our room, working on the map of Elvore once again. Violet had nearly finished the castle and I was almost done with the trees. Fee Fee sat on Violet's desk, pushing his nose into her box of colouring pencils.

I wondered if our walk together had appeased Violet, at least for now. And yet her strange silence, after what she had said earlier this morning, was causing me to feel nervous. Was she going to make me ask her what she knew? Surely she was aware of my anxiety.

The door opened and Emmeline stormed in with a face like a thundercloud. 'Piff, how could you!'

Violet looked up. 'What?'

'Siggy has been loose in the park for hours. It took Jennings *forever* to get him back to the stables. It's been a complete nightmare. Siggy was right up by Top Farm. There are tools and all sorts lying around up there. He could have hurt himself. And imagine if he'd made it to the road. He might have been killed.'

Violet's eyes widened. 'What do you mean, loose? How?'

'Because of you, of course,' said Emmeline. 'You didn't secure him. You left the stable door open.'

Violet went rigid. 'No, I didn't. I bolted the stable door. I know I did.'

'Well, you can't have done. No one else has been to the stables. It must have been you.'

Violet looked to me for help.

I pretended to be bewildered by the whole situation. I shook my head. 'I don't know,' I said. 'I didn't actually see you bolt the stable door.'

Emmeline was still glaring at Violet. 'I know it must have been an accident, Piff, but really, how could you be so careless?'

Violet was red in the face. She squeezed her eyes shut. When she opened them, we were both still looking at her.

'I put the bolt across, I know I did.' Her voice was adamant.

'Well, you clearly *didn't* bolt it,' said Emmeline. 'In fact, you're often doing this, aren't you? Getting muddled. Making mistakes. Just think what could have happened to poor Siggy.'

Violet looked stricken. Emmeline's words had touched a raw nerve.

I stared down at my hands. I felt awful, thinking again of the voice in Violet's head, the voice that told her she wasn't good enough, that she was always making mistakes, that she needed to undo all the bad things she had done.

'I'm sorry, Emmi,' Violet whispered.

Chapter Eighteen

W E WERE IN THE LIBRARY after dinner, Emmeline pacing up and down in front of the fire. Laura sitting on the Chesterfield squeezing a rubber ball attached to a scent bottle.

'Her rituals are getting worse,' I said.

'She could snap at any moment,' said Laura nervously.

Emmeline looked over at her sister. 'Will you stop squeezing that thing, Lolly? You're making the whole room smell of Shalimar. I can hardly breathe.'

'What are you all taking about?'

Violet stood in the library doorway.

'Why, Piff,' said Emmeline calmly. 'There you are. We were wondering where you'd got to.'

'I know you were talking about me,' said Violet, her gaze darting nervously around the room.

'Of course we weren't, darling,' said Laura quickly. 'You must stop being so paranoid about things.'

Violet swallowed. 'I'm not being paranoid. I know what you all did. And now I've got proof.'

'What are you talking about?' snapped Emmeline.

Violet dug into the pocket of her cardigan and produced a tiny toy soldier. I knew what it was at once: the Major General. I saw Robin on the snow. The Major General next to him. Emmeline picking up the toy. Putting it in her pocket.

'I found it in your room,' Violet told Emmeline.

Emmeline's eyes narrowed. She rested her cigarette in the cut-glass ashtray on the mantelpiece. 'And what, *exactly*, were you doing in my room, sneaking about, going through my things without permission?'

'But this isn't yours though, is it?' said Violet. 'It belonged to Robin. He never went anywhere without the Major General. It means you must have been with him when—'

'Violet, that's enough,' said Emmeline.

I looked over at Laura. She had gone pale.

Violet took a few challenging steps towards Emmeline, her shoulders squared, still clutching the toy. 'I know why you're all in here whispering. I know what you did.' Her lip trembled. 'I don't know why you don't just tell me. I've told you: *I know.*'

'Know what?' said Emmeline.

I held my breath.

'I know one of you shot Robin,' Violet said to Emmeline, who was turned to the fire. 'One of you killed him. I know you lied to the police. I even covered for you. But I'm not going to lie any more. I'm going to tell Daddy and the police everything I know. They'll want to talk to you, and then you'll have to tell them the truth. Robin deserves it.'

No one spoke. I could hear the fire crackling, the clock ticking. The smoke from Emmeline's cigarette spiralled upwards to nothing. Lord Claybourne's father in his gloomy

Victorian attire looked down on us from his portrait above the mantelpiece.

Emmeline exhaled deeply then turned to Violet, her features calm and composed. She gave Violet a pitying look. 'Oh, Piff. You still don't remember, do you? The real truth is it's *us* who have been covering for *you.*'

Violet blinked, then knitted her eyebrows together. 'What are you *talking* about?'

Emmeline smiled sympathetically. 'Gosh, you really have got yourself into a muddle, haven't you? I thought as much,' she added sagely.

Violet opened her mouth then closed it again. I had no idea what was going on, but when I looked to Laura she was nodding, giving Violet that same, awful, sympathetic look.

'You've been in shock,' Emmeline said. 'It's no surprise really, is it? After what happened. You begged me to let you have a go with the gun. Of course we all knew it was an accident but still, it's upset you terribly.'

The colour drained from Violet's face. 'What?'

'You haven't been yourself since,' interjected Laura weakly. 'Surely you can see that?'

'You must have thought he was a deer or something,' said Emmeline. 'You weren't wearing your glasses. And I *told you* you weren't ready to handle a shotgun.'

I felt a horrible clenching in my stomach.

Violet stared at us.

'We had to protect you,' Emmeline continued. 'Oh, I know you're far too young to go to prison,' she said quickly. 'But you'd be sent to one of those horrendous schools. You know, for wayward children. It would be awful, far worse than Heathcomb.

This school, well, you hear about the things that go on in these kinds of places, don't you? And of course the other girls wouldn't be from the same background as you. They'd despise you. In fact, I'd be quite worried for your safety.'

Violet was still staring at Emmeline. She opened her mouth. 'I ... You ... Y-you're lying.'

'I'm afraid it's really quite common,' Emmeline said, reaching for the Freud volume she'd left face down over the sofa arm. 'It's our minds, our *subconscious*, trying to protect us. We repress those memories that are just too horrific for us to recall. A sort of blanking out. I've been reading about it for some time now – it happened to Anna O – and of course as soon as I saw the way you were behaving, how you seemed to have absolutely no know-ledge at all of what you'd done, I knew that's what had happened to you. You'd blanked it out. It was lucky, really, that I realised. I was able to think quickly and cover for you. But unfortunately repressed memories can cause all sorts of problems. It's why you've been feeling so unwell, so confused.'

Violet looked from Emmeline to Laura, and then at me. I couldn't meet her eye.

'You're lying,' she whispered. 'I didn't go out to the woods that day. I wasn't even there.' She turned to me. 'Tell them, Gilly.'

I bit my lip. My stomach was in pieces and I felt as sick as Violet looked. But if I went against the sisters now I'd be throwing their friendship away. I could be responsible for the breaking off of Emmeline's engagement, perhaps even for sending Laura to prison. I knew it was too late, now, to turn back. I had to agree with them, stand by them. 'I'm afraid it's true,' I said quietly.

Violet stared at me in disbelief.

'You really don't remember any of it at all, do you?' asked Emmeline, her voice soft. 'Poor Piff. You were in such a state. Don't you remember how the shot knocked you to the ground? How you dropped the gun? At first we were all far more concerned about you – you'd fallen over in the brambles, you see, but then we went to look to see if you'd got anything ...'

'You left him there,' whispered Violet.

'*We* left him there,' Emmeline corrected her. 'We had to think quickly. We had to protect you.' She shook her head. 'You were numb with shock. We had to carry you back to the house. Don't you remember that?'

Violet was blinking rapidly. 'That was another time,' she said. 'That was when I hurt my ankle in the woods. I got it caught in a trap. You and Gilly helped me back to the house.'

Emmeline shook her head again. 'You're confusing the two events. I wasn't there that day. Just like I wasn't in your room last night.' She turned to me. 'Tell her, Gillian.'

All three of them were looking at me. I struggled to form my words. 'Emmeline wasn't there that day. It was just us. I helped you back to the house.'

Emmeline nodded sadly. 'You've been getting *very* confused recently, haven't you? Misplacing things, imagining scenarios that never even happened. And then today, with Siggy ... We didn't want to tell you ... But I'm afraid you killed Robin.'

'You're lying,' Violet whispered, her voice hoarse.

I was hot and dizzy. It all made finally sense. Those horrible things we'd said and done to Violet since the accident. I thought of Emmeline's words: *We must keep Violet unsettled.*

255

We absolutely cannot have her voicing her suspicions. We need to make sure she won't be believed.

Emmeline touched Violet lightly on the arm and Violet flinched. 'I really am sorry, Piff. It's a terrible thing for you to have to come to terms with, I know. I thought perhaps it was for the best, that you'd managed to blank it out. We would never have even told you if you hadn't pushed and pushed, and begun making accusations about the rest of us. Because, of course, given that it was you who fired the gun, *that* just isn't fair.'

I snuck a glance at Laura. She was sitting, perfectly poised on the Chesterfield, her hands neatly placed in her lap. She caught my eye then looked away.

Violet's face had gone pink. 'That's not how it was,' she said. 'It *can't* be. I was here, in the house, working on the map of Elvore. I heard a gunshot.'

'I'm afraid not,' said Emmeline. 'That must have been another time. Really, it's quite common. You suffered a trauma and now your mind is playing tricks on you.'

Violet took a step back.

'We were all there,' said Laura quietly. 'We would hardly have left you behind, would we? You walked ahead of us with the gun. You were so pleased to be having a go with it.'

Emmeline reached for her cigarette then sat down next to Laura, facing Violet. 'You were overexcited, of course. I partly blame myself. I should never have let you have the gun.'

Violet had made fists with her hands. 'It's not true,' she whispered.

Emmeline stood again. Taking the fire poker, she casually nudged a log into the middle of the flames. 'And when we got back to the house, you went straight upstairs to your room. It was clear to me you were completely unable to process what had happened. We didn't know, then, quite how bad it would be for you, that you would repress the entire memory of the event, but we made the decision not to say anything to you about what had happened. We couldn't put you through it,' she said kindly. 'That's why I took Robin's soldier. We had to hide it from you.' She threw the end of her cigarette into the fire.

'We knew it would taint your whole future,' said Laura, her voice faltering slightly.

'We needed to protect you,' said Emmeline. 'We would never have told you what really happened if we hadn't been so concerned you were going to say something silly to Father or the police, something that could put us *all* in jeopardy. But you most of all.'

Violet was staring fixedly at a point on the library shelves behind the sofa, her fists still tightly clenched, her shoulders rigid. Suddenly she leaped up, emitting a horrible growl. She grabbed the fire poker from the stand where Emmeline had just replaced it and rushed towards Emmeline. A flash of terror crossed Emmeline's face as the curved tip of the hot poker came dangerously close to her left cheek. She caught Violet's arm.

'I hate you!' Violet screamed, struggling with Emmeline. 'You're liars. I hate you. I hate all of you!'

Violet's knees buckled. She crumpled, sobbing into Emmeline's chest. Laura was taking the hot poker from Violet who hardly seemed to notice as it was prised from her hand. Emmeline steadied herself. She put a tentative arm around Violet's shoulder and patted it awkwardly.

I stood there, my heart pounding, watching Violet cry in her sister's arms. The fear on Emmeline's face was gone and she was now soothing Violet, comforting her, murmuring something into her ear.

Violet lifted her head. Her face was puffy and streaked with tears. 'Is this real?' she asked. 'Is any of it real?'

Chapter Nineteen

THE CATERERS HAD ARRIVED FOR the ball. Boxes of wine and great platters of food were being unloaded from a van. 'No, take that *around the back*,' I could hear Mrs Frith saying. Ethel and Mary were decorating the lounge hall. Up on ladders, they were hanging flower garlands and dusting the chandeliers. It was the first time I had seen Mary at work since Robin's death. We weren't to speak of Robin, Lady Claybourne had instructed us. We weren't to give Mary sympathetic looks or treat her any differently than we had before. She needed to get back to work, to be doing something to occupy her mind.

Men in white gloves were creating a champagne fountain in the lounge hall, carefully arranging a large number of glasses on a table in the middle of the room. The band was setting up in the gallery above the hall, tuning instruments, putting up music stands.

As I surveyed the busy scene, I felt light-headed. The figures dusting and rearranging the furniture, the vases of flowers and dyed pampas grass, the dust motes floating in a shaft of weak winter sunlight, all felt as distant and as unreal as a dream.

Violet hadn't come out of her room all day. She'd missed all her meals.

I'd left her alone all morning, telling myself it was for the best, but I couldn't stop thinking of what we had told her and how it appeared to have broken her. I'd felt, these last few days, that she'd been getting smaller and smaller, like a set of Russian dolls I'd once played with. I'd never seen her so lifeless, so diminished. It wasn't right of us to leave her up there under her bedclothes, murmuring to herself. I had no idea what I was going to say, but I knew I couldn't put it off any longer: I had to go to her.

Upstairs, I found the door to our bedroom opening. Lady Claybourne stepped onto the landing, followed by a tall man with a thick reddish beard peppered with white. He was carrying a Gladstone bag and holding his hat. The doctor, I presumed. Although a different one to the man who had come when Violet caught her ankle in the trap. Panicking, I opened the door to the linen cupboard, slipped inside, then quickly pulled the door shut behind me. I blinked, adjusting my eyes to the darkness. I could see shelves of linen and towels. There was an old woody smell along with a hint of dried lilac and camphor. I wrinkled my nose.

'I'm afraid we do need to keep an eye on her,' I heard the doctor say.

'But what can be *done*, Dr Roach?' asked Lady Claybourne, her voice low and urgent.

I pinched my nose fearing I might sneeze. What on earth would I say if they found me in here?

'She needs to rest,' Dr Roach said. 'I am sorry to say her symptoms aren't all that uncommon in girls of her age:

emotional outbursts, listlessness, these delusions you say she's had. Unfortunately, girls prone to this sort of thing are typically overly imaginative, sensitive, and passionate.'

My eyes began to water as I struggled hard to stifle my impending sneeze.

'Yes, that's Violet,' said Lady Claybourne. 'And she *fidgets* dreadfully.'

'She's a bold rider, I presume?' asked the doctor.

'What? Oh no,' said Lady Claybourne. 'Violet never did well on horseback.'

'Still,' said Dr Roach.

I felt my urge to sneeze subside and breathed a grateful sigh of relief.

'It's just such an important time for the others,' said Lady Claybourne.

There was a pause and I pressed my ear against the door.

'I assume you'll be at the ball tonight, Doctor?' Lady Claybourne asked.

'Yes, of course.'

'I had hoped school would help, that it would smooth away any ... rough edges,' Lady Claybourne went on wearily. 'But she seems worse than ever.'

'It's been a difficult time for you,' said the doctor. 'To have such a tragedy here, at Thornleigh ...'

'And now *this*,' said Lady Claybourne. 'I really can't have Violet creating difficulties for Emmeline and Laura. I've their futures to think of too.'

'Of course,' Dr Roach replied smoothly. 'Some young girls struggle with adolescence but I've seen many come through it and turn out to be the most charming of young ladies.'

'Still, something will have to be done,' said Lady Claybourne firmly. 'I must speak with Emmeline.'

I waited until their footsteps had receded along the passage, before letting myself out of the linen cupboard.

Standing outside our bedroom door, I hesitated. Was it better to leave Violet alone? Perhaps she should rest. Hadn't the doctor said so? The truth was, I didn't want to confront Violet. I knew it was cowardly but I couldn't face it. I couldn't bear to see what we had done to her. Despising myself, and with a heavy heart, I turned reluctantly away from the door.

*　*　*

I left the house via the boot room and found myself stepping out into the crisp, cool air. I needed to be outside, to get away from all the activity in the house. I needed to breathe.

I strode across the muddy park, my boots squelching on the damp grass.

When I reached the edge of the woods and the lake, I stopped for a moment and stood staring into the murky depths, and at the frosted, bent reeds. A few scarlet rose hips were clinging to a branch, the only violent colour among the grey and the white. Two mallards, a male and a female, were paddling across the smooth surface of the water.

After I had circled the lake, I found that instead of walking back to the house I was heading in the direction of Frank's cottage. I wanted to at least be close to it for a moment, to see the smoke rising from the chimney and to imagine Frank, cosy inside, sitting at his table whittling away with his knife or reading one of those battered old Hardy novels. I hurried along the edge of the beech woods, feeling grateful to now be out of the view of the house. Coming close to the cottage and the open gates, I stopped, frozen. A black Wolsey with the little blue police plaque on its top was parked outside Frank's cottage.

As I watched, the cottage door opened and there was Frank, head bowed. To my horror, I saw he was handcuffed. He was being led towards the car by Detective Gamble and Constable Sparrow, one on either side of him. He wore a blank, glazed-over expression. Why wasn't he protesting? Telling them they'd got it wrong? Then just as Constable Sparrow was opening the car door, Frank looked up and saw me standing there. Our eyes met. He gave a small nod as if nothing at all was out of the ordinary. All I could do was gape wordlessly as the car's back door was slammed shut and Detective Gamble and Constable Sparrow climbed into the front of the vehicle.

I turned away before they could see me.

*　*　*

I ran back up to the house as fast as I could. I had to tell Emmeline and Laura. Emmeline would know how to make this right. There must be something we could do, something we could say. We had been mistaken. Frank had been walking *away* from the woods. He wasn't carrying a gun after all. We'd all got it wrong, there was no need to *arrest* him. It was all a big mistake. I shouldered my coat off, throwing it in the direction of the peg, kicked off my boots.

I found Emmeline in the lounge hall arranging lilies in a vase.

'I've seen Frank,' I told her, breathlessly. 'He's been arrested by Detective Gamble. I saw him get in the car.'

Emmeline selected another stem and clipped its end. 'Are you sure he was being *arrested*, Gillian? He may have only been being brought in for questioning.'

'I saw handcuffs,' I said, remembering the way Frank's shoulders had been forced forward.

'Well,' said Emmeline slowly, 'they're probably hoping they'll get a confession out of him which they won't.'

'Because he didn't do it!' I said.

Emmeline glanced up at the musicians in the gallery. 'There's no need to get worked up,' she said. 'He'll probably be home by nightfall. They don't have any evidence.'

I looked towards the windows. The winter sky was already turning pink. It seemed unlikely they would be bringing Frank home before dark. Would he have to spend a night at the police station? Would they keep him in a cell? The thought made me feel cold inside.

'And I'm sure Frank Marks can take care of himself. It's not like he hasn't seen the inside of a cell before,' Emmeline added cattily.

I pictured Frank in a small room, being questioned by the police officers. Although Constable Sparrow was too young, Detective Gamble had most likely served in the war. I couldn't imagine anyone down at the station being too friendly towards a conscientious objector. I remembered what the sisters had said: *Everyone hates him. Feelings still run deep around here.*

'Is Violet in her room?' Emmeline asked.

'She's been in there all day,' I said. 'She's refused to speak to me.'

'I expect she'll come around,' said Emmeline. 'And she'll need us when she does. But I really do think you should be

careful about associating with Violet tonight. She has a reputation for being a little odd, as we well know. The last thing
you want is for people, the *right kind* of people, to see you as
a friend of hers and dismiss you.' She smiled at me. 'I'm only
trying to look out for you, Gillian. It's time for you to shine
on your own.'

I weakly returned her smile. I felt terrible about Violet and
extremely worried about Frank. It hardly seemed like the
moment to be thinking about my social aspirations. I reminded
myself that Emmeline was being kind, trying to look out for
me, and that I should value her advice. Tonight *was* a chance,
the kind that didn't come along often, for me to meet who
Emmeline considered the 'right kind of people'. I didn't want
to let Emmeline or myself down. I couldn't afford to waste
opportunities. And yet there was a tightness in my chest when
I thought of Violet. A part of me wished I could shut myself
away from everyone, find a way to disappear.

Footsteps behind us. 'There you both are.' Lady Claybourne
was carrying a bundle of fabric. 'You should think about getting
ready, girls. Ethel is heating the curlers for Laura.'

'I'll just finish up here,' said Emmeline.

'Beautiful,' said Lady Claybourne, beaming at the lilies. 'It
will be splendid tonight, I just know it will.' She turned to me.
'Gillian, why don't we go up and see if we can rouse Violet?'

* * *

'Violet. Why are you still in bed?' Lady Claybourne said crossly.
'And why have you ignored Gillian all day? Don't pretend that
you haven't.'

Violet turned around and stared dully at us both. She looked dreadful – pale and sickly. Her hair was sticking up and her lips were dry and cracked. She was holding Fee Fee tightly on her lap, methodically stroking his ears.

Looking at Violet, I was having difficulty breathing. I didn't want to be here. I only wanted someone to do something about Frank. I couldn't understand Emmeline's lack of concern and wished I'd pushed her into taking some kind of action, rather than letting myself get distracted with her talk of Violet and the ball. How was she able to remain so focused on the ball, anyway, when Frank was with the police? How could she be so sure it would all come to nothing? I took a deep breath, trying to imagine I possessed Emmeline's calmness and certainty.

Violet stared at her mother. 'I'm not going to the ball,' she whispered.

'Oh, I think you are,' said Lady Claybourne darkly. 'Dr Roach says it's nothing but your nerves. You're to come downstairs and behave like a normal young lady for once in your life. I won't have you hiding away up here and everyone asking me where you are. I've brought you your outfit,' she said, laying the bundle of fabric in her arms on the bed. I could see now it was a dress. Layer upon layer of white and pink taffeta. The bodice a thick, silky blue. Huge, ruched, puffy sleeves.

Violet emitted a choking sound from her throat.

'Little Bo Peep,' said Lady Claybourne.

'I can't wear that,' Violet said weakly.

'Of course you will. We'll tie white ribbon around one of your father's walking canes to give you a crook.'

Violet dropped her chin to her chest as Fee Fee jumped from her lap. She stared vacantly at her hands.

'And there's a cap,' said Lady Claybourne. 'Ethel altered it for you. It ties under your chin.' She laid a frilly mob cap with a large pink ribbon on top of the dress. 'Do call for Ethel if you need any help dressing. She's fixing Laura's hair.'

After Lady Claybourne had left us to dress, there was an uncomfortable silence.

At any other time, the whole scene with the dress might have been amusing, but chancing a quick glance at Violet sitting numbly on her bed, her shoulders slumped, my insides churned. I longed for the feisty, passionate, full-of-life Violet I knew so well. I could see her, back at school, entering our dorm room, throwing her suitcase onto her bed. *If we're stuck together we may as well stick together.*

I wanted, desperately, to apologise, to tell her the truth, but of course if I did that Violet would know I had lied. That we had *all* lied. Violet needed to believe what we had told her for the good of us all.

'There's something I need to show you,' I said instead.

Violet barely looked at me as I took the folded newspaper cutting from the drawer of my night table and handed it to her. Her eyes scanned the short article.

'We kept it from you,' I said, trying to control the wavering in my voice. 'We didn't want you to come across it in the paper and realise it was something you'd done. It's funny, isn't it? How you always look to see if you've done anything bad, and now here it is, something you *did* actually do.' I took the article from her then replaced it in the drawer.

I had to turn away from Violet then. There was an ache in the back of my throat. But this was what Emmeline had meant for me to do when she handed me the article, I was sure of it.

'We had better dress,' I told her briskly, but she didn't move, just stared at the wall as if she hadn't heard me.

I had so been looking forward to wearing the dress Laura had found for me but now my chest felt heavy as I reached for it. It was a beautiful shimmering gold. Laura had told me she'd worn it for a winter ball a few years ago. *It will be perfect for Cinderella, Gilly. You simply have to wear it.*

I'd only just slipped it on when the door opened and Laura appeared wearing a red lace-fringed dress and a velvet cape. She put a large vanity case on the dressing table.

'You look beautiful,' I told her.

She did a little twirl. 'Why, thank you, Cinderella. I'm Little Red Riding Hood, of course.'

She was the most glamorous little Red Riding Hood I'd ever seen.

'I hope you don't meet the wolf tonight,' I said.

Laura laughed. Then she noticed Violet who was slowly putting on the Little Bo Peep dress. When she had managed it, she sat on the edge of the bed, staring at her twitching hands. The dress was truly hideous; layer after layer of pink and white frills, an unflattering corset across her narrow chest. Her bonnet looked ridiculous.

'Goodness,' said Laura, swallowing hard. 'Little Bo Peep, I guess.'

Violet said nothing. I exchanged a glance with Laura.

'Look, Piff,' Laura said uneasily. 'I know how awful it all is, truly I do.' She paused and I wondered, just for moment, if she was going to tell Violet everything, tell her what really happened, but then she cleared her throat. 'It's knocked us all for six. We were all terribly fond of him. But it was an accident, a fluke, one of those horrible things ...' She trailed off. 'We couldn't tell anyone it was us. I mean, *you* ...' She blushed, and bit her lip. 'We couldn't let it spoil our lives, we just *couldn't*,' she said desperately. 'And I am sorry you ... blanked it out, that we had to tell you like that. I know we can't forget what happened, but tonight is important to Mummy. We *have* to try to move on, to get back to normal.'

Violet still said nothing. Her brow was tightly creased, and I could see she was doing her rituals.

'Well,' said Laura, standing. 'I've brought my makeup.' She turned to me. 'I thought I could do yours, Gilly. What do you think? Shall I?'

'Yes, please,' I said.

'Violet?'

Violet flinched. 'I don't want makeup,' she whispered. The words seemed to have caused her a great effort. Her eyes were big and round. *There's something wrong with her*, I thought. *There's something wrong with her and it's our fault.*

'Fine. I'll just do Gillian's then.' Laura gave Violet a cross look. 'You're going to have to pull yourself together, Piff. You do know that, don't you? You're going to get over this and move on like the rest of us have had to. You've really no choice.'

*   *   *

I watched from the landing window as a steady stream of motor cars rolled up the mount, long slants of rain illumin- ated in their headlights. The slamming of car doors, the opening of umbrellas. Higgins was stationed by the front door to take the damp coats, and Mary and Ethel would no doubt be busy serving drinks on silver trays alongside the catering staff.

I remembered Boxing Day morning. How we had all watched from the tower bedroom – the activity in the park, the hunters arriving. I thought of how happy I'd been to be at Thornleigh with Violet, to be spending time with the sisters. I thought of how much had changed since then.

I could hear the band starting up. The house seemed to be finally coming alive, ablaze with colour, light and music, fizzing and humming with energy.

I caught a glimpse of my reflection in the landing mirror. I hardly recognised myself in my golden dress. Laura had created waves in my hair and my face was powdered, my eyelids shimmering, my lashes longer and thicker. I pushed my shoulders back and smiled slowly and seductively at my reflection. I could almost pass for a model in a magazine. *Every girl must get a chance to be a princess*, Laura had said that first evening at Thornleigh. And Emmeline: *Your first night in society. A big moment for you, Gillian.* Would I really have changed anything about the last two weeks if it meant I couldn't have this moment? For a split second, I couldn't be sure.

I went back into our room. 'Don't you think we should go down now?' I asked Violet. 'The guests are arriving.'

With barely a glance at me, she rose silently from the bed. Together we made our way downstairs. Violet kept her head bowed, her hands clasped tightly in front of her. I felt embarrassed to be with her. The feeling had been creeping up on me for some time. Perhaps Emmeline was right: advising me to distance myself from Violet. It just seemed so cruel, especially on top of what we had done, what we had told her. Now, I reminded myself, was not the time to think about it.

The lounge hall was beautiful. This was the sort of occasion Thornleigh had been built for. I wondered how many people, over the years, had danced in the great hall, how many romances had blossomed under the dazzling chandeliers. I could imagine the upstairs bedrooms, no longer dusty and closed up, but full of guests. The servants' quarters stuffed with chauffeurs, maids and valets. Tonight, there were traceable echoes of the past in the present. Life was slowly being breathed back into the house. Its scars less visible under the glitter and sparkle of the ball.

People were milling around in their costumes: soldiers in red, queens with rouged cheeks, tzars, painted natives, Eastern princesses, and a Viking with a shield and sword. I saw Dr Roach, although he was wearing an ordinary brown suit with a top hat and I couldn't tell what he had come as. Guests were stopping to admire our outfits. A heavily made-up woman was pawing at Violet's dress. 'Don't you look lovely, dear.' Usually this would have irritated Violet, but tonight she bore it silently without even flinching. It was as if she had gone somewhere else in her mind.

The band was playing in the gallery. Guests were gathering around the champagne fountain.

We edged our way through the crowd. I thought Violet was behind me but when I turned around she'd gone. I scanned the room but couldn't see her anywhere.

Lady Claybourne was flitting from one small party to another. She was dressed as Queen Elizabeth in a huge Tudor dress with a frilled collar and a gold crown. Her jewels sparkled under the chandelier lights. Lord Claybourne was wearing a striped football jersey and a patch over his eye.

'A pirate.'

I turned to see Laura standing next to me, holding a champagne flute, following my gaze.

'Ah,' I said.

'Not very imaginative but we mustn't expect too much from poor Daddy. I suggested we dye the jackdaw red or green to give him a parrot but Emmeline said absolutely not. She said it would be traumatic for him.'

I wasn't sure if Laura meant for Lord Claybourne or for the jackdaw.

'Can you do that?' I asked. 'Dye birds?'

'Of course,' said Laura. 'Lord Berners at Farringdon dyes his pigeons all sorts of beautiful colours. It amuses him.' Laura was still looking at her father. 'Daddy doesn't like this sort of thing much. Parties. But he bears it well. There were great parties here in the past.'

I looked around for Violet. Where had she gone?

A momentary hush fell over the guests. Emmeline had appeared at the top of the staircase to a chorus of oohs and ahhs. She wore a column of white silk and a crown made of thorns and paper snowflakes. The dress cut across her collarbone and I could see several fine white scars snaking their way along her bare shoulders. They only made her more beautiful, more unusual. Poised, radiant and resplendent, she floated down the staircase, smiling at her admirers.

'The belle of the ball,' I heard someone exclaim.

'The Snow Queen,' Laura whispered to me.

'She looks wonderful,' I said.

'Doesn't she,' replied Laura. 'Absolutely divine. Although we can't see the real splinter of ice in her heart, of course.'

I glanced at Laura to see if she was joking but she was completely straight-faced.

Lady Claybourne was beaming proudly. At Emmeline's entrance, the band switched to a different tune, the fiddler starting first, then the others joining in, the music confident, romantic, reminiscent of a previous era.

'I wish Mummy would get with the times and let them play swing or jazz,' said Laura with a sigh. 'I'm going to find Charlie, and perhaps another drink.' She glanced around the room. 'You'll be all right, won't you?'

'I'll look for Violet,' I said.

'Good idea. How was she? After I left.'

'Just the same.' I lowered my voice. 'Laura, do you think she really believes—'

'Shh,' said Laura. 'Not here, Gilly.'

I nodded, and Laura smiled. She touched my shoulder before dashing off. Charlie Chester-Barnes was with a group of his friends over by the piano. He saw me and gave a little wave. I waved back, then began to squeeze my way through clusters of people, all in their costumes and finery. I saw Mary carrying a tray of canapés and looked down, avoiding her eye, a thickness in my throat.

I wondered if perhaps Violet had gone down to the kitchen to try and find something to eat. She usually had such a good appetite and was constantly ravenous, but today she'd hardly eaten a thing.

I took the backstairs, the sound of the music fading. Bare walls. A chilly flagstone floor. A smell of old cooking. As I stood at the arched entrance to the kitchen, Mrs Frith, spatula in hand, and the caterers who were busy arranging tiny pieces of fish on a huge platter, all stopped and stared at me.

'Can I help you with anything, Miss Gillian?' asked Mrs Frith brusquely.

'Oh, no,' I said, immediately embarrassed. 'I was just looking for Violet.'

'She wouldn't be here, miss,' said Ethel quietly.

'No, of course not. I'm sorry to have troubled you.'

I left quickly, my cheeks pink.

Upstairs, back in the hall, I scanned the room again but there was still no sign of Violet.

'There you are, Gillian.'

I turned to find Emmeline behind me. She had a young man with her. The man had thin blond hair, pockmarked cheeks and a large nose. He was wearing a tunic and black boots. I guessed he'd come as a medieval knight.

'This is Gillian Larking,' Emmeline said to the young man who gave me a swift nod. 'Gillian, this is Hector Burns.'

'Oh, hello,' I said, thinking it nice of Emmeline to introduce me to the glamorous people she knew. I remembered her comment about eligible bachelors and felt my cheeks flush.

'Would you like to dance then?' the man said, leaning in close to me.

I looked around but Emmeline had gone.

'Oh,' I said, unsure. 'I suppose we could.'

He held out his hand and I followed him to a spot in the centre of the room. We began to shuffle around with the other dancers. He held me stiffly. Our knees knocked together several times. I murmured an apology but he didn't seem to hear. Then he got more enthusiastic and swung me about a bit. Finally, he drew me in. I was relieved the swinging had stopped, but now he held me too close.

We came to a natural pause and I quickly extricated myself from his arms. One of the caterers passed with a tray and Hector grabbed two glasses of champagne and handed one to me. I drank mine thirstily. It was cold and refreshing and meant I didn't have to talk with him for a moment or do any more dancing. As I gulped down the champagne, he looked at me with new interest.

'Gillian, is it?'

'Yes.'

'Cambridge?'

'Oh, no,' I said, blushing. 'I'm still at school. I'm a friend of V—' I quickly checked myself, remembering Emmeline's advice. 'A friend of the family.'

'Me too. In a way,' he said. 'Well, my parents are. Can I get you another glass?'

I shook my head, remembering how I'd felt after drinking with Laura. 'No, thank you.'

He looked disappointed. 'How about we go out for a breath of air then?'

We headed for the French doors. It was freezing outside. Hector draped his jacket over my shoulders which I thought extremely gentlemanly.

We stood shivering at the edge of the patio, looking at the thin slice of moon. I waited for Hector to produce a cigarette as I'd assumed he'd wanted to go out for a smoke.

'Let's go over here,' he said, surprising me by taking my hand and leading me across the patio.

His hand in mine was soft and limp, and oddly unpleasant. He led me around the corner, then all of a sudden I found myself forced against the wall with Hector pushing his mouth against my neck and pawing my dress. I froze. His hands seemed to be everywhere all at once and I yelped as he grabbed at my bosom. I tried to catch his arms to stop him pulling my dress any higher over my thighs. He was making strange panting noises.

'Get off!' I said, giving him a shove.

'Oh, come on,' he said, pressing me against the brickwork and pinning my arms at my sides. His breath smelled of cheese.

'Let go of me!'

'I saw you across the room—' - he was murmuring in my ear, as if I hadn't spoken '—and I thought, now *there's* a girl I'd like to have a good time with tonight.'

I stomped as hard as I could on his left foot and he yelled, letting go of me. Taking the opportunity, I broke free and ran, his jacket slipping from my shoulders and landing on the damp grass as I did so.

'Prig!' he yelled after me.

I stumbled, shaking, back into the lounge hall and found myself once again in the middle of the ball. Tears pricked the backs of my eyelids. I felt dizzy and disorientated. I had made a man shout at me. I hadn't behaved as he'd expected me to. Every bone in my body had been screaming at me to get away from him, and yet I doubted myself. Perhaps I had behaved childishly. Perhaps I wasn't as worldly as I'd liked to believe. How would Emmeline or Laura have reacted? Would they have known what to do? Would they have laughed it off? Managed to untangle themselves in a more dignified manner? Would they have been more grateful a man had wanted them?

I felt sure they would not be feeling as I did now: sick, faint, and itchy all over. The whole encounter couldn't have taken more than a few minutes, and yet I was disgusted with myself. I could still feel Hector's hands climbing my thighs, that squeeze of my breast . . . I clutched my stomach. A heaviness I couldn't shift had settled there. Neither could I shake the feeling I had been somehow contaminated.

The music played on. The dancers danced. The champagne flowed. I searched for a friendly face, something to steady myself with, but could find no one. Where *was* Violet?

Finally, I saw Emmeline over by the champagne fountain talking to one of the gentlemen who had been at the Boxing Day hunt lunch. The thought of that awful lunch caused a dropping sensation in my stomach.

Laura made her way over to me with Charlie in tow.

'Good to see you again, Gillian,' said Charlie.

I tried to smile but I was finding it hard to focus. My ears had gone funny, as if I was under water.

Laura leaned in close to me. 'Did you go out for a smoke with Hector Burns, Gilly? I thought I saw you . . . You must be careful of Hector. He's got a bit of a reputation with girls, if you know what I mean. Emmi's told me all about him.'

I tried to process what Laura was telling me. Surely Emmeline couldn't have known what Hector might try to do to me when she'd introduced us? But then there was a loud gasp from somewhere behind me. The sound of a single glass falling to the floor. Painted faces, hats, masks, all turning in the direction of the doors. Hands flying to mouths.

Violet was walking steadily into the middle of the room cradling a soft grey heap in her arms. At first I thought she had spilled something on her clothes. She was covered in it. Her hands, that awful dress. She even had a smear on her face. Then I saw what she was holding. Fee Fee, limp in her arms. The blood was everywhere, on her dress, her arms, dripping down her legs and onto the floor. In her right hand, she clutched a bloodied kitchen knife.

The entire room froze. No one moved.

'I had to,' Violet murmured. 'I had to undo it all. I had to.'

Emmeline appeared at Violet's side. 'You can't undo it,' she said quietly, carefully taking the knife from Violet's fingers.

As if finally coming to her senses, Lady Claybourne screamed. All at once the room buzzed and hummed as people rushed forward towards Violet, trying to see or trying to help. Several ladies still had their hands to their mouths or were clutching their husbands. The band had stopped playing. Violet stumbled a few paces into the champagne fountain. As I watched, the entire pyramid of glasses fell down around her.

The last I saw of Violet was Charlie wrapping his jacket over her shoulders and Emmeline, Laura, Charlie and Dr Roach ushering her out of the room. She still clung tightly onto the bloody remains of Fee Fee.

Chapter Twenty

I T WAS COMING UP TO midnight when I was summoned to the library.

Inside the lamps were on but there was no fire. The two doctors both stood as I entered. Dr Roach, of course, had been at the ball, had witnessed Violet's terrible entrance, but I didn't know this new, much younger, doctor. Why a second doctor was needed when Dr Roach was already here, I had no idea.

'Ah, Gillian,' said Dr Roach.

I slowly crossed the room. I felt overly hot.

'This is Dr Spinlow,' Dr Roach said. 'A colleague of mine. In fact he completed his training with me, didn't you, Spinlow?'

'That's right,' said the younger doctor, a little nervously.

'There are certain – situations, Gillian,' Dr Roach explained. 'When a second doctor is needed to assess a patient and give an opinion along with the first.'

I gave him a blank look. I had no idea what he was talking about. I was incredibly tired. My limbs felt shaky. I had stayed up as Emmeline had told me I might be needed. I hadn't seen Violet since she had been escorted from the ballroom. No one had told me a thing.

'Please, sit down, Gillian,' said Dr Roach.

They took an armchair each. I perched on the Chesterfield. One of the lamps was casting a shadow across the rug and I stared at it. I could feel my heart thumping.

'You're not in any trouble,' said Dr Roach, perhaps noticing my nervousness. He cleared his throat. 'I imagine that being a smart girl, Gillian, you understand Violet isn't at all well right now.'

'Lady Claybourne said that perhaps she's coming down with some—'

'What I mean, Gillian,' said Dr Roach, 'is that it appears to us that Violet is not too well *in her mind.*'

I said nothing.

Dr Spinlow spoke. 'We've heard from Lady Claybourne, and Violet's sister, Emmeline, who have both told us about Violet's recent behaviour.'

I looked up.

'But,' said Dr Roach quickly, 'we understand that *you* are a close friend of Violet's, and who better to notice any changes in her behaviour than her friend?' He gave me an encouraging smile.

A coldness ran through me.

'Do *you* believe Violet's behaviour has changed recently?' he asked.

I tried to think what Emmeline would want me to say. Should I say no, that all was fine? Or should I admit that Violet's behaviour had recently been odder than usual, that she seemed to have disappeared into herself? Wouldn't he ask me why I thought that was? I could hardly tell him it was because we'd told her she'd killed someone. Unlike the police interview, Emmeline hadn't warned or prepared me for this.

'Yes,' I said in a small voice. 'Violet hasn't been herself.' I paused. 'Although she's always been – imaginative.'

Dr Roach leaned forward a little. 'That's exactly what we'd like to talk to you about, Gillian. Violet's imagination. Unfortunately, she's made some rather wild and disturbing claims.'

My sweaty hand was tightly gripping a handful of the fabric of my dress. I could have changed after the ball but I'd felt too numb to bother. Now I felt foolish, sitting here in a skimpy, sparkling garment in front of these two very serious men. I could feel the doctors' eyes on me as I tried to regulate my breathing.

The room was very still. These men were doctors. I could trust them. This was my chance to put it all right. I should tell them, now, what happened that day in the woods, how we decided to keep it from everyone, from Violet, what we had done and said that had caused my friend to doubt her own memory. If I told them now, it would all be over. I could leave Thornleigh and never come back. But then who would I be? Plain shy Gillian from Form B. And everyone would know not only what I had done, but what Emmeline and Laura had done too.

'Violet gets confused,' I said quietly. 'She makes up stories.'

Dr Roach leaned forward. 'So it isn't unusual for Violet to fabricate events?'

I tugged at my dress then swallowed hard. 'She has this whole world, in her head. It's an imaginary world. She asks me to play it with her.' I bit my lip. 'I don't always want to,' I lied. 'It seems – childish.'

Dr Roach raised an eyebrow. 'You think yourself too old for such games?'

I nodded, straightened my back a little.

'Please, Gillian,' said Dr Roach kindly. 'Tell us more.'

I shifted on the smooth, worn leather of the Chesterfield. My left leg was trembling and I concentrated on trying to still it. I took a deep breath. 'To Violet, the games are quite real. They always have been. Of course I knew the games were all fantasy. But Violet ... She can be very convincing ...'

The two doctors exchanged a glance.

Dr Roach coughed. 'And has Violet ever said anything about voices in her head?'

I frowned. 'She always knows what's happening in Elvore. That's the name of it, her other world. She knows what's happening there because the characters tell her.'

'I see,' said Dr Roach. 'So the voices she hears are those belonging to the characters in this – imaginary world?'

I nodded. 'But then there's also the, um ...' I could feel my hands sweating.

'Go on, Gillian,' said Dr Roach.

I stared at his shiny brown shoe as they waited for me to continue.

'Well, Violet has her rituals, you see. Her undoings.'

Dr Roach gave me a steady look. 'Rituals? Undoings?'

I wanted to scrunch myself up very small on the sofa. They were both staring at me. 'That's what Violet calls them. She has to do things.'

'What sort of things?' said Dr Spinlow, leaning forward.

'Oh, well, you know ... Counting on her fingers, and touching doorknobs three times before she enters a room, going through her lists in her mind. That sort of thing.'

Dr Roach studied me for a moment. 'Has she always done these – rituals – Gillian?'

I took a deep breath. 'For as long as I've known her, yes. But I think before too. She worries she's done something bad. The rituals – they're a way of somehow undoing the bad things she's done, even though they weren't really bad ... Or else they're a way of preventing terrible things from happening.'

'And someone tells her to do these – *rituals*?' Dr Roach was saying. 'A voice in her head?'

'Yes, I think so,' I said uneasily. 'A voice in her head.'

There was a pause, and then Dr Roach said, 'Well, I think that will be all, Gillian.'

I stood awkwardly. My dress had stuck to me.

He gave me a brief nod. 'You've been most helpful.'

As I was leaving the room, I caught a glimpse of the clock on the mantelpiece. It was a minute past midnight. We had entered into the new year.

* * *

That night I slept in a strange bed in one of the guest bedrooms. Laura told me Lady Claybourne thought it best I stay in another room. I still had no idea what had happened to Violet.

In the morning, I opened the curtains to a different view of the park. I drew in a breath. There, emerging from the woods, was a stag, its head lifted, its majestic antlers on display. For just a moment, it seemed to be looking straight at me. But then it turned and slunk away into the mist.

I scrambled to get dressed and then hurried down to breakfast.

Lord and Lady Claybourne were already in the dining room with Emmeline: Lady Claybourne pushing scrambled egg crossly around on her plate, Lord Claybourne reading the paper. As usual the Claybournes were all dressed for the day, looking their normal, immaculate selves.

'Really, you'd think it would be quite simple, wouldn't you?' Lady Claybourne was saying. 'She knows I like a splash of cream and a little salt. I don't think the salt has been anywhere near these eggs, and she's certainly not used cream.'

'Send them back, dear,' said Lord Claybourne, feeling around the paper for his toast, 'if they are unsatisfactory. I am sure Mrs Frith will make them again for you.'

'Oh, no, I wouldn't want to *trouble* her,' said Lady Claybourne.

'Really, Mother, you must,' said Emmeline. 'She should know how we take our eggs by now.'

'Most likely they were made by Mary,' said Lady Claybourne. 'I've told Mrs Frith not to let that girl anywhere near breakfast, unless it's to wash the dishes. She's completely useless.'

I sat down and was pouring myself some tea.

Emmeline passed me the milk. 'Happy New Year, Gillian.'

I blinked. 'Happy New Year,' I said. I quickly scanned the faces of the Claybournes for a sign, something that might tell me what had happened to Violet. I found nothing.

Lady Claybourne gave me a tense smile. 'Sleep well?'

I said, uncomfortably, that I had.

Laura slunk in wearing her fur coat and looking green about the gills.

'I wish you wouldn't wear that at breakfast,' said Lady Claybourne.

'Well, I wouldn't, if it wasn't *freezing*.' She reached for the coffee pot then looked blearily around the table. 'Where's Violet?' she asked tentatively.

'Mary is getting her up,' said Lady Claybourne. She put her cutlery down with a clatter.

Emmeline smiled sweetly at Laura. 'Would you like some kedgeree?' she asked.

Laura gave Emmeline a dark look. 'Just coffee. Thanks.'

Lord Claybourne sipped a hot cup of tea, the steam rising up into his face, misting his spectacles. 'I'll tell Ethel to light a fire in the drawing room after breakfast,' he said.

'In the library, please,' said Emmeline.

The dining room door opened and Mrs Frith entered, red-faced and wheezing, carrying a tray of extra toast, and poached kippers for Lord Claybourne.

Lord Claybourne cleared his throat. 'Could Olivia have her eggs again, please, Mrs Frith? She likes a splash of cream and a little salt.'

Mrs Frith put the toast and kippers down. ''Tis no problem at all, your Ladyship,' she said, sweeping Lady Claybourne's plate off the table whilst giving the back of her head a venomous glance.

'Well,' said Lord Claybourne, after she had gone, 'I think the party was enjoyed by all.'

The rest of us stared at him.

There was a discreet cough. Higgins was at the dining-room door. 'Your Ladyship, the car is here.'

Lady Claybourne blinked. 'Already?' She hesitated then dropped her napkin onto the table. 'Yes, of course. Thank you, Higgins.'

As she passed her husband's chair, Lord Claybourne reached out, catching Lady Claybourne's arm. The gesture startled her. I had never seen the Claybournes touch or embrace, had never witnessed any affection between them. They skirted around each other, kept to their own quarters.

'Olivia,' he said, 'we can still put a stop to this.'

Lady Claybourne hesitated. She looked to Emmeline and then, without a word, turned away from her husband.

Lord Claybourne sat for a moment, his shoulders slumped, his breakfast and his paper abandoned. He pulled his napkin from his collar, then walked resolutely after his wife, his cane tapping against the floor. After exchanging a glance, Laura and Emmeline got up too. I followed them into the hallway.

The front doors were open. Higgins was standing in the porch. Lady Claybourne and Dr Roach were at the bottom of the stairs. Outside on the drive was a motor car with the back doors open.

Mary appeared with Lady Claybourne's white fox fur . 'Your coat, your Ladyship,' she said, draping it over her shoulders. 'There's a chill with the door open.' Her voice lacked any strength or feeling and I noticed she'd lost weight.

'Yes, thank you, Mary,' said Lady Claybourne, reaching into her pockets. 'I wonder where my other glove is?'

'I've not seen it, ma'am.' Mary's lips trembled and she pressed them together.

Violet appeared at the top of the stairs looking dazed and confused. The cardigan she wore over her nightdress was slipping off her shoulder. Her hair was unbrushed. On one side of her, hanging onto her arm, was a large, matronly woman wearing a nurse's uniform, with grey stockings and black, sturdy lace-up shoes. On the other side was a dark-haired man in a white doctor's coat.

They began to escort Violet down the staircase and towards the open door. Some kind of realisation seemed to have dawned on her. She blinked, her eyes damp and overly bright. She cried out, breaking free of the nurse's grip.

'I won't go, I won't!'

Both the nurse and the doctor rushed to catch Violet's arms as she struggled to pull away.

'You can't make me. You can't. I won't go!'

She writhed under their grip.

'Let me go. You're *hurting* me!'

Dr Roach rushed forward to help as Violet shouted and lashed about, her socked feet kicking against the staircase. I could see the tendons standing out in her neck as her cries for help grew more desperate.

'I'll be good. I'll be good!' she cried. She was shaking violently. Her face was flushed, her hair sticking to her damp forehead. When she saw it was no use, that she wasn't going to be able to break free, she began to scream, the sound of her screams piercing and terrible.

I felt a painful pressure in my chest from where I had forgotten to breathe. Finally, I stepped forward, but Emmeline caught my arm. Laura had her hand over her mouth.

Dr Roach was stepping away now as the doctor in the white coat and the stout nurse had managed to capture Violet's arms and legs and were half carrying, half dragging her across the entrance hall. She spat in the direction of the nurse. Her face was purple. '*No, no, no, no, no, no,*' she screamed.

Lord Claybourne was clutching his stick, his knuckles white. Lady Claybourne had averted her eyes.

Violet was taken down the front steps and bundled into the car. A restraint had been placed over her hands. The nurse was in the back of the car with Violet. The doctor in the white coat was outside, speaking to Dr Roach, but I couldn't hear what they were saying. Then the doctor got in the front next to the driver. Higgins was calmly closing the car door, as if he was seeing the little party off for a picnic.

We were all outside now. The engine started and I could hear Dr Roach murmuring something to Lady Claybourne about 'groundbreaking treatments'. I caught a glimpse of Violet's tearstained face at the car window. She was looking at me, her eyes desperate and pleading. *Do something, Gilly.*

After the car had gone, we stood there uselessly.

'Come,' said Dr Roach. 'Let's not all get cold now.'

We went numbly inside. Higgins shut the door behind us.

As we all stood in the entrance hall, silent and stunned, Mrs Frith came up the stairs holding a silver tray. She stepped towards Lady Claybourne. 'Your eggs, your Ladyship. Just how you like them.'

Chapter Twenty-One

18th March 1939

Dear Gilly,

I hope all is well for you back at school. I apologise, for I know it has been some time now, since you left us, but here I am, writing to you as I promised I would.

Violet remains at Bancroft Hospital which Mummy says is really the best place for her at the moment. We hope, of course, that she is having a nice rest and receiving the treatment she needs. We haven't been to visit her yet as the doctors don't advise it.

I'm afraid I must tell you that Frank Marks confessed to accidentally shooting Robin when he was out rabbiting on Boxing Day morning. He is to be tried for involuntary manslaughter next month. A prison sentence is expected. We heard from Father that a spent cartridge was discovered by the police near to the spot where Robin was found in the woods. The same cartridges were found in Frank's cottage. Perhaps he felt he had no choice but to confess. We really don't know. We hope, of course, that given Robin's death was an accident, the sentence won't be too harsh. Frank has been in prison before and will know something of what it is like. He'll never be able to return to Thornleigh, but I've heard he has a brother up in the north country, a miner, who may be able to secure him work on his release, whenever that may be.

Hugh Cadwallander has proposed to Emmeline and they are to be married in May. This has been a source of great joy to us all as you can imagine. Emmeline will not be returning to Oxford but I am sure she will have plenty to keep her busy as a new bride!

I hope you stay in touch and I wish you all the very best.

Yours faithfully,

Laura

I carefully folded the letter and put it back in the envelope. I was cold all over. 'Violet has gone away for a rest,' Lady Claybourne had told us.

'How long will she be there for?' I'd asked.

'A few weeks I should think,' Lady Claybourne had replied vaguely.

Each morning since my return to school, I had woken wondering if it would be the day Violet would return to Heathcomb, herself again.

'You won't be here long,' I'd told Beatrice Averly, my new roommate, when she arrived with her suitcase, polished shoes and neat ribboned bunches. 'My friend will be back very soon.'

Beatrice was quiet and tidy. She enjoyed lacrosse, kept her swimming medals next to her bed, and fell asleep immediately after lights out. She was nothing like Violet.

I couldn't believe Violet had been away from home for two months. *She'll be going mad*, I thought. Will she be able to go out for the long walks she likes? Will she be able to work on her map of Elvore? Does she have *Peter Pan*?

And Frank ... I put my face in my hands. We'd all said we'd seen him with the gun, but it was my fault the police had arrested him. I'd taken the cartridges from the cottage. But I couldn't understand why Frank had confessed to something he didn't do. It didn't make any sense. And what was Laura talking about? Frank couldn't go up north and work down a pit in the dark all day. He belonged at Thornleigh. He loved the woods and the land, the trees and the lake, and the still, misty mornings. They were a part of him, he had said.

My chin was quivering and I wiped my eyes with the sleeve of my pinafore.

As much as the horrifying news the letter imparted had upset me, so had its formal tone and brevity. Laura might as well have been writing to a distant relative, and I didn't believe her for a minute when she'd written 'I hope you stay in touch'. It seemed clear to me that they wanted nothing more to do with me. Had my time at Thornleigh meant nothing to Emmeline and Laura? What about *cousin Gilly*? Who was I now, without them? I was nobody. I was back where I started, in my dull, hopeless life.

Only it was worse than that.

I had lost my friend.

* * *

291

Late that night, when Beatrice was snoring softly, I got up and left our dorm room.

The night air was cool and sharp. I propped the door open with a brick then crossed the roof to the edge, wrapping my arms around myself and remembering how Violet had stood here six months ago, telling me how wonderful it would be here at night with the stars.

Nos contra mundum.

Us against the world.

I had wanted Emmeline's approval, had longed, more than anything, to be accepted by her. She was everything I'd wanted to be. I had trusted in Emmeline, and because of that I was responsible for destroying my friend.

I missed Violet. Unpredictable, precocious, overly passionate, terribly anxious and strange as anything – I missed all of her.

When I'm around you, Gilly, I don't need to do so many rituals.

She had been getting better and then, because of us, she had been sent away.

We had been told that, at Bancroft, Violet would get the help she needed. After all, normal sane young women do not slaughter their pets with kitchen knives. We had lit a match under Violet's deepest fears and insecurities then stood back and watched her burn. And for what? In order to protect ourselves and what others might think of us.

I loathed Emmeline then, but more than that, I loathed myself. I had betrayed Violet in the worst possible way.

I took a step up onto the walled edge of the roof, lifted my arms and closed my eyes. How pleasant it would be to walk right off. The sensation of falling swiftly through the cold night air. I wouldn't even scream. Tomorrow, they would find me in the shrubbery. Nothing but a tangled mess of broken limbs and twisted nightdress.

I stepped down and away from the ledge. I had never been brave. But then perhaps it wasn't bravery. Perhaps it was the most cowardly thing I could do.

But neither could I stay here.

Everywhere I went – our dorm room, the dining hall, the art room where Violet had got upset over her flowers, the chapel where she'd once asked me if I ever had the urge to shout out blasphemy – in all places I was reminded of her.

I no longer wanted to take my school exams, and I certainly didn't want to follow in Emmeline's footsteps and apply for university. I didn't want to do anything Emmeline had done.

Just a few days ago, a hush had fallen over the dining hall as Miss Tankard had turned up the wireless and we heard that Hitler's troops had marched into Prague. The broadcaster implied what we all feared, that Hitler had no intention of honouring the Munich Agreement. There were murmurings that war was inevitable now.

If there was to be a war then I was going to be a part of it. And in being a part of something greater than myself, in putting myself forward, serving my country, and helping those who may find themselves in need, perhaps I could somehow begin to atone for the terrible thing I had done.

Back in my room, I dressed by the light of the candle then packed my suitcase. I left a note on my bed, explaining that there was no need to panic or send out a search party, that I was going to my aunt's residence in London.

All the doors were locked, of course, but I found an unsecured window down in the kitchen and, after throwing my suitcase onto the wet grass, I climbed out and set off across the playing field towards the lane. I had a little emergency money in my suitcase. When I reached the station, I would curl up in the waiting room until morning when I would purchase my ticket and take the first train to London. I had completed the journey enough times with Aunt Ada that I knew the way. Aunt Ada would be furious, of course. No doubt she would write to my father. I didn't care. I wasn't ever going back.

Part Three

Part Three

Chapter Twenty-Two

1942

ONE AFTERNOON, THREE YEARS LATER, I was walking along Cadogan Gardens when I heard my name. 'Hullo, Gillian.'

I hadn't even meant to walk that way home but the King's Road was closed off due to an unexploded bomb – UXBs we called them. They were a huge irritation; streets constantly being shut off by wardens, buses diverted, crowds of people standing about, waiting for the bomb squad to arrive.

I turned at the sound of my name. A young fair-haired man in uniform was crossing the road, coming towards me, smiling.

At first I couldn't think who he was. We had a Canadian soldier billeted with us, a cheerful hulk of a chap, and I was always bumping into his friends, but this man was in a British uniform: Royal Air Force. And his voice was vaguely familiar to me, although his accent was not the London one I had grown accustomed to. His vowels were most definitely upper class. It was only when he grew closer that I recognised him.

'Charlie,' I said in amazement.

'I knew it was you,' he said. 'How have you been, old gal?' He beamed, looking genuinely pleased to see me.

'Fine,' I replied, blinking. An image of him at the New Year's Eve ball, rushing over to Violet, ushering her out of the room, made me feel unsteady. I hadn't thought about that night in a very long time.

'This is something, isn't it? Bumping into you.'

'It is,' I stammered.

'Don't tell me you're living here in London these days?' Charlie said, still grinning. His smile revealed even teeth and good dentistry. His uniform was neat and pressed and he wore a yellow daffodil in his lapel. He had retained his boyish good looks and cheerful demeanour.

'Yes,' I answered, recovering myself, 'just around the corner. Chelsea.'

Charlie whistled with admiration. 'Plenty of safer places to live, Gilly.'

'I know, but . . .' I trailed off. I needed to be here, needed to be at the heart of it, to do what I could. I didn't know how to articulate this to Charlie.

Charlie nodded. He understood. I knew that the uniform he wore, the part he was playing in the war, could most probably have been prevented. No doubt his father could have found him an essential job, pulled various strings if he'd needed to, to make sure Charlie didn't have to fight, yet here he was.

'How long have you been in London?' he asked me.

'The spring of '39.'

'Golly. You've seen it all then,' he said.

'Yes. I'm with the Red Cross.'

We looked at each other.

'And you?' I asked, gesturing to the uniform.

'Bomber Command. Squadron Leader now, in fact,' he said sheepishly, yet clearly proud of his rank.

'That's wonderful, Charlie.'

Charlie shrugged. 'It helps if you went to the right schools, of course.'

'I'm sure that's not all there is to it,' I said diplomatically.

Charlie laughed. 'No, it turns out there's quite a lot involved with keeping a six-thousand-pound Halifax in the air. And that's without the bombs.' He chuckled. 'They sent me over to Canada in '39, not long after I knew you, to complete my training. I flew Tiger Moths over the mountains. You wouldn't believe how beautiful it was up there, Gilly.'

'I really can't imagine.'

'Since then I've completed two tours. I'm a rare statistic. A lucky charm.' He smiled sadly then straightened his shoulders. 'Not that I've told you any of this, of course.'

'I haven't heard a thing.'

'I've got a few days leave. That's why I'm here. You know that Laura and I married, don't you?'

I shook my head. I hadn't heard anything about any of the Claybournes since that letter from Laura. What with leaving school, the war, recently turning nineteen – I felt like a different person. Though seeing Charlie, the mention of Laura's name, had brought me sharply back to Thornleigh, to the Claybournes, to something I had tried so hard to forget.

'That's lovely,' I said, smiling brightly. 'Congratulations.'

Whatever my feelings about Thornleigh, I *was* pleased for Laura and Charlie. I'd always thought they'd make a lovely couple and it was clear to me, even back then, how they felt about each other.

'Just you wait until I tell Laura I ran into you,' Charlie said. 'She'll be delighted. She often talks of you.'

I didn't know what to say. I doubted it was true and assumed Charlie was only being polite.

'Laura often says, "I wonder how Gilly is getting on these days." You must pop over and see us some time. She'd love it.'

'Oh, I . . .'

'It's difficult for her,' Charlie said quickly. 'I'm away a lot, you see. Between you and me, I think she could use an old friend, someone not part of her usual set, you know?'

I blinked, then quickly nodded. I certainly didn't think Laura would consider me 'an old friend'. But Charlie was right, I was definitely not part of Laura's 'usual set'. Even with the war on, I knew the upper classes, most of them anyway, were determined not to give up their dinners and dances and long weekends at their friends' country houses. But then I felt a pang of sympathy for Laura as I pictured her waving Charlie off, the endless waiting for news, the dread of an official-looking letter. Laura, I knew, would be half out of her mind with worry when Charlie went away. I looked at him, at his kind blue eyes, cheerful smile and neatly pressed uniform and felt glad she had married him.

'How are Lady and Lord Claybourne?' I enquired politely.

Charlie's face dropped. 'Oh, gosh, Gilly, didn't you hear?' He touched the back of his neck.

'Hear what?' I asked.

'They're dead.'

I stared at him.

'I'm afraid they both drowned. Almost three years ago now.'
I stared at him. 'Drowned?'

Charlie rubbed his forehead. 'They were on the *Athenia* in
'39. Do you remember it?'

I told him I did. The sinking of the *Athenia* in the Atlantic
had been one of the first great tragedies of the war. It was said
to have been sunk by a German torpedo that hit the engine
room. I remembered how, on reading the paper that day, it had
felt like we truly were at war.

'A witness said they made it into a lifeboat, but that there
was an accident . . .' Charlie trailed off.

I could hardly bear to think of it. Lady Claybourne scram-
bling for a lifeboat in her pearls and furs. Lord Claybourne
standing on the deck, surrounded by chaos. The smell of smoke
from the engine room, the shouts and cries and weeping. The
water creeping up onto the deck. The papers said the passengers
had been singing 'Roll Out the Barrel' as the ship went down.
Then I remembered Lady Claybourne's fear of water, how she
never went near the lake, and shuddered.

'Of course it was terribly hard on Laura and Emmeline,' said
Charlie.

'Yes,' I said, wondering why he had omitted Violet. It was
difficult to take in. I suppose if I had thought of the Claybournes,
I would have imagined them all still there in that great crumbling house. Lord Claybourne opening his paper, eating his
kippers. Lady Claybourne sweeping through the house, giving
instructions to the servants.

'Are you and Laura at Thornleigh then? Or Emmeline . . .'

'Gosh, no.' Charlie ran a hand through his hair. 'Thornleigh
was requisitioned. The military are there doing God knows

what. Helping themselves to the wine cellar, I should think. Emmeline and Cadwallander have bought a little place in Buckinghamshire. And Laura and I are in Richmond. I didn't want her in London,' he added hastily, 'but she loves the city. She's in the WVS and does all sorts. I get awfully worried about her when I'm away. The town hall was hit, you know. And most of Peldon Avenue has gone. I wish she'd use the damn shelter but she doesn't want the neighbours to see her in her curlers.'

I smiled. That sounded like Laura.

'Look, you must give me your address, Gilly. She'll be pleased as punch to hear I've bumped into you.' He took out a tiny notepad and pen and thrust it towards me.

I jotted down my address and he studied it carefully. 'You're not far at all.'

'It's my aunt's house. She's staying with a friend in Shropshire.'

'I'm sure you and Laura will have plenty to talk about,' he said, tucking the notepad into his pocket. 'I can't wait to tell her I've seen you.'

After he'd gone, I stood on the pavement for a moment, trying to take it all in. Lord and Lady Claybourne, dead. Emmeline married to Cadwallander. Laura and Charlie, just down the road in Richmond. And Thornleigh, of course. I pictured tanks rolling down the mount, soldiers studying maps in the lounge hall, planning attacks. Men in uniform, playing cards and smoking in the library.

I wondered what Laura's reaction would be when Charlie went home and told her he'd seen me. Would she really want to get in touch? I very much doubted it.

I expect, like me, she wanted to forget.

And yet, I couldn't help thinking of Violet. I'd never had a friend like Violet, before or since, and I often found myself wondering what she was doing. Laura would know, of course. Seeing Laura again would give me an opportunity to ask her about Violet.

I knew Violet would definitely have wanted to get involved with the war, even if it had meant lying about her age as I initially had. I could imagine her in the Land Army or the Timber Corps. Was she out there, somewhere, digging up fields, felling trees, or draining fenland? Or perhaps she was here in London, volunteering at a different hospital or working the telephones at a local fire station. I might have passed her in the street and not even realised it.

I shook my head. I knew that if Violet had really wanted to get in touch, she would have found a way. And I was sure I would hear nothing from Laura.

I had a brief, fleeting thought that it might actually be a comfort to see Laura, to remember I had not been the only one who had witnessed the events of that winter, to know I really *had* witnessed them, and to see the guilt and pain I carried with me reflected in the face of another. Would Laura feel the same?

* * *

Not long after I'd arrived in London, and as soon as the war was announced, Aunt Ada packed her bags and went to stay with her friend, Winifred, in Shropshire. Before she left, she tried to persuade me to come with her, but I'd refused. I'd come to London to do my bit, not to run away, even though, of course, that was exactly what I'd done by coming to London in the first place.

303

Although Aunt Ada had not been happy about my decision to leave Heathcomb and temporarily move in with her, when the war came I think a part of her was secretly glad to have someone looking after the house. Not that there was much I'd be able to do if it did take a hit.

Terrified of invasion, of German parachutists, Aunt Ada had hidden the knives, maps and the best biscuits in the cupboard under the stairs, leaving me strict instructions. *Don't let them at the garibaldis, Gillian. And remember there's always the gas oven, and plenty of pillows in the linen cupboard.* My aunt thought that if the Germans should land, the quickest way to do myself in would be to stuff pillows against the kitchen door and put my head in the oven (Aunt Ada was not optimistic about the war).

Aunt Ada's house was not large but it had two spare rooms. The first was occupied by a man from the Royal Canadian Army Service Corps who had been billeted with us. A girl called Moira quickly took the second room. Moira worked for the Air Ministry. We got on well and often shared our meals. During one of the first nights of the Blitz, the night they bombed the docks, we crawled out of Moira's bedroom window and sat on the roof, watching the German planes dropping more and more bombs into the burning inferno on the horizon that we knew to be the East End. It looked like the whole city was on fire. The red-orange glow made the sky so light it felt like daytime.

I got a job working in a stationery shop on the King's Road. The shop was owned by Mr Smith, a portly man in his fifties. Business was good. A lot of people write letters during a war. And of course we sold those awful black-edged cards you saw in the front windows of people's houses, an indication that they had suffered a loss.

There was a spotty boy called Douglas who did the deliveries and the unpacking. He was seventeen, about to turn eighteen, but there was little chance of him being called up as he'd had polio as a child and his right foot dragged. Then there was Sheila who was having a fling with a US serviceman called Hank. Sheila was worried Hank might ask her to marry him and put her in a dilemma. Although they drove her 'up the bleedin' wall', she was close to her family and wasn't sure about leaving them all to go off to live in Utah with Hank's family (where was Utah? we wondered). We looked it up in the library and found a picture of a town with wide streets and not many trees.

'What about prairie fever?' I asked.

'Don't be daft. There's no prairies. Only mountains, see?'

We'd both peered at the picture.

'Have you travelled before?' I asked Sheila.

'Only to Margate,' she said. 'We go every summer.'

I looked at her and she quickly shut the book. 'Well, anyway, he might not ask.'

I then decided I would volunteer part-time with the Red Cross. Firstly, I had to complete twenty hours in a hospital. Some of our patients were bomb victims from the East End. Beneath even the newly instated nurses, we VADs were given all the worst jobs: emptying bedpans, changing bandages, bathing filthy, shocked patients, many of whom had lost their homes and their families. The shifts were long and it was gruelling, often upsetting, work.

Determined to be useful, I volunteered for extra hours and all the worst jobs as if it would somehow make a difference, as if I could convince myself that, despite the terrible thing I had done in the winter of '38, I was still, somehow, a good person, someone I could like.

There was one awful evening when I had arrived at work only to be told I was needed downstairs in the morgue. There had been an afternoon raid and a bomb had landed on a church. A great many people had been sheltering in the crypt and were literally blown to pieces. It was my job, along with a few other of the girls, the mortuary attendant and a young, pale-faced doctor, to try to assemble the body parts for burial, or at least do the best we could so the victims' loved ones could imagine they were burying their complete relatives. A large number of those killed were women and children and it was awful, trying to match up various small limbs, making piles of coats and tiny hats.

'Bit of a jigsaw down here tonight, ladies,' the mortuary attendant had said. 'You'll need your handkerchiefs.'

He was right; the smell was terrible. I joined one of the girls outside and smoked a cigarette, trying to replace the stench with something more palatable.

That night I ran a scorching hot bath, not caring how much water I used. And then I cried, hugging my knees to my chest and sobbing desperately over the utter pointlessness of it all and how much I despised myself.

After my weeks at the hospital, I was posted to a casualty clearing station in Balham. The more severely injured went to the hospital and I found myself dealing mostly with shrapnel injuries. There was a woman who was brought to us one night after a particularly bad local raid. She wore a huge floppy hat and was badly bruised and shaken. She told us something had hit her on the head and that she'd put the hat on to cover 'the scratch'. We gave her a cup of strong sugared tea and sat her down. 'This is what I need, love,' she said, sipping her tea. 'I'll be right as rain in just a jiffy.' When we removed her hat we found the top of her head missing. She died half an hour later.

On the nights I wasn't at the clearing station, I went out. Sometimes with Moira, sometimes with Shelia from the shop, or with a group of Red Cross volunteers. Café de Paris, The Four Hundred, The Old Florida: I frequented them all. People were being blown to smithereens every night and there didn't seem much else for it but to go out, to dance, to go home with a man which, I am ashamed to say, I often did. Not that I looked particularly hard for men, but when they came, when I recognised that glance across the bar or the dance hall, or felt a hot hand on the small of my back, a whisper in my ear, I usually went. Sex obliterated my thoughts of the war, and of Thornleigh, of Violet, Frank and Robin, even if only for a short while. These encounters were fleeting, often awkward and embarrassing. I went home and scrubbed myself raw but never felt clean. I was occasionally reminded of Hector and his horrible groping hands.

The narrow, sheltered life I had led at Heathcomb, surrounded only by the daughters of wealthy gentlemen and a handful of downtrodden teachers, seemed very far behind me, a different world altogether. I sometimes wondered if I had left the girl who had gazed listlessly out of grubby classroom windows, who had stuffed gristly pieces of meat in her pinafore dress, and who had befriended Violet Claybourne, completely behind; that somehow she was still there at school, but that I was here, now an entirely different person.

I knew what happened at Thornleigh had changed me, that I might very well be living a completely different life had I not been so obsessed with the fading grandeur of Thornleigh Hall, had I not been so desperate for Emmeline's affections, so eager to fit in where I did not belong. I wished I'd had the courage to stand up for what I knew was truly right.

But I had not.

And now I was here, unable to shake the feeling that my soul had shrunk, along with the sense I was wading through thick tar each day. I often cried for no apparent reason. Perhaps, I thought, other people did not live like this. Perhaps there were people who had made better decisions, who were happy, even. The concept of being happy, of moving through life with ease, felt as remote and alien to me as an image of a faraway land on a projector screen at the picture house.

And so I went on, wearing myself out, trying not to think too much, trying to keep the self-loathing at bay. I had imagined Emmeline, Laura and Violet were doing the same, that seeing me would only bring about the return of memories we would all rather not face.

When, several days after bumping into Charlie, a letter from Laura did arrive, I could hardly believe it.

Chapter Twenty-Three

L AURA'S LETTER WAS SHORT BUT enthusiastic. *So lovely to hear you're in London. How marvellous! We absolutely must meet for lunch, darling. My treat, of course.*

I very nearly didn't respond. But then I thought again of Violet, of how much I would like to know how and where she was. And I suppose I couldn't help remembering enjoying Laura's company when I had been at Thornleigh. Despite all that had happened, when I looked at Laura's handwriting, I felt a tug at my sleeve, a whisper in my ear. *Cousin Gilly.*

And so that was how the following Thursday afternoon – my afternoon off – I found myself walking into the dining room at The Ritz. Even though we were in the middle of a war, the room was surprisingly busy. Waiters in crisp white shirts sashayed among the tables where attractive women in furs and pearls, men in smartly tailored suits or in navy or khaki uniforms, sat eating and drinking as if they didn't have a care in the world. Clouds of smoke gathered around the diners. Statues of goddesses in demure poses were placed in the alcoves. Pink marbled walls. Beautifully draped, gold-trimmed curtains complete with swags, tails, and pelmets. I had worn my smartest dress and my best hat but even so the dress was rather worn.

I finally spotted Laura at a table in the corner by a large urn. Seeing her there, amidst the soft lighting and scent of expensive cigarettes, I thought I was dreaming. I had come to think of the Claybourne sisters as ghosts, existing solely in another life, another time. Seeing Laura, the edges of the room blurred into a single point and I felt as light as air. She gave a little wave.

'Gillian, darling. How wonderful. Can you believe it? How have you *been*?' She gave me kisses in the French way.

I smiled despite myself. She was just as I remembered her. 'Oh, you know ...' My voice cracked with emotion. So much had changed for me, I had no idea where to begin.

It was also quite a shock to hear Laura's voice. I'd spent so long working at the stationery shop and nursing the East-Enders at the hospital, it felt odd to be in the presence of an upper-class voice once again, that familiar debutante drawl the Claybourne girls, and many of the girls at Heathcomb, had possessed.

We sat down. Laura was wearing a mint-green dress, a fox neckpiece and a stylish little hat. There was a bottle of tonic water on the table, I was surprised to see, but then it was the middle of the day. I helped myself after she gestured to it, feeling relieved that at least it wasn't going to be a boozy lunch.

'It's been a long time, hasn't it?' I said.

'Indeed it has! You look adorable. All grown up!'

Although in my ordinary life, I did feel a grown-up, in the presence of Laura, I suddenly felt the awkward, dowdy schoolgirl once again.

'It's very nice in here,' I said glancing around. 'You could almost forget there was a war on.'

'Exactly.' Laura smiled. 'That's why I love it.'

'I'm surprised they can keep it open,' I stumbled on.

Laura looked at me. 'People have still got to *lunch*, darling.'

'I suppose so,' I said with a smile.

'We must protect our pleasures, Gilly. What else have we got? Hitler can't take everything, you know. Especially not cocktail hour. We must lunch for England, darling.'

I tried not to laugh; she looked so serious.

'And of course there are all sorts in here.' She lowered her voice. 'See that chap over there?' She pointed to a man in the corner. 'An Iranian arms dealer.'

'Really?'

She nodded. 'And the King of Albania has rooms here, apparently.'

'I'm so pleased you married Charlie,' I blurted out.

Laura reached across the table and squeezed my hand. Her hands were pale and small and I noticed she wore a gold wedding band and a large sapphire surrounded by diamonds.

'It must be an awful worry . . .' I continued. 'Charlie fighting.'

Laura lowered her eyes. 'You can't imagine, Gilly. He's gone off again now. A base somewhere in Yorkshire. This damn war . . . I don't even know where he flies to half the time, or when. They can't say, you know.'

'I am sorry.'

She let go of my hand and reached for the menu. 'Let's order something, shall we? They've still got lobster if you'd like it. But of course we can only go for three courses. That's all they're allowed to serve these days.'

'Lobster?' I said faintly. Most of my meals had consisted of a slice of Spam and half a baked potato. I had learned to live

EMILY CRITCHLEY

with a constant gnawing at my stomach. I hadn't eaten chicken in three months, let alone three courses, let alone *lobster*. I picked up the menu and blinked at it, 'I think one course will be fine,' I said, feeling overwhelmed.

'Perhaps I'll order for us,' said Laura breezily. 'What about the salmon? One of the guests has it sent down from his estate. It will only be on the menu for a few days.'

'Lovely.'

Laura glanced around the room. 'Of course it isn't anything like what it was, not after the Italian waiters and the head chef were rounded up and packed off. Poor things.'

I nodded, then after a moment said, 'I was sorry to hear about your parents.'

A flicker of grief crossed Laura's face. 'Thank you. It's still so funny to think that we're orphans.' She paused, took a sip of water. 'They thought they would be safer abroad. We've got relatives in Canada. Second cousins or something.'

'Yes,' I said, remembering the moose head in the lounge hall at Thornleigh.

'Emmeline married Cadwallander, of course,' said Laura, changing the subject. 'But I'm sure you know that.'

'Charlie mentioned it.'

'They're living at a place called Wynscott. It's really quite something, although Emmeline calls it their "country cottage".'

'Was Chaseley House requisitioned too?'

Laura took another sip of water. 'It's a boys' school. I haven't seen it myself but apparently the ballroom is full of metal cots. They were lucky. Hugh could see what was on the horizon, and as soon as war was declared he offered Chaseley up as a school. He thought small boys were likely to do less damage than soldiers, although who knows?' She gave a little laugh then smiled sadly. 'We weren't so fortunate with Thornleigh.'

'I heard.'

Laura sighed. 'All we can do is wait it out, and then go in and see what the damage is. Well, Hugh will, seeing as it belongs to him now, really.'

'Does it?'

'Of course. It's Hugh and Emmeline's. Hugh always had his eye on Thornleigh, although even he couldn't have foreseen that Mummy and Daddy would go *quite* so quickly. Though to be honest, what with all the taxes and everything, I'll be surprised if Emmi and Hugh can keep it on along with Chaseley but I'm sure they'll come up with some scheme or other.'

I was a little shocked to hear this. I'd always thought Emmeline marrying Cadwallander would mean Thornleigh was safe, but there hadn't been a war on then.

Our food arrived, served by two waiters, one of whom placed my napkin in my nap with a flourish. The large fillet of salmon was mouth-watering. I had roast vegetables cooked, I could see, in real butter, some fancy little potatoes, and gently steamed watercress and samphire.

'This salmon is delicious,' said Laura, tucking in. 'It's so nice to have samphire in season again.'

'How is Emmeline?' I asked.

'Oh, she's all right. She's just, you know, *Emmeline*.'

'Does she have children?'

I imagined Emmeline to have had quite the little brood by now. An heir for Hugh and a couple of spares, no doubt.

Laura swallowed then set her fork down. 'No, actually, she doesn't.' She lowered her voice. 'They've tried. For a long time now but ...' She shook her head. 'Well, I don't really know. She's seen all sorts of doctors, apparently. But I don't know any more than that.'

'Oh.' I imagined Emmeline had wanted it all: a husband, an estate complete with servants, an active social life, *and* children, even if those children did spend most of the day with their nanny. Knowing the sort of person Emmeline was – fiercely determined, concerned about social status – I was sure she would feel she had failed. Her inability to have children with Hugh must be a great source of frustration to her, as well as sadness. Still, I found it difficult to muster much sympathy for Emmeline after what she had done.

'They'll carry on trying, I expect. And you know Emmeline. When she wants something ...'

I did know, although it was not something I wanted to remember. 'Are you sure it's her?' I asked. 'I mean, Cadwallander might not be—'

Laura waved a hand in the air. 'Yes, one *has* heard of such things. As I say, I don't know anything about it, really. She doesn't exactly confide in me these days. I only think ...' She hesitated for a moment. 'Well, I suppose what I mean is that if it *was* him, if there was a way Emmeline *could* then she would.'

I thought I knew what Laura was getting at. A quick, passionate affair, a subsequent pregnancy. Yes, I thought, a little guiltily, Laura was right, if there was a way, Emmeline would make it happen.

I felt that despite all our small talk and catching up, we were avoiding the elephant in the room. I got the sense that Laura felt, as much as I did, that we would have to acknowledge, at some point, our shared secret. Perhaps, I thought, Laura even *wanted* to acknowledge it. Having a secret can be lonely. Perhaps that's why she invited me here.

As if guessing something of my thoughts, Laura looked down into her lap. 'It changed everything for me, you know, Gilly.' 'What happened that winter. I know it might not seem as if it did ... But it did. It changed the very core of me.'

She looked up and our eyes met.

'I understand,' I said softly.

Laura pulled at the sleeves of her dress and lowered her gaze. 'I went very cold on Charlie for a while. I wasn't sure I still wanted to marry him. I didn't feel I deserved to live a normal, happy life after what I did. But then, after a time, when I saw how miserable I was making us both, I decided that perhaps, by loving Charlie, I might be able to redeem myself. Oh, I know I can never make it right,' she said quickly. 'But I thought to myself, if I can just love this one man with all my heart and do right by him for as long as I have, then perhaps I can find a way to live with what happened. Do you really understand, Gilly?'

'I do,' I said, thinking about the long hours I worked, arriving home each evening bone-tired, unable to think about anything at all.

'But we have to carry on, don't we?' Laura said, tracing the rim of her glass with her finger. 'Because it's all so beautiful and extraordinary. That's what I tell myself, anyway.' She dropped her hands into her lap. 'We never forget,' she said quietly. 'We never forget those moments that changed everything. But it's no good looking over our shoulders, is it? Because we'll only fall flat on our faces.'

My chest hitched and I wished I could reach across the table for Laura's hand. 'It's difficult,' I managed to say.

'You see, Gilly, every day when I wake, I reach for Charlie and I try to love him a little better.' Her voice quivered. 'And then I tell myself it was an accident. I say it to myself over and over again: *It was an accident.*'

'It was,' I whispered. 'Of course it was.'

'And after that...' she said, 'after Robin ... well, I don't know, it all just sort of spiralled ...'

We sat in silence for a moment or two. The waiter appeared to take our plates.

Laura forced a bright smile. 'Charlie said you were with the Red Cross?'

'I man a First Aid Post at a casualty clearing station, and I'm sometimes called in to the hospital when they're short-handed.'

'That must be very hard work, Gilly.'

I told her about the endless folding of linen and cutting of gauze bandages. Then I told her about the East Enders we'd received at Cheyne Hospital who had lost their homes and all their possessions, of bathing an old woman whose leathery skin was so encrusted with dirt and grime, the bathwater turned black. I told her about a recent night in the hospital: the patients had been terrified of a nearby raid and several of the ward sisters had performed the cancan in order get them laughing.

'I really admire you, Gilly. I do a bit for the WVS. I helped to organise a lot of the evacuees early on, but I don't think I could be a nurse.'

'I only do it in the evenings. I work in a stationery shop during the day. On the King's Road.'

Laura's eyes widened. 'Goodness, really? You *work.*'

I smiled again. Work wasn't a part of Laura's world, not the kind of work I did anyway. 'I've decided I'm going to leave at the end of the summer and apply to become a full-time VAD if they'll have me.'

'That's very admirable, Gilly.'

'I feel I must do something.'

Laura nodded. 'I felt the same recently. I wanted to help more with the war effort, especially with Charlie away ... but now, well, it's not really possible ...' She gave me a small smile. 'Must find the ladies' room,' she said, sliding elegantly off her chair. 'It only seems five minutes since I last went.' She paused, then leaned over and whispered in my ear. 'In fact, Gilly. I'm pregnant.'

'Oh, Laura, that's wonderful!'

She grinned at me. 'About eleven weeks they think. Charlie is thrilled to bits.'

'Of course he is.'

She smiled again then rushed off to find the loo, leaving me with her good news.

Sitting there alone in The Ritz dining room, feeling happy for Laura, I wondered – if we'd told the truth about what had happened that morning in the woods – would Laura be sitting here now, happy, excited, expecting her first child? Perhaps she would. But then again, perhaps she wouldn't. If what she'd done, the truth of that terrible accident, *had* been known, might Charlie's parents have put their foot down over the marriage? Might Laura, under the strain of an inquiry, or even an arrest, and under the public gaze, have fallen to pieces?

I thought it odd that Laura hadn't yet mentioned Violet. I hadn't either, but I think I was hoping Laura would mention her first. Or perhaps, curious as I was about what had happened to Violet, I had also been content, for such a long time, with my imaginings. Happy to picture Violet out on some farm in the West Country, rolling up her sleeves, milking a cow. Or as a nurse, perhaps, driving a van full of medical supplies across a muddy French field.

Laura returned to the table.

'It's lovely news, Laura. It really is.'

'You'll have to come and see it,' she said cheerfully, 'when it arrives.'

'I will.'

'Gosh, I'd love a cigarette right now,' said Laura with a sigh, 'but Charlie has got this mad idea in his head that smoking might be bad for the baby. I told him, everyone smokes, darling, but he's quite set on it, so I've given them up. It makes me feel dreadful. If ever there was a time I could do with a cigarette, it's been these last few weeks.' She laughed. 'But you go ahead and smoke, Gilly.'

'It's all right. Thanks, though.'

Laura took a sip of her tonic water.

'How is Violet?' I asked.

Laura paused, her drink halfway to her lips. She seemed surprised by the question. She blinked and glanced down at the tablecloth. 'Well, I'm afraid I don't really know,' she said eventually.

My shoulders stiffened. 'You don't know?' Of course there was a war on, but still I had hoped Laura would have *some* idea how her sister was. I rubbed my eyebrow. 'But, I mean, what is she doing? Where is she?'

Laura pulled at the fur neckpiece at her throat. 'Well, she's at Bancroft.'

I stared at her, my skin tingling. 'What?'

'She gets the treatment she needs there,' Laura said quietly, not meeting my eye.

I continued to stare at her.

Laura looked uncomfortable. 'It's supposed to be a really excellent facility . . .'

I felt a clenching in my stomach. 'You mean,' I said, 'she's been in there *all this time.*'

Laura nodded, bit her lip.

'But that's . . . over three years.' The room was closing in on me, colours blurring, and yet the laughter and the clinking of glasses sounded far away.

Laura said nothing, only exhaled deeply.

'She only went in for a rest,' I said, my breath catching in my throat.

'I know,' said Laura. Her eyes met mine for a brief moment, then she looked away again. 'God, I did try, Gilly,' she said, wrapping her fingers tightly around her glass. 'You've got to believe me. It was just after Mummy and Daddy died, I thought we could get her out. Charlie and I sent a doctor and a lawyer up there but . . .' She trailed off. 'It didn't come to anything. The doctors said Violet needed to stay, that she wouldn't be able to cope if she left. I told them. I said we'd take care of her but . . .' She shook her head. 'They were insistent. And then, the following week, Emmeline and Hugh came steaming over to our house, parking the Rolls-Royce out on the street, almost hitting the lamp post. Emmi said we shouldn't have meddled, that they received regular updates on Violet's treatment. Then I asked about the money. Hugh and Emmi dealt with all Mummy and Daddy's affairs after their deaths. They said I shouldn't have to bother with any of it, that it would be too much for me, too upsetting. There was money left for Violet, you see. Daddy had seen to that. Emmi said they had

Violet's treatment covered, that her money was in some sort of fund. Both Emmi and Hugh spoke to Charlie and me as if we were children. They told us they had it all in hand, and we weren't to be contacting Bancroft, that it would disrupt Violet's treatment.'

I didn't know what to say. I was feeling quite ill.

'You don't understand,' Laura said on seeing my expression, a note of desperation in her voice. 'You only knew Emmi for a short time. You don't know what she can be like. And Hugh Cadwallander, he's a powerful man, a man who gets his own way. He does whatever Emmi wants him to, and she thinks Bancroft is the best place for Violet.'

'Have you been to see her?' I asked, the words choking in my throat.

Laura swallowed hard. 'Only once. A few months after she went in. Just after I wrote to you.' She paused, then looked up at me. 'It was awful, Gilly. Violet ... She was drooling and her eyes looked all strange. She tried to say something to me but her words were slurred. I couldn't understand her. It was so distressing, so I left. Then we had a letter arrive telling us it was better for Violet's health if we didn't visit. We would only upset her. They told us they had a treatment plan, that they were giving her insulin to calm her down and something else, they said.' She furrowed her brow. 'Some new treatment involving electric shocks. Apparently it brings people back to themselves, makes them nice and calm, that's what the doctor said. But it takes time.'

I was staring at Laura, yelling at her in my mind: *But there was nothing wrong with her! We made her think she was mad. We told them she was mad!*

'You've got to understand,' Laura said desperately. 'Once she went into Bancroft, Mummy never spoke of her. And after a while, even Daddy stopped too. It was as if she was dead or had never existed. A few times I heard Mummy call me her youngest daughter.'

I felt a squeezing of my ribcage, a pressure between my eyes.

'I mean, they can't all be wrong, can they?' Laura was saying. 'Surely they wouldn't have said all of that about new treatments and calming her down unless she needed to be there?'

I shook my head. I didn't know. All I knew was what we had done, and all I could think of was Violet strapped to a bed, a nurse sticking probes in her or injecting her with needles. She'd be livid. No wonder they thought she needed calming down. And what if she couldn't go outside? She'd hate that. She needed her long walks, the outdoors, fresh air.

I put my hand to my head and stared down at the table linen. It was too terrible: us here, having lunch, and Violet . . .

'Listen, Gilly.' Laura reached across the table and held my hand in hers. 'I'm sorry, it must be an awful shock to you. I suppose I thought you knew. You were there when she . . .' She swallowed again, as if she could force down the memories. Violet's screams, the way she writhed and kicked and spat as the nurse dragged her down the stairs, her tear-stained face at the car window.

'After the baby is born, and when the war is over – surely it can't go on for much longer now? – we'll try again. We'll get another lawyer. We'll go and get her, Gilly, I promise. We'll do it together.'

Laura, I saw, wanted me to forgive her for not doing more, for not standing up to her parents, to the doctors, to Emmeline and Cadwallander. But I understood it must have been impossible for her. And she was wrong; I did know what Emmeline was like. Emmeline manipulated those around her until she got what she wanted.

I nodded and squeezed Laura's hand. I wanted to believe it, that perhaps we could still, somehow, rectify what we had done.

Oh, Violet, I thought. *I'm so sorry.*

Chapter Twenty-Four

TWO MONTHS AFTER I'D HAD lunch with Laura, the house next door took a direct hit, killing our neighbours. The houses were terraced and the bomb blew some of our roof off too. I managed to get under the bed and cowered there, my hands over my head as great chunks of plaster and masonry rained down. When it all went quiet, I called out to Moira who told me she was in the hallway. Grateful to hear she was alive, I wriggled out from under the bed, covered in a horrible grey dust that had got in my eyes and mouth. Looking up, I saw the gaping hole in the roof and the dark night sky. After that night, we took rooms above a pub until it was safe to return to the house. I had to write a letter to Aunt Ada explaining what had happened.

Although I had not seen Laura again, I thought often of her promise: *We'll go and get her, Gilly. When the war is over.*

I read the announcement when it appeared in the newspaper:

Mr and Mrs Chester-Barnes are delighted to welcome the arrival of a healthy baby boy to be christened Henry William Bartholomew. Mr Chester-Barnes is the son of eminent businessman Walter Chester-Barnes. Mrs Laura Chester-Barnes is the younger sister of Countess Cadwallander of Chaseley House.

I was pleased for Laura and could picture her siting up in bed in a sun-filled room, surrounded by pillows, holding her tiny son, marvelling at his miniature toes, his new wrinkly skin, the miracle of him, and that he was all hers. Charlie would be there, perched on the end of the bed, grinning in that boyish way of his, gently putting a finger out for the baby to grasp, telling everyone he knew what a cracking little chap he was.

I sent a card, posting it to the address in Richmond. I did not go and visit Laura as she had said I must. I suppose a part of me still felt that perhaps she had only invited me for lunch that day because, after I'd bumped into Charlie, she thought she was obliged to. Charlie obviously knew about Violet, where she was, but I was quite sure he knew nothing else of the secret we shared, of what Laura would be reminded of each time she saw me. I was also incredibly busy at the hospital and overseeing the repairs to the roof and I suppose, for all those reasons, I hadn't gone out of my way to visit Laura.

The war was dragging on and had become a grim normality. There was a man called Ian Farley, a second lieutenant in the navy, who used to take me out when he was home. It started in the usual way, but he had wanted to see me again: wanted, he said, to *get to know me*. We had grown fond of each other. He was easy to be with and I looked forward to his letters which were full of trivial news that was supposed to amuse and reassure me. When he had leave, Ian took me to fancy restaurants with linen napkins and red-shaded lamps on the tables. I still went dancing, but I no longer went home with men. I thought that if the war ever ended and I was able to see more of Ian, something might come of the attachment. He had talked about us getting a place together, getting married. I had only smiled, preferring to keep my feelings to myself for the time being, but I liked the thought of living with him, of seeing him make his coffee every morning, his toothbrush next to mine in the glass by the sink, of watching him go off to work in his civilian clothes, and I knew I wouldn't want to stay at Aunt Ada's forever, especially if she returned from Shropshire.

Despite having Ian in my life, thoughts of Violet, of what had happened to her, plagued me, and I spent many sleepless nights turning it all over in my mind as the guns boomed and the sirens wailed. Could it be possible that Violet really had been unwell? That she did need to be at Bancroft? Was it truly the best place for her? And yet we had told Violet she had done a terrible, terrible thing. Hadn't we? My memories of what had really happened at Thornleigh had become fuzzy. I had shut them out for such a long time that they had taken on an air of dreamlike unreality.

One Wednesday morning in July, I decided to visit Laura and the baby. No longer could I bury my head in the sand and forget what I knew about Violet.

The sun was shining and along the edge of the Anderson shelter Aunt Ada's sunflowers were in full bloom. I thought I might take the train to Richmond, walk around the park, see if Laura was in. If she wasn't, well, it wouldn't matter too much. I'd have had a walk in the sun and seen where she lived which would be interesting enough.

I set off feeling optimistic. I had decided that Laura would be pleased to see me. After all, hadn't she insisted I come over once the baby was born? I realised that it had, in fact, been eight months since the birth. The newborn I'd been imagining would have turned into a chubby, crawling baby boy, no doubt grabbing at everything in sight. I smiled at the thought. I was still desperately searching for justification that we had done the right thing that day in the woods, that by saying nothing, we had somehow saved Laura, enabled her to go on and live the life she'd wanted.

I arrived in Richmond a little after one o'clock. I decided to call on Laura first, thinking we might be able to take the baby out for a walk around the park in his perambulator. The house was quite grand, although I remembered Laura telling me they only had the top floor. Climbing the steps, I rang the bell and waited patiently.

The door was eventually opened by a stern-looking woman with grey hair swept back into a severe bun. She glared down at me.

'Is Laura – Mrs Chester-Barnes – at home?' I asked.

'She isn't taking visitors,' came the curt reply.

I felt cross at this dismissive response. 'If you could tell her it's Gillian Larking, please.'

She pushed the door to and I could hear her climbing the stairs, muttering to herself.

A few minutes later she appeared again and reluctantly held the door open for me. When we reached the top floor, she gestured to a closed door. 'She's in the sitting room.' The woman paused and glanced me over as if assessing me for something. 'It's best not to tire her,' she said, before turning on her heel and marching off.

I shook my head then pushed the door open, finding myself in a large room full of heavy antique furniture that looked as though it had been brought in from somewhere else. I realised it had. The eau de Nil button-back sofa with the dark wood trim had been in the library at Thornleigh. It was a shock to see it. For just a moment I was back there: a fire crackling in the grate, snow softly falling outside the window, Emmeline pacing in front of the fire in one of her long pale dresses, her forehead creased in concentration, a sick, anxious feeling in my stomach.

But then there was Laura rising from a chair over by the open bureau, coming to greet me. She was wearing fashionable loose wide-legged trousers, a silk blouse, and a single strand of pearls at her neck. Her hair had grown almost to her shoulders.

'Gilly,' she said happily. 'I can't believe it's you. How lovely. What are you doing here?' Her pleasure at seeing me appeared to be genuine, although she looked tired.

'I was in the area,' I said, feeling suddenly embarrassed, not wanting to admit I had made a special journey on a whim.

As she hugged me I noticed she had grown quite thin which, after her pregnancy, surprised me.

'I'm sorry about the housekeeper,' she said. 'She's terrifying, isn't she? I keep thinking I ought to let her go but it's difficult to get people these days, and she was good when ...' She trailed off then gave a little nervous laugh. I noticed her face was without colour and although I knew it had been a long winter for all of us, she looked as though she hadn't been outside in a while.

'She is rather frightening,' I agreed.

'Sit down.' Laura gestured to the sofa. 'How lovely to have company. And on such a beautiful day.' She looked absent-mindedly towards the windows.

'I hope I haven't disturbed you,' I said, glancing at the bureau where she had been sitting. I wondered if she had been writing a letter. Perhaps to Charlie.

'Oh, no.' She smiled at me. 'It's been some time, hasn't it? Since we had that delightful lunch.'

'It must be eighteen months or so.'

Laura nodded and fiddled with the cuff of her blouse.

I glanced around the room but could see no sign of the baby. Maybe he was sleeping.

The door opened and the stern housekeeper entered with a tray of tea. She put it on the sideboard, gave me a reproachful look, then quickly left. Laura seemed distracted; she'd hardly noticed the tea tray. I poured for us.

'Thank you,' Laura said when I handed her a little teacup with trailing roses around the rim. 'How have you been, Gilly?' she asked. 'Tell me everything.'

I told her about my work, about the house next door that had been hit. I told her about Ian and Laura gripped my hand and said, 'How wonderful, darling. We must meet him.' I didn't want to talk about myself, but she seemed so keen to hear it all. I wondered if she had been away and had recently returned to London; she didn't seem to know much about what was going on with the war. Perhaps, as with several other people I knew, Laura had stopped listening to the wireless as it made her feel too downhearted.

As we talked I realised there was something different about Laura. It was hard to say exactly what it was. She was more subdued. She'd lost her sparkle. Or at least it had dimmed. I told myself she was probably just tired, the baby was wearing her out, but I couldn't shake the feeling that she had changed in some fundamental way. Like a painting left too long on a windowsill: she had faded slightly.

Laura still hadn't said anything about the baby and I began to feel uneasy. Where was he? I had a horrible, sinking feeling that something dreadful had happened.

'Laura,' I said quietly. 'Where is Henry?'

Laura paused then set her teacup down. 'Well, he's at Wynscott,' she said lightly. 'With Emmeline and Hugh.'

I felt immediately relieved. The baby was fine. Perhaps Laura thought it safer for him to be in the country for a while. Maybe Laura was only in town as Charlie was due leave.

I was thinking all of this when she let out a little sob.

I looked at her, surprised. Her shoulders were shaking and she quickly covered her face with her hands. I moved closer to her and touched her arm. 'Laura. Goodness. I'm sorry.' I couldn't think what I had said to upset her. 'What is it?'

She produced a handkerchief from her sleeve and was dabbing her eyes. 'No, *I'm* sorry.' She sniffed. 'Really, what must you think of me. It's just I haven't had a guest for so long ... I never cry. Really, I don't.'

I sat, blinking at her. I didn't know what to say.

'Is it Charlie?' I asked.

Laura stood and went over to the window where she lifted the sash, letting a burst of cool air into the room. She located a packet of cigarettes on the bureau then lit one with a shaky hand. So she'd taken up smoking again.

'It's everything,' she said finally.

I waited for her to go on but she only stood there, gazing out of the window, taking tiny, quick puffs on her cigarette.

'It's true, I miss Charlie dreadfully.' She paused and took in a deep breath. The smoke from her cigarette curled upwards. 'Although I can't think why he'd be in any rush to return to me,' she said at last.

'Laura.' I shook my head. 'Why ever would you say that?'

She exhaled out of the window and, without shifting her gaze from the sky, said quietly, 'It was fine at first, you know. The first few days. It was wonderful. Everything was perfect.' She went to the open bureau then handed me a photograph in a small silver frame. The photograph showed Laura in a pale dress, looking down at the tiny, swaddled bundle in her arms, blissfully serene, the love for her newborn son radiating out of her.

'It's beautiful,' I said. 'Laura, you look ... wonderful.'

Laura nodded. She took the photograph from me, replaced it in the bureau, then returned to the window.

I held my teacup in my hands, watching her.

'But then it wasn't wonderful anymore,' she said, bringing the cigarette to her lips. 'I couldn't work it out, why I was feeling like I was. I had this constant terrifying sense of dread. It ... surrounded me.'

I waited for her to go on. Outside, a bird was chirping. Someone rang their bicycle bell.

'I felt afraid *all* the time,' she said.

I watched as she tapped ash out of the window then turned to look at me. 'I don't know how to describe it, Gilly. It was as if every drawer in my head had been flung open and all my undergarments and goodness knows what else were flying about untethered.'

I knitted my brow, trying to process what she was telling me.

Laura stared at a patch on sunlight on the floor. 'You know, Gilly, I sat on the end of my bed one morning and realised I didn't know how to put my blouse on.' She took another long drag on her cigarette and turned back to the window. 'I couldn't stand for him to be near me,' she said softly.

'Who?' I asked.

Laura glanced at me then looked away again. 'Henry,' she said.

I frowned and she must have seen.

'I didn't understand either,' she said quickly. 'I had wanted him so much, you see. I loved knowing he was there, growing inside me, waiting to meet him. And when I saw him, well, as I said, it was all wonderful at first, but then it wasn't.'

'And this came on after Henry was born?'

She nodded, then crushed the cigarette into an ashtray on the windowsill. 'I know it's dreadful to say,' she whispered, 'but I didn't want him anymore.' Laura paused. 'I wished he hadn't been born.' She turned and looked at me, her eyes big and round. 'That's what you've got to understand, Gilly. I mean, who would think such a thing? They'd put him in my arms and I thought I was going to die. The feeling came over me again: the panic, the fear. I couldn't *breathe*. I felt as if my chest was going to explode into a million pieces.'

'But I'm sure lots of new mothers—'

'No,' she said, cutting me off. 'It got worse. I went on for weeks and weeks, living with those dreadful feelings. The nursemaid had to do everything. I could barely look after myself, let alone Henry. I could tell she thought I was unnatural, the worst mother she'd ever known. Then I started to have these thoughts ...'

331

I stood and walked slowly towards her. 'Laura, what do you mean? What kind of thoughts?'

'Well,' she said, letting out a nervous laugh, 'I thought the walls were speaking to me.' She shook her head, then stared blankly at a spot on the windowsill. 'It sounds absurd now, doesn't it? But that's what I thought. Then I told Charlie I had been given the devil's child as a punishment.' She looked at me and I could see her eyes filling with tears. 'You know,' she whispered, 'because of Robin, because of what I did. Of course, Charlie didn't understand. He didn't know what I was talking about.'

I took her hand. 'You know that's ridiculous,' I said.

She nodded. 'I do *now*. But it was different then. I was confused all the time. I had all these terrible thoughts rushing about in my head.'

'What did the doctor say?'

She gazed at me. 'I wouldn't let Charlie call anyone. I didn't want a doctor. I was frightened. After what happened to Violet . . .'

She gave me a desperate look, then crossed the room and sat on the sofa. 'You never saw Violet there, Gilly. You don't know what it was like. I begged them not to call any doctors. I said I just needed time and rest, but still I knew something terrible was happening to me, that Henry wasn't safe with me. I had more terrible thoughts. Truly awful ones. That I'd throw him out the window or stab him with a knife. It was like Violet, really . . . You remember, how she always thought she might do something bad, but she never did?'

I nodded.

'Only I didn't think of that at the time. I was wrapped up in all my horrible visions.'

332

Neither of us said anything.

'Emmeline came,' Laura said, finally. 'They organised everything, Emmeline and Hugh. They stepped in like they always do, taking over, making plans. Charlie had taken leave when I was unwell, but he had to go back in the end. Hugh and Emmeline found a nurse for me. They sent Mrs Hinchcliffe over from Wynscott. That's the housekeeper,' she whispered. 'She's stayed on. And then they took Henry back with them. They said it wasn't safe for me to have him here.' She paused and stared into her lap. 'They were right, of course.' She shook her head. 'It took such a long time,' she said. 'But after a while I *did* begin to get better.'

'You were very brave,' I said. 'Going through something like that on your own.'

Laura gave a small smile. 'It was as if, finally, a layer of the fear and the dread lifted. I began to have hours when I felt quite normal. I took to walking in the afternoons. I walked everywhere, all over London. Just walking and walking. All those bombed houses, craters in the road, air raid wardens yelling at me, I hardly noticed them. The walks seemed to help.'

'And now?' I asked.

She smiled at me. 'I'm better now,' she said firmly. 'Much better. But Gilly.' She gripped my hands in hers. 'Oh, Gilly, I miss him terribly, you can't imagine. It's a constant pain in my heart. I simply can't explain it. I've got his little cot next door, his perambulator. All his favourite things. Oh, you wouldn't believe how much I miss him. The way he used to wriggle up my chest, his little milky burps, how he'd throw his arms above his head when I put him down in the cot.' She dabbed at her eyes with a handkerchief. 'I was so grateful to Emmeline and

Hugh at the time. Knowing Henry was safe and being looked after. Both Charlie and I were grateful. But ...' Her chin trembled and I squeezed her hand. 'Now,' she said, her voice breaking, 'now I'd like him to come home.'

From the room below, I could hear a clattering sound, footsteps pacing the floor. The edges of the curtains fluttered in the breeze where Laura had left the window open.

'How long has it been since you saw Henry?' I asked.

'It's been seven months,' she said calmly.

I drew in a breath. 'Have you spoken to Emmeline? Does she know you're better? Does she know you'd be able to cope with Henry now?'

Laura looked into her lap. 'I've tried to call her, but she always puts me off. Last time I called, she said it wouldn't be a good idea to upset Henry's routine.' She exhaled deeply. 'That's why I have to go over there. It's the only way.' She looked at me, her eyes suddenly clear and focused. 'I want you to help me, Gilly. I realised it as soon as you walked into the room. I haven't been able to do it on my own, but now that you're here.' She smiled at me. 'I know you'll be able to help me.'

I was taken aback by this. 'Don't you want to wait for Charlie?'

She shook her head. 'Charlie believes Henry is safe with his aunt and uncle in the countryside. He's risking his life every night, Gilly. Flying right into the heart of the enemy. I can't think about it ... I certainly can't write to Charlie and upset him. He needs my letters to be cheerful when he's coping with so much. I can't tell him how desperate I am, how this is tearing me apart, not when Charlie believes I'm so much better. I can't worry him like that right now. But I also can't wait any longer for Henry. It's eating me up inside. I can't go on like this. I *need* him, Gilly. He's my son.'

'When?' I said, blinking at her. 'When do you want to go?'

'The last Saturday of the month,' Laura said firmly. 'Hugh always visits his mother on the last Saturday of the month and Emmeline never joins him. I think it will be better if only Emmeline is there.'

This was only ten days away.

She gripped my hands in hers. 'Please say you'll help me, Gilly.'

Chapter Twenty-Five

I TOLD THE WARD SISTER I had a family matter to attend to. I rarely asked for time off and she was happy to let me go for the day as long as I could find another nurse to cover my shift.

'Can you drive?' Laura asked as soon as I arrived in Richmond. She was in her hat and gloves, ready to go.

'I can drive,' I told her. Aunt Ada had taught me when I'd first arrived in London. At that time, I had no real desire to learn but she had insisted, telling me a woman could never be independent unless she drove. Aunt Ada was one of a generation of women who, after the Great War, had learned how to make a life without a husband. There were times when I quite admired her. She had sat in the passenger seat of her Ford, discreetly holding onto her hat as I blundered around the streets of West London. I passed my test but, when the war broke out, Aunt Ada took her car down to Shropshire and I hadn't driven since.

'Great,' said Laura. 'I can too. Charlie taught me. But I don't have a licence.'

'I'd better drive then,' I said.

The Beauford was open top and we wrapped our scarves around our heads to stop our hair from blowing about. I borrowed a pair of Laura's sunglasses.

The roads out of London were quiet. Petrol was still on ration and people weren't supposed to be making unnecessary journeys. I didn't ask Laura how she'd managed to get the fuel to take us to Wynscott.

It was a hot day. My bare legs stuck to the leather car seat. The hedgerows were full of elderflowers and meadowsweet. Laura sat quietly next to me, holding the map and a brown teddy bear.

'Henry's,' she explained.

When we got into Buckinghamshire, she began to direct me along the narrow lanes towards Wynscott. 'Turn right here at the postbox. Yes, that's it, I remember this lane. I'm sure it's left just here.'

Laura was gripping the teddy bear tightly. 'What if he doesn't like me?' she asked softly.

I glanced at her, then looked back at the road. We were driving through a village, passing a small green with a duck pond and weeping willows. 'Of course he'll like you,' I said gently. 'You're his mother.'

'That's what I keep telling myself.'

When the house came into view, Laura pointed it out. Red brick. Four tall chimneys. Pointed arches over the windows. It was a commanding presence in the surrounding countryside and I remembered how Laura had said Emmeline referred to it as 'our little country cottage'.

We drove up the long driveway, parked at the front of the house, then walked up the path lined with laurel hedges. The sun was shining, casting shadows from the mature trees across the grass.

Laura gazed up at the house.

She knocked on the door using the large brass knocker and we waited, Laura with her handbag hooked over her arm. She was still clutching the teddy bear.

I was surprised when Emmeline herself opened the door. She was wearing a belted cinnamon-coloured dress with a pair of matching heeled shoes. The dress was calf-length, as was the fashion, and I remembered those long, pale Edwardian-style dresses she used to wear. She looked the same, only a little more refined. Her grace, poise and that inherent coolness she possessed were all still visible.

Emmeline was clearly startled. She blinked at us then raised an eyebrow.

On seeing her, I felt a surge of emotions. I despised Emmeline for what she had done to Violet, for how she had drawn me in and convinced me she knew what was best for me, but I also felt a strange elation at seeing her again. I angrily swallowed it. How could I still admire this woman? After all she had done? No, all I felt towards Emmeline was a white-hot rage. I hated her.

'Laura.' Emmeline's voice faltered but then she smiled, recovering. 'And Gillian too. What a surprise. You should have let me know you were coming.' She stepped back to let us in, still smiling, albeit a little stiffly. We stood in the large vaulted hallway. Up the stairs was a gallery landing. I could see Laura glancing around, no doubt wondering where Henry was. The house smelled faintly of lilies and furniture polish.

'You're lucky I heard you knock. We've been in the garden.' Emmeline smiled brightly then turned to me. 'It's been a long time, hasn't it, Gillian?'

I felt my jaw tense. 'It has been a while,' I said tersely, remembering again how much I had wanted both Emmeline and Laura to like me, to be my friends, my sisters. And still I was entangled with them, because of what had happened, because of what we had done.

Emmeline looked from me to Laura. 'Well ... I'm so glad you two are still in touch. I didn't know.'

I could feel the colour rising in my cheeks. 'So you've been here since the start of the war? How nice,' I said, with a hint of sarcasm.

If she caught it, Emmeline decided to ignore my tone. She waved a hand in the air, gesturing to the house. 'It's suited us perfectly these last few years. It was rather drab when we arrived but we made the best of it. I took some of the curtains from Thornleigh.' She stopped and looked at me again. 'You've grown up, you know. It suits you.'

I could feel myself blushing against my will. Damn Emmeline. I reminded myself that her opinion of me meant nothing to me now. It was difficult to believe that after all the time that had passed, all we had gone through together that winter, she was standing here making pleasantries with us. Remembering what we were here to do, I felt a flutter of anxiety in my chest.

'I'll ask Nellie to bring us some lemonade, or perhaps tea if she can manage it. Nellie's new. Still getting to grips with things. It's so hard to find girls nowadays.' Emmeline paused, studied us closely. 'I wish you'd have let me know you were coming. Still, there's a little of the honey cake left. We've got

eggs here at least. One of the benefits of living in the country.'
She smiled again. 'It *is* lovely to see you, Gillian. You'll have
to tell me what you've been doing with yourself. I've always
thought fondly of your stay with us.'

My stomach tightened.

'We don't want tea,' said Laura through gritted teeth. She
had been standing quietly next to me, clutching her large black
handbag and the brown teddy. 'Where is Henry, Emmi?'

'Henry?' said Emmeline 'Well, he's up in the nursery with
Nanny. It's almost time for his nap.'

Laura turned on her heel and began to march up the
staircase.

Emmeline's face darkened. 'Really, Lolly,' she called after her,
'it's most unsuitable for you to come over here like this—'

Laura turned around and glared at her sister. 'I've come for
Henry,' she said. 'And I don't care if it's *unsuitable* for you. He's
my son.' She was at the top of the stairs now, looking wildly
in both directions.

Emmeline brushed past me – I caught a whiff of her perfume,
a musky floral – and ascended the stairs after Laura who was
dashing along the landing, frantically pushing doors open.

The nursery was a large bedroom at the back of the house.
The walls had been papered above the dado with a circus design;
lions and lion tamers, elephants on tiny stools, scantily clad
women on trapezes. There was a cot, a nursing chair, a rocking
horse and an open toy chest. Henry was sitting on the floor
holding a toy car, waving it in the direction of his mouth. A
young woman in a grey pinafore dress was kneeling next to
him, presumably the nanny. 'That's it, Henry,' she was saying,
'broom broom.'

Laura gasped and put her hand over her mouth. 'Oh, *Henry*.'

The nanny stood, alarmed.

'Oh my God, he's sitting up,' said Laura. She took a step towards Henry but Emmeline darted in front of us and stood next to Henry as if shielding him from danger. He dropped the car and tugged at Emmeline's skirt.

'Mama,' he said.

Laura gasped.

'His first word,' said Emmeline proudly.

Henry looked from us to Emmeline, unsure.

Laura had gone pale. 'You've taught him to call you that?' she said, her voice hoarse.

Emmeline sighed then turned to the nanny who was watching us all. 'That will be all for now, Maud. You may be excused.'

After giving us one final curious glance, the girl quickly left the room.

Laura was visibly shaking. She bent down, dropping the teddy on the floor, her handbag still hooked into the crook of her elbow. She held her arms out. 'Henry, darling ...'

Henry whimpered and hid behind Emmeline's skirt. After a moment Laura stood up, rejected, her legs trembling.

'Really, Laura,' Emmeline said. 'This is most selfish of you. Can't you see it's upsetting for Henry? I think it would be best if you left.'

Laura stared at her sister, her eyes oddly bright and feverish. 'I'm not going anywhere. Not without Henry.'

Emmeline smiled thinly. 'You're forgetting you aren't well. Your nerves—'

'There's nothing wrong with my nerves anymore. You've no right to keep him here.'

'I'm afraid that you are mistaken,' said Emmeline curtly. 'It's all in order. Well, it will be soon. Hugh and I are sorting out the particulars.'

'What are you *talking about*,' said Laura.

I put my hand on Laura's arm, trying to calm her, but she shook me off.

'You must understand,' said Emmeline. 'To Henry, I *am* his mother. You couldn't cope, remember? We've got everything Henry needs here. He'll have a wonderful life. Hugh's buying him a pony. He'll go to Eton, of course, when he's old enough. Just like Hugh did.'

'You're mad,' Laura said softly.

'You can't do this,' I said to Emmeline. 'It isn't right. It isn't ...'

Emmeline ignored me. 'Don't you see, Lolly – all we can give Henry that you can't? He'll have the best of everything here with us. Don't you want that for him? Don't you want him to have the very best?'

Henry had begun to crawl across the rug and, despite the tension in the room, was now making a grab at something in his toy chest. 'Gigi,' he said, triumphantly pulling out a small white toy rabbit.

Laura watched him then turned to Emmeline again. 'I know I wasn't well,' she said. 'But I'm better now. I'm much better.' She looked back at Henry and I could see how painful it was for her to watch him and not be able to put her arms around him, to breathe him in. I felt a stabbing in my chest.

'A mother should want what's best for her child,' said Emmeline.

Laura stared at her. 'Of course I want what's best for Henry,' she snapped.

'Really? Because one wouldn't know it to hear you talk. You're really being very silly about all this.'

Laura blinked. 'He's my *child*.'

'This is Henry's home,' Emmeline went on. 'This is all he has ever known. It could be quite damaging to him, to drag him away from everything that is familiar and safe. It could have implications.'

A flash of confusion crossed Laura's face. Then she shook her head. 'I won't let you do this,' she whispered.

'And you've got to think about what it would mean for Henry – having a mother of unsound mind. Mothers need to be strong and let's face it, Lolly, you've never really been that, have you? Children have to come first. They need stability, security and moderation. You've always been a deeply unsettled person.'

Laura's mouth dropped open. 'But I am settled. I'm married. I—'

'And what about your drinking? The stealing?'

'I won't listen to this nonsense,' said Laura fiercely.

Emmeline sighed. She bent down, stroked the top of Henry's fluffy head, then turned to look at us again. 'This really doesn't have to be difficult, Lolly,' she said wearily. 'Of course you can *make it* difficult, if you must. You can make it a strain for everyone. But in the end, nothing will change. We've got the doctors' records. We did call a doctor, you know. A friend of Hugh's. He observed you several times. We can make a case, if we need to. Hugh's friend can testify. It's quite clear you're unfit.'

Laura took a step back. Her whole body was trembling. Her hands fluttered and her eyes darted from Henry to Emmeline.

I realised what Emmeline had done. Of course, Emmeline always had a plan. She always got what she wanted. I felt a terrible rage boiling inside me. It was all Emmeline's fault: Violet, and Frank. Now poor Laura.

My heart was pounding. I lifted my chin. 'You can't do this,' I said to Emmeline. 'It's a terrible thing to do. Henry belongs with Laura and Charlie.'

Emmeline raised an eyebrow. 'If you don't mind, Gillian. This is a family matter.' She cocked her head. 'But then you always did want to get involved, didn't you?'

My stomach hardened. I could feel myself biting down on my bottom lip.

'You think you're the picture of innocence, Gillian,' Emmeline went on. 'You tell yourself you were led along, that you had no choice. But the truth is, your life before us was quite colourless. After what happened that day in the woods, for the first time in your life, you felt as though you were actually a part of something, didn't you?'

'I don't know what you're talking about,' I said. But her words had made an impression on me. That winter. It had been like a camera lens snapping into sharp focus. I had felt life rushing at me a million miles an hour, just as I'd always longed for. It was both terrible and nerve-wracking, but also electric. What did that say about me? But *of course* I wished none of it had ever happened. Didn't I? This, I reminded myself, was what Emmeline did. She planted seeds of doubt in your mind then watched them grow.

'Besides,' said Emmeline, turning to Laura, 'Henry will stay here with me because you owe me, remember? After what I did for you. Covering for you like that.'

Laura brought a hand to her face.

'You really have no idea, both of you. How close those police officers were to working out that it must have been us. *One* of us,' she said, looking pointedly at Laura.

'I don't owe you anything,' Laura whispered.

Emmeline laughed. 'Oh, but you do, Lolly, don't you?' Her face changed. 'Don't you see? You killed my son and now I must have yours.'

I froze, my mouth falling open. I looked back and forth between the sisters, astonished.

Emmeline was watching me. 'Oh, no one told you?' she said breezily. 'Of course Mother wanted it all covered up, wanted him sent away. But Father wasn't keen on it. He thought we should bring Robin up in the house, give him an education. Poor Father, he'd always wanted a boy. And Mary was there, of course. She'd lost her own child late in her pregnancy but no one in the village knew.' Emmeline shrugged. 'It had to be kept a secret. I had to marry Hugh, you see, to save Thornleigh.'

'You *hated* Robin,' said Laura through her tears. 'You could never even bear to look at him. The only thing you ever did for him was name him.'

'Well, I didn't get much of a chance to do anything for him, did I?' said Emmeline flatly. 'Seeing as you killed him.'

I squeezed my eyes tightly shut then opened them again. This wasn't happening.

Laura was reaching into her handbag, pulling something out. She clutched the gun with both hands, pointing it at Emmeline.

For a moment, Emmeline looked startled, but then she laughed. 'Goodness, is that Father's service revolver? Wherever did you get it?'

'I'm taking him back,' said Laura, through gritted teeth. 'You can't have my son. I won't let you. I'm not leaving without Henry.'

'And what are you going to do, Lolly, shoot me?' Emmeline looked amused. She held herself perfectly still and upright.

I could feel my heartbeat loud in my ears. The barrel of the gun was right next to my elbow, hovering there in Laura's shaking hands.

'Yes,' said Laura, calmly, 'if I have to.'

'Laura ...' I tried, but my voice came out a faint croak.

'Yes, listen to your friend,' said Emmeline. 'She covered for you too, remember?'

Laura ignored Emmeline. She lifted the gun, her index finger hovering over the trigger. 'Give him to us,' she said, 'and then we'll leave.'

'And I'll call the police,' said Emmeline in a bored tone. 'I shouldn't think you'll get very far.'

'You can't call the police. He's my son.'

'I shall tell them, of course, that you're quite mad. It runs in the family, don't forget. And we've got the doctor's statement. You'll be institutionalised. Charlie won't have any say in it, I'm afraid.' She paused. 'Or, if you shoot me, you'll go to prison for murder. Henry will be without you either way.'

Laura glanced at Henry who had abandoned his rabbit and was watching us all, sensing something was amiss. His chin wobbled.

Emmeline was right, and we both knew it.

'Laura ...' This time she blinked: my voice seemed to have got through to her. I placed my hand over hers then began to gently lower the gun. At first she resisted but then I felt her hand go slack. Once the gun was pointing at the floor, I carefully removed it from her.

'Thank you, Gillian,' said Emmeline.

Laura fell to her knees and began to weep, covering her face with her hands. After a moment she managed to pull herself to her feet and fled the room. I could hear her running down the stairs. She'd left the teddy bear abandoned on the floor.

I looked at Emmeline. She had bent down to pick up Henry who had begun to make little whimpering noises. 'There, there,' she was saying. 'Just a bit of silliness, darling. It's all right, she's gone now.'

I held onto the bannister for support, the gun still in my hand, as I made my way down the staircase and out the front door after Laura.

I found her sitting in the passenger seat of the car, staring blankly ahead. I climbed in beside her. The sun was still shining, the steering wheel hot to the touch. I didn't know what to say and so I said nothing. Wrapping the gun in my scarf, I placed it carefully under my seat then began to back slowly out of the drive.

What could we have done? Emmeline had thought it all through as always. Would Laura and Charlie try to fight Emmeline and Hugh when Charlie was back? Surely they could afford lawyers? No doubt Emmeline and Hugh would have better ones. But Laura would fight. She had to. There was nothing more we could do today but Laura would get Henry back. She was his mother. I had to tell myself this.

Laura did not cry again. At one point on our journey back to London she cleared her throat and said, her voice oddly chipper, 'I shall have to place an advert in the paper about the perambulator. Henry will be too big for it soon. Someone else will want it, especially in these times. It isn't at all fair of me to hang onto it.'

'Laura,' I said gently. 'You don't need to think of anything like that now.'

She said nothing else.

As we drove, I thought about the gun under my seat. I decided I would take it with me and drop it into the Thames.

We arrived in Richmond. Laura took the car keys and thanked me politely for driving, as if we had been out enjoying a pleasant afternoon in the countryside together. She seemed calm, almost serene.

I should have known.

Five days after our visit to Wynscott Laura received a telegram telling her Charlie's plane had been lost. I saw his name in the paper. *Missing in action.* I asked Moira if, working for the Air Ministry, she could see what she could find out. She had returned from work, shaken her head grimly. Charlie, she said, had been on his way home after completing a mission over the Ruhr when he was picked off by a Messerschmitt. He had managed to keep the plane in the air for quite some time but had eventually gone down over the North Sea. It had been almost ten days and none of the crew had been found. 'I'm afraid there's no chance at all,' Moira had said sadly. 'I am sorry for your friend.'

I tried to get in touch with Laura but when I went over to the house, the housekeeper told me, firmly, that she was seeing no one at all.

Three weeks later she drove her car off a cliff.

Part Four

Part Four

Chapter Twenty-Six

1999

Dear Mrs McCune,

I am writing to you at the request of my aunt, Violet Claybourne. This is a somewhat tricky letter to write. I have only recently become acquainted with my aunt. Up until six months ago, I knew I had one aunt who died in a car accident during the war – I have a picture of her holding me when I was just a few days old – but knew of no others.

I am writing as I believe you might have known my mother, and my aunts, and I am hoping you will be able to help us.

Six months ago I received a telephone call from an administrator at a hospital in Wiltshire. They informed me that, due to the new Community Care Act, they were closing, and that all of their patients, some of them who had been at the hospital for a great number of years, would no longer be able to live there under the care and supervision of the hospital staff. They told me they were, in fact, one of the last remaining institutions of their kind in the country.

I suspected they were looking for me to support some charity or other, but the lady on the other end of the telephone told me I had misunderstood the reason for her call. She was calling, she said, to check when I would be able to collect my aunt, or if I, as her next of kin, would be planning to organise her care. Of course, I told her, there must be some mistake. I didn't have an aunt. But she was quite insistent. They had all the paperwork. I was the only relative of Miss Violet Marie Claybourne they had been able to make contact with.

I won't bore you with the details, but after various lengthy investigations on my side, I came to understand that the information was correct, that Violet Claybourne is indeed the third child of my grandparents, Olivia and Giles Claybourne. As you can imagine, I was thoroughly startled to learn I had a living aunt, even more so that no one had thought to tell me. But I understand, of course, that those were different times.

My Aunt Violet has now been living with my wife, Phyllis, and I for the last four months, although we plan to find suitable accommodation for her before the end of the year.

Going to see my aunt that first time, we didn't know what to expect. You see, the hospital where she had been living, Bancroft, was a hospital for the mentally ill. We were surprised to find her quite calm, aware of what was happening to her, and of the hospital's closure. It was only me she was unaware of, having never been informed of my existence. We had that in common. If I may be frank, Violet was not at all as we had imagined. You would not know, by looking at her or talking with her, that my aunt is mentally unwell. She occasionally becomes confused, but that is to be expected, given her age, and the recent changes in her daily life.

Violet has said very little to us about the past, about how she came to be at Bancroft, or what her life there was like. She did, however, recently mention you, telling us you were a friend from long ago and asking if we might be able to find you.

This investigation into your whereabouts took a little time and effort but, seeing as it is the only request Violet has made of us, we felt we should oblige.

My aunt was delighted to learn that we had an address for you. She would have written herself but her eyes are not so good these days. I cannot stress how much we would love to hear from you. We are also living in London. Perhaps we could meet? I would certainly like to learn more about my aunt and how she came to be admitted to the hospital. As her new official carer, I requested access to my aunt's medical records but they are scant, to say the least. There is no one else we know of who would have been around at the time, and it is our hope that talking to you will help us shed light on the mystery. Violet is silent on the subject and, at this point, we are fearful of probing too much and upsetting her. I also know she would very much like to see you. It would be a comfort to her, I believe, to speak with someone from the past, someone who knew her before her time at Bancroft.

I look forward to hearing from you in due course.

Yours sincerely,

Henry Cadwallander.

My first thought had been that it simply couldn't be true. I put the letter back in its envelope and hid it behind the fruit bowl for several weeks. Was this because to accept the letter's truth was to finally have confirmation of what I had known, on some level, all along – that the events of the winter of 1938 had determined the next sixty years of Violet's existence, had completely obliterated, for her, the luxury of an ordinary life?

* * *

Several days after my impromptu return to Thornleigh Hall, I sit at my kitchen table in the warm, spring sunlight, the letter spread out before me. White daffodils with yellow trumpets stand in a vase on my windowsill. The kitchen smells of toast and marmalade.

Could Violet really have been in Bancroft all this time? The thought is inconceivable, and yet it is here in front of me in black and white.

Who is Violet now, after all these years? Does she really want to see me? I find it hard to believe. And yet it is written there, in Henry's letter ... I realise that, if Violet does want to see me, at the very least, I owe her that.

* * *

The café is on the top floor of a central London department store. Henry's suggestion. He needed, he told me, to do a little shopping, 'pick up a few bits' was, I think, how he phrased it. Would I be able to meet Violet for a cup of tea? He would remain in the department store should I need anything. Violet, he told me, was coping much better now with what he referred to as 'the outside world'. They had done a few dry runs and she was apparently comfortable in cafés. He would collect Violet when he was finished with his shopping. He would be no more than an hour and would leave his mobile telephone number with me in case I should need him. I did not tell Henry I had no mobile telephone of my own, having never seen the need to invest in one.

I arrive at the café first. I hate being late and did not want to rush, my nerves already fraught. It is not a good idea, anyway, to rush anywhere at seventy-five. That's the one thing no one ever tells you about getting older: your balance goes. Rushing around is for the young. I feel heavier these days too, which is absurd because I am sure there is less of me; my bones are losing density, my hair is thinner. I was never tall but I'm sure I am shrinking, like a pair of woolly socks left out in the rain. Still the heaviness. I am reminded of an old piece of rock – one of those slabs that geologists or whoever they are, study. The layers of time are pressing down on me.

I sit at a table for two in the most secluded corner I can find, watching a mother with a toddler as she tries to pierce her child's juice carton, the child wriggling around on its chair, climbing onto the table. It's almost twelve o'clock and the café is full of ladies of a similar age to me in twos and threes, wearing beige cardigans, many of them already tucking into lunch. These days the ladies no longer wear hats and gloves, but they still lunch. Laura would be pleased.

I've been feeling nauseous for days, ever since I picked up the telephone and spoke to Henry Cadwallander. My muscles are twitchy, I haven't been sleeping well, I'm sure I am experiencing heart palpitations. Subjecting myself to such anxiety cannot be a good thing at my age. You never know what small instability of the body might finish you off, which blood vessel might rupture, major artery clog, or what might finally nudge that silently festering clot up to the brain. Sitting here in the café, waiting for Violet, I have the urge to unfasten the top button of my blouse, let a little air in, but no one wants to see more of a mature lady's neck than is necessary.

Then I see him. A man in his mid-fifties wearing an expensive-looking shirt and jacket. Hair greying at the temples. Blue eyes. Still handsome. He smiles and it is a smile I recognise. *Hullo, Gilly. I thought it was you.* For just a moment I am nineteen years old. A man in uniform crossing the street, coming towards me. But of course it isn't Charlie. Charlie never got the chance to grow grey.

I stand, a little unsteadily.

'Gillian?' Henry Cadwallander asks, unsure.

'Yes,' I croak, attempting to clear my throat.

Then I notice an old lady, slightly dumpy and with mad white hair, standing behind Henry, wearing a maroon raincoat.

I try to move forward but my body doesn't obey me and I find I am trapped between the table and the hard plastic chair, my mouth open like a fish.

'This is Violet,' Henry says, stepping aside, producing her like a magic trick. 'My aunt.'

If we're stuck together we may as well stick together.

'Yes,' I say stupidly, because it is. A changed Violet, but still very much Violet.

Violet looks at me, her expression difficult to read. 'Hello, Gillian.'

I try to speak but find I am unable to form any words. I manage, at least, to shut my mouth.

'Well,' says Henry glancing from me to Violet. 'I expect you two will have some catching up to do.' He winces slightly, as if remembering why this would be so, but then he bumbles on. 'I'll be in electronics, should you need anything. Or perhaps menswear. But I expect you'll stay here, won't you? Shall we say an hour, and then I'll be back?'

Like small children, we both nod.

Once Henry has gone, Violet glances at the empty table and frowns. 'You haven't ordered anything?'

'Oh, no,' I say. 'You have to go up and order.' I gesture towards the counter where a few people are moving trays along, peering at the jacket potatoes, chilli con carne and lasagne.

Violet follows my gaze and, for a moment, she looks perplexed. Then she breaks into a smile. 'Like school,' she says. Before I can reply she asks, 'Tea, then?'

'Yes, but let me—'

'I'll go. You stay here,' she says firmly, as if concerned I might disappear.

'At least let me get this.' I reach for my purse, uncomfortable with the thought of Violet buying me a cup of tea.

'No,' she insists. 'Anyway, it's on Henry.' She moves off towards the counter, and I have no option but to wait for her to return. I study the grey tabletop but find myself sneaking little glances at Violet as she shuffles along in the queue. It really is her, the Violet I once knew, radiating out of this old woman with curly, snow-white hair and bright green eyes. The same frown, the same quick, spritely movements, the same voice even.

She returns to the table with a tray, carefully puts it down and pulls out a chair.

'You look the same,' she says, finally.

'So do you.'

She smiles and begins to pour the tea.

I watch her, wondering how on earth to begin. 'How is it? I ask. 'At Henry's?'

'Oh, it's fine,' she said cheerfully. 'I've got my own room. Isn't that nice?'

There is something childlike about her: the delight she takes in passing me my teacup and setting the milk jug on the table, the thrill of having her own room. I realise that, for the rest of us, lives have been lived: marriages, divorces, children, jobs, travel, illness and loss, experiences that irrevocably change a person, but for Violet time has stood still.

I watch her open a sugar packet and tip the contents into her tea. She reaches for the second packet then hesitates and gives me a questioning glance. 'You don't want this, do you?'

I shake my head. I haven't taken sugar in my tea since before the war.

'Funny, sugar coming in packets. Everything is in packaging now. Even vegetables. Henry's fridge is full of strange foods. I had an avocado yesterday,' she says proudly. 'At Bancroft, our food was served to us, so I never saw how it all arrives wrapped up in plastic these days. And there wasn't a lot of variation; cottage pie on Monday nights, beef on Tuesday, fish and chips on a Friday ...' She takes a sip of tea. 'We weren't allowed sugar in our tea.'

'It must be so strange,' I say. 'After all that time—'

She raises an eyebrow. 'It's certainly that.'

What can I possibly say to Violet? How can we begin to discuss what happened to her? My breathing is rapid. I am half expecting her to throw the teapot at me.

She clears her throat. 'It's the talking I'm still getting used to. I've never talked as much.'

'You always talked a lot.' I hesitate. 'When I knew you – before, I mean.'

She smiles. 'Yes, I did, didn't I? I suppose that must have changed.'

She takes another sip from her steaming cup of tea.

'I was worried at first,' she says. 'About leaving Bancroft. It was my whole life, you see.' She pauses, lowering her gaze. 'I thought I would end up on the streets. I thought I'd most likely starve or freeze to death. I didn't know how I was going to live. But then they contacted Henry.' She looks up at me.

There is a thickness in my throat. I think, suddenly, of all she has missed: refrigeration, television, miniskirts, The Beatles, the Moon landing, punk rock, the Berlin Wall, *Neighbours*. It's mind-boggling.

'"Your nephew," they said. "Your sister Emmeline's son."' She pauses, takes another sip of tea. 'But of course he isn't Emmeline's.'

'No,' I say.

She looks closely at me and my face tingles under her scrutiny. If only I had tried harder. If only I hadn't given up. It had seemed impossible at the time. I had no legal right to try to get Violet out, and Emmeline would have fought me at every turn. Still, I know I failed Violet. I tug at the sleeve of my cardigan. 'How did you know?' I ask. 'About Henry, I mean?'

'Well, he looks just like Charlie Chester-Barnes, doesn't he? Only older, of course. And then I heard about Laura.'

I take in a deep, shuddery breath. 'You mean, you didn't know?'

She shakes her head. 'No one thought to tell me. I never thought it strange Laura didn't visit as no one visited.'

'But surely, Emmeline . . .'

Violet gives me a small, sad smile. 'Emmeline washed her hands of me a long time ago. She erased me.'

'She didn't *ever* visit?' My voice trembles.

Violet gives me a steady look. 'It was a big shock,' she says. 'To learn of Laura's death.'

I feel light-headed. Laura drove off that cliff fifty-six years ago and yet, for Violet, the grief is evidently still new and raw. All that time, she hadn't known a thing. How could Emmeline not have *told* her?

'I tried,' I say, a hint of desperation in my tone. 'After the war. I telephoned and said I wanted to visit you. They told me it would upset you, that you weren't to have visitors, that you – weren't well.' I stared into my tea. 'Then, a few years later, I tried again. They wouldn't even confirm you were still there. I thought perhaps you'd left.'

'Nope,' says Violet, playing with the sugar packet. 'I was still there. I think Emmeline and Hugh made sure I didn't receive any visitors, and the hospital wasn't exactly keen on it. Most people there were like me. Either without relatives or with relatives who wished to forget about them.'

It hits me, full on in the stomach, as if for the first time: the utter pointlessness of it all, the life Violet should have had, and the life she had actually lived. 'I'm so sorry,' I whisper.

Violet shrugs. 'I got used to it. Bancroft was my home. They asked me once, I think it was in the early eighties, if I wanted to leave, and I said I wasn't sure. You see, by then Bancroft was all I knew. And with no one on the outside to help me, well, how could I leave? How could I ever learn to do all the things for myself that had been done for me ever since I'd arrived? I wasn't always unhappy. We had a bakery, and a garden with fruit trees. We kept chickens. I loved my chickens. Percy and Matilda were my favourites. Only Percy was a girl, of course. And the man with the library trolley used to come on a Wednesday. We had a television. I learned a lot from the television,' she says thoughtfully.

My stomach clenches. 'You make it sound quite nice,' I say faintly.

She gives me a sharp look. 'It wasn't always. People died. Quite often. And every now and then a warden would take against you for some reason or other and make your life hell.'

Violet tears open the packet of biscuits she'd bought and offers me one. Ginger nuts. I shake my head.

She takes a small bite, chews and swallows. 'They did terrible things to me there, Gilly, if you really want to know. Especially at first. They strapped me down and electrocuted me. We all used to dread it. You never knew, you see, when they were going to do it. They'd say "No breakfast for you today. It's your turn for treatment. Keep your nightgown on."' She looks down at her hands. 'I can still smell it. The spirit solution they tipped onto cotton wool and held against our temples. It used to drip into my ears. I can't stand anything wet in my ears now.'

I wince.

'I used to do a lot of the cleaning, especially in the earlier years. The wards, the day room, the kitchen. I worried about germs. And cleaning kept me occupied. I would pray that if I could just mop the floor well enough, perhaps they'd let me off treatment, but they never did.'

'That's awful,' I whisper.

'And there was talk of an operation to remove a damaged part of my brain, but luckily that didn't come to anything, though I saw it happen to some of the others. It all got rather hippy in the seventies. There was a lot of art and discussions about our inner journeys. At Bancroft it was best to keep your personality to yourself. Like school, really. I had a few friends over the years, but you had to be careful. The more sane you appeared, the more the doctors thought you were mad.'

I search for a tissue and dab at my eyes. Violet watches me curiously but says nothing.

'You know it wasn't you, don't you?' I manage to say. 'That day. In the woods.'

'Yes,' says Violet calmly. 'You have a lot of time to think in a mental hospital. I realised, after a while, what Emmeline had done. She'd made me feel I was going mad. She told me I'd been there, that I killed Robin. And I believed her because, at that time, and for many years afterwards, I didn't trust my own mind.'

I swallow the bile at the back of my throat. 'I really am so sorry,' I say. My words sound hollow. How can they ever be enough? 'We all did it,' I whisper. 'It wasn't just Emmeline. We all played a part.'

'But it was her idea.'

'It was me,' I say. 'I told the doctors about your rituals. I told them you heard voices in your head.'

At the table behind us, someone is pulling out a chair, scraping it across the floor. Violet gives me an amused look. 'Goodness, Gilly. You don't think it was *your fault*, do you?' She shakes her head. 'It wasn't you. Nothing you could have said would have made a difference one way or the other. By then Emmeline and Mummy were determined to get me out of the way. I was an embarrassment to Mummy. And Emmeline thought I would say something about Robin which would scupper her chances with Cadwallander. I'm not sure Mummy would have gone through with it though, if it wasn't for my behaviour that final week, and what I did at the ball. I think I probably did go a little crazy.' She laughs, then sighs. 'Poor Fee Fee. I've never forgotten him, you know.'

'But you would never have done that, if we hadn't—'

'Please, Gilly.' She waves a hand in the air.

We look at one another.

'She made me believe I was responsible for what happened to Frank too. She wrote and told me.'

'Frank.' It was strange to be saying these names aloud after such a long time, after pushing it all away for so many years. Frank's name was thick on my tongue.

'Poor Frank,' Violet says with a sigh. 'He was the perfect scapegoat.'

'Emmeline said it was just a diversion,' I whisper. 'Something for the police to think about so they wouldn't look too closely at us.'

Violet pours a little tea into her cup. 'I always liked Frank.'

I nod tearfully then swallow hard. 'You know, I wondered for a long time why Frank didn't say anything about seeing us there, heading for the woods with the gun. Because he *did* see us.' I pause. 'I've had time to think about it too.'

'And?' says Violet.

I think of the figure in white heading towards the woods, the dropped glove in Frank's cottage, Frank's eyes meeting Lady

Claybourne's as he ascended the mount with Robin in his arms, how I had run to the cottage after lunch and had blurted it out: *We've done something terrible. Laura* . . . The look in Frank's eyes: concern, panic, *fear*.

'Frank and Lady Claybourne,' I say. 'There was something going on, wasn't there?'

Violet lifts her tea to her lips. 'Mummy was a terrible flirt when she was young. I don't think my father ever satisfied her. And when he returned from the war, well, Daddy wasn't ever really the same. Frank was good-looking, you know. And it would have excited Mummy. Sneaking off down to the cottage like Lady Chatterley.'

'Laura was Frank's daughter,' I say, finally articulating what I had suspected for so long.

'Yes, I'm pretty sure,' Violet says. 'She didn't look much like Emmeline and me, did she?'

'Frank wanted to protect her,' I say slowly. 'All along Emmeline told us *she* was protecting Laura but in the end, it wasn't really Emmeline protecting her at all, it was Frank.'

'Possibly,' said Violet. 'We'll never know for sure.'

I rub my forehead as Violet takes a second biscuit.

'And Robin was Emmeline's. I'm assuming you know, Gilly.'

I nod. 'The tutor. They were in love.'

Violet snorts, scattering a few crumbs across the table, then shakes her head. 'Who told you *that*? Laura?'

'Yes.'

She sighs. 'That was Laura all over. Ever the romantic.' She pauses, looks out of the window, then returns her gaze to me. 'Our English and Languages master was an old letch.'

I blink in surprise.

'He took a special interest in Emmeline,' Violet continues. 'She was bright. Extraordinarily so, as you know. He knew how to encourage her intellectually, something our parents had certainly never done. Mummy didn't place much value on our studies. And Daddy was just so *distant*. He didn't know how to be around us. Well, then came Mr Lempstead. I remember how Mummy said he had the perfect experience, he'd only ever taught girls, you see. There was some problem with his reference. I don't think it ever came through. He told us the previous family he'd worked for had moved to Italy and that was why they couldn't be reached. In the end, Mummy liked him so much, she hired him anyway. He was charismatic. Even a little flamboyant. He used to wear these hats ... Not that he was the type Mummy would go for. She preferred her men, the ones she had her affairs with anyway, steady and rugged, and a little rough around the edges, like Frank. But still, Mr Lempstead knew how to flatter Mummy, bowing to her, and talking to her about her flowers and her parties. Mummy was blind to what was really going on in the schoolroom.'

Violet pauses, finishes her biscuit. 'I walked in once. He was sitting very close to Emmeline. I could see his hand resting on her thigh. I thought that odd. But I was only a child, I didn't really know how to make sense of what I was seeing, of the feeling I experienced whenever Mr Lempstead was in the room. An uneasiness, like a cold hand creeping up the back of your blouse.' She shakes her head. 'I don't know why he didn't try anything with Laura. Perhaps he thought her too unpredictable. She might scream or innocently say something to Mummy about him rummaging around in her skirts. But Emmeline knew that the things Mr Lempstead was doing to her could never be told to Mother or Father. To anyone.'

'That's terrible,' I say.

Violet stares into her teacup. 'Emmeline changed around that time. She became subdued and withdrawn. She seemed to disappear into herself, into a place the rest of us couldn't reach. I knew it had to stop, that Mr Lempstead had to leave, but I didn't know how to make it happen. Then there was that night. I heard the footsteps outside my door.'

'The butterfly room,' I say, memories returning to me thick and fast. I see Violet standing outside the door to the butterfly room, telling me she doesn't like to go in there.

'It was awful,' says Violet. 'Even in the dim light, I saw the look on Emmeline's face, completely blank, as if she had gone somewhere else in her mind. And Mr Lempstead huffing and grunting, and his eyes, his awful, hungry eyes.' She shudders. 'I screamed and screamed. I tripped and dropped the lamp. It shattered on the rug and started the fire. Emmeline blamed me for her burns. And she hated me for seeing what I did.'

'And then Robin ...'

'No one realised for several months. I overheard the maids talking, saying that Emmeline had become a heifer, that even her shoes didn't fit her anymore, that she must be sneaking into the pantry at night. I thought nothing of it. Then it became clear. It was too late by then, of course, to do very much. Mummy thought Emmeline should be sent away to have the baby but Daddy was worried about her travelling, and I don't really know how it was all arranged, but in the end it was decided she would stay. I think Mummy wanted the baby to be adopted. But Daddy put a stop to it. One of the only times he stood up to Mummy. I do wonder if he asked Mummy to bring Robin up as hers. If he did, she must have refused. Probably to spite him. Or maybe she thought she was too old, that people would talk. Either way, relations weren't very good between my parents by then. And there was poor Mary who lost her baby around the same time. The whole village knew Mary was pregnant with Ned Barrow's child. Ned who died in the fire trying to save our furniture. I suppose it was a sort of compromise. Robin would live with us as Mary's child, but Daddy would be able to put him through school. I think he hoped Emmeline might take Robin back one day.'

'Do you think she ever would have?'

Violet sighs. 'I don't know. I doubt it.'

'Laura told me Emmeline was struggling to conceive with Hugh Cadwallander.'

'I don't know anything about that,' Violet says. 'But I think Robin's birth was difficult. When he was born, Emmeline could hardly bear to look at him. She couldn't cope with the shame, and he was a constant reminder of it. She couldn't cope with the fact that Mummy knew about Mr Lempstead, knew she was no longer *intact*, although of course Mummy didn't *really* know what had gone on, that Emmeline hadn't been able to say she hadn't wanted any of it. I think Emmeline hated herself for what happened. She was clever, you see, which made it worse. She hated that she had allowed herself to be manipulated in such a fashion.'

'It's terribly sad,' I say.

Violet gives me a steady look. 'It doesn't excuse her behaviour. It doesn't excuse what she did to me, to Laura.'

'No,' I quickly agree. 'Of course it doesn't.'

We sit in silence for a moment or two.

'So what have you done with yourself, Gilly? You married, had children, I suppose?'

I nod. 'I married my first husband, Ian, after the war. We had two girls, Angela and Susie.' I smile. 'Ian and I were happy enough when the girls were small. At least, we made it work. But we married quickly because that's what people did then, and because it felt like a miracle to be alive at all. But we were really quite different, Ian and I, in a way that didn't always work. We parted perfectly amicably when the girls left home. They were outraged, at first, but they came around. I fell in love and married Graham.' I smile. 'Graham, well, Graham was everything.' I experience a familiar pang of sadness and attempt to clear my throat. 'Angela has two girls of her own, Daisy and Rebecca, and Susie has a little boy, Peter. My grandchildren are getting quite grown up themselves these days . . .' I pause and look into my teacup. 'Graham died last year.' I stop talking and Violet watches me carefully.

'I'm sorry,' she says. 'About Graham. Did you work, Gilly? Did you have a career?'

'I was a VAD during the war,' I tell her. 'But I gave it up soon after, and then I had the children. I didn't work when they were young – no one did then. When they were older, I took a secretarial course. I worked in a solicitor's office for fifteen years. It was fairly dull work, I suppose, but I liked feeling useful again, and the independence it brought.'

Violet smiles, enjoying the rather ordinary and distilled details of my life, but I feel dreadful knowing how privileged my life has been when Violet's was stolen from her.

'Do you think you'll tell Henry?' I ask. 'About Laura. About who he really is?'

Violet presses her hands together in her lap. 'I think I probably will, yes, when the time is right. I think I need to do it – for Laura.' She pauses for a moment, perhaps thinking of her sister, then leans forward. 'Listen, Gilly, there is one more thing. It's why I wanted to see you. I'd like you to help me with something.'

'Of course,' I say quickly. 'Anything. If there's anything I can do—'

'I'd like to go and see Emmeline.'

'Emmeline?' I look at her in surprise. 'Oh, I thought—'

'No, she's alive,' says Violet. 'Henry goes to see her a couple of times of week. I haven't asked him to take me as I think he believes it might be upsetting for the both of us. You see, Emmeline isn't well. She's not quite – how can I put it – she's not quite the full ticket anymore. Henry says he isn't sure she even knows who he is.'

I don't know what to say. It is difficult to believe the person Violet is talking about could be Emmeline.

'But even so,' Violet continues, 'I'd like to see her. I'm sure you understand.'

Do I understand? Not really. But how can I refuse? I have so much to atone for, I barely know where to begin. What I really want to say to Violet is *Will you forgive me for what I did?* Or perhaps more importantly, *Will you forgive me for what I did not do?*

But forgiveness seems childish and inadequate, and all I can think is: *Yes. Yes, of course I will take you.*

'I thought we could go this weekend,' Violet says.

Chapter Twenty-Seven

I T'S A SUNDAY MORNING AND the roads are quiet. Of course I can't remember the exact route and, anyway, the roads are different now: the M25 has been built, for one thing. But once we are in Buckinghamshire, I recognise a few landmarks; a church, a roundabout, a pub. Graham used to say I never forgot a place. He wasn't one for flying, and we spent many a summer driving to Cornwall, Wales, Yorkshire, or the lakes, me in the passenger seat with the map, giving directions, a flask of tea wedged in behind the handbrake.

Eventually, we find ourselves driving through the village with the green and the weeping willows. '*Turn left at the duck pond,*' I can hear Laura saying, but when I glance over it isn't Laura next to me, but Violet.

'Did you say something?' I ask her.

'No,' she says. 'But we must be nearly there.'

Wynscott has hardly changed. It's just as I remember it. Some of the laurel hedges have been cut down and the windows and doors have been replaced but, really, it is no different to how it was on that stifling hot day in 1943. I notice a 'For Sale' sign staked into the front lawn, advertising the name of a salubrious-sounding estate agent. A cherry tree is in full and beautiful bloom.

'Henry's selling it,' Violet tells me as we pull into the drive. 'He's found a home for Emmeline. Somewhere that will take her in.'

She made her sound like a stray dog.

'The care home is in Crouch End,' Violet goes on. 'I suppose it's a bit of a trek for Henry coming over here twice a week. And they'll use the money to pay for her care. He says I'll get a flat, once the sale has gone through. In fact, I'm going to be quite well off by the sounds of it. There was money in a trust for me too. It seems Daddy didn't completely forget me.'

I am glad to hear this.

We pull to a stop on the drive. I look up at the house. 'Is Emmeline still able to live on her own'? I ask.

'Oh, Henry says there's a whole team of people. Carers, cleaners, gardeners. He says it all costs a fortune.'

'And Hugh. I suppose he—'

'Hugh's been gone for fifteen years now, Henry told me. There was an age difference between them, don't forget. Emmeline refused to move at first of course, when she became ill, but now ...' Violet shrugs. 'Now she barely knows what's going on, apparently. The carers and the cleaners come in six days a week and Henry and Phyllis usually visit on a Sunday, but today they're having lunch with friends.'

'Henry doesn't know you're here?'

'No one knows I'm here.'

We get out of the car and make our way up to the front door. Violet produces a large set of keys from her pocket and begins to try one after the other.

'Did you take those from Henry?' I ask, frowning.

She ignores me and carries on fumbling.

'Can't we just knock?' I say. 'We might give her a fright, barging in like this.'

'She's been told not to answer the door,' says Violet. 'And she's not allowed outside on her own. Apparently, she keeps wandering off. People have found her, walking up the lane in her nightdress, stumbling around in the dark. She made it all the way to the pub once. I know Henry worries about her not getting enough fresh air – he always takes her out on a Sunday – but they can't risk it, her wandering off on her own, so they lock her in. Ah, here we go. This is the one.'

The door opens and we step into the hallway. There is a sweet, musty smell, like potpourri, or flowers on the turn. Dust motes float in the air, caught in a shaft of light from the stained-glass window. I look around, at the vaulted ceiling, the staircase Laura had dashed up, the landing she had run desperately along, searching for Henry.

Violet closes the door behind us and it clicks shut. I feel like a burglar, sneaking into someone's house uninvited. The air is very still. From somewhere I can hear the steady rhythmic ticking of a clock. I think of the grandfather clock at Thornleigh: that little boat that swung from side to side, caught forever in a storm.

We wander through a large beamed kitchen with a terracotta floor, then find ourselves in an overheated sitting room off the kitchen. I imagine there to be another, more formal, living room somewhere.

Sitting in a green armchair is a tiny white-haired woman wearing a floral dress, an oversized cardigan, grey tights and slippers. The television is on – a gardening programme – and she stares vacantly at it.

In my mind, Emmeline has remained the way I knew her when I was fifteen: elegant, confident, fiercely intelligent, self-assured. It is difficult to believe that this diminutive old woman in a shabby dress, in this stuffy room, is Emmeline. And yet it is. I can see it in the sharpness of her features, and how there still remains about her a faint air of poise and entitlement. But she is also terribly frail. I think of the three of us, how time has marked and shaped us. Laura avoided it all. And yet we are the privileged ones.

Emmeline looks at us, not so much with surprise but with acceptance, as if she has been expecting us. 'The roses need cutting back,' she says. I glance at the television screen where a man is holding a handful of carrots, brushing the dirt from them. There is no sign of any roses.

Violet stands, staring at Emmeline as if searching, in this tiny bird-like woman, for the sister she once knew. 'Hello, Emmi,' she says finally. 'We've come to visit you.'

'You're not the usual one,' Emmeline says, looking hard at Violet.

Violet perches on the sofa, reaches for the remote and switches the television off. Emmeline makes no protest, only blinks. 'Tell the boy the door is stuck again.'

Violet leans forward. 'Emmi, it's me, *Violet*. Your *sister*.'

I think perhaps there is a faint flicker of recognition, but then Emmeline is placing her arms on the sides of her chair, trying to get up. 'I'll put the kettle on,' she mutters. 'The sandwiches have sand in them.'

Violet and I exchange a look.

'It's all right,' I say quickly. 'I'll do it. You stay there.'

Emmeline, with barely a glance in my direction, sinks back into the chair.

I feel grateful to be in the kitchen, to be doing something useful. I also want to give Violet and Emmeline a few minutes alone. I wonder if there is something Violet wants to say to Emmeline, even if Emmeline isn't able to understand.

I find a Denby teapot and decide to make a pot. There is a note on top of the hob rings on the AGA that says, 'Do Not Touch!' When I look in the fridge for milk, I notice several pre-prepared meals in oven dishes wrapped in cling film. Someone has attached notes to each of them with microwaving instructions. I find a tray propped up against the fridge next to the kettle and set the tea things out.

In the sitting room, I am relieved to find Emmeline and Violet still sitting quietly, just as I left them. I pour the tea. Emmeline stares into her cup as if the contents mystify her. Eventually, she takes a few tiny sips.

'I'm staying with Henry,' Violet tells Emmeline.

There is no reaction from Emmeline.

'I'm not at Bancroft anymore. Remember Bancroft? The hospital?'

Emmeline flinches at the sound of Violet's voice.

'You told Mummy I should be sent away. Don't you remember? You were worried I might become a nuisance. You left me there, even when you could have got me out. Then you took Laura's baby. Don't you remember that, at least?'

Emmeline stares at us both then looks to the windows and shakes her head. 'There's no birdseed,' she mutters. 'I've told him before.'

Violet sighs.

I reach out and place my hand on Violet's arm. 'I'm sorry,' I say. 'Whatever you came for, I don't think—'

'It's all right, Gilly,' says Violet. 'I just needed to see her. I needed to try.'

I nod. We were too late, I think. But if we weren't, would Violet have got what she wanted from Emmeline? Recognition of what she had done? An apology? I doubt it.

'No one ever comes,' Emmeline says loudly, pushing her teacup and saucer onto the side table.

'Well, we're here now,' says Violet.

I glance around the room. On the dresser there is a black-and-white photograph of Emmeline and Hugh Cadwallander's wedding. Emmeline is wearing a long-sleeve silk gown and holding a bouquet of tall-stemmed flowers. It is almost as disconcerting to see Emmeline in the photograph, looking as she did when I knew her, as it is to see the tiny old lady sitting here in the flesh. There are other photographs too: Henry in a prep-school uniform; Henry, about sixteen or so, wearing cricket whites; Henry in a powder-blue suit sporting a bushy moustache and standing next to his own bride who wears a white minidress and a flower garland in her hair.

Violet puts her teacup on the tray and stands. 'Let's go out,' she says to Emmeline. 'Henry is worried you don't get enough fresh air. You can show me the garden.'

I am not sure about this idea, fearing it might distress or confuse Emmeline, but what can I say? And Emmeline seems to understand. She looks towards the windows then allows Violet to help her to her feet.

We leave the warm snug and the kitchen and find coats and boots by the back door.

'This will do,' says Violet, pulling a heavy, ancient-looking waxed cotton jacket down from the peg rail. Emmeline looks suspiciously at it but then meekly holds her arms out. 'That's it,' Violet says, helping Emmeline into the coat then zipping her up to the chin. Emmeline shuffles out of her slippers and we help her into a pair of wellington boots. Her stick-thin legs look almost comical sticking out of them.

I put the door on the latch then follow the pair of them outside, Violet steering Emmeline by the elbow. She opens a side gate and we step onto the lawn.

The garden is huge and secluded. A few empty urns stand about on the patio and there is a table under green tarpaulin, held down by a plant pot. The edges of the tarpaulin flutter in the cool April breeze. A swing seat covered in a faded fabric hangs from under a plum tree full of white blossom. I imagine Emmeline, a younger Emmeline, sitting on the patio in the summer, wearing a sun hat, sipping a cold drink as Henry runs about on the grass. But had they lived here then? Or had they lived at Chaseley? Had Emmeline ever really been happy? I wondered. Had she convinced herself that Violet's incarceration and Laura's death had been nothing to do with her? Had she really loved Henry as her own? Or had he been merely an acquisition, like a new horse, or an apartment on the French Riviera, the right dress for the right party, something she simply had to have. Did she really believe she had given him a better life than he would have had with Laura? Had she, by loving Henry, believed she had redeemed herself for giving up Robin?

We would never know.

As we head further down the garden, Emmeline mutters to herself. Violet takes her arm.

'Oh, look,' says Violet as we walk.

We hadn't seen it when we'd been up by the patio as it was sunken slightly, just out of view, but now ahead of us we can see a lake.

'It's just like Thornleigh,' says Violet. 'I can see why they went for this place.'

The lake *is* a little like the lake at Thornleigh, although not quite so large, and without the dense woods behind it, only a line of trees that separates the garden from the fields and countryside beyond. The lake even has a wooden jetty, although there is no sign of a boat.

'Swimming,' Emmeline says suddenly.

Violet laughs. 'It's hardly the weather,' she says.

I wonder if Emmeline is remembering something, a time when she swam in the lake, or when she watched Hugh and Henry splashing about in the water. I picture a hot summer's day; towels on the jetty, a pitcher of lemonade. I wonder what is going on in Emmeline's mind. What prompts the random words and phrases? Are there moments when the broken connections fuse into place? Henry told Violet Emmeline is still lucid at times but perhaps he was only being hopeful. Is Emmeline fully lost, now, in some other world, a world that is unreachable to anyone but her? Is she stuck in a different period in time? If so, which has she chosen? If she even has a choice at all.

Violet steps onto the jetty. She still has hold of Emmeline's arm. I follow them and we stand taking in the blossom-covered trees, the fluffy bullrushes. Emmeline, at the edge of the jetty, shuffles her feet a little as if cold. She turns to face us, looking from me to Violet, perhaps wondering again who we are. I am about to say we should probably return to the house.

It all happens so quickly.

Violet takes a step back then gives her sister a sharp shove.

A flicker of surprise crosses Emmeline's face. She raises her arms and, for a split second, her hands seem to claw at the air. Then she is falling backwards. A terrible splash. A spray of water.

I gasp, my mouth falling open, my breath caught. I catch a glimpse of something under the surface, a flash of white from Emmeline's hair, a faint thrashing, but all too quickly there is nothing. Just the still, dark water.

I make a strange noise at the back of my throat, cover my mouth with my palm. I glance wildly about. We need to act quickly. Surely there must be a life ring, a large branch. Something we can use.

These thoughts are foolish. Even if there is a life ring, there is no way an elderly lady of eighty-three could possibly grab hold of it. I have the mad idea – some inherent instinct to save a fellow human being – that I must go in after Emmeline and drag her out. But I find I can't move. My limbs have frozen, my reflexes too slow, and of course, I realise, if I went in, if either of us went in, we would surely never get out ourselves.

Violet is staring at the water. She looks mildly surprised.

'Violet,' I whisper. 'What have you done?'

She doesn't answer me.

We stay there for several minutes. Emmeline had been there, right next to us, and now she is gone. The surface of the water is calm, unbroken. A gust of wind rustles through the long grass at the water's edge.

Violet begins to back away from the jetty. She turns and steps onto the lawn. I follow her, trying to speak but unable to form any words. I glance over my shoulder as if I might see Emmeline, but there is no one there, just the lake and the trees. I want to rush back, to save Emmeline somehow, but I do not.

Calmly, Violet begins to make her way across the lawn.

'Violet,' I say desperately, 'we have to—'

'It's all right, Gilly,' she says, taking my arm. 'Come on now.'

I find myself walking alongside her, walking away from the lake. Three girls in the woods. The sound of a gunshot. The absence of a scream. *I think it would be best if we returned to the house.*

When we reach the garden gate, Violet stops.

'If it's all right with you, I think I'll wait in the car,' she says, as if nothing at all has happened. 'You just need to wash the tea things up, put them away exactly where you found them. Put the chain across the front door. I'll lock it from the outside. Oh, and leave the back door open.'

I look numbly at Violet but she is already opening the garden gate, heading for the drive.

I glance again in the direction of the lake, then back to the house. Too stunned to do anything else, I do exactly as Violet has asked, my movements slow and automatic. Just like before, all those years ago, I know what is required of me.

I go into Wynscott alone. I wash out the teapot and the mugs, dry them with a tea towel, put the tray back where I found it. I wonder whether to put the television on, then decide to leave it off. I pull the chain across the front door then exit via the back door, leaving it open.

Violet is sitting, huddled in the car. 'Can you put the heater on? I couldn't work out how to do it. It's got rather chilly.'

I start the engine and switch on the heat. The car is running but I can't seem to drive it.

I turn to look at her. 'Violet,' I say, 'what's going to happen to us?'

Violet smiles. 'Oh, Gilly. You always were a worrywart.' She glances at the house. 'I told you, she's wandered off before. She shouldn't even be living on her own, really. Someone will realise she's missing. Probably not until tomorrow. They'll find her, of course, if they drain the lake. Or if she floats. But that coat was rather heavy, and I put a few ornaments from the mantel-piece in the pockets.' She pauses, then looks at me. 'Don't worry, Gilly. No one knows we were here. Anyway, who's going to suspect us? Two old biddies.' She chuckles.

'I can't do this, Violet. I'm sorry, but I can't. I have to go back.' I glance towards the house. Why haven't I moved? Why am I still sitting here?

'No, you don't, Gilly,' Violet says softly. 'You don't have to do anything at all.'

A gust of wind blows, shaking blossom from the cherry tree onto the drive. I grip the steering wheel, my knuckles bone-white.

I failed Violet all those years ago. Then Laura asked for my help and I failed her too. Is this how I can redress the balance? Perhaps Emmeline did deserve it. Justice at last. For Frank, for Violet, for Laura. But how will I live with myself? Even when time passes and this becomes another part of my past. How will I go on knowing I could have done something to help Emmeline, but didn't?

I had once hoped that the Claybourne sisters might become my family, that they would give me access to the kind of life I had hardly dared to dream of, a life of wealth, ease and privilege. But in the end they had used me, each in their own way and I had been happy to oblige.

Would any of it have happened at all, I wonder, if Lady Claybourne, less concerned about social appearances, had let Emmeline and Laura ride that morning? Or did it happen because of a man who, sitting in the schoolroom one morning, decided to put his hand on his pupil's knee just because he could?

As young women back then we were powerless. Even the Claybourne sisters with their wealth and social status were not immune to the expectations of their class and gender, or to the power of men. Emmeline had longed for that power. She had wanted everything she felt she should have, no matter the cost to herself and to those around her.

And what remains, now, at the end of it all?

I think of a photograph of a young woman holding her newborn son, her expression a mix of joy, love and fear. Fear, perhaps, because her baby is now not only a part of her but a part of the world, a part of the mess and of the chaos. 'Because it's all so beautiful and extraordinary,' Laura had said, before she sailed off the edge. Perhaps that's all we can do: keep our minds and hearts open, try to avoid as much destruction as possible, allow ourselves a little self-forgiveness, do our best to guide our children before we, like Laura, sail off the edge.

Somehow, I will live with what has happened here today, just as I have lived with everything else for such a long time.

What other option is there? This too, will eventually become a part of me.

People often say of a painful memory or experience, that it 'belongs to the past'. Does it? I wonder. In my experience, the past does not readily absorb what we would prefer to forget: our less than fine moments. They are still there, those moments; an unforgivable word said to a loved one, a terrible mistake, a moment of human weakness or cruelty. A cold December morning, a single gunshot, the cry of the crows, followed by sixty years of silence. A terrible splash. We carry these moments with us, these little familiar hauntings, the worst parts of ourselves, and we justify why they occurred because if we did not we would not be able to carry on.

This too I will justify to myself, somehow.

I will carry on.

'Gilly?' says Violet quietly next to me.

I glance at her. She looks cold and forlorn, not at all capable of what she has just done. 'Yes?' I whisper.

'Do you think we could – do something, sometime?'

'Do what?' I ask, my voice cracking.

'Oh, I don't know,' she says. 'Go out for tea, perhaps. Or to the pictures?'

I stare straight ahead, at the long driveway, the low hedges, the cherry blossom sprinkled across the lawn.

'Yes,' I say. 'I think we could.'

Violet nods.

There is still so much I don't know about Violet. Will I get the time to find out?

There is a moment's silence.

'Gilly?' She reaches out and touches my arm.

I turn to look at her.

'I think I'd like to go home.'

I nod, then release the handbrake. We roll down the drive and I put my indicator on to turn right out of the gates, even though there isn't a single car to be seen.

I realise that, for Violet, I don't know where home is.

I drive her anyway.

Acknowledgements

Thanks to my agent, Hayley Steed, to my editor Sophie Orme, and to my U.S. editor MJ Johnston. Thanks to the team at Bonnier Books UK, including Clare Kelly and Misha Manani. Thanks to Sourcebooks in the U.S., particularly Anna Venckus. Thanks to Caroline Hogg, Mina Yakinya and Sandra Ferguson. Thanks to my family for always supporting my writing, and to Martin for giving me time and space to write, your advice on 1930s shotguns, your excellent culinary skills and so much more. Thank you to my writing friends (you know who you are — we must meet up again soon). Thanks to the booksellers and librarians who work so hard to get books into the hands of readers. Thank you to my readers; without you this would not be possible.

I am grateful to various works of non-fiction and memoir. These include: *The Long Weekend: Life in the English Country House Between the Wars* by Adrian Tinniswood, *Terms & Conditions: Life in Girls' Boarding Schools, 1939-1979* by Ysenda Maxtone Graham, *Oleander, Jacaranda: A Childhood Perceived* by Penelope Lively, *The Female Malady: Women, Madness and English Culture, 1830-1980* by Elaine Showalter, *Because We Are Bad: OCD and a Girl Lost in Thought* by Lily Bailey, *The Man Who Couldn't Stop: The Truth About OCD* by David Adam and *A Chelsea Concerto* by Frances Faviell.

**Read on for an extract from
Emily Critchley's compelling debut mystery,
One Puzzling Afternoon.**

A mystery she can't remember. A friend she can't forget.
On a suburban street filled with secrets, eighty-two-year-old
Edie Green must face her past to discover what happened to
her friend Lucy, who went missing years before . . .

'Gripping, heartbreaking'
The Sun

'Beguiling . . . Beautifully written'
Heat

'A captivating and poignant book'
Marianne Cronin

'A real page turner'
Louise Hare

'A mystery deftly woven with tension and compassion'
Beth Morrey

1
2018

I FIRST SEE LUCY THEDDLE STANDING outside the Post Office on Tuesday afternoon. Looking exactly the same as she did in 1951.

I am on my way in when a young man accosts me, carrying a tray and wearing a paper hat.

'Free sweets,' he says, pushing the tray under my nose.

'Free sweets?'

'It's our open day,' he explains, gesturing to the small shop squashed between the Post Office and Sandy's Shoes. The shop used to be a key cutting place. Before that, it sold sports equipment and school uniforms. The sign over the door now reads: *RETRO SWEETS. ALL YOUR CHILDHOOD FAVOURITES.*

'No, thank you.'

'Oh, go on. One won't hurt.' He nudges the tray towards me.

I peer down and there they are: Parma Violets. I reach for them. I can't help myself. 'These used to be my favourites,' I murmur, but the man isn't listening. He has spotted another customer and dashed off. *'Free sweets!'*

I unwrap the tube and pop one of the tiny discs in my mouth. The taste is sweet and soapy. They remind me of spring flowers and warm days, of cycling down to the sea with the sun on my face, of secret whispers and kept promises.

That's when I see Lucy. She's standing next to the postbox wearing white ankle socks and the school uniform we used to wear: a green pleated tunic over a blouse. Her hair is in two neat plaits; she's carrying her satchel and her violin case.

'Oh, hello, Lucy,' I say.

A woman in a blue coat is coming out of Sandy's Shoes. She gives me a sympathetic smile. It's a look I am familiar with, one I don't like. When I glance back at the postbox, Lucy has vanished. I blink then crunch the sweet down, swallowing hard. A chill runs through me and I shake my head, trying to push the image of her from my mind; she's nothing to do with me anymore.

I quickly shove the rest of the Parma Violets into the pocket of my mackintosh and enter the Post Office, shuffling forward past the stationery and up to the counter.

'Ah, good morning, Edie.'

'Hello, Sanjeev.' I am pleased to have remembered Sanjeev's name, pleased it had been there for me instead of that awful void that exists, more often now, where a familiar word should sit.

'And what can we do for you?' Sanjeev smiles whilst behind him his good-sized wife is busy pasting labels onto packages.

What was it I came in for?

'I'll have twelve stamps, please.'

Perhaps I came for stamps. Everyone can always use a few extra stamps.

'Keeping well, are we, Edie?'

Sanjeev speaks loudly, probably because of the glass partition. I can tell by the way he leans forward that he wants his voice to carry.

'Very well indeed,' I reply, trying to match his loudness.

'Autumn now,' he says.

'Leaves everywhere,' I offer.

He slides the stamps to me under the glass and I pay for them. I notice the collection box and the tray of red paper poppies with their green plastic stems. It must be that time of year again, the time for remembering. I slide a pound into the collection box then fix a poppy to my buttonhole.

'Take care now, Edie,' Sanjeev says cheerfully.

When I exit the Post Office, the boy with the sweet tray is offering a drumstick lolly to a man on a mobility scooter. I look around cautiously but can see no further sign of Lucy. Above me, the clouds are gathering; there is a gust of wind and I shiver, pulling at my coat.

As I pass the newsagents and the rack of papers outside, a headline catches my eye: *Local School to Close*. The words mean something to me, only I can't think what. I lean in, peering at the photograph of a grey, imposing building. Then I remember – it's Daniel's school. The secondary school where he works as the deputy headmaster. Daniel says the school isn't closing but *merging*. Another school is getting a big development and all the children from Daniel's school are joining that one. Daniel could work there, but he doesn't want to. I frown, unable to remember why.

At home, I pick a bill up from the doormat, edge my coat off and place my shoes on the rack Josie recently insisted I buy. When you reach my age, everything becomes a trip hazard.

I go straight through to the kitchen to put the kettle on. Ordinarily I'd wait for Josie, but the events of the morning, seeing Lucy, require a cup of tea before Josie's arrival. Whatever happened to her? I feel I should remember but I can't. I roll her name around in my mind. *Lucy Theddle, Lucy Theddle.* It feels strange, forbidden, and I bite my lip trying to quell the unease that squirms in my stomach.

Josie finds me, fifteen minutes later, sitting in my chair in the living room sipping from the mug Daniel bought me last Christmas. It has a sketch of a cityscape and the word *Stockholm* written in a delicate script. A gift from his latest city break.

'Hello, Edie,' Josie bellows at me from the hallway. 'Have you been out?' She pokes her head round the living room door and peers in at me.

'The Post Office,' I say.

'What for?'

'Stamps.'

Josie frowns whilst shaking her coat off. She's holding a tiny collapsed umbrella and it gets caught in her sleeve. 'I could have done that when I go to the shops tomorrow.'

I attempt a shrug but find my shoulders don't obey. My joints, nowadays, often ignore my instructions.

'Not got the telly on?' she asks, looking at me suspiciously. Josie cannot understand how anybody would want to sit in a living room and not have the television on.

'No,' I say. 'I was thinking.'

'Thinking?' Josie repeats the word with some wonderment. 'Well, that would be nice, wouldn't it?'

Not waiting for my reply, she scoots off to the kitchen then returns wearing my apron. 'I'll just do this bit of washing-up, Edie, take the rubbish out for you. Then I'll make us a cuppa. Oh. I see you've already made one.'

'I'll have another.'

She nods, disappears. I can hear her rattling around, turning on the tap, the sound of the cupboard door opening and closing. She's probably looking for the Marigolds.

Josie comes for two hours, four days a week. Expensive. But worth it. It was Daniel's idea, and I was most against it at first but I've got used to her now. I enjoy the way she bustles around, making sure she earns her nine pounds an hour – a perfectly reasonable rate, Daniel tells me. She isn't my carer, just to clarify. She helps out with the household chores. Daniel insisted on hiring her and I went along with it. Of course, I'd never let Josie go now I have her. She's a single mother, you see. She needs the extra income.

Josie was reluctant, at first, to sit down and have a cup of tea with me, during *working hours* as she calls them. She soon changed her mind when I persisted, although she often stands, leaning against the door frame, or else she perches on the sofa arm, as if she isn't really stopping, only pausing. People don't like to take breaks anymore, I've noticed. They have to keep busy, as if something terrible will happen to them if they stop.

I push myself up from the chair and move unsteadily into the hallway. My kitchen, these days, is very beige and very clean (Josie is fond of bleach).

She's at the sink with her back to me, her shoulders slightly rounded, her dark hair tied with a thin red band.

'I saw Lucy Theddle today.'

Josie jumps and turns around. 'Oh, Edie. I thought you were in the living room.' She recovers herself and continues rinsing a fork under the tap. 'Who's Lucy Theddle then?'

'She disappeared in 1951.' As I say the words aloud I feel surprised that this is something I know, and by my certainty.